PRAISE FOR *LOLA*

WINNER OF THE JOHN CREASEY
(NEW BLOOD) DAGGER AWARD

NOMINATED FOR THE EDGAR AWARD

"A fine, brutal debut thriller." *Mail on Sunday*

"A debut as fast, flexible and poised as a chef's knife. At its best it has the lithe energy of a Lee Child novel, combined with Dennis Lehane… an unshakably engrossing read… Love is vibrant and clear-eyed, an exciting new west coast observer."
New York Times Book Reviews

"A tough, enterprising and vulnerable heroine, Lola gives the reader an unvarnished insight into ghetto life." *Sunday Times Crime Club*

"A brilliant debut, a bleak and cynical noir set in the patriarchal gangland world of LA's South Central, with smack-dealer Lola pulling her gang's strings as she does whatever it takes to survive." *Irish Times*

"*Lola* is a raw, dark and claustrophobic tale, but also a powerful and moving one. It's a long time since I've felt so connected to a character's emotions and motivations in a novel."
Gilly Macmillan,
New York Times bestselling author of *What She Knew*

"Intense, gritty, and breathlessly paced, *Lola* is a thriller that's been elevated by exquisite writing and deep character development."
Booklist

"Stunning… This powerful read is at once an intelligently crafted mystery, a reflection on the cycles of violence and addiction, and a timely mediation on the double standard facing women in authority."
Publisher's Weekly (Starred Review)

"An unbelievably smart mystery."   *Newsweek*

"I have never read anything like *Lola*, magical and microscopic in scope. An art book, a lens, a page turner, a provocative examination of the many cities that are one city, Los Angeles… Melissa Scrivner Love is bursting with talent and style."

Caroline Kepnes, author of *You* and *Hidden Bodies*

"A glorious invention, the Latina daughter of Lisbeth Salander and Walter White, on a lifelong tear of revenge after being pimped by her mother for drugs and then living with the double invisibility of her gender and her race."   *Kirkus*

"I fell hard for Lola in all her fierce and broken beauty, her reckless and necessary hardness, her bottomless capacity for loyalty. Don't miss this ride."

Joshilyn Jackson,
New York Times bestselling author of *The Opposite of Everyone*

"An absorbing tale that blends compassion and a bracing realpolitik into a fascinating account of one woman's unquenchable will to not only survive but thrive."   *Irish Times*

"With prose that's just a joy to read and a protagonist I'd welcome in my corner any time, *Lola* is a terrific first novel, one of the best I've come across in years."

S.J. Rozan, Edgar-winning author of *Ghost Hero*

"One of the best written crime dramas to be published in quite some time."   *Associated Press*

"Achingly beautiful… But Scrivner Love does better than Steig Larsson by creating a female character who is not just standing up to males, she's actually reconstructing gender for herself and her community."

Milwaukee Journal Sentinel

"A gritty, tightly plotted masterpiece that doubles as a whirlwind tour of some of the many different sections and tribes of L.A."

Los Angeles Weekly

AMERICAN HEROIN

MELISSA SCRIVNER LOVE

A Point Blank Book

First published in Great Britain and Australia by Point Blank,
an imprint of Oneworld Publications, 2019

ISBN 978-1-78607-536-9
ISBN 978-1-78607-537-6 (eBook)

Printed and bound in Great Britain by Clays Ltd, Elcograf S.p.A.

Oneworld Publications
10 Bloomsbury Street
London WC1B 3SR
England

Stay up to date with the latest books,
special offers, and exclusive content from
Oneworld with our newsletter

Sign up on our website
oneworld-publications.com

MIX
Paper from
responsible sources
FSC® C018072

For Mom and Dad
For David
For Leah and Caleb
For bright futures everywhere

AMERICAN HEROIN

PROLOGUE

Christopher has to roll the back window down when Scott lights his first cigarette. They aren't even at the end of his block in the foothills of Hollywood. The houses on either side are tricked out for Halloween—lit ghosts and pumpkins, talking witches with hair the texture of straw, headstones and cobwebs. The sick bright-orange light from the 76 station's circular sign is only a glow from here, half-way up the residential street. Behind Christopher, the two-story brick fairy-tale house where he lives with his parents gets farther and farther away. Christopher squeezes his head out the window, not think-ing to roll it down more, because he doesn't want to appear weak to Scott. Or because he isn't thinking tonight. If he were, he would never have gotten in the car.

Above him, the centuries-old trees on both sides of the street fold in a welcoming hug. There's a Gelson's across from the 76. A few steps away is a coffee shop, a comedy club, and a restaurant famous for crepes and coffee.

"Where's Karen?" Scott asks before he exhales in a swishing puff.

"She had to study. Biology test next week. Mrs.—"

"Ruiz. Yeah, I had her too."

"Fuuuuuuuuuuck," the teenager in the passenger seat says. "She was hot. Hard, but hot."

Christopher knows this kid's name is Erik. Erik and Scott are both seniors at Harvard Westlake, where Christopher is a sophomore. Erik's father, like Scott's, is a TV director who travels nine months out of the year, skipping from show to show—New York, Vancouver, Atlanta of all places. Both Erik's and Scott's mothers don't work.

"Outside the home." Christopher hears his own mother correcting his thought. "They don't work *outside the home*."

He doesn't know why he thinks of his mother now. She wasn't home for dinner. Christopher can't remember the last time she was. She hasn't texted to ask where he is. She wasn't there to stop him. Even as he thinks it, Christopher knows this is only an excuse.

"How far is this place?" Christopher asks Scott.

"An hour in traffic. Shouldn't be a problem tonight, though."

"Fucking traffic," Erik says.

Christopher has heard a rumor that Erik got a perfect score on his SATs. It's difficult to believe in this car, on this night, past midnight, when Erik's vocabulary consists of "fuck," "hard," and "hot."

Christopher should be studying for his biology test too. He should be with Karen, sitting on her bed, her bedroom door a careful crack open so her parents, both ob-gyns, can keep a careful ear out for the act that keeps them employed.

There's a billiards bar just east of the exit for the 101 South. His parents always share a laugh when they pass it, and his mom touches his dad's hand. There's something remembered there, something that doesn't include him. Something from before.

"Dude, you're going south, remember?" Erik pipes up. "There."

Even though Christopher isn't yet old enough to drive, he can tell it's a tricky exit—eight lanes of traffic, or it seems that way, and Scott needs to get over quicker than he can to merge onto the freeway.

Maybe there's still time to not make it.

But Christopher wants to make it. He knows somewhere deep down, beneath his roiling gut, that what they're doing tonight will save him.

He thinks of Karen's bedroom, the scratchy floral cover with its pinks and purples, the laced ruffle that reaches from the bottom of the mattress to the top of the floor. He thinks of the things he wants to do to Karen but can't because he looks at her bedroom and still sees someone innocent.

But the truth is, he is innocent too.

It's just his mind that's fucked. He can't stop the dark thoughts, of the things he wants to do to Karen, where he wants to stick things, how he wants to make her scream. He thinks these things, and he feels guilty after, and he is alone.

He used to consider slitting his wrists.

That was before Scott slipped him his first tab of X.

"You think they got places to eat?"

"What?"

"Where we're going," Erik says. "I'm hungry."

Christopher has met Erik only a handful of times before to-night. Like Erik, Christopher's a smart kid, but he's too young, too inexperienced.

Christopher still thinks about his mother when he's going to score heroin for the first time.

"Yeah, Mexican food," Scott says, and Erik barks a quick laugh to let Scott know he's safe telling a racist joke here. But Erik's laugh stops short and turns to a sigh. He must realize what Scott said is wrong.

"I don't think we'll be hungry. After," Christopher says.

"What, have you done this before?" Scott asks. Christopher catches the older boy's eyes in the rearview mirror. Ice blue. Even in the dark, Christopher can see them.

"No. I just . . . I've heard."

"Probably from Monty," Erik says.

Monty is their dealer. He can get the small stuff—pot, X, acid. He's a twenty-one-year-old criminal-justice student at a community college in Simi Valley who draws his morality line at selling heroin. More likely, he doesn't have the connections.

"Monty doesn't do heroin," Scott says.

None of them has either.

Christopher doesn't know why Scott and Erik have decided to-night is the night they snort poison powder. He doesn't even know for sure why he said yes—only that something inside him needs to change. He needs a reboot, an upgrade, and, while he's smart enough to know heroin has never done that for anyone, he is also desperate enough to try.

He wonders if his mother would rather have an addict son or a dead one.

"What's it called again? The place we're going?"

"Huntington Park," Scott says.

"Never heard of it," Erik says, as if he's heard of every L.A. nook and cranny where a person can buy heroin.

It takes twenty-nine minutes now, just after midnight, for Scott's car to make the journey from the Hollywood Hills to Huntington Park. Christopher has no particular affinity for Hollywood proper, a place where blobs of tourists meander in shorts that reach to their knees, clicking selfies and eating at chain restaurants even though they're in L.A., for fuck's sake, a food mecca. A cheap-food mecca. The tiny pale pastel stucco houses with overgrown lawns and bars on the windows aren't what these tourists expect.

The 101 moves at a crawl through downtown, where Christopher turns his head to see the members of the L.A. Philharmonic painted down the entire side of a skyscraper staring at him—the violin player with her sprayed-stiff chestnut hair, the cello player in a tux, gray hair slicked back. Are they playing now, while he's riding in the backseat of Scott's Range Rover to score heroin? No, it's too late for that.

Scott takes exit 1A off the 101 onto Seventh Street, then heads south on Santa Fe Avenue, a street Christopher has never heard of before tonight. A lot of the houses here wouldn't be out of place in Hollywood. They are the same pale pastel stucco—yellow, blue, peach—with bars on the windows. But here, there are no tourists. Every soul on the street is Latino. A fat man with a name tag embroidered on his work shirt stops to let his pit bull take a shit. A teenage boy and girl sit on a curb, stealing a make-out session under a streetlight. At a red light, Christopher hears laughter in short, violent gasps from the open windows of the corner house.

When they get to the intersection at Santa Fe and Zoe, Christopher takes in the Mexican restaurant across the street—Avila's El Ranchito—with its red-and-green awnings and its chili-pepper

Christmas lights. It's now he sees the true distinction between Hollywood and Huntington Park. The restaurant is bordered by an empty parking lot, at least ten spaces deep, five across. And according to the sign, the parking is free.

There is no such thing as free parking in Hollywood, even when the business that operates the lot is closed. Of course, it's silly to pretend he's coming from Hollywood. He lives in the Hills above the tourist trap, but it might as well be on the other side of the country.

"This is where they sell," Scott says.

Christopher has not thought until now that he should ask Scott where he got his intel. He should know better, given his background. He should be smarter. Christopher's parents have been shelling out a good forty grand a year for his private school education since at least kindergarten, and here he is without the good sense to ask if this heroin score could be a setup.

"At the restaurant?" Erik asks. "Like, with complimentary chips and salsa?"

Also racist, Christopher thinks, but these guys are seniors, and he wants what they've come here to buy.

"No, the restaurant's got nothing to do with it," Scott corrects. "It's closed. See."

Erik peers out the window as if he's going to see the darkened windows of Avila's El Ranchito light up and open, spilling mariachi music and drunken laughter.

When the light in front of them turns green, a kid rounds the corner on a bike he's at least a foot too tall to be riding. He's maybe fifteen, Christopher's age, though it's hard to tell because he's so thin, and the bike is a kid's bike, with an oversized seat and no hand brakes. Christopher knows because his father bought him a similar one when he was six.

"That one of them?"

"I don't know," Scott says.

Christopher thinks that if he were leading this operation, he wouldn't admit to not knowing. He would also have done his research, starting with the members of the gang they were buying from.

The kid gets close enough to see their features through darkened glass, but he doesn't look at them. Instead, he swings his bike in a slow circle, then loops right into a figure eight. Christopher hears the whoosh of his tires out the window. It's graceful, the dance the kid's doing on his bike, slow and heavy like he's moving underwater.

Christopher hadn't realized until now how tired he is.

"You think he saw us?" Erik again.

"I don't know."

Jesus, Scott, Christopher wants to say.

"What do we do?"

"I've got the money," Scott says, as if someone has asked him about it. But no one has.

The kid is coming back now, so close to the driver's side of the Range Rover he could scratch the paint with his fingernail if he wanted. Christopher imagines he would want to, if their positions were switched.

"Drop it," Christopher hears, but it isn't Scott's voice or Erik's. It is lighter, tinged with the slightest accent. It must belong to the kid on the bike.

Scott scrambles for the plastic grocery bag, a relic from several years ago, before Los Angeles banned them from supermarkets and drugstores. Christopher wonders if Scott's parents' housekeeper has a stash of them somewhere, a ball of bagged bags shoved in the back of the cabinet under the kitchen sink. His parents' housekeeper does.

Scott looks both ways for passing cars, like he's crossing the street instead of checking for cops or thieves or both, but the night is quiet. He drops the plastic bag out the driver's-side window in time for the Latino kid on the bike to turn and swoop it up, then disappear around the corner.

No one speaks. They wait, the seconds dripping as slow as water from a broken faucet you trick yourself into thinking is fixed, or the hiccups you think you've beaten.

Erik sighs, and Scott's knuckles turn white as they grip the steering wheel.

"You know who he was?"

"No."

"You think he wasn't with them? Like, maybe he just took our money?"

Scott doesn't answer, probably because he's sick of admitting he doesn't know.

"Maybe we should go," Christopher ventures, but only after he sees the dashboard clock click through a full five minutes.

"We can't let them get away with that," Erik says.

Christopher doesn't have to ask who he means by "them." To Erik, it is a blanket expression for "other." Black, Latino, even Asian, if he's talking about drivers. But Erik doesn't recognize this about himself. If Christopher were to point it out now, Erik would be embarrassed.

Scott's hands run the length of the steering wheel, leaving spots of sweat. At the intersection, the light goes from red to green.

Then an older dude appears, twentysomething, black hair, a short block of muscle, jaywalking with his hands in the pockets of his baggy jeans. He is whistling a pop tune Christopher can't place—Pitbull? No, Lady Gaga. He skirts the Range Rover, but he doesn't touch the car. He doesn't look at the boys inside. He keeps walking and whistling, and Christopher, like Scott and Erik, doesn't breathe until the man disappears behind the candy-colored stoplights of the next intersection.

"The fuck?" Erik again.

"We should go," says Scott.

"Wait," Christopher says. He steps out of the car to retrieve the baggie from behind Scott's front driver's-side tire. "He left it for us."

The red lights are flashing now, Christopher thinks, even though he isn't looking directly at them. They are coming from behind him. What he is looking at is only their reflection off the glittery black of Scott's Range Rover.

"Holy shit," a voice inside the car says, but Christopher doesn't know if it's Erik or Scott or both.

Christopher straightens up to his full height—six feet. He fumbles at his door, wondering if Scott is going to gun it out of here without him. But Scott is frozen at the wheel. Christopher fastens his seat belt and says, "Go."

Scott hesitates. Now Christopher sees the LAPD black-and-white, its red lights whirring and flashing, its sirens whoop-whooping, and for a split second Christopher thinks how these alarming notes could be the beginning of an aggressive ice-cream-truck jingle.

But they're not. They're the cops. And they're coming for Christopher, Scott, and Erik.

"Scott, you have to drive," Christopher repeats.

"Shit," Erik says.

A split second before the black-and-white is upon them, she appears. Latina, cargo pants, a white tank top. She is tiny, one arm spilling dark blood. She has her hair pulled back in a long rope of black braid. She stumbles into the street, and the black-and-white has to slam the brakes to keep from hitting her. The cops' fender comes to a halt inches from her knees.

Christopher can't see her face, only the back of her, but from here, it doesn't look like she flinched.

"Help!" she cries out. "Help." It's more of a bleat this time, as if she's tailoring the volume of her voice to meet the expectations of the officers who exit the cruiser now.

The sight of her wakes Scott up. He yanks the wheel left, flipping a U-turn and hitting the gas as soon as the Range Rover is square.

"Who the hell was that?" Erik asks.

ONE

BUM DEAL

Lola wakes up in pain. The gash on her arm is several days old, but Lola doesn't do painkillers.

The morning after the incident, she had gathered her men in the Crenshaw Six's clubhouse, a vacant ground-level apartment downstairs from this one. There was silence when she walked in. Jorge didn't bother to crack a joke. Marcos was speaking English so the newer lieutenants Manuel and Ramon couldn't understand. They all knew they'd fucked up. Their boss was wearing a bandage. She had saved their corner crews from the police. She had played the damsel in distress, a role that exhausts her even when she doesn't bleed for it.

"I had to cut myself," Lola could have said. "I had to make it look like I have some asshole boyfriend who wounded me. I had to make the cops believe he ran away before they'd leave me alone. Those white kids only got out because I had to sacrifice."

Lola doesn't have a hard rule against selling to white kids. There are plenty who don't drive spanking-new Rovers with a Harvard Westlake decal. There are plenty who won't be offered a plea deal for identifying the gang members who sold them the shit that would ruin their lives faster. The difference is money. She doesn't allow her men, and, in turn, their foot soldiers, to sell to rich white kids. They are dangerous. They will tell the police what they want to hear for fear of the opening of a record, a closing of a college application, the shutting off of a privileged future.

She did not go after Ricky, the boy on the bike, because it was not his fault. He was given an order.

This time, it was Marcos, Ricky's lieutenant, the only member of the Crenshaw Six to have done hard time before Lola's baby brother, Hector. He had taken the beating hard for the first three seconds, resisting the urge to fight back, to rip each other member of his gang to shreds, but Lola had seen the control there, the ability to stop himself, to relax into the pain. She had loved him in that moment.

Now she can hear the television going in the living room. Lucy must be awake, propped up on oversized couch cushions with her bowl of cereal, taking care not to spill milk. Lola has told her it doesn't matter if she spills, but Lucy remembers the one time Lola scolded her for it. A mistake, Lola knows, but that scolding is what Lucy will carry with her for life. In the scheme of the little girl's childhood scars, Lola must console herself with the fact that the ones she inflicts will be the faintest. Rosie Amaro, Lucy's biological mother, a junkie whose greatest accomplishment in life was taking Lola's advice and ending her own shitbag existence, set a low bar for motherhood.

Lola throws back sheets twisted from last night's romp. Over two years after her last relationship ended, she has not allowed the one man she's permitted in her bed to sleep there. "Bed" is a generous term for her sleeping accommodations, a mattress and box spring on a floor carpeted in beige. Her walls are white. There are no curtains, only blinds, to shift the morning sunlight from cheerful yellow to flat gray. Three unpacked boxes are stacked against the mirrored closet. She has lived in this apartment for almost two years, but she refuses to call it home.

Lola stands and stretches her fingers up to the ceiling, then swings one sinewy arm across her flat chest. She watches her small muscles strain under her skin, then relax. She switches from the right arm to the left, taking care not to split the wound open. She sucks air in through her teeth and counts to ten. She has never understood how these two things help alleviate pain. But they do.

Before she and Lucy moved here, to the bottom of the U in this two-story horseshoe-shaped courtyard complex, Lola had lived in the same house for a decade, a house a mere three blocks from this place, which is neither house nor home. It was the house where she fried empanadas every Sunday, the house where she raised her baby brother, Hector, from the age of eleven. It was the house where her older boyfriend Carlos bought her a cake from a grocery-store bakery to celebrate her high school graduation, and the house where she later shot Carlos between the eyes for initiating Hector into his gang, the Crenshaw Six. It was the house where Lola had Hector arrested for a murder she committed, a betrayal she still tells herself was for her brother's own good.

It was the house she shared with Garcia, her last boyfriend, until he fell back in love with Kim, the prior love of his life. It is the house where Lola destroyed that love with $5,000 and the truth—that Garcia witnessed Lola shooting Carlos, Kim's brother, between the eyes, and did nothing. Kim had moved out of the neighborhood and set herself up somewhere inland, Bakersfield or some other smog shit town where $5,000 went further than here, in Huntington Park, a South Central–adjacent suburb of L.A.

"Mama!" It's Lucy, who's on the cusp of eight but still calls out to Lola with the sweet neediness of a toddler. Lucy is smart. The teachers at Blooming Gardens, the private school in Culver City that costs Lola upward of $35,000 a year once "voluntary" donations are factored in, have told Lola that Lucy is reading at a fifth-grade level. She knows her fractions and long division and even some basic computer coding. It is only when calling for Lola, her mother of two years, that Lucy regresses.

"Be right there, *mija!*" Lola calls back.

Lola takes stock of her small body in the closet doors that double as mirrors. A thin scrim of dust coats the glass, the only sign of age in this place, but Lola can still get a clear picture of herself. Twenty-eight years old, no more than five-foot-three, ninety-eight pounds, some of that weight accounted for by her long, rope-thick black hair. Right now, Lola is wearing only part of her standard uniform—a ribbed white tank and white cotton underwear. She'll fish her olive-green cargo pants off the floor before she goes into the living room to greet

Lucy. Lola doesn't know if covering her own skin helps ease Lucy's trauma or makes the little girl repress it, but she figures the least she can do is shield Lucy from the sex that happens in this house.

Last night, Lola cranked up the white-noise machine in Lucy's bedroom for the half hour her male guest was present. She kicked him out of bed the second after he rolled off her, giving him some coffee for the three-block trek back to his place.

Like Lola's own mother, Lucy's mother pimped her daughter out for drug money. Lucy will never have a normal relationship with sex, no matter what Lola does. This fact makes Lola sad, but it also takes away some of the pressure she would feel if Lucy hadn't been messed up before they ever met.

Now, Lola finds Lucy in the beige living room. The new and neutral feel of the apartment is still present after almost two years here. Lola imagines the beige was meant to calm the nerves and tension brought on by poverty, but all the color does is remind her this place is not her home. It might feel cozier if Lola were to paint the walls a warm red or cool ocean blue, but in order to paint, Lola has to feel she will stay here.

Lucy sits on the chocolate sofa, her cereal, soggy with sweetened milk, forgotten on the coffee table in front of her. Even though Lucy is past toddler clumsiness, Lola has capped the table's sharp corners with rubber, aware even as she did so that childproofing was coming far too late in Lucy's life.

Lucy is reading a book called *Matilda* by someone named Roald Dahl. Lola has taken a peek at the pages, delighting in the pranks the girl genius Matilda plays on her used-car-salesman father. Lola knows some men who need a little surprise super glue in their life, though Lola would aim it lower than their hats. Lola plans to keep reading the book whenever Lucy puts it down, which is not often. Lola's daughter reads in stolen moments, like now, when she should be finishing her breakfast but instead is devouring a book in the television's bright morning glare.

Onscreen, an anorexic blond news anchor chirps about a new high-intensity workout craze, then lowers her voice an octave or two to describe L.A.'s token morning hit-and-run. In the early hours of this particular morning, November 1, a mother and daughter walking their dog were struck and killed in a pedestrian crosswalk. Onscreen, the lone witness, a man on his way to a morning factory shift, swears it was a black Mercedes that did it, although the car sped away too fast for him to get a look at the plate. Lola watches this morning's local man, for there is always a local man, shake his head about the need for yellow flashing lights to mark the pedestrian walk. The "local man" is brown, as were the victims. Lola's not holding her breath for those yellow warning lights.

"Who will write the letter?" It's Lucy, her eyes scanning a page of *Matilda*, left to right, left to right.

"What letter?"

"To petition the city," Lucy says. "For the lights."

"You watching this?"

"It's loud."

"You can turn it down," Lola says, even as she lifts the remote and clicks the volume down ten notches.

"Sorry."

"Wasn't bothering me," Lola says. There are many conversations between the two of them like this—Lucy voicing a problem, Lola fixing it instead of letting Lucy figure it out for herself. Lola is careful with discipline—she knows the normal mother of a normal child might scold the child for blaring the television while reading. She's heard the initials from fretful parents of Lucy's wealthy West Side classmates—ADD and ADHD—but after Lucy's hellish formative years, not being able to focus on any one specific horror might be a blessing.

"The letter," Lucy reminds Lola, relieving Lola's temporary concern about ADD.

"The guy on the news can write it."

"He says he works fourteen hours a day and doesn't own a printer."

"He can email it," Lola says.

"What if he doesn't know how to email?"

"Would you like to write a letter to the city about the crosswalk?"

"He's not going to do it. Shouldn't someone?"

Lola wants to tell Lucy they can't fix everything, that Los Angeles is a sprawling mix of beauty and plastic and blood and sex and broken bones and horns blaring and homeless people sleeping under overpasses and tempers boiling and waves cooling, that somehow it all goes bright and happy and sometimes it hurts people, grinds them down to nothing. Lola wants to tell Lucy that there are too many problems in their own neighborhood—immigrants living in fear, underpaid, off-the-books workers scraping together enough pennies to bring families from Mexico to Los Angeles in backs of trucks hot as ovens, and gang violence . . . some of it perpetrated by Lola herself.

"Someone should. But we have to get to school."

"Okay," Lucy says. She slides off the sofa tummy first so she doesn't fall. She is small for her age, since her asshole junkie mother never bothered to make sure she had enough to eat. It was Lola who taught Lucy to slide off the overstuffed cushions tummy first, to make sure the floor was there before she jumped. It is a habit the little girl holds on to despite her feet almost touching the floor as soon as she turns over.

"You need to eat something," Lola says.

"I can finish my cereal."

Lola can tell by Lucy's tone that she doesn't want to waste food, but she also doesn't want to eat the cereal. Lola doesn't blame her. Who wants those little *o*'s after they're milk-logged and mushy?

"I'll make you eggs," Lola says, and Lucy leaps into her arms and hugs her so tight it hurts.

"Thank you, Mama," Lucy says, her voice a sweet whisper, her lips close enough to brush Lola's ear when she speaks. She smells faintly of sweet cereal milk and sleep and last night's shampoo.

"You're welcome, baby girl," Lola says. "Why don't you go get dressed and I'll have your plate ready when you're finished?"

"Okay," Lucy says, moving at a run back to her bedroom, where she shuts the door. Even though it's only her and Lola in the apartment, Lucy likes to keep the doors closed when she's naked. Lola has never commented on this habit because she understands it. That being said, if Lucy ever does decide to parade around their apartment with nothing between her bare body and the air, Lola will keep her mouth shut. No judgment. Ever. That is Lola's first rule of parenting.

In the kitchen, Lola pulls eggs and half-and-half and butter from the small humming refrigerator and cracks the eggs into a cheap skillet charred brown on the bottom from gas flames. Unlike the stove in Lola's old home, this one is electric, the valves beneath the burners glowing red in even circles, like pretend fire.

The knock at the door comes three minutes later, at the exact moment Lola needs to stand close to the eggs scrambling in the skillet to keep them from browning.

"Just a minute!" she calls.

She is scraping the yellow fluff across the nonstick surface when the second knock comes. She turns her head toward the door this time and yells, "I said one minute!"

When she turns back to the skillet, a piece of egg has gone brown, and Lola mutters, "Shit, shit, shit," as she flicks the brown piece into the trash and transfers the remainder to Lucy's plate.

She has seen skulls pressed flat under tires and knife wounds fester because their victims can't go to hospitals. A browned egg shouldn't bother her, and it doesn't. It is the person she knows is knocking that grates at her.

She strides to the front door, gripping her spatula like a weapon and spoiling for a fight as she opens it.

"I said one fucking minute," Lola says.

Lola chose this particular second-floor apartment for its vantage point. In front of her, the complex's shitty courtyard, dotted with uneven pebbles and dusty brown grass, stretches all the way to the street, the two long legs of the U-shaped building bordering it on either side. Lola might not be able to keep her enemies away from her home, but she can sure as hell see them coming.

Her mother is a different story.

Lola should have known there would be trouble when she acquired the apartment directly beneath her own for Maria. Two summers ago, a rival drug lord named Darrel King kidnapped her mother, giving

Lola something like seventy-two hours of precious peace. But Lola had to waste resources getting her mother back, including Hector, her baby brother, who, for reasons unknown to Lola, still harbors a blind spot of unconditional love for their mother. Hector's failed, and un-authorized, attempt at a rescue mission led to Darrel King's death at Lola's hands. Now Hector is doing time for Lola's crime, and keeping Maria close is the only way Lola can assure her former junkie mother never gets to play damsel in distress again.

"Good morning," Maria Vasquez sings, her voice lovely and lilt-ing. It still sends a shiver up Lola's spine, and she always feels a drop of acid tingeing her cheeks, lighting them up in pain, whenever her mother speaks. Lola learned in childhood that a peaceful good-night story or song did not equal a peaceful good night.

Now that her mother has been off heroin for several years, Lola finds Maria's quest for health and wholeness both annoying and gut-ting. Lola wants her mother to acknowledge she fucked up raising her children. She wants Maria to apologize for pimping Lola out to get her fix. She wants Maria to acknowledge it is she, not Lola, who is responsible for her son, Hector, landing in prison.

Lola has come to terms with the fact that this apology will never come.

"What time is it?" Maria asks when she sees Lola's raised spatula. Lola glances at the watch on Maria's wrist, the one her mother is too lazy to read for herself, and dreams of beating Maria's black hair with her cheap plastic spatula, leaving soft-cooked egg crumbles to rot there.

"Oh," Maria says, and glances at her watch. "Sorry." An apol-ogy, but never the one Lola wants. "Seven thirty. Doesn't Lucy have school?"

"We're trying to get out the door," Lola says.

"Right," Maria says, but she stays planted on Lola's doormat, which Lola purchased when she and Lucy moved in last year. On it, a brown pit bull declares, all visitors must be approved by the dog. Lola is certain Valentine, the pit bull who is probably curled up in Lucy's bed snoring as the little girl dresses, does not approve of Maria. Yet here her mother stands, waiting for an invitation that will be issued only after the silence gets too awkward.

"You need something?" Lola asks.

"Not me. Jorge's cousin."

Lola thinks of Jorge as the Crenshaw Six's jester, the man who cracks a joke, poking fun at himself, right before he slides the knife between your ribs. Jorge gets caught up in his codependent relationship with Yolanda, his girlfriend of many years, who wouldn't think twice about beating Jorge with a cheap plastic spatula like the one Lola's holding. Still, it strikes Lola as odd that Jorge hasn't mentioned a cousin needing her help.

"Shouldn't Jorge be the one telling me about this cousin of his?"

"Yolanda said he didn't want to bother you. Said he'd been enough trouble lately."

Lola glances at her bandaged arm but doesn't acknowledge her mother is right.

"She's pregnant."

"Yolanda?"

"The cousin. They thought she got the flu. Won't go away, so they say they need some of those antibiotics. I told her she shouldn't be doing that. The more you use those things, the less effective they become."

"Where'd you read that?"

"The computer." The fact that Maria doesn't even know to call it the Internet confirms what Lola suspected—her mother is full of shit.

"Does your computer have an MD?" Lola can't resist the opportunity to make Maria feel stupid.

"What?" Maria stares at Lola with her big, blank brown eyes, and Lola thinks of cows blinking and chewing in a field. Lola wonders how much of her mother's mind remembers what she did to her daughter, or, rather, let others do to her, and for how much heroin.

"Nothing," Lola mutters, because all her little jabs at Maria add up to nothing when her mother doesn't realize Lola is making fun of her. "Tell Jorge's cousin to come by the party tonight."

It is November 1, Día de Los Muertos, and tonight Lola is throwing a party for her small square of Huntington Park. The neighbor-hood will build *ofrendas* for deceased loved ones, decorating them with the orange marigolds, flower of the dead, that Lola is having delivered later today. The food will be catered—sandwiches piled with salami and cheese, encased in thick Italian rolls. There will be craft beer and a cupcake bar and candy for the kids, who will load up on free sugar and thank Lola before becoming their own parents' problems at bedtime.

This is Lola's first time hosting a party since the barbecue she and Garcia threw at their old place. That night, there were burgers and Coronas, ceviche and salsa. The food was homemade, not catered. That night, the cops swarmed the house and arrested Hector.

"But she's here. She needs your help."

It is the first of the month, and, although Lola's door is always open to concerned citizens of her neighborhood, the first is the day she has found to be most popular for problems arriving at her doorstep—the rent is due, or people want to make a clean slate, leave bad relation-ships, stop drinking or doping. She's fixed every problem from a sec-ond grader whose candy was stolen by the school bully to a desperate family man who owed money to the wrong gang. She's cared for her people, and she doesn't need to remind them of their obligation to her when she passes them on the sidewalk or in the market aisle.

"I don't see her," Lola says after a cursory glance around the court-yard, where she spots Señora Ocampo, a hunched woman of sixty who sprouted gray streaks in her black hair even before she turned thirty, watering foliage she must think is flowers but is really just weeds. Señora Ocampo has a debilitating case of rheumatoid arthritis and had no health insurance, until her daughter approached Lola on the first day of September and pleaded her case. Mr. Hernandez, a janitor at the local elementary school who's supporting his family of five on $400 a week, shuts his thin board of a front door behind him, juggling a small paper lunch sack, a red thermos, and a baby. He raises a hand in greeting, and Lola smiles and waves back from her second-floor perch. She has groceries delivered to this family every week, anonymously, but Mr. Hernandez's wife knows who sends the bags of tortillas and eggs and fresh fruit and vegetables. It was she alone who approached Lola on the first day of October last year, asking Lola to please help her family because her husband would not take food stamps, or, as Mr. Hernandez had called them when his wife begged, charity. Now Lola watches the man shuffle to his truck with the baby and his lunch, unaware that she provides him with the food inside. To him, his wife has become an expert in the art of couponing, and he can say to her, "See what happens when you pay attention to the cost of things?"

Lola makes sure the people in her neighborhood have enough, because they are her people, and you can't be queen if you don't take care of your people. You must give them everything they need. It is the things they want that they must get for themselves.

"She's right here," Maria says, producing from nowhere a pregnant woman in a purple cotton dress, a black shawl failing to conceal the bowling-ball lump at her center. She must have been standing to the side this whole time. Lola can learn from this—danger does not always come from straight ahead.

"*Hola,*" says the pregnant woman, and Lola wonders how much of her conversation with Maria she overheard. What kind of daughter must this woman think Lola is?

"Hi," Lola says. She is more guarded in English, pausing to choose her words despite it being her first language. "How can I help you?"

"It's my husband," the pregnant woman says. "He's in prison."

"I can't get anyone out of prison," Lola says.

"Please," the pregnant woman says. "You don't understand."

Lola has heard that she doesn't understand many times. Most often, the statement comes from someone who's pleading for a life, sometimes their own at the wrong end of Lola's gun, sometimes for someone else's, usually an addict relative or an incarcerated child or a kid lured into a gang life they want to leave but can't.

"Mama." It's Lucy, dressed for school in jeans and a plain cotton T-shirt. She has scraped her hair back into a neat ponytail and decorated it with a single flower. Lola wants to ask where she got the flower, something purple and feminine, but right now she has to scold her mother, delay the pregnant woman, and get Lucy in the car.

"I'm sorry," Lola says to the woman with the bowling-ball belly. "I wish I could help you get your husband out of prison. But I have a meeting. And then we have to get to school."

The pregnant woman hugs the apartment complex's concrete wall with one hand, supporting herself against the prickly surface, painted the pale pink of undercooked salmon. She lets Lola pass, but, in the process, Lola is able to get close enough to hear the woman's breath, labored and uneven, as if Lola has dealt her a blow. Lola's arm accidentally brushes the woman's belly as she passes. Does she feel a kick there? Can that be? Is the baby making its own plea to her?

When Lola is halfway between her front door and the staircase, the pregnant woman has caught enough breath to call after her.

"I don't want you to get my husband out of prison. I don't want my husband to get out of prison. Ever."

Lola stops at the head of the stairs. "Why?"

She hates that she already knows the answer. The pregnant woman's husband is an abusive bastard who will beat her and her baby, even before the baby has a chance to become a child. The story is so common Lola wonders how the police can live with themselves, letting men, white and black and every color in between, beat their women and children. She imagines some cops, the empathetic ones, can't live with having to let these men go. That's where alcoholism, divorce, and swallowing guns comes in—when you realize the good you do will never erase the evil of the world.

"He hits me," the pregnant woman confirms. She attempts to cup her huge belly in her small, swollen hand. "And he will hit her."

Her. A little girl. Another victim. Unless Lola intervenes.

In the kitchen, Lucy notices the woman's low, protruding belly for the first time.

"You're pregnant," Lucy says.

"Yes," the woman says.

Lola sees Lucy's eyes narrow as she stares at the woman's stomach. Is she trying to see through the cloth and skin, down through layers of blood and veins to the baby's face?

"What does it feel like?" Lucy asks.

"Lucy . . ." Maria starts to chide, but Lola scrapes the leg of a kitchen chair on tile, and the noise jolts Maria. She doesn't have to look at Lola to know her daughter means for her to shut up, to let Lucy ask questions about this world and how it works.

Lola has often wanted to ask the question herself, how it feels to carry another life inside you before that life separates and is released into a vicious, inescapable world. She wonders if her children would be fucked even before they made their exit. She does not know her father, and her mother is an addict. She does not know if it would be right to unleash that genetic cocktail, even on a space as cruel as earth.

"It feels . . . fine," the woman responds.

Lola finds herself wishing for a clearer answer, although she knows she shouldn't care. She swallows a pill at the same time every day and asks her only current partner to wear a condom, all so she doesn't run the risk of ending up like this woman.

"Come on, *mija*," Maria says to Lucy, taking the plate of eggs. "Let's go eat in the living room."

Maria and Lucy leave, and Lola gestures for the woman to pull out the chair across from her at the table.

"Do you need something to drink?"

"I'm fine, thank you."

"You should stay hydrated."

"I do."

"What's your name?"

"Camilla."

"And what do you think of your cousin?"

Camilla doesn't catch the wink in Lola's voice, the one that should let anyone listening know Lola thinks highly of Jorge, because all the pregnant woman says is "He is a good man."

There are many adjectives Lola can call upon to describe Jorge, but "good" isn't even in the first hundred that jump to mind. He is a good man, Camilla is right, or as good as a banger with an average amount of blood on his hands can be, but that good is buried deep under layers of sediment and molten rock. That good is Jorge's inner core, his center. It is hidden even from him.

Maybe he is different with his family, Lola thinks, then feels a pang at the thought that Jorge is not her family but her soldier.

"You said you want to make sure your husband stays in prison."

"That's right."

"What's he in for?"

"Six months ago, we were at a bar."

Alcohol. Men. Sweat. Violence.

"My husband, Martin, got upset with another man."

"Why?"

"Because the man tried to buy me a drink."

"So it was a bar fight."

Camilla shakes her head.

"The man left. And Martin said we're going too. I thought maybe he would fight him outside. But Martin headed for our car. I thought he was taking me home."

Lola is silent. She wants to give Camilla the space to confide in her.

Camilla stops and looks around at Lola's yellow kitchen. "This place is nice," she says. *It isn't,* Lola thinks, not to her, but the color on the walls is cheerful and the oven cooks meat evenly. Nobody who lives here gets beat up here. To some people, this fact alone would make Lola's apartment a palace.

"What happened next?" Lola prods.

"Martin told me to get in the car." The pregnant woman stops to lower her head. Lola wonders if this means she is ashamed to continue.

"And did you?" she tries.

"Yes."

"Then what?"

"We . . . Martin followed the man. He was in his car too." The woman looks up, as if she has reached the end of her story.

"Did Martin kill the other man?" Lola asks.

"No."

"What did he do?"

"He beat him."

"But not to death?" Lola is trying to get to the issue here, what is so bad about a man taking up for his woman.

"No. The man . . . his name is Brandon . . . he's in a coma. He will be, forever, unless his family decides to take him off that machine that breathes for him."

Now Lola understands the horror of this particular ass-whooping. While she might have sympathized with Martin's position were he not a wife-beating piece of shit, she does not approve of Martin's half-assed actions. If you set out to beat a man, beat a man, but allow him to walk away. If you set out to kill a man, kill a man. No man deserves to breathe and not live.

Then again, no man should be fighting another man over a woman, as if she is property to be stolen and retrieved.

"I see," Lola says.

"He's in for attempted murder. It would be murder, if his—Brandon's—parents pulled the plug. But they won't. They don't believe in that kind of thing." Here the woman gives a toss of her hand to indicate "that kind of thing," parents taking away their child's last breath, letting him rest in peace as they wrangle with killing their own child.

"What do you want me to do?"

"Martin's up for parole this month."

"He's only served six months," Lola says, detecting a note of naïveté in her voice she needs to check.

"Overcrowding . . . first offender . . . good behavior . . ." Another glib wave of the woman's hand, as if it's all bullshit, but this time, Lola thinks, it is.

"Where's he at?"

"Locust Ridge." The pregnant woman meets Lola's eye as she says it, and Lola catches the quick lick of her lips, the anticipation of Lola's response to these two words.

Lola keeps her face still. She releases her hands, which she didn't realize she was holding in two tight fists.

"I think I can help you," Lola says. "I know I can."

"How?"

"You came to me. You know how."

The woman bows her head again, nodding this time. "You're right. I'm sorry."

"And you know the risk if you talk after—you give birth shackled to a prison bed. You willing to risk that to make sure Martin never meets his daughter?"

The woman hesitates. She opens her mouth, about to say something, then snaps it shut, fast as a steel trap. "Yes." She has swallowed whatever confidence she was about to share with Lola. The result is a greenish tint to her face, and Lola can see beads of sweat beginning to pop like tiny, clear kernels of corn on her forehead.

The pregnant woman leaves without saying goodbye. Lola wonders if she has to stop in the stairwell to vomit. She feels her own stomach churning, something about this meeting not sitting right.

It isn't the fact that a pregnant woman asked Lola to murder her husband. It is something Lola's mind can't pinpoint, no matter how many times she plays the meeting over in her head. Jorge . . . good man . . . Martin . . . Brandon . . .

When Lola looks up from the kitchen table, the sun is too high in the sky, and she has to hurry out the door to get Lucy to school on time.

Still, her mind spins the replay . . . coma . . . half-ass . . . good behavior . . . overcrowding . . . Locust Ridge.

The prison Jorge's pregnant cousin named is the same prison that houses her baby brother, Hector. Today is the day she has scheduled to pay him a visit. Today, she will have Martin killed.

TWO

INSIDE MAN

After she drops Lucy off at school, it takes Lola three and a half hours to make the drive from Huntington Park to Locust Ridge Prison. The landscape is desert, dirt, and mountains. Outside Los Angeles County, the traffic moves at a steady clip, and Lola puts Flakiss on the radio and rolls down the windows. The wind whips her hair into sharp needles that prick her cheeks and eyes. She stops at a gas station she knows from countless prior trips has a clean bathroom and buys Vitamin Water and a bag of salted almonds. She has a routine for this trip now, one she makes every month, unless Lucy has an activity that requires her supervision or support.

In the reception area, she goes through the standard security check. She raises her hands above her head and lets the male guard pat her down. He even runs his gloved hands through her hair, which is frazzled and sweaty all at once from the drive. He knows her name but still calls her "ma'am." In here, it is not a term of respect, but a token term that lets her know he's in charge and she should follow his instructions. She knows his name, Rooney, and calls him by it. She has offered to share her almonds with him many times, and many times he has refused.

The visitation room is long and low, with bad, bright light and a row of chairs facing glass. There are dividers between the chairs, but they only give the illusion that you're having a private conversation if you lean forward and put your elbows on the hard shelf. Even then, you're just fooling yourself, thinking nobody's watching or listening.

This is a room full of eyes and ears. It is for seeing and hearing, but not for touching. The room stinks of pine cleaner and stale doughnuts, two smells that could be familiar and comforting, if never enticing. In here, they cause bile to rise from Lola's stomach to the top of her throat.

When she reaches her designated visitor's booth, Number Six, Hector is already seated across from her behind glass. He has his hands in his lap, so she can't see the cuffs there. She doesn't know if he's hidden his shackles on purpose, to protect her, or if the move isn't a conscious thought. She decides to believe the latter, because Hector must know she doesn't need protection. She's no weeping female, like the woman two chairs down, an older black woman in orthopedic shoes. Lola guesses from the age of the man across from her, late forties, that the man is the woman's son. Most violent crimes are committed by perpetrators in their twenties, though Lola can't remember the source of the statistic now. Maybe she made it up. Still, the thought makes her wonder how long the older woman has been making the trip to see the man Lola has decided is her son. How long can a mother cry for her lost child?

"Hey," Hector says, his hands on the shelf now, because he's lifted the receiver and pressed it between his ear and shoulder. Lola sees he is, indeed, cuffed, and realizes that it does bother her to see her baby brother having to use his ear and his shoulder as he would a hand to hold a phone receiver.

She tries not to think about his trigger finger, which she cut off as punishment for a fucked-up drop two years before.

Lola lifts her own receiver and presses it between her own ear and shoulder, in solidarity with her brother.

"You look good," she tells him, as she does every time she comes to visit, and she means it. Two years in prison have grown Hector from boy to man in a way Lola tried but failed to do at home. His black hair is long and glistening. He's pulled it into a small knot at the nape of his neck, but if he were to let it down, Lola knows it would fall to his shoulders in straight, silky strands. His face is graveled with black stubble. Biceps strain at the seams of his orange jumpsuit. His shoulders look wider. His eyes, once wide pools of brown that begged for anything Lola would give him—ice cream, forgiveness, mercy, dinner—have shrunk to black slits. There is no question in Hector's eyes now. Is that what makes a boy into a man?

"Thanks. You too," Hector says, but Lola knows this is a perfunctory compliment. Hers is too, but she usually takes time to assess the truth of her words after she says them. Now Hector doesn't spare her a second glance. She wonders if he's worried looking her in the eye will turn him back from man to boy.

"You won't look at me," she notes, because this is not usually the case when she comes here. Lola might have landed Hector here, behind bars, having turned him in to the cops for a murder she committed, but Hector had done so much other unforgivable shit in the name of her gang, of her, that the realization she'd sacrificed him brought him a flood of relief. All along, Hector had been begging her not for mercy but for punishment.

"Oh," Hector says, and she sees the change in him as he sits up straighter and points his black-slit eyes at hers. He doesn't apologize. He just corrects his behavior and moves on. Lola sees that prison has not only changed her brother from boy to man, but from civilian to soldier.

Good thing, she thinks, *because he's about to get his first order in his new habitat.*

"How're they treating you?"

"Fine."

"Not good?"

"It's prison," Hector says. "We're here to be punished. Nobody to blame but ourselves."

And me, Lola thinks, *me who went at Darrel King's throat with a broken beer bottle, who drained his lifeblood with a shard of pretty green glass. But only because you made me do it, Hector. You charged him, you made Darrel draw down on you. You made me clean up your mess. I saved your life, then I let this place take it.*

Hector will be out in ten years, maybe less. He will be almost thirty. He will have missed his twenties, the decade white people are allowed to make stupid mistakes that transform into good stories—hookers, coke, wild parties—but for which all others must pay.

"Anyone giving you trouble?"

"Nah, Lola, you don't have to worry about me. I'm good in here."

Lola wants to correct him. Yes, the Crenshaw Six are a more powerful force than they were two years ago. They've got more corners, more powder, more cash, and a more dignified white lady partner—a DA, even—but they're not MS-13. They don't have an extensive network of prison connections that offers protection and a chance to sell drugs and turn a profit even in prison. In prison, the only thing that allies Hector with anyone else is the color of his skin. Brown. Does that make him an automatic black-headed stepchild of MS-13 or any of the countless other Latino gangs? Do they keep the black men at bay and the Aryan Nation from shivving Hector in the shower? Is protecting her brother an automatic afterthought for them? And if so, will the day come when they're not there to save him?

"Lola," Hector says, leaning forward in a way that, if they weren't separated by glass and his hands weren't cuffed in front of him, he would take her smaller one in his. His flesh would surround her, reassure her in its meaty heft. For once, Lola knows her baby brother would cover her, instead of the other way around. "I'm good."

"Okay," Lola says, swallowing the lump in her throat so fast it aches.

"You got everything for the party tonight?"

"Just gotta pick up the sandwiches," Lola says.

"Sandwiches, huh? White-people food. From a deli in Santa Monica. Bay Cities, was it?"

"Yeah. Who told you that?"

"Mom wrote me an email," Hector explains. When Hector was sentenced to Locust Ridge, Maria took it upon herself to get an email address. She went behind Lola's back and picked AOL. Lola had wanted to tell her no one uses AOL anymore, but Maria had proudly written out a check for $25 to the service Lola hadn't known anyone could pay for, pressed a stamp on the plain white envelope, and walked it to the corner mailbox herself. When Lola had tried to question her mother, Maria had held up a hand and demanded she stay out of her business. Fine, Lola had thought, I'll stop paying your rent, I'll stop cooking your dinner, I'll stop knocking on your door every morning to make sure you haven't ODed. Lola had kept her mouth shut, though, something about centuries of daughters across cultures respecting mothers compelling her to stay silent, and when night fell, she had made tacos al carbon for Maria.

"You know why she got AOL? I told her nobody uses that shit anymore," Hector says.

"Yeah, I told her that too. You know she pays for it?"

"The fuck?"

"Writes a check every month. Probably going in the pocket of some Nigerian prince."

"Yeah, probably."

"Mom's set in her ways," Lola says, and she likes that she and Hector are discussing their mother's annoying, yet harmless, Internet habit, as opposed to her potentially lethal heroin habit. For a moment, they could be any two siblings in any suburban living room, rolling their eyes at an aging parent out of equal parts annoyance and affection. Unlike any two suburban siblings, though, if someone's ripping Maria off, collecting twenty-five bucks a month, Lola will find that someone and make sure it doesn't happen again.

"Didn't expect to see you today," Hector observes. "Thought the party'd keep you busy."

"Not too busy to see you." It's true, Lola had planned to come here today, even before the pregnant woman showed up with a kill request. *Convenient timing,* Lola thinks, although, to be fair, Camilla hadn't demanded she deliver the order today.

"Something else going on? With Mom?"

And now they're back to Hector and Lola, the two children of a junkie, always looking over their respective shoulders in case Maria decides to pawn all her shit and stick a needle between her toes because the veins in her arms are shot.

"Yeah."

Hector sits up straighter.

"Not with Mom," Lola reassures him. "With . . . work."

She has to be careful here. There's a guard in every corner, each one standing stock-still so they can hear the inmates' conversations. She has never given an assassination order in front of so many officers of the law, if prison guards count as officers of the law. She makes a mental note to check this fact later.

"What's up?"

"A woman came to see me," Lola says, and she paints a smile on her face and freezes it there so she can hold up her phone. She has photos of Lucy here, and she scrolls through them as she talks. "She's had a rough time with her husband."

Hector laughs at a photo of Lucy on the sofa, her ankles crossed, trying to read a paperback Dickens Lola found at a yard sale, pristine from non-use. Lola doesn't want to mix Lucy up in this, though. She keeps scrolling.

"This woman needs help."

"How?"

"Her husband's in here. Maybe you know him." Lola arrives at the photo the battered woman showed her. It was a hard copy, and Lola had snapped a digital photo of the paper photo laid on her kitchen table. No texts between the pregnant woman and Lola.

The woman's husband is paunchy, at least two decades older than Camilla herself, with thinning black-and-gray hair. He has a mustache that doesn't hide the extra fat in his face. His black eyes glint with something like happiness, and the right corner of his mouth is twisted up in a smile. He is sitting in front of a giant birthday cake, frosted white, with too many candles to count. Lola has looked at the photo several times, wondering if Camilla took it, if the glint in his eye and the turned-up corner of his mouth were indications of love for her or mere possession.

"Yeah," Hector says. He leans forward, and Lola notices one of the guards shifting his weight.

"Sit back," Lola says through gritted teeth.

Hector does.

"I've seen him," Hector says, more certain now.

"See that birthday cake?"

"Yeah."

"No more candles for him," Lola says, and she doesn't know if she means for the poof of air that escapes her lips to punctuate her order. *Lights out, motherfucker.*

She expects a pause from Hector while he considers. Instead, he says, "That's what's up."

It takes Lola a second to decode this new slang Hector must have picked up inside. She realizes it is not a question, but an acceptance.

The corner guard is walking toward them, someone over a loud-speaker saying that visiting hours are over, and that inmates must return to their cells.

Lola swipes forward in her camera roll, bringing up another picture of Lucy. She wonders if the prison guard thinks she is Hector's woman, that this is a child they share. She wonders, too, if Hector's actual woman, Amani, has visited him here, or if she did the smart thing and forgot their forbidden romance once it went from difficult to impossible.

"How's Amani?" she tries as she rises from the hard plastic chair.

"What?" Hector is surprised. Lola has never asked after his woman, a smart black girl who would be harmless if her brother didn't run with an opposing gang . . . A gang whose leader Lola had executed to save her own brother's life.

"Amani. Has she been to see you in here?"

Hector lowers his head again, and Lola knows before he says it that no, Amani has not been to see him. She is on the outside, reading and studying and trying to make a better life for herself. Like Hector going from boy to man, Amani has gone from girl to woman.

"No," Hector says. Then, his only challenge to her thus far, "That make you happy?"

"No," Lola replies, surprised at her answer, because she knows it is the best thing for both Hector and Amani. Yet standing here, across from her handcuffed brother, his head bowed now that she's reminded him of his heartbreak, she can't be happy that the thing she stayed up nights wishing for has finally come to pass.

THREE

OF THE DEAD

The courtyard of Lola's apartment building is bursting with orange marigolds and skulls. It is night, November 1, Día de Los Muertos. Time for her party. Her men have transformed what was this morning a dusty brown courtyard into a walkway of a shrine. Citizens of the neighborhood are preparing to pay tribute to their dead. Lola has provided the flowers, the food, and the skulls. Her people will bring the ritual.

Hector was correct. She purchased the food at Bay Cities—sandwiches on hot, fresh bread. When she got home with the food, she had enlisted Maria to keep the chicken parmesan and the meatballs warming in the oven. The cold cuts were distributed among the building's tenants—turkey and Havarti in what little space the Hernandez family had in their refrigerator between the orange-juice concentrate and the processed-cheese singles stacked in slick plastic; Black Forest ham in Señora Ocampo's refrigerator, which appeared to hold ten stalks of celery and nothing else; pasta salad and hot-pepper spread in Lola's own kitchen. Now, her men are delivering the food from apartment refrigerators to the courtyard, where she can see them placing foil roasting pans packed tight with wrapped sandwiches on long, paper-clothed tables.

"Nah, nah, man, you gotta cut a hole in the foil *before* you travel with this shit. Else it gets soggy," Jorge tells Marcos, who has recovered from his beating and holds a hot roasting pan with nothing but paper towels for oven mitts. Maria still pulls that shit, thinking a paper towel will protect her from four-hundred-degree metal. Lola wonders if sociopaths like Marcos and recovering addicts like Maria appreciate the extreme feel of metal singeing skin. Is it the only safe thrill that makes them feel alive? Or do they like it because it makes it feel like they are being punished for the sins they won't admit they've committed?

"Sorry," Marcos says, and when the ex-con sets the large roasting pan on the table and raises his hands in half surrender, half pain, Lola wonders if she can actually see the red burn marks on his palms, or if she is imagining them. If Marcos is in pain, he shakes it off, because in the next instant, he has found a steak knife on the table and has begun to cut careful slits in the foil to let the steam off the meatball subs.

"Nice work, man," Jorge says.

"Thanks," Marcos replies, and Lola realizes she likes watching her two soldiers work in unison to keep bread from getting soggy.

"Nothing sexier than a man with food," Lola calls out. She considers it polite to let her men know when she is watching them. She wants them to feel free to vent, as long as it's not in front of her. It is normal to complain about the one who calls your shots. She would be suspicious if they didn't complain about her. But if she hears it, she has to take action, and there are no warnings from HR in the career path they've chosen.

Jorge glances left and right, then makes a big show of craning his neck across the courtyard, which is empty except for him and Marcos.

"Don't see any men here," Jorge says.

Lola laughs even though she knows the joke is belittling to her sex. She doesn't know if it's an instinct, or the desire to preserve Jorge's sense of humor. He isn't always on the mark, but she needs him to keep trying to keep things light.

"We got any tortillas?" Marcos asks.

"Tortillas?" Jorge starts. "This shit's Italian, man. It's called Bay Cities Italian Deli. No tortillas in Italy. Ain't that right, Lola?"

"That's right," Lola says.

"Oh," Marcos says, and his disappointment shakes Lola.

She doesn't notice the handsome Mexican man with the high

cheekbones and the rippling biceps until he's upon her. It is not that he tackles her or hugs her. He doesn't need to touch her to cover her whole body with his presence.

His name is Manuel. She bothered to learn it only after he half-assed his boss, Juan Gomez's, orders to hold her down and inject her with black-tar heroin two years ago. Manuel cut his teeth as a hench-man for Los Liones cartel, but since Lola stabbed the cartel's leader in the throat, Manuel has pledged his loyalty to her.

She has been sleeping with him for over a year, although in this case, it is appropriate to say there is no sleeping involved. They are fucking. They aren't talking or cuddling or planning. It is fifteen minutes, maybe twenty, of tearing each other apart, of pounding and sweating and moaning, then it is over. He vacates her bed as soon as she has pushed him off her, even though he is spent, his body stuck to the sheets and mattress, craving rest.

"Up, up!" she will say to him, and there is always a five-minute period of groaning and rolling over, of convincing her he is about to put feet to floor and tiptoe out of her bed, out of her apartment, leav-ing no trace behind to confuse Lucy . . . or Lola.

It is Lola who brims with energy after, pulling on a robe and wanting to scrub the floor or prepare food for the busy week ahead.

Is that why she keeps going back to him? To increase her produc-tivity? Is he her secret elixir? A good-luck charm? If so, can she cut him off at any time, like she promises herself, without repercussions?

"*Hola*," Manuel says now. He has his hands in the pockets of his dark jeans. He is tall, six-foot-six, and the knowledge of how much space he takes up causes him to conserve in any way possible—hands in pockets, shoulders hunched, head down. He can stretch to his full height when he needs to intimidate, but now, at this family carnival, he does not want to frighten the children.

"*Hola*," she says. She feels Marcos's and Jorge's eyes on her and her new comrade. The blending of her Mexican and American sol-diers has been a process. Manuel's English is poor, although Lola has caught him working on it in his car. He must have bought a language program, because she can sometimes hear a crisp American woman sounding out words—"cat," "dog," "kitchen," "lunch"—when she approaches his driver's-side window. Unbeknownst to Manuel, she often waits to hear how he sounds these words out, to catch his mistakes, but she always stops when she feels a catch in her heart at his effort. He is learning this language to make her proud. If she admits that to herself, she can't keep kicking him out of her bed.

Next to Manuel, Ramon stands, wrinkled hands clasped behind his back. Ramon is in his sixties, his face a map of craggy, sagging skin. He has clean white hair and clipped nails. Even tonight, a night of celebration, he wears his standard uniform of short-sleeved sky-blue collared shirt and navy-blue work pants. It's the kind of shirt designed to hold a name patch, but Ramon does not let just anyone know his name. He is Lola's cleanup crew, the man who can disappear guns and drugs and bodies. In a pinch, he can forge a passport or a driver's license. He does his job so well that, when he has scrubbed out a weapon or a substance or a life, it is hard to find the slightest evidence it ever existed. He, too, came to Lola from Los Liones, but, unlike Manuel, Jorge and Marcos have accepted him. Ramon rarely speaks, in English or Spanish, and he is too old and has seen too much shit to take part in petty power games. He does his job without complaint, with pride instead of passion, and he goes home to an apartment Lola has never seen, but which she imagines is clean and sparse, like him. Ramon is not a threat. Ramon is not sleeping with his boss.

Lola is not naïve enough to pretend she doesn't notice the dynamic here. Manuel and Ramon stand with her above the courtyard, looking down on Jorge and Marcos.

"Yo, boss," Jorge calls. "You wanna come taste these tortas?"

Lola feels a surge of gratitude for Jorge, smoothing the waters, using a word both the American and Mexican parties can stomach.

"Yeah," she calls back, and she takes the stairs two at a time, her arms at her sides, her two men behind her.

"I tasted it first. No poison," Jorge says, and when Lola laughs, she sees that for once he was not joking.

"What's wrong?" Manuel asks in Spanish.

"Nothing, yo," Jorge answers in English. "We're all good here."

She has not had a chance to recount her meeting with his cousin Camilla, or the hit she called on Camilla's husband. Maybe that is the cause of his tension, but Lola wants tonight to be a party, absent the tribulations of gang rivalries and language barriers and domestic violence.

Lola sinks her teeth into the warm bread of the sandwich. The tomato juice stings her tongue before escaping the side of her mouth. Manuel hands her a napkin. She ignores him. She is not a child. She can clean up after herself.

When the neighbors see Lola in the courtyard, doors begin to open. Children pour onto the shitty dead grass like horses let loose from a starting gate. Soon, Lola's square is full of shouting children running back and forth. In contrast, the weary adults step out tentatively, pulling shawls and jackets over their shoulders to protect them from the slight chill as the sun falls in the fiery sky.

Señora Ocampo stands over a crying child who has skinned his knee.

"That's what happens when you run too fast," she scolds him in Spanish, but the next second the older woman is bending to the ground, whispering to the child that cake and kisses will make it all better. When the old woman kisses his knee, the child stops crying and is back on his feet, running and yelling that someone should pass the ball to him.

Mrs. Hernandez nudges her chubby kindergarten son and her scrawny first-grade boy out the family apartment's door. She carries two daughters, the toddler on one hip, the baby on the other. Lola doesn't know where the Hernandezes' teenage daughter is, but suspects she will make an appearance fashionably late, in a tidal wave of adolescents who are equal parts passion and apathy. Mr. Hernandez follows his wife and their gaggle of children with shoulders hunched from a hard life's work.

When Mrs. Hernandez lands in front of the food tables, she stops, and Mr. Hernandez smashes into his wife.

"Sorry," he says.

"Don't walk so close to me," she reprimands him.

"Sorry," Mr. Hernandez repeats, and Lola doesn't know if she sympathizes with Mr. Hernandez, who should have been looking where he was going, or Mrs. Hernandez, whose husband has impregnated her five times. Is it any wonder the wife is put off by her husband's touch when she has to scream at her fat son not to eat dessert first, then beg her skinny son to please take some sandwiches, all while a toddler is screaming "poop" in her ear and a baby is yanking at her stringy hair?

"Where is Carmen?" Mrs. Hernandez asks her husband about their teenage girl.

"*No se*," he says. Of course he doesn't know.

"And where are the tortillas?" she continues, as if the unexplained absence of both her daughter and her carbohydrate of choice are of equal concern.

"I don't know," her husband says again.

I don't know. Sorry. I don't know. Sorry. Watching this husband and wife, Lola is happy for her empty bed, for her mornings with just Lucy. She doesn't want a partner who doesn't know, who is sorry. She doesn't want to have to ask the questions that make up marriage and family—*are we out of milk, can you take out the trash, what time do you think you need to leave to make sure the kids get to school on time?*

Lola intercepts Mrs. Hernandez with a polite smile. "These sandwiches are from an Italian deli," Lola explains. "The bread is baked fresh daily. My mother and I kept it warm for tonight. Please, try them."

Mrs. Hernandez flushes the darkest red a Mexican American woman can. She did not expect Lola to hear her question about the tortillas.

"They look bloody," Mrs. Hernandez's scrawny six-year-old says. He has pried the top layer of bread from one meatball sub and is staring at the red meat swimming in its bright-red sauce.

"Abel," Mrs. Hernandez hisses.

"Abel," Mr. Hernandez sighs.

"It's okay," Lola says, because she sees Mr. Hernandez's hand clench into a fist behind his back. He is a timid man here in her courtyard, but he has a wife who bosses him around and refuses his touch, and Lola to pay for his groceries. He is poor. He can't support his family. Lola would not find it hard to believe that a man like that might strike a child to give himself the illusion of control.

"We have turkey and Havarti too," Lola says.

"It's fucking good," the fat five-year-old son chirps, his mouth open, his cheeks full as a squirrel's saving nutrients for winter.

"What's Havarti?" the skinny one asks.

The entire Hernandez family, from baby to daddy, looks to Lola for an answer.

"Cheese," Lola responds.

The scrawny kid drops the meatball sub back onto the tray, causing his mother to cry out in disgrace.

"Abel, you touched that sandwich. Now you must eat it," Mrs. Hernandez says in tense English. Lola catches the woman's glance— she wants to make sure Lola is watching her reprimand her son for ruining the food she has provided.

"It's okay," Lola repeats.

"Abel, try the turkey."

"I don't—"

"Abel." It is Mrs. Hernandez again, her voice a bark now, and from the way Abel snaps up a napkin and shoves the turkey sandwich in his mouth, Lola knows that it is Mrs. Hernandez, not her husband, who has raised her hand to their children.

There was a time when Lola would have sought revenge immediately. Now she files what she has deemed fact away for future use. She will take care of the problem, but she is running an empire. She must delegate some of her people's issues to the soldiers she trusts.

When the scrawny Hernandez kid spits his wad of turkey sandwich onto the dead grass of the courtyard, Mrs. Hernandez's hand does fly up and across her son's cheek.

Mr. Hernandez yelps for his wife to stop, but she doesn't. She hits her asshole child, over and over, no longer with the back of her hand, but with her belt, which has come off in the confusion.

Lola darts between the two, catching a smack of the belt on her hip that stings, before two large hands are placed on her waist, removing her from the conflict that isn't a conflict, because it isn't between two adults. It is abuse.

"The fuck?" Lola shouts, but no one hears over Mrs. Hernandez's yelps and Abel's wails.

It is Manuel, standing in his full height over Mrs. Hernandez.

"You will stop now," Manuel says in heavily accented English. He plucks Mrs. Hernandez off her son, yanks the belt from her hands so hard she cries out in pain.

"The fuck," Lola repeats, quiet enough that no one hears. She is glad, because this time the words come out halfhearted instead of angry.

She isn't referring to the courtyard clusterfuck, because there is a different man approaching now. He emerges from a dark-blue sedan, a sensible car with no chrome or rims or tinted windows. He wears denim as dark blue as his car, with no tears, and his short-sleeved plaid button-down is tucked in at the waist. He carries a bright-white casserole dish covered in foil.

He no longer belongs here, but Lola recognizes him.

"Lola," he says, and her men turn to him even though she swears his voice is just as soft as hers. Maybe men recognize the smooth baritone of one of their own better than a woman with a question in her voice.

It is Garcia, her ex, the man she lived with for three years in the little house three blocks over, the man who pretended to lead the Crenshaw Six while Lola pulled the strings from the shadows. The man who was content to toss and turn beside her until Lola decided she wanted to come out of the shadows and receive credit for her work.

"I brought flautas," Garcia says.

Lola senses everyone's eyes on the white casserole dish, the familiar fried food inside. She hears flies buzzing over the now-soggy sandwiches. She doesn't look to see how many are left.

"Who is he?" Manuel asks in Spanish. "Should he be here?"

Jorge and Marcos exchange glances. Lola sees Jorge lick his lips, and she knows he would like some flautas.

"No," says Marcos. Lola can't help but notice her men are speaking to one another, and the observation pleases her.

"Christina made these," Garcia continues, starting to peel back the foil.

"What are you doing here, man?" Jorge asks.

"I heard there was a party—"

"You invited to this party?" Marcos asks, the corner of his mouth curling up in a cruel half smile.

"No, but I was in the neighborhood—"

"You were here with food prepared by a woman?" This is Manuel, in broken English. Lola hears the uncertainty in his voice that would be skepticism in his native tongue. In English, he is just trying to make sure he understands the situation.

"Good fucking point. You're just in the neighborhood with a dish full of flautas?" Jorge nods approval to Manuel, who stands a little straighter.

The whole courtyard waits for Garcia's answer. He is caught, his shirt stiff with starch, his face shaved free of stubble, his tattoos covered.

"I'd like to speak with Lola alone," he says.

"No."

"No."

"No fucking way, you piece of shit." Jorge.

But Lola walks toward her ex. She knows he wants something from her. She needs to respond to his presence, not just let her men do it for her.

"Boss—"

"It's okay."

Manuel puts a hand on her shoulder, but she shakes it off.

She reaches Garcia.

"Why are you here?" she asks in the same soft voice no one heard before.

"I . . . I wanted to see you."

"It's been two years."

"Too long."

"Not really."

Garcia laughs like he doesn't believe her, but she is telling the truth.

"Give me that," Lola says of the casserole dish. Garcia hands it over.

Lola lifts the foil, looks at the flautas inside. They are fried to a crisp golden brown, not a single charred black piece. She could not have achieved such culinary perfection. Then again, she doesn't allow fried food in her house.

Lola turns the dish over and lets the flautas spill to the ground.

The courtyard is quiet. Somewhere else in Huntington Park, a child shouts, a fire truck blares, a car's brakes screech.

"Go now," Lola says.

If Garcia had come to her in private, she would have more time to find out what he wanted from her. She is not fool enough to think his appearance is a random coincidence. She is also not fool enough to think he just couldn't stay away from her. It has been two years, and he has a new woman named Christina who likes him enough to fry a pan full of flautas for a party to which she's not invited.

But Garcia approached her in front of her soldiers and her civilians, and she had to send him away ashamed.

She keeps the casserole dish. He retreats to his car. And when he pulls away from the curb, the Hernandez children start to eat the flautas from the ground.

FOUR

IMPOSTOR

The next morning, Lola wakes with a headache so sharp it makes her forget her bandaged arm. It is early, just before her alarm. She will need to wake Lucy up soon.

The knocking is soft, but Lola is a light sleeper. She has been since childhood, knowing to be on her guard especially when unconscious.

She pulls on a sweatshirt and slippers because there is a chill in the air.

Jorge stands on her threshold, holding a paper sack of oranges.

"*Hola,* boss," he says.

"Early."

"I know. Wanted to catch you before you took Lucy to school."

"The fuck?" Lola jerks her chin at the fruit. Jorge is not one to bring groceries.

"Oranges."

"No shit."

"From my cousin."

"Oh," Lola says. She would never have accepted payment from the battered pregnant woman. Any favor a citizen asks of Lola is free, at least in terms of cash. Her people pay her back in favors when called upon. Sometimes Lola wants information. Sometimes she asks them to betray their own family members. No one knows what Lola will want from them, or when she will want it. Have faith, she tells them, believe in me, and I will not steer you wrong. Two years in, and no one has ever told her no.

"She's real thankful you agreed to see her."

"Uh-huh," Lola says, thinking of everything she must do to get her daughter out of bed and presentable for school: pee, wash hands, help stir the eggs, spread sunflower butter and jam on toast, ice pack for lunch.

"Her husband, man, what a trip," Jorge says.

"Yeah, well," Lola says. "Same old shit. But he's taken care of."

"Huh?"

"Her husband. I took care of him," Lola says, because even if the battered pregnant woman's piece-of-shit husband has yet to suffer at the wrong end of Hector's shiv, Lola finally has faith in her baby brother.

"How'd you do that?"

Lola gives Jorge a sharp look. He is allowed to take orders, he is allowed to voice his opinion when asked, but he can't question her methods when she either didn't ask or it's too late to change them.

"It's just . . . she wanted me to bring the oranges up first. Make sure now's a good time. To meet you."

"What?"

"Oh, that's her now. Marisol!" Jorge calls out to a woman who is all stomach, waddling across Lola's courtyard in a stretch-cotton dress. She has the same black hair and brown skin as the woman who sat across from Lola at her kitchen table yesterday, but now Lola remembers—that woman, also presumably nine months pregnant, didn't waddle. That woman didn't need to stop in the baked heat to catch her breath.

"I'm . . . so sorry," the woman gasps from below. "I sometimes get dizzy."

"That's your cousin?" Lola says to Jorge.

"Yeah. Marisol. My piece-of-shit uncle's daughter. Married a piece of shit like her father. Now he gotsta go."

"Is her husband in prison?"

"Prison? Shit no. He beats women, not cops. No judicial system got time to waste on that."

Lola is quiet. Jorge shifts his weight from left foot to right and back again in the stretch of seconds it takes her to feel bile bubble from her stomach to the top of her esophagus.

"You know, I'm not saying that's right. I think it's a shame the system lets men get away with that." Her silence has made Jorge step up on a soapbox, and, while Lola believes he means every word he's saying, she also sees he doesn't like to admit his own opinions here, on her doorstep, in public. Jorge is a soldier. He takes orders. He makes her laugh. He keeps his opinions to himself.

"Jorge," Lola says at last, and he stops talking, his shoulders sagging with relief. He does not want to be the one to effect social change. He will leave that to her.

"A woman claiming to be your cousin came to see me yesterday morning."

Jorge wants to ask a question but thinks better of it.

"She got to me through Maria," Lola says, because she knows Jorge was going to ask how someone could get to Lola without an introduction. The confession feels good. She wants Jorge to call her an idiot. She wants him to tell her she should have known better. Because she is, and she should have. *But the woman was huge,* she wants to say, *belly out to here, claiming her husband would have raised his hand to a tiny baby.*

"Aw shit," is all Jorge says, meaning to be quiet because he knows how Lola feels about her mother, which is interesting, because Lola isn't sure herself.

"This woman—Camilla, she called herself—claimed she was having problems with her husband. And that he was in prison."

"Was?"

"Is. Maybe." Lola stops and takes a few deep breaths. She has to stop stumbling. "He was eligible for parole soon. She asked me to make sure he never got out."

"Which prison?" Jorge asks. He is putting together the pieces, thinking ahead, feeling a shit storm on the horizon like a tingle of heat up a dog's spine before an earthquake.

"Locust Ridge."

"Aw shit." Again.

"We don't know who she really was or why she really wanted that man dead. We have to get a message to Hector. Call it off."

Marisol reaches them at this moment, huffing and puffing at the top of the open stairwell's concrete steps. She's wearing a purple cotton dress and flip-flops. She leans over, scrunching up her big belly over swollen ankles.

"I'm . . . sorry . . . Lola . . . I mean, Ms. Vasquez," Marisol gasps.

Lola knows she needs to be on the road, figuring out how she can speak to her brother on a day with no visiting hours, but she can't look at this woman without wanting to whisk her inside and sit her on the sofa with a glass of icy lemonade. So that's what she does.

Once Lola has Marisol situated on the sofa, her feet propped up on an overturned wicker laundry basket, Lola leads Jorge into the kitchen.

"I should hear her story," Lola says.

"She got a husband who beats her. And he'll beat the baby too, soon as it cries. That's her story. Same as the other woman's, minus the prison."

"I'll fix it."

"'Course you will," Jorge says. "That's a twenty-dollar fix. You got a baseball bat and men with guns. You'll get him out the neighborhood. But she's here, with her lemonade, and he can't get to her."

Lola knows he is right, and she loves that Jorge can make his own opinion sound like a pep talk, steering her in the direction he knows is right but would never tell her.

"Now. How can we get a message to Hector?"

"We can't. No visiting hours for two more days."

"What about email?"

"He can check his email once a week."

"Okay, okay. We can work with that."

"On Sunday."

It is Wednesday. Whoever Jorge's fake cousin wanted dead will be that way by Sunday.

Lola thinks of driving to Locust Ridge at a hundred miles an hour, of claiming a woman's hysterical love for her brother, letting them see emotion trump a cold, calculated plan to save a man, a criminal, she doesn't even know. But it is rush hour. Traffic out of Los Angeles will be moving at a crawl. Even if she were to arrive at Locust Ridge at a decent hour, the guards will let her flop like a caught fish on a cold floor.

She needs special treatment.

"Jorge," she says, digging a burner phone from a stash under her kitchen sink. "Go get Maria, please."

"You got it, boss."

He is gone by the time she is dialing the number.

Andrea picks up, a bit breathless, on the first ring. She sounds like Lola has caught her in the middle of something she shouldn't be doing . . . like trafficking drugs to the people she is supposed to protect and serve . . . Or exercising at work. Or having couch sex in her office.

"It's me," Lola says.

"Hello." Andrea is cautious not because she doesn't recognize Lola's voice, but because she does. Lola finds it strangely satisfying, not having to state her name for an L.A. deputy district attorney to recognize her.

"I have to see my brother."

"You can," Andrea says. "At visiting hours."

"You think I don't know that?"

"No," Andrea says.

It's only then Lola realizes Andrea must have someone in her office, someone she can't tell to fuck off so she can deal with her illicit side business.

"I need to get him a message. Or . . . get him out."

Andrea's silence keeps Lola talking.

"He might be in danger. If . . . I don't get to him in time."

"For a funeral?"

"What? No . . ." Lola wants to feel like she's in command of this conversation. But she does not have the power to access her brother without Andrea, who's got the power of the DA's office behind her.

They are fifty-fifty partners in finance, but when it comes to the bureaucratic trappings of California correctional facilities, Andrea's the one in charge.

"Of course you can request temporary release for the death of your mother."

At that moment, Maria walks into Lola's kitchen carrying a plastic sack of avocados. Lola's mother ignores the fact that Lola is holding a phone to her ear.

"From the community garden," Maria says.

Six months ago, a squat house with barred windows stinking of meth sat on the lot next door to Lola's apartment complex. A chemical miscalculation by the amateur meth cooks led to a fire, the house burned down, and the owners—whom Lola never met—were relegated to either coffins or prison. Lola transformed the place with the bare hands of others, but she paid her workers. Now there is a community garden next door instead of a lab that manufactures shitty meth.

"Whose death?" Lola says to Andrea, just to hear it again.

"Your mother's," Andrea repeats.

Lola licks her lips at the fantasy, then sees the fear on Maria's face and feels an instant pang of guilt.

"Who's dead?" Maria asks.

Lola covers the flip phone's mouthpiece with her hand, unsure if this move will mask her voice, and says, "No one. Hypothetical."

She sees her mother attempting to mouth *hypothetical,* and turns her back, because watching Maria struggle only compounds her own guilt.

"What do I need to make that happen?" Lola says to Andrea.

"A death certificate. But it has to be an official copy."

Lola thinks of Ramon, her cleanup man. His cartel career involved not only disappearing dead bodies, but live ones as well. It was Ramon who created masterpiece passports for fleeing criminals or refugees or their loved ones. Ramon could provide escape from revenge or prison or pain. In that way, he is a true artist. He can forge a death certificate, although Lola doesn't know that she can have him put Maria's name on it. It would feel too good.

"What about a grandmother?" Lola mumbles to Andrea.

"That'll work too," Andrea says.

"Do I get it to you?"

"I can make sure it goes to the appropriate department." Lola can sense her partner doesn't want to say more with someone else in the room. "I need to go now," Andrea says. "Talk soon." And she's gone.

"I don't know about these avocados. They smell like metal." Maria sniffs the skin of one of the deep-green fruits.

"Then throw them out."

"A waste."

"If they cause food poisoning, they'll be wasted anyway."

"Huh," Maria says, trying to wrap her head around her daughter's observation.

"Mom. Sit down." Lola gestures to one of the kitchen chairs.

Maria obeys before she thinks to ask "What's wrong?"

"The woman you brought here."

"Jorge's cousin?"

"She wasn't Jorge's cousin. His cousin is that pregnant woman in the living room."

"Oh," Maria says. She doesn't seem surprised or apologetic. Lola needs to make her mother feel something, preferably bad.

"You brought her to me. You vouched for her."

"I told you who she told me she was," Maria says.

Both women are sitting up straight now, and Lola takes the jolt she gave her mother as enough.

"Okay. That's fine," Lola says in a tone she hopes conveys to Maria that it's not, but she catches her mother nodding agreement. In Maria's mind, as usual, she has done nothing wrong. "But I need you to think. What else did she say?"

"Just that she was pregnant."

"Mom."

"She had walked here."

"She was that pregnant and she walked here? How far?"

"Well, it couldn't have been that far. She looked really pregnant to me."

"Yes, she looked that way, but she lied about everything else, and she walked, and she wasn't out of breath, was she?"

"No," Maria admits.

Lola has never been pregnant, but her mother has, at least twice that Lola knows. *What was it like,* she wants to ask her mother, *carrying me inside you? What did you feel? Doesn't having carried a child qualify you to tell when another woman is lying about it? Shouldn't you know better than me? Shouldn't I have known better about you?*

Instead, Lola asks, "Is there anything else you remember?"

Maria scrunches up her eyes like a child waiting for a surprise. But when she opens them several seconds later all she says is "I'm sorry. There's nothing."

Lola nods, and her mother knows that is her cue to rise. Maria has reached the doorway to the living room when she turns, patting the pockets of her jeans, which are small but still baggy. Years of heroin have made Maria's body not hold on to food.

"She did drop this."

Lola sees the white rectangle of paper and feels a pissed-off pang that her mother gets to be both the one who fucked up and the one who saved the day. Or maybe Lola is pissed at herself for trusting her mother in the first place. She takes the receipt from Maria and scans it. It's from a liquor store several blocks away. Lola looks to see what the woman bought. Cheap vodka. A bag of straws. A candy bar.

When she reaches the bottom, her heart begins to beat faster. She reads the total, and only then does she allow herself to check the payment method. Credit.

"Yes," Lola says.

"What?"

"She paid with a credit card," Lola explains.

Maria peers over Lola's shoulder. "She bought vodka. Pregnant." Maria dares to cluck her tongue in judgment of the woman Lola suspects might have called a hit on a somewhat innocent man, but most likely would not pimp her own children out for drug money.

"Piece of shit," Lola says, the closest she will ever come to insulting her own mother. But as usual, Maria doesn't realize Lola's words are meant for her, and, even if she did, Lola would deny it.

"Her credit-card number is blocked out. With the little X's," Maria notes.

"Not the last four numbers," Lola says, grateful she needs only a piece of the puzzle to start seeing the whole picture.

FIVE

THE CALM BEFORE

The weekday crowd of surfers, unemployed actors, businesspeople on early breaks, and construction workers who have been working since six overwhelms Lola every time she ventures west to Bay Cities. Many of the deli's patrons are beachgoers, tracking sand and saltwater from the doors to the glass case that runs the length of the store. Some wear suits. Others, yoga pants. Here, they all take a number.

Lola spots her partner, Andrea Dennison Whitely, several surfers over, staring at the chip rack as she waits for one of the men working the carvers behind the counter to call her number. Lola watches Andrea's green eyes flit from sea salt to barbecue and back again. After a few rounds of indecision, an oddity for the prosecutor, Andrea grabs both bags at once.

"Twenty-seven," a man barks, and Andrea steps up to the counter. Lola can't hear the other woman's order from here, and she shouldn't be paying so much attention. The two of them—one brown, one white, one a drug dealer, one a prosecutor—should have no business together that doesn't involve bars between them.

It bothers her that they've met here several times over the course of two years, but Lola doesn't know what Andrea orders. It's not like they can sit at one of the concrete tables on the patio overlooking Lincoln Boulevard. Instead, they get their sandwiches in sacks and sneak out back to discuss whatever urgent business has brought them together in the flesh.

Until Lola became her partner in the drug-trafficking business, she had not known Andrea smoked when she was stressed. She was not stressed often.

Today, a plastic bag slipped over her wrist, Andrea lights up as soon as Lola lands with her own bag.

"Not hungry?" Lola asks.

"Busy week," Andrea says.

"Trial?" Lola tries again.

Andrea shakes her head and sucks in a lungful of tar and nicotine. When they first began working together two summers before, Lola would have respected Andrea's silent command that the time for Lola to question her was over. Today, with her brother in jeopardy and Andrea able to open the prison gates, Lola plans to keep prodding. They may not be able to sit across from each other at a Bay Cities table, but they are partners.

As Andrea takes another suck on her cigarette, Lola notices the changes in the woman's physical appearance. She doesn't look older than her thirty-seven years, based on the birth date Lola had learned peeking at Andrea driver's license when she opened her wallet to pay for lunch at one of their early meetings. She doesn't seem stressed. Her skin is milk pale, her nose pert, her eyes a burning green, all somewhat permanent qualities, even though this is L.A., where plastic surgery is ubiquitous to even the most noble of professions.

No, it's not Andrea's skin or her facial structure. It's her hair, Lola thinks, two shades darker, so brown it could be mistaken for black in the right light. Andrea dyed her hair. Many women—or, in the case of Los Angeles, all the women—her age do the same. They cover up grays, they delete the signs of age, they go lighter. Blondes have more fun. But darker? Who takes chestnut locks and blackens them?

Lola looks to her own braid, a thick rope of silky black laid over her shoulder like someone posed it that way. It is almost the same color as Andrea's. Could it be the woman is trying to emulate her? No, Lola thinks, Andrea doesn't want to be anyone but herself.

"Did you dye your hair?"

At first, Andrea pretends not to hear the question, instead taking a large bite of her sandwich. When hot peppers escape the bread, she pinches them between two purple nails and pops them in her mouth. Her appetite has returned at a convenient time.

Two years ago, Andrea had dispatched her faithful dirty cop, Sergeant Bubba, to the doorstep of Maria's old apartment. There, he had delivered a message—a time and place for Lola to show up. Lola knew the orders came from Andrea. She had also known she hadn't wanted to work for anyone but herself. Still, after the two weeks she had that August, she knew the value of stability, especially given the little girl who'd been learning to play with a dollhouse—the one Lola stole from Blooming Gardens—in the corner.

"I don't want to work for you," Lola had told her.

"You wouldn't work for me. You'd work with me. We'd be partners."

"Fifty-fifty?"

"That's what partnership is."

Two years later, outside Bay Cities, Lola has started to realize that even though she and Andrea split their profits fifty-fifty, the balance of power might be off. She can't get into Locust Ridge to see her own brother without Andrea making a call to the warden. She can't know what kind of sandwich Andrea orders here because they can't both have a seat at the same table.

"I felt like a change," Andrea says, flicking her darker hair over her shoulder. "Something in the air, right? Something not quite right. You feel it too, don't you?"

Andrea meets Lola's eye for the first time, and Lola has to look away. Andrea does that sometimes, looks into your soul and sees it naked. It can be frightening.

Andrea's mood matches the gray day, and Lola wants to get out of the West Side, where the cloudy sky doesn't match the multimillion-dollar real estate. Gray sky goes with her neighborhood—poverty and people trying to scrub permanent filth from crumbling homes. Here, knowing for sure she has killed someone she shouldn't, it is unsettling.

Lola had tried to call Hector multiple times, with constant transfers, dropped calls, and flat-out refusals her only response from Locust Ridge. She had tried on a frantic tone, thinking that would help, but it only made the guards and administrators who were the gatekeepers of the phones at Locust Ridge sigh louder and enunciate their words more clearly, separating them into pinprick syllables that all spelled the same answer: No.

Finally, at ten o'clock last night, the landline in Lola's apartment had rung. She had snatched up the receiver before the first shrill tone died.

"Yes, I accept," she had said, because she was expecting the automated woman's voice telling her she had a collect call from the correctional facility.

She had wanted to say, "Please. Don't do it," as soon as she heard Hector's breath on the line.

But before she could, he had said, "It's done."

"Okay," Lola had said instead.

An older couple comes out the back door of Bay Cities now, the man banking left, the woman right, spectacled eyes searching for their car in the small parking lot. The man sees Andrea, but she doesn't see him back. The man doesn't stop looking at the two of them, though, eyes squinting, as if he can't believe there are two women out back sharing a cigarette. As he inches closer, Andrea leans toward Lola.

"And what did he say to you after he hit you?"

The game Andrea has begun is an old favorite. Prosecutor, victim, white, brown. If anyone recognizes you, make them think we're here on legit business.

"He said he was sorry . . . that he would never do it again," Lola replies, bowing her head so low Andrea, and the eavesdropping old man, can see the careful part down the center.

"And then what?"

"Then I . . . I don't remember anything. He must have put something in my drink."

Andrea stubs her cigarette out against the dumpster, biting the inside of her right cheek to keep from saying something she'll regret. Lola has found Andrea never says something she'll regret. She is a woman who expects every word to make its way into print, be it hard copy or online. She speaks in euphemisms and code when she's referencing her drug business. Otherwise, she is partial to sound bites that outline injustices for women and minorities. On good days, she expresses empathy—she has taken Lola's hand in hers when outside eyes land on the two of them.

"I can help you," Andrea says. "But you've got to trust me."

"Funny. He says the same shit."

Andrea hefts her lunch sack farther back onto her forearm, a signal that she is going to walk the fuck away if Lola doesn't lay off the passive-aggressive jabs. But Andrea is a tough lady. A few flirty barbs from Lola should ping off her thick skin like drops of water on leather. Unless Lola has gotten at a truth even she doesn't understand.

The old woman calls the old man over to their car, and they inch out of the parking space with the care of people who should not be driving.

"So did you find out? About the guy?" Lola asks, the purpose of this meeting. She wants to know whom she might have had killed and why.

"Yes," Andrea says, waving the question away as if it's a pesky fly. She is irritated. Maybe at Lola. She lights up again.

"What's going on?"

"Shit at work."

"Which work?"

"This shit show," Andrea says, gesturing with her cigarette hand to all of Los Angeles.

Lola doesn't bother to point out that this could apply to either her legitimate job as a prosecutor or her domain as a drug lord. Instead, Lola waits. She has never been one to fill silence. She lets people do that for her, and she listens.

"Los Liones is gone. We took down their leader, they can't get their shit together."

Two summers ago, Lola slit Juan Gomez's throat with a piece of glass she found lodged in her foot. Andrea was pissed Lola didn't leave him alive so she could prosecute the man who led Los Liones.

"You understand I'm speaking as a prosecutor now," Andrea says, and Lola does, appreciating the fact that Andrea will not speak her crime aloud. That would be foolish, despite the damage to Lola's ego.

"It took two years, but there's a new game in town. A different cartel."

"What cartel?"

"Rivera. Started up in Colombia by a man named Paulo Cortes. He developed an organization that handled every aspect of the business—growing, harvesting, transport, marketing, sales. If Paulo had lived, maybe you could have learned something from him."

Lola stays silent. Andrea's speech is beginning to sound less like a history lesson and more like a reprimand.

"This cartel, Rivera . . . They got to Texas. But apparently the Lone Star State wasn't big enough, and now they've come west. It's Manifest Destiny with heroin. They're violent, no one knows who the leaders are. Same story, different fucking day. It's like goddamn Whac-A-Mole in this town." Andrea grinds the sucked-up cigarette under her heel and plucks it between her fingertips, and Lola isn't sure if she's hesitant to litter or just doesn't want to leave DNA.

"You've got competition," Lola says, understanding the smoke and the hair dye and the lingering dread.

Andrea is holding a fresh cigarette and a hot-pink Bic, but Lola doesn't know where either prop came from. She has just realized Andrea is not carrying a handbag.

"We do," Andrea says. "But that's beside the point. I'm talking about competition for my resources. I can't prosecute wife beaters and rapists and child molesters if I'm out trying to turn these cartel kids on their superiors. Goddamn drug war. Fucking useless." Andrea lights the third cigarette. Lola has never seen her this out of sorts.

"Funny thing for a prosecutor to say."

"What? You think a goddamn thing we're doing is working?"

"Who's 'we'? The law?"

"Yeah."

"Don't know about that side of things. But I know I'm making money."

"You have a daughter. Is that what you would say to her?"

Lola doesn't know how to answer the question. Until this moment, she has not considered that there will come a day when Lucy asks what Lola does for a living, and that Lola will have the power to destroy the little girl's life whether she gives her the truth or a lie. If it's the truth, Lola will have opened up a potential for her daughter to take over what could become a family business. If it's a lie, Lucy will never know the true Lola, the Lola who is a mother and a drug lord, who, by the time Lucy asks the question, will have built an illegal empire that spans the multitude of cities that make up Los Angeles, from desert to coast. If it's a lie, Lola will never get to say to her daughter—
All this, I did for you.

"I don't know what I'll tell her."

"You and every mother out there," Andrea says, gesturing to the chain-link fence that serves as a barrier between the alley and the row of houses and apartment buildings beyond. Lola knows her gesture is meant to encompass more, to encircle every mother, every parent, in Los Angeles, her city, but it reminds Lola they are just two women hiding in an alley where no one can see them, plotting to take over the world.

"You said you knew who he was. The man." *The one I had killed,* Lola finishes the thought.

"I already told you," Andrea says.

Andrea has started toward her apple-red Audi, slicked between two SUVs parked over the lines.

"You told me about a cartel, and Manifest Destiny, and that I could have learned something from their leader if he were alive."

If he were alive.

Andrea stops and speaks with her back to Lola.

"Have you figured it out yet?"

Lola has. She has killed a man named Paulo Cortes, one of the founders of the Rivera cartel.

Lola has done what men do. She has started a war, and she doesn't even know why.

SIX

SWAP

The waiting room for visitation is colder today, or Lola is anxious, she's not sure which. She has her arms crossed over her stomach, her hood up because she didn't have time to dry her hair before she set out on her journey here, to Locust Ridge. It is Saturday. She has a forged death certificate for a fake *abuela* in her hand. She isn't sure it will be enough. She has tears, if she needs them. If she'd thought about it, she would have rummaged through a neighborhood consignment shop for a plain black dress and worn it here, to make the fake funeral seem imminent. Lola can't remember the last time she wore a dress, any dress, not just a black one that indicated mourning. But has she truly buried anyone she was supposed to grieve? She never knew her father, her mother is still alive and awaiting relapse, her brother is in prison. She shot her first love, Carlos, between the eyes, and had her new soldiers prove their loyalty to her by abandoning his body in the Angeles National Forest. Even if she had wanted to make a show of grief for Carlos, there was never a body over which she could cry.

"Lola Vasquez," the female guard calls from behind smeared glass.

The five-step journey from stiff plastic chair to smeared glass and guard takes far too long.

"What's your purpose here today, ma'am?" the female guard asks. She is black and bulky, not mean, but not nice either.

"I need to get my brother. For our *abuela*'s funeral."

"Special request?"

"Yes, that's right."

"You want to see the warden?"

"Yes," Lola says, trying to sound more sure than she is.

The warden's office is smaller than she would have expected, and there are piles of files on every surface. The phone is ringing when she enters, but the warden's secretary seems more concerned with the malfunctioning coffee pot. She bangs on the metal sides, begging it to "Come on! Come on!" She is a thin, nervous woman in a pencil skirt and sweater vest, reminding Lola of a librarian, or what she has read about librarians in books.

"Sit down," the secretary says to Lola when she catches her staring.

Lola does. The phone keeps ringing. Lola keeps her arms crossed even though it isn't cold in here. When she checks the forged death certificate, she spots her own sweat staining the edge.

The man who enters is small, no more than five and a half feet tall, wearing a suit two sizes too large for his hunched frame. Muddled chestnut hair lines the bottom of his bald skull, and he has a mustache to match. Lola catches sight of a white powdered crumb stuck in the patch of thick facial hair right under his nose, and for a second, she thinks, *Cocaine.* Then she hears the crinkle of plastic wrap, the labored chewing of someone trying to hurry their breakfast doughnut as the warden says, "Ms. Vasquez. I'm Warden Thorpe. What can I do for you?"

"My brother . . . it's my brother. Or my grandmother. She died. Passed away." Lola hands over the forged certificate with trembling fingers she hopes can be attributed to grief and not fear of getting caught. She doesn't care about prison time. She wants to get her brother out of here before the Rivera Cartel has time to retaliate.

"Hector Vasquez," the warden says, and the way the man says her brother's name, she can tell this warden has no fucking clue who Hector is. Good.

"Yes."

"Must be an ideal inmate 'cause I haven't heard his name."

"Thank you."

"Did you raise him?"

"Yes," Lola says, but where there should be pride, she feels the sting of insult. What stereotype does she embody, here in the warden's office, a Latina begging for her convict baby brother's right to grieve? What assumption has Warden Thorpe made about her, sitting across from him, that he felt not only the need, but the right, to ask her if she and Hector came from a broken mother whose mantle Lola had to take up at so young an age?

Lola must keep her eye on the prize—getting her brother out of this prison before the cartel can avenge one of their founding fathers' deaths. She decides to use her meeting with the warden, however brief it may be, to gather some intelligence.

Warden Thorpe is perusing the death certificate, jotting notes in a spiral notebook. His computer, a large, loud desktop, dings with an email, and the warden immediately turns to his screen, his mouth half open in equal parts anticipation and concentration, peering over his spectacles instead of through them. Lola decides to hold her question until he has finished hunting and pecking a response. When she hears the whoosh of the email beginning its journey, she pounces.

"Do you have many? Ideal inmates?"

The warden gives her a kind smile. "Not nearly enough."

"What makes an inmate ideal?"

The warden shifts in his seat, and the chair's metal frame bounces and squeaks under even his slight frame. "Obedience. Quiet. Patience."

"And a bad one?"

"Everything else," the warden says, and Lola's not sure he's joking until he throws his head back in a laugh that sends him dropping back in his chair. It is only now she realizes this man finds her attractive—he is trying to impress her.

"Who's the worst?" she presses, determined to ride this wave of good fortune.

The warden sits up straighter now. He folds his hands together and leans toward her. "The worst is gone now," he says.

"What did he do?" Lola leans forward, letting the warden see her tongue tickle her lip in anticipation. It is a poor substitute for the cleavage she wouldn't show even if she had it, but it works.

"Organized crime. Drug running. Torturing, maiming. Women and children." The warden looks into Lola's eyes as he says all these words, craving her response. At least he's not someone who insists that, because she's a little lady, she shouldn't have to hear these things. She's Latina. She raised her convict baby brother. He knows, and maybe even appreciates, that she has seen some shit.

Lola is also sure he wouldn't say this shit in front of a white woman.

"And he got out?"

"Somebody shivved him," he says, watching for the proper hardening of her face, the apathy of a ghetto girl.

"Oh well." She shrugs, and the warden likes this response so much she thinks for a second he might take her hand.

"Your brother will meet you at the gates in ten minutes. Please have him back in seventy-two hours."

Lola doesn't know what she was expecting—demand for a blow job, a hand job, some kind of job. Instead, Warden Thorpe has gone back to his computer, where he taps out another email and yells for his throwback secretary, whose name is Mona, to call the guards and get Vasquez ready for temporary release.

Lola stands, and he notices and stands too. He offers his hand first. "It's been a pleasure, Ms. Vasquez," he says.

"Thank you."

When she is almost to the door, the warden calls after her, "Tell Andrea I said hello. Though I hope you don't have cause to go back to her again soon, right?"

Now Lola knows the score. The warden has tolerated her and her request because Andrea made a call. To him, she is just another "ideal inmate," a brown woman who keeps her head down and does nothing to attract attention.

When Lola arrives at the gates, she finds a guard with a mustache, thin frame, and spectacles identical to the warden's. She wonders if they are related, but then she is hearing the buzzer, followed by the name "Vasquez" called in a deep baritone as the bars slide open, and she is seeing an inmate in an orange jumpsuit walk through the open space where before there was a cage.

But the inmate is not her brother. It is a fat Mexican with capped teeth, a man with a good twenty years on Hector.

"Here he is. Your brother," the guard sneers at her, and she knows this man is in on the swap.

She also knows that wherever Hector is, he is no longer in this prison. The Rivera Cartel must have taken Hector to a second location long before Lola arrived here and sat across from the Warden.

The cartel has begun its retaliation against her, and Lola has no choice but to join the war she began.

SEVEN

BATTERED

The storage facility Jorge's harmless thief of an uncle owns is dark, even during the day. When cash from her partnership with Andrea began rolling in almost two years ago, Lola had doubled the amount of money Jorge was slipping to his uncle to make sure no customers were around when the Crenshaw Six needed to use one of the facility's twenty units.

"For this amount?" Jorge's uncle had said. "Take one side. Anytime. I'll keep the customers away."

"You only got ten customers?"

"Economy's shit. People don't got extra stuff to store," Jorge's uncle had claimed.

Lola hadn't been present for the conversation, but she knew enough about Jorge's uncle to know his customers—lower-middle-class residents of Huntington Park who would rather be dragged naked through the streets than give up that one basketball with the Michael Jordan signature that could be worth some dough, if it weren't deflated and dinged and forged. No one in Lola's neighborhood de-clutters. They hold tight to what little is theirs, and they store overflow crap in a cheap facility like this.

Lola has been known to use the keys Jorge got from his uncle to peek inside some of the units, and she's not surprised at the junk she finds—cheap scalded pots with blackened bottoms, chewed-through cat toys, cartons of baby onesies to be passed down through generations, but not for another decade. Until then, they stay here, suspended in time, useless to wailing, starving, cold babies.

It was the onesies that aligned Lola with Jorge's uncle. He has been in the storage game long enough to know that many of his customers, once their things are out of sight, never think to retrieve them. They just need to know they're here, sealed shut in darkness. So what harm is he doing if he takes a few things, not for himself, but for the greater good? Jorge's uncle is a kind of junkyard Robin Hood, stealing shit from his own storage facility and making sure it goes to someone who can use it.

When Lola had mentioned the onesies to him, he hadn't asked what she was doing here or why she was snooping around his customers' belongings. Instead, he had said, "Show me."

She had, and he had done a quick stretch of his arms before hoisting the box, which couldn't have weighed more than two or three pounds, and removing it.

"What will you do with it?" she had asked.

"I know a guy, just lost his job, and just had a baby. Bought all the onesies in newborn size, but the baby's fat as shit."

And that was that. Jorge's uncle had given the Crenshaw Six free rein on one of the facility's two hallways. Ten units to themselves. And none of the facility's legit customers could hear what was going on inside one of the Crenshaw Six units if they came to retrieve something from their unit on the other side. That never happened, though. Once an item was relegated to one of these units, it was gone for good, a body buried in the dirt, useless but treasured, never to be seen or touched again, because who wants to see a loved one turned to rot?

Now Lola and Manuel walk together down the Crenshaw Six hallway. A few weeks ago, Lola had given Ramon cash to replace the lightbulbs and repair some pipes that leaked sludge onto the concrete floor. Lola hasn't been here since she assigned him the task, but now she sees Ramon has done a meticulous job, buying bulbs with enough light to illuminate any pitfalls, but not enough to give the illusion of comfort.

Manuel isn't talking, and she wonders if there's something on his mind, or if this is how he behaves when he's about to do what they're about to do. She likes to talk a bit before, to surprise her soldiers with questions about their personal lives. The problem with Manuel is, as far as she knows, she is his personal life. She is fucking him, she is kicking him out of bed, and then she is falling easily into blissful sleep, alone. She doesn't want anything more, especially not while she's raising Lucy, so there is nothing to press with him here, no wondering when they might make it official. She wants this fuckfest strictly off the books.

"Are you hungry?" she asks, but the question sounds more like an invitation than she would have liked.

"No," he says, but only after he's searched whatever he can see of her face and determined that is what she wants him to say.

"Okay."

They stop in front of Storage Unit Number 7. This is Lola's unit, the one she works most, the one where she shot a woman between the eyes two years ago last summer. She feels comfortable inside, she knows how many strides it takes to pace from one side of the unit to the other during an interrogation. She has found that pacing keeps her calm, but it makes her subject nervous and, therefore, more likely to babble.

Lola nods to Manuel, who keys open the padlock, unrolling the metal door with a ripping clang that reveals the woman who claimed to be Jorge's cousin. She wears a stretchy cotton dress and a baby bump, and she's sweating even though outside the November day is pleasant. There is no air conditioning here.

"Water," Lola says, and Manuel tosses her a bottle from the pack they keep in the corner. "Thank you."

Manuel knows that is his cue. He disappears, rolling the door shut, and when the final rumble of metal dissipates, all Lola can hear is the woman's labored breathing. She is frightened.

No one has touched her yet, because Lola wants to be clear on certain facts first.

"Drink this," Lola says to the woman who may or may not be named Camilla as she hands over the water. No one has tied her up, because she's too scared to run.

The woman gulps the water so fast Lola thinks she will choke. In a few seconds, the whole bottle is gone, and the woman's breath comes in gasps, as if Lola has been holding her underwater instead of quenching her thirst.

"Stand up."

The woman obeys.

"Take off your clothes."

"What?"

Lola stays quiet. The woman accepts the silence for a moment, then does as she's told, unwinding from her lengths of cotton, down to her bra and underwear . . . and the fake pregnancy belly that helped her win Lola's compassion.

"Why are you still wearing that?" Lola asks. "Con's over."

"People are nicer when I'm wearing it."

"Nicer how?" Lola asks, more for her own curiosity than to solve a mystery that will help her brother.

"They sometimes give me free shit. Snacks and water. A seat on the subway."

So this woman is one of the handful who use L.A.'s poor but empty and, therefore, clean excuse for an underground public transportation system.

"I'm giving you free water. And I did you a favor. A big, fat fucking favor."

"I'm sorry, I know." The woman stands before Lola, dimples of fat in her stomach visible now that her belly lies discarded on the cold concrete floor.

"I didn't ask for anything in return. I did what you asked."

"I'm sorry," the woman repeats, and Lola can hear her crying now.

Lola takes a folding chair from the corner and shakes it open. She sits backward on it, her hands on the chair's headrest, her head tilted as she contemplates the woman in front of her—flabby arms, toned calves, dimpled tummy, stringy hair. She sees bruises too, yellow and purple pools of blood deep under the skin.

"Who's been hitting you?" Lola asks.

The question gets the woman's attention. When she looks up at Lola, she is not only crying but sobbing, snot bubbling at the edge of her left nostril.

"Please don't kill me," she says.

"What's your name?"

"Flora."

"Flora, I asked you a fucking question. Who's been hitting you?"

"My husband."

Lola sighs, indicating both her displeasure with Flora's answer and her unwillingness to fall for this scam again.

"See, Flora, that's weird, 'cause last I heard, your husband's in prison, and you asked me to make sure he never got out."

"I know, I know." The woman's breath catches one, two, three times in her chest, punctuated by a wail of a sob that Lola waits out, chin on her hands, peering up at Flora like she's a curious specimen to be examined and explained.

"You lied to me," Lola says, because she wants to see where Flora's narrative will go now that she's painted into a corner, stuck on Lola's turf in bra and underwear, belly discarded, men with guns two units away.

"I did. But only about part of it."

"The part where you ordered a hit?"

"Yes, that part."

Flora isn't looking Lola in the eye, but Lola can tell from the woman's tone that she doesn't realize that is the only part that matters. Not the hit itself, but that Lola ordered her own baby brother to carry it out.

"But the other part . . . the part about my husband and the road rage and him beating that man . . . that part was true."

"So your husband is in prison?"

"No." Flora looks up again, and Lola thinks this woman is good.

She knows when to look her captor in the eye. She knows this part of the story will count with Lola. "He's home. With me."

"Nobody called the police?"

"Of course someone called the police. But Johnny, that's my husband, scared that other guy so much he wouldn't ID him. Nobody ended up doing anything . . . until you."

Flattery. Lola would let Flora continue with the compliments if she didn't have so much other shit to do.

Lola hears a machine whirring to life across the hall, where Ramon has set up a makeshift printing press. It is this machine that forged the final death certificate for Maria's mother, a Mexican woman whom Lola never met. All she knows about Rosita Vasquez is that she spoke no English and used to slap a young Maria across the face for minor infractions like breathing too loudly in a quiet room. Apple, tree, not far, and all that, Lola thinks, then squashes it when she feels her heart speed up, her stomach churning. Lucy, she thinks, cycle of abuse, apple, far, tree. Then she remembers that, for all her failings as a mother, Maria has never laid a hand on her. She left that to the men in her life, the ones who brought her heroin, and they never hit Lola either.

"Where's Johnny now?" Lola sighs, wondering if shouldering someone else's burdens will always help her shutter her own.

"At home. He lost his job. He's been drinking a lot."

"Jesus Christ," Lola says, because how many times does she have to hear this story, with its identical piece-of-shit men and their drinking habits and their taking their drunken frustrations out on the vulnerable?

"She said she could make it stop."

The pronoun springs Lola from her chair, where she's been playing at a casual cool she can no longer pretend. Flora has surprised her.

"She? A woman sent you to me?"

"I don't know her name. I only saw her once. After the police came when Johnny had . . . done something to me."

Lola feels her brain pulsing against her skull, working hard to tell her the puzzle is already put together even as she is still figuring it out. Woman. Sent her. Domestic violence. Showed up after the po-lice. Power to make it stop. Cause.

It takes Lola almost an entire silent minute to pull up the photo on her phone, because Jorge's uncle hijacks Internet from the sweatshop next door.

"Is this her?" she asks Flora.

And Flora says, "Yes. She said you wouldn't be able to resist offing a man beating a pregnant woman."

The photo Lola has shown her is of Andrea.

EIGHT

TEXAS GIRL

It is past four when Louisa Mae's mother pulls up outside the school in her silver Mercedes wagon.

"It's used, but it'll do." Her father had beamed when he brought it home for her mother, who hadn't been surprised, and, instead, received the gift with a tight, polite smile. "Don't you like it?" her father had asked.

"Oh, yes. The color is lovely."

"It's a Mercedes."

"It's perfect."

Louisa Mae was old enough to hear the unspoken question in her mother's tight smile—*How can we afford it?*

Today, Ms. Flannery has waited outside the private school where Louisa Mae's parents transferred her last year. Ms. Flannery teaches history. She isn't married, but she lives with a man, Louisa Mae knows, because she heard her mother whispering about it to Casey's mother on the kitchen telephone at the beginning of the school year.

It is early November now, Halloween having just passed. Louisa Mae and her brother, four years her junior, had dressed as an apple and an orange. Louisa Mae had wanted to be a kitten or a pop star, but her little brother, a mere eight years old, hasn't taken to the new school as well as his seventh-grade sister.

"I don't want to trick-or-treat," he had claimed, although Louisa Mae knew he did. Her brother likes all kinds of candy, even Tootsie Rolls and candy corn. He is plump. He needs to play football, their father claims, to toughen him up. But this is small-town Texas, where even the eight-year-old version of the sport might involve broken ribs and concussions, little boys in helmets to keep their skulls from crushing, all those little bodies out for blood.

"We'll go together," Louisa Mae had said. "As something stupid. Cats and dogs. Apples and oranges. So no one can make fun of us because we know it's dumb."

Her brother had liked that idea.

"Here's your mother," Ms. Flannery says now, even though Louisa Mae is already halfway from the school steps to the car. Ms. Flannery shivers, pulling her brown wool sweater tight around her even though it isn't that chilly. "Louisa Mae?" she calls out right before Louisa Mae opens the passenger door. "You sure everything's okay?"

"What?"

Ms. Flannery thinks of articulating further, then shuts her mouth. "Nothing. I just . . . have a good night."

"Thank you for staying with her." It is Louisa Mae's mother, Mary, popping out of the driver's seat and speaking to Ms. Flannery with one leg still on the floor mat and one hand still on the wheel. She will be in a hurry to get home, get dinner on the table for Louisa Mae's father.

"It wasn't a problem," Ms. Flannery says, and Louisa Mae sees her teacher cast one more glance the Mercedes's way as her mother shoos Louisa Mae into the front seat and under her seat belt. Click. Shift. Zoom.

"I'm sorry I was a late," Mary says. "I had . . . the bank called."

Louisa Mae knows only that this means there is a question of money. She doesn't know if it is money needed for the house or the car, or if one of her father's businesses—a chain of Western Unions across the southwest region of Texas—is the culprit.

She just knows it will not be the night to ask her father the questions the girls at school put to her today.

Their house is a three-story brick, set back a good distance from the road. Her mother had planted saplings on each side of the circular blacktop driveway last spring. They have since lost the few leaves they sprouted, little puffs of yellow and orange her mother raked and tossed into the big green trash bin herself in a single morning.

"I'll need you to help your brother with his homework before dinner," Louisa Mae's mother says, casting a glance in the rearview mirror as if she expects her father early tonight. As if someone is chasing her.

"Sure," Louisa Mae says.

Maybe she can ask her mother.

"School was weird," she continues.

"Oh?" Louisa Mae's mother inches the Mercedes into the three-car garage, overly cautious even though there is nothing to hit. Hers is the only car.

"Yeah. Casey was asking me about Dad."

"What about him?"

"Just what he does for a living."

"He operates a chain of Western Unions. He's received national acclaim from the company," Louisa Mae's mother recites.

"I know."

"And isn't that what you told Casey? She should know. Her mother and I are friends."

"No, she knows. She just said . . . she meant his other living."

Louisa Mae's mother must mistake the gas for the brake, because she bangs the car into the wall the garage shares with Louisa Mae's father's den. There is a swift crumple of metal and a whelp from Mary.

"Oh, shit," Mary says. "Shit, shit, shit."

Louisa Mae doesn't bother telling her mother it's just a scratch, that they have insurance. She is twelve. She doesn't know if it's just a scratch. She doesn't know how insurance works. Does this go on her mother's driving record? Will it disqualify Mary from driving on future school field trips?

Of course, that is the least of their worries.

"We'll tell your father after dinner," her mother says, as if this will make it better. As if a steak and a Scotch will make his blood boil less.

In the kitchen, Mary drops a thick pat of butter on a grill pan. She salts and peppers a thick cut of beef Louisa Mae can't name. It is only when the meat is sizzling in the pan, red blood turning gray because her father eats steak only well done, that Louisa Mae realizes her mother said *we'll* tell your father after dinner. She has made Louisa Mae complicit in her mistake.

Was it the question she asked, about her father's other living? Had it distracted her mother? If the question had the power to crash a car, didn't that mean there must be some truth to it?

"Go help your brother," Mary says.

Louisa Mae finds him at the dining room table, math worksheets spread out in front of him. He has completed the first long-division problem, but is stuck on the second.

"You're supposed to be good at math."

"What?" He looks up, caught, then sees his older sister leaning against the doorframe, casual, as if he doesn't need her here.

"You wear glasses. Doesn't that mean you're good at math?"

"Ha-ha," he laughs. "You're so funny—"

"You remembered to laugh."

"But there was no joy in it."

Louisa Mae thinks this is an odd thing for an eight-year-old to say, even her brother. He must have read it in a book.

She looks at the problem that has him stuck and makes a nonchalant observation. "I always hated the problems where you have to carry one. It's like, just one, why do we have to have a leftover?"

Her hint clicks for him, and he scribbles on the worksheet.

"Did Mom send you in here?"

"I was bored anyway."

They finish the worksheet this way, with Louisa Mae looking across the table at the china cabinet, the circles of pale blue on matching white dinner, salad, and dessert plates. The stacks look even—twelve each—but surely that can't be. The china, Mary constantly reminds anyone who will listen, is from her grandmother's wedding, a good fifty years prior.

Is it possible to keep something so delicate for that long without breaking a piece?

He comes in at five after six, as he does every night, loosening his tie, complaining of traffic, taking the Scotch her mother offers him and downing it because he feels a man of his stature should like Scotch. When they have all gone to bed, Louisa Mae knows, he will crack open a Pabst and kick back in his recliner watching old highlights on ESPN.

He comes into the dining room, kisses Louisa Mae on the top of her head. She scratches the place afterward, preferring to mess up her hair all by herself. He tousles his son's hair and claps him too hard on the back.

"Good day at school? Good, good." He doesn't wait for either of his children to answer.

"Dinner!" their mother announces, as if they are three houses away instead of a single room. She doesn't want to be accused of letting the food get cold because she mumbles. Louisa Mae's father is always telling Mary to speak up.

"The steak is perfect," Louisa Mae's father pronounces after the first bite.

Mary smiles. "Thank you."

Louisa Mae's brother starts to eat. Louisa Mae herself wonders, just for an instant, if now might be a good time to ask the question the girls at school asked. But she can read a room, especially her own family's dining room. Now is not the time.

"How was school?" her father asks again.

Mary's eyes flit from her husband to her daughter and back again. A warning Louisa Mae doesn't need.

"Good," she says, eyes on her plate, which holds spaghetti and meatballs instead of steak. Louisa Mae knows that means there was a sale on ground beef at the supermarket this week. Her mother buys meat for herself and her children on sale. She pays full price for her husband's steaks.

"What was that?"

"Good."

"No," her father says, jutting out his chin to gesture to Mary, as if he's identifying her in a police lineup. "That look your mother gave you. What's she up to?" He smiles. It is cruel.

"Nothing," Mary hurries to answer before her daughter can. But

Louisa Mae wants to tell her mother that she shouldn't bother. Louisa Mae can take better care of herself and her family than her mother ever could.

Her father has never raised a hand to her. Yet. She's not foolish enough to believe this is because she knows better how to navigate his moods. She knows her days as a little girl are numbered, that soon she'll be a young woman, poised to leave. It is then she will become a threat to him.

"Nothing? You believe that, Louisa Mae?" Her father turns to her, his cruel smile shifting sideways so there is a touch of mirth, as if they are on the same team, as if they together will beat her mother later.

"No," Louisa Mae says, and Mary lays her napkin in her lap and places her forehead on her clasped hands as if she's praying. *This is the end,* her pose screams. *Please take me, God.*

"See that, Mary? We've got a good girl. One who tells her father the truth."

Louisa Mae sees the rise and fall of her mother's back, coming in uneven waves, her spine hiccupping. Her mother is crying.

The image angers Louisa Mae. Mary is a good mother. She makes sure her children have full bellies and clean clothes and good educations. She kisses them when they fall and hugs them tight before bedtime.

She just can't fight a monster all alone.

"Casey asked me about your other business," Louisa Mae says, looking right at her father. She's always thought of his eyes as blue, but tonight, they are as gray as a winter sky, and cold too.

Her father is up from the table in an instant.

Mary says nothing, just keeps her head down, as if the blow won't connect if she doesn't move.

But it does connect.

"Mom!" It is Louisa Mae's brother, who knows better but has let emotion get the better of him.

No, Louisa Mae wants to tell him, *you can't do that.*

But when she looks at him, he's already whispering, "I'm sorry, I'm sorry, I'm so sorry."

It's okay, Louisa Mae almost says back, but she doesn't have time, because their father has heard her little brother.

Before tonight, he has not raised a hand to his son either.

This changes quickly. Louisa Mae marvels at just how quickly one can go from not being to being a victim of physical abuse. She wonders if her own father's transition from man to monster was as swift, if once he'd hit a woman he knew he could never go back on the sin and so doubled down.

"No!" Now it is Louisa Mae letting emotion get the better of her, as her father's hand comes down on her baby brother. Again. Again. Her baby brother whimpers, which makes her father angrier, and Louisa Mae looks to her mother, who still has her head bowed, even though there is blood dripping from her nose to her plate of spaghetti and meatballs.

Louisa Mae has to fix this.

She knows the combination to the gun safe. Her father is too much of a showman not to take his guns out and let his children admire them. He told her and her brother the names, vicious combinations of letters and numbers that meant death. He showed them how to push a bullet into the chamber and send it to go "Bang."

Her fingers tremble on the gun safe's key pad. She knows the combination well—it is her birthday, as if her father knew his daughter might one day need to open this safe to protect herself from him.

She has a recurring dream where she needs to call a friend, Casey, maybe, to come get her, to save her and her family, but she can't get beyond the first three numbers because there is someone chasing her, or because her own memory fails.

She can't let this be like the dream. She can't fail.

She has the gun in her hands, cool metal on skin, when she hears a long, low moan. Is it her mother or her baby brother?

She runs, gun in hand, dragging it along like a lazy dog on a leash. Why is it so heavy?

When she gets back to the dining room, her mother is in the same position. And her brother is lying motionless on the floor.

Is he playing dead? He must be, Louisa Mae thinks, he is so smart.

Just not great at math. But he can write stories. He has a vivid imagination. He can escape that way, and now it looks like he has.

Except when Louisa Mae looks for the rise and fall of her brother's back, she can't see it.

"No," she says.

Her father has his back to her, his hands on his hips, looking out the window to the road, which is so far away no one can see into this house, can see what has just happened in full view of anyone who bothered to drive up in their car and peer through the first lit window they saw.

But no one has come looking for her father.

Once she lifts the gun, she finds, it is not so heavy. It has become her accomplice.

She shoots her father in the back, the gun telling her yes, yes, this is the way. The gun telling her, *I will help you make it right.*

When her father crumples, Louisa Mae is standing up straight.

NINE

WHITEWASH

It is almost eight o'clock on Saturday night when Lola re-enters the Los Angeles city limits, looking forward to ending her journey from Locust Ridge. She and the fat Mexican masquerading as her brother have exchanged mere grunts about the Civic's temperature—too hot, then too cold. He told her his name once they got rolling on the freeway, Lola pushing the pedal past eighty out here where there is no traffic.

"My name is Allen," he had said. "I have a family. Please don't kill me. I am a pawn."

Lola knows all of this is most likely true, but she can't make decisions based on "most likely." It is only after Lola drops Allen off at the ground-floor apartment where her men will keep him under strict watch that she has a second to contemplate her next move.

The strip mall across the street from one of the two corners Ricky runs is almost completely dark. In other parts of Los Angeles, strip-mall marquee signs listing businesses from sunless tans to Subways stay lit at night, proprietors willing to shell out extra bucks to advertise to tipsy drivers and working-class citizens waiting for their bus. Here in Huntington Park, Lola is the proprietor. She owns the strip mall. She owns all the businesses that populate it. She can clean cash even when the lights are off.

The Laundromat, the sole business open twenty-four hours, now spills only dim light into the parking lot. Inside, a weary woman transfers sopping, dingy T-shirts and underwear from washer to dryer. Lola makes a mental note to have the maintenance man check the spin cycle on all the washers as she walks the lot's empty spaces, the faded white of the parking lines sprinkled over the cracked, black asphalt like powdered sugar on a dark chocolate cake.

She has come here to let the Rivera cartel find her.

Lola finds a bench at the edge of the parking lot, where a black Nissan Sentra with windows so dark Lola knows the tint can't be legal rests. She hears the squawking of a radio inside, not music, but a man's voice. A comedian? A political pundit? All she hears is noise.

Could the Rivera cartel have sent this car for her?

She hopes so.

Across the street, she sees her boys. Two of them, Jamie and Rodrigo, take subconscious turns sitting and standing on the bench opposite Lola. Jamie sits, Rodrigo stands. They are not supposed to pace, to betray nerves of any kind, but Ricky is not here to watch over them, to remind them they can do better than show scared.

It must be the Nissan making them nervous, because they must think what better car for an undercover cop to drive than one impounded for illegal tint? The original owner must be a gangbanger or a wannabe. In Lola's years of experience, she has found wannabe bangers more dangerous than actual criminals, people who want so badly to belong to the life they are willing to cross whatever line in the sand they never thought to draw for themselves.

Across the street, a decade-old Benz pulls to the curb, Lola's curb, and Lola doesn't have to hear the driver's voice to know he's a kid, a white kid, no more than seventeen, a carful of girls surrounding him. She guesses he has told them he has connections, that he can get them whatever they want, and she feels a pang of sadness—or is it guilt?—at her own rules. Her soldiers don't usually sell to rich white kids, because the consequences aren't worth the risk. Cops care when white kids OD. Though Jamie and Rodrigo themselves are barely seventeen, they don't use and they don't sell to white people their age or below. But maybe tonight, with Ricky not here to watch over them, they will cross that line, as Ricky himself did last week.

Jamie swaggers to the car, one hand in his pocket, and Lola can hear him bark his standard opening line, "Yo, you lost?"

She hears a jumble of words spilling from the white kid's mouth, sees from the car's interior light the girls, all three blond, exchanging looks, wondering if the driver will keep his word, wondering if they will have to reward him. Lola sees the yearning in the girls' eyes, sees they want this deal to go down, but that they also don't, because if it does, they will feel an obligation to the pimply-faced dude in the driver's seat.

There's a long silence as Jamie looks from the driver to Rodrigo, who stands, frozen, in the lone street lamp's glow. Rodrigo is a scrawny kid in baggy jeans and a black jacket. Lola puts his weight at all of 110 pounds. She knows he eats everything he sees but can't put on pounds, and she knows his parents couldn't afford to feed all five of their growing kids even though they each worked two jobs. Last year, Rodrigo's little sister had tested at genius levels in math, science, and reading. Rodrigo, concerned she would end up squandering her potential as a ghetto girl, had approached Lola and asked for a job to help put her through school. She hadn't wanted to put Rodrigo on the street, but the boy kept coming back, week after week. Finally, he showed her a photo of his sister, beat by girl bullies for being smart. Rodrigo wanted to put her in private school, where she'd be safe. He wanted his sister to have a future, the one thing Lola couldn't begrudge anyone who could see that survival on its own was not enough.

Now, stuck in the streetlight's crosshairs, Rodrigo debates—make the sale or not. From her perch, still unseen by her boys, Lola wills him to make the right decision. Normally, she would love nothing more than for a carful of white privileged, pimple-faced trust-fund teens to get hooked on the white powder that, if nothing else, helps level the playing field. But ever since last Saturday, when her boys caught heat for selling to the white kids in the Range Rover, the whole gang is on strict orders not to make the same mistakes. The LAPD, or at least the city bureaucracy behind the establishment, wants to preserve the city's trust-fund kids, the ones with bright futures and the upbringings that will allow them to change the world.

If the Crenshaw Six sells to white kids during the city's latest crackdown, it will be Lola's gang, not the white kids, who find themselves behind bars.

She hears the Nissan's radio again, and she can hear a Mexican man bitching about his nagging wife in Spanish. Stand-up comedian, she thinks.

Then Rodrigo gives a brief shake of his head, and it's like he's passed the ball off to Jamie, whose head whips back to the Benz. His words ring clear in the night air, "Get lost," and relief floods every inch of Lola's body. The absence of adrenaline, that chemical that means she's got to save someone's life, is her own drug.

Deflated, the pimply-faced kid rolls up his window and drives away, the three blondes' lips set in grim lines. Have those three ever tried coke or heroin? Lola wonders. Was tonight an adventure, a one-time thing they assumed would never come back to bite them in the ass because of their privilege? With coke, maybe, but heroin—heroin doesn't see privilege.

When the Benz has turned the corner, the driver careful to flick on his turn signal before applying the brake, Lola can't sit on the bench any longer. She didn't come here to spy on her soldiers, but she feels the need to praise them for making the right decision.

"Hey," she calls, jaywalking because there are no cars, and the light is red.

"Oh shit," Jamie says when he recognizes her. She pulls her hoodie down even though he's already made her face, because tonight, she does not want to stay hidden.

"Ms. Vasquez," Rodrigo says, and the formal title breaks her heart. This kid should be going to college, she thinks, not charged with making a life for his sister—even if that charge is coming only from himself.

"Hey . . . ma'am," Jamie says, mirroring Rodrigo. If he'd been alone, Lola guesses he would have called her Lola, but Jamie doesn't have a mother or a father to tell him how to address his boss. He has a senile great-aunt who's pushing ninety. The old woman hoards cats, too many to count, and the apartment where Jamie grew up reeks of feline piss and shit. As Lola approaches him now, she can smell the Tide on his hoodie. Jamie is meticulous with his grooming, but, try as he might, there are always stray cat hairs visible on his clothes—white on black. He has fought a losing battle since the day he was born. His mother took off, his father went to prison for armed robbery. Now Jamie is good at making sure he has clean clothes. He is punctual. He turns a profit and obeys Ricky, from what Lola's heard, but, unlike Rodrigo, Jamie never had a shot at getting off this corner.

"Nice work. Turning that gringo away," Lola says. With her lieutenants—Jorge, Marcos, Manuel, Ramon—she would never have thrown around a term like "gringo." It seems juvenile, to call a white person that if she's not speaking full Spanish. But these soldiers are boys, not yet out of high school. If Lola finds out they've been ditching class to peddle powder, she'll have her men jump their asses out of the Crenshaw Six, and they know it.

Rodrigo goes from rumpled to ironed flat, remembering that he should accept a compliment from his boss instead of shrugging it off like it's nothing. "Thank you," he mumbles. Next, Lola will have to work on not only standing tall but speaking clearly.

"Yeah, man, no problem," Jamie says.

Rodrigo clears his throat.

"What is it?" Lola asks.

"I just . . . haven't seen you out here. It's late. There's that Nissan over there . . ." Rodrigo trails off.

"Finish your sentence," Lola says.

"Oh, shit," Jamie says, under his breath, as if he's watching a one-sided MMA fight on pay-per-view that just went so wrong the doctor had to be called into the octagon.

"I just—"

"No. There's that Nissan over there and what?" Lola keeps her voice level, a tactic she finds frightens people more than screaming. A woman screaming connotes fear, powerlessness, everything she can't show anyone—her enemies, her soldiers, the law-abiding citizens of Huntington Park who depend on her, her mother, her daughter.

"There's that Nissan over there and I'm worried the person inside might see you."

Lola shoots the kid a half smile, her head tilted, and when she reaches out her hand to knock him on the shoulder, Rodrigo breaks into a wide grin.

"Not so hard, huh?"

"No, ma'am, Ms. Vasquez," Rodrigo says, going from grin to gulp again in a way that lets Lola know he might have her approval for now, but he's not going to take it for granted.

"You guys packing?" Lola asks.

"Always," says Jamie. If Lola showing favoritism to her star soldier bothers him, Jamie doesn't show it. More likely, he knows what he is and what he'll always be—the bottom rung. If he's lucky, he'll run this corner one day, but Lola doesn't see potential for even a full block. Still, she doesn't waste any sadness on this fact, because Jamie accepted his background role in the world long ago.

Jamie shows her the glint of a weapon in his waistband. Rodrigo does the same, but his jeans are too loose on his malnourished frame, and Lola worries the gun will spill down his pants, dropping to the asphalt with a surprise shot. Rodrigo sees the concern on her face and adjusts his pants so the weapon is more secure.

"I've got a belt at home," he explains. "I forgot it."

"Wear it next time."

Rodrigo nods, head bowed.

"Where we going?" Jamie asks.

"Across the street," Lola says. She looks both ways before crossing, even this late at night, when she can hear the buzzing of engines from the freeway a mile away but hasn't seen more than a single car cross the intersection between them and the Nissan since she greeted the boys. She finds both her arms coming up in a cross, one blocking Rodrigo, one blocking Jamie, an instinct honed over the past two years of imagining the horrible things that can happen to a child. A little foot stepping into a crosswalk, a car's driver thinking they can make the light. No malice. Just an accident. But Lola does not believe in accidents. She believes in keeping her arms guarding her child and her soldiers.

She believes that Nissan is parked across the street because the Rivera cartel sent it to keep watch on one of their new rival's corners. She does not believe they came here expecting to see the boss out here. To the soldier inside, she must look like a mother pulling her bad boys home.

"Hey," she says, her voice raised louder than she would prefer. She wants to surprise the Nissan's driver, though. She wants to let him—because she knows from the sexist Spanish stand-up and the bravado to play it loud past midnight in a neighborhood not his own that the driver is a man—sweat. She wants him to wonder why this woman is coming at him with her arms held out, a walking Jesus, two wide-eyed schoolboy soldiers pretending they know how to keep her safe, both too young to know she is the one protecting them.

Lola catches her first glimpse of the driver through the front windshield—male, brown skin, mustache she knows without seeing up close he should shave. She doesn't get a chance to see more, though, because the man throws the Nissan in reverse and guns the car backward out of his parking space.

The hiss and pop that follows makes Jamie jump, Rodrigo freeze. In an instant, Rodrigo has his weapon drawn on the Nissan's windshield, aiming for a kill shot, because, in his mind, he's just heard bullets whiz, and he knows they didn't come from him or Jamie. Jamie is slower, Lola notices, and she didn't care for the jump that came with the loud noise, as if he's a normal adult entering his own surprise party.

"Cool it," Lola says to Rodrigo.

"I don't think I should put the gun away, Ms. Vasquez," Rodrigo says, because he still hasn't figured out what the noises were that came from the car, or why the Nissan has stopped moving ten feet out of the parking space.

"Fine. Keep it ready. But no shooting unless I say. Stay right here," Lola says. She takes off at a light jog, and Rodrigo and Jamie watch her, too scared to ask each other what the fuck just happened, and what the fuck is currently happening.

Lola doesn't bother knocking on the driver's-side window. She reaches for the door—unlocked . . . the balls on this idiot—and yanks it open. The driver falls out of the seat, but that can't be. No one took a shot. Did they? She takes her eyes off him for a second, glimpsing the source of the pops and hisses—four deflated tires. Her eyes whip to the front of the car, where the tire spike she placed before she sat on the bench rests, sharp and ready for its next gig. She'll get her boys to bring it home.

"Stand up, motherfucker," Lola says.

The man doesn't. He is bent down on hands and knees like a dog. His spine shakes. Is he crying? Lola takes a step toward him. There is something in the way his back bends, the way his left hand splays out more than his right on the night-black asphalt. She recognizes the noise coming from his shaking body. This motherfucker is laughing.

She fights the urge to pull the baby blade from her cargo pants pocket. She should slit his throat right here, but slit throats spill blood, and she needs this asshole to help her find Hector.

Except he is not "this asshole." She knows him. She feels the familiar way he gets to his feet, a lumbering plod followed by a lithe jump, as if he's gone from old man to young in the process. She remembers it from the way he got out of her bed, their bed, for years.

"Hey, Lola," Garcia, her ex-boyfriend, says as he turns to face her. The words and the mustache make him seem more cartoon villain than former lover. She can't be sure, but she thinks she detects the fermented reek of alcohol on his breath. Has he come here, to her neighborhood, drunk?

She doesn't return his greeting. Behind her, she can feel that Rodrigo and Jamie know something is happening because nothing is happening. A beginner banger would take a standoff as reason to shoot. She should let them know it's okay. But Garcia is drunk, and, therefore, braver than he ever was when they were together. In this altered state, he might convince himself he is a match for her.

"She tell you about me?" Garcia says, and Lola doesn't know if she got good deciphering her ex-man's drunk slurs during the three years they shared a creaking double bed, a mismatched set of washer/

dryers, and fluids—blood, sweat, snot, piss—so that the liquid pulsing through one would have one day ended up in the other.

"No," Jamie says. He hasn't picked up that there's anything wrong here beyond the potential rival gang lieutenant seeking a showdown.

But Rodrigo can tell there is something between Lola and Garcia. He would have been younger when they were together, middle school even, but everyone knew that Garcia had left his girl Kim after she miscarried the baby he was afraid to have anyway.

"Can't stay with a woman who can't carry," Lola remembered the wrinkled women around the neighborhood saying five years ago, eyes peering down spectacles at expiration dates on milk cartons and Cotija cheese in the corner bodega, not knowing she was watching and listening. She hadn't corrected them, hadn't explained that it was Garcia's fault Kim had miscarried in the first place. He had blown the red light at Maywood and Gage, plowing into a pickup and causing Kim to bleed out their child before the ambulance arrived. It was around that same time that Lola found Garcia on her doormat. She had known when she let him in that day, wet from rain and the destruction of his future as father and provider, that he would not leave until things broke between them. Did she always know they would break, even then, with him standing on the threshold? Or had she hoped the two of them would one day sit on the porch of a larger place in Huntington Park, not talking as their rocking chairs creaked, handing sections of the *L.A. Times,* a newspaper to which she had never bothered to subscribe, back and forth? Had she heard gunshots then, in that fake future, or had her fantasy self transformed her neighborhood into a place of children's shouts that stemmed from play instead of anguish, the blood that came from little bodies from the normal scrapes and scars of childhood rather than the trauma of violence and abuse?

"You're Garcia." Rodrigo speaks, because Lola can't think of a single thing to say to this man crumpled on the pavement, drunk with laughter and nostalgia and the power of letting Lola know he now works for the rivals she never meant to have.

"Yeah. That's me. You hear I used to live here? With her?"

"Yeah," Rodrigo says. "Heard you couldn't let your woman be the boss."

Lola bristles at Rodrigo's statement, but he is right—Garcia couldn't be both her soldier and her partner. He was fine pretending to be the boss to the outside world, but as soon as extenuating circumstances—a fucked-up drop, $2 million in missing heroin, $2 million in missing cash—made it clear she was the true leader, Garcia had been suspended, fruit cocktail in Jell-O, not knowing his place in the gang or in his own home. He hadn't wanted to contradict Lola—that went against his nature as a soldier—but he also, on some level, wanted to feel safe telling her what to do. Unfortunately for him, he was too chickenshit to separate Lola the leader from Lola the girlfriend, and, therefore, the partnership he had wanted with her, in the bed and out, had proven impossible.

"You doing more talking than she ever let me do." Garcia barks a mean laugh.

Lola feels her hand raise, not directed at Garcia, but at Rodrigo, who has overstepped his boundaries, whether or not he was just trying to prevent the silence and dead air that came from her inability to speak. When she turns to him, she sees Rodrigo's eyes widen, she sees his arms come up to shield his face. He is terrified. He is a kid in a dark bedroom, his stomach curdling when the door opens and light from the hallway shines in, an adult coming for him. He is Lola. He is Lucy. He is any child abused by an adult, parent or otherwise, and Lola feels shame course through her veins, her heart speed up, a fresh sweat on her brow she should not let Garcia see. Maybe he is too drunk to remember anything tomorrow.

"Lola," Garcia says. "Take me home."

She whips the blade from her pocket and slices Garcia's cheek open from ear to mouth. He screams, a high-pitched, awful scream, and Rodrigo peeks out from behind his raised arms, realizing that Lola has not laid a hand on him.

"Oh shit," Jamie says, although this entire time, he has not removed his hands from the pockets of his jeans.

"You get the fuck off my turf," Lola tries whispering in Garcia's ear, but his screams drown her voice. She tries again, louder, getting so close to the ear on the cut side of his face that she can smell the metallic tinge of his blood, still spilling from cheek to concrete. "Tell whoever you're working for at the Rivera cartel to get the fuck off my turf."

For a second, Garcia looks too confused to feel pain, but Lola can't tell if the confusion comes from having never heard the name or surprise that Lola knows the name of the cartel that sent him to get close to her.

"Pretty ballsy of you to show up at my party with your fucking flautas. Now it makes sense. You're working for them."

"Fuck you," Garcia says. When he spits in her direction, it is blood, but he is too drunk to have much aim. The blood-and-saliva mixture lands somewhere near Jamie's foot, and he sidesteps it even though it hasn't hit him. His hands come out of his pockets. For a second, Lola thinks he might rush Garcia, tackle him to the ground, and bash his head against the asphalt. Jamie does not like it when his shoes get dirty.

"Fuck you," Garcia repeats.

"You already have," Lola says. "And you didn't learn the one thing I thought I taught you."

"What?" Drunk, desperate Garcia asks her.

"You fuck me, I always fuck you back."

She is halfway across the parking lot again when she hollers back to her ex, "Tell your boss I want to see him."

"I don't have a boss no more. I got a woman. And this one can cook."

Rodrigo and Jamie freeze. Lola hears Jamie sucking in air as he puffs out, "Shit . . ."

Lola keeps her back to her ex. She sees the tired-looking woman frozen with her laundry basket, watching the scene outside. Lola doesn't recognize her.

She hears the slam of Garcia's car door as he kills the engine and grabs the keys. She can't hear his footsteps, but she hears his mutterings—*Fucking bitch, goddamn piece of shit, fuck you*—getting softer. He is retreating.

When he is gone, the woman steps out of the Laundromat. She has pulled on a hoodie. She drops her laundry basket at her feet.

"Sorry to disturb you," Lola says. Still, this woman is not from the neighborhood. This woman has expertly colored hair and clean skin and perfect square nails painted pale pink. This woman stands up straight.

"Actually, I came here to find you," the woman says. She leans over the piles of clean laundry, sending black shirts flying across the concrete as she digs out a weapon and levels it at Lola.

So I was wrong, Lola thinks. *Garcia isn't working for them.*

Can it be Garcia just wants her back? The question isn't worth posing now, when she has stepped into a puddle of leaked oil in the strip mall parking lot, and there is a woman holding a gun in her face.

"You will get in the car," the woman says. She speaks the accented English of a Mexican American who spends most of her time south of the border. Her dress is faded pink. Beneath its loose cotton, Lola can detect almost no outline of a body. There are no tree-trunk thighs or even a pouch of an abdomen. This woman is lean enough that she leaves no trace in the cotton.

The car she points out with a quick flick of the end of her gun, as if she knows Lola won't have the opportunity to run, is a Lexus SUV, white, not black, with tinted windows. Lola didn't spot it in the parking lot before because the vehicle is just turning in now, meeting the end of the woman's gun halfway. A compromise.

Rodrigo and Jamie have their own weapons drawn. They are behind Lola still, one on each side, but the woman in the pink dress doesn't acknowledge them.

"You will get in the car," the woman repeats.

"My soldiers won't allow that," Lola says, not knowing if it's true. They are boys. Dealers. She wants Rodrigo to go to school, to get off this shithole corner.

"Damn straight we won't," Rodrigo tries, but no one bothers to respond to his mumbled assertion, a declaration he most likely heard from the movies, or from Jamie, who heard it in a movie. There is no television at Rodrigo's apartment. His parents pawned it long ago.

"These are children," the woman says.

"Let them go," Lola says, because there is no point in faking the boys' ability to protect her anymore. If the woman lets Rodrigo and Jamie go, they will run to the real soldiers, the men—Manuel, Jorge, Marcos—but it will be too late. Lola will be in a Lexus on her way to—where? South of the border? A Tijuana brothel? The desert? Where her brother is? But where is her brother?

"They will not go," the woman says.

Lola knew she would, but she had to try. Jamie, she thinks, would have left. Rodrigo would have stayed and ended up dead, being loyal to her. Now she can tell herself he's staying here under duress, on the wrong end of this woman in the pink dress's gun.

There is a quiet buzzing then, and the Lexus's sunroof opens. Another woman emerges, equally nothing under a blue cotton dress. She has a sniper rifle. She doesn't need it, from this distance, but, like any other cartel, the Rivera cartel must go in for showboating in their violence.

The driver of the Lexus, too, is a woman, Lola sees now.

"You have noticed," the woman in the pink dress says with no trace of a smile.

Lola doesn't ask the question that's on her lips—Why? It is a betrayal to her sex, to think of them as weaker, to think of them by their sex at all here, in the dark parking lot of the strip mall she owns, where loaded guns are the only power necessary.

She could take these women, Lola thinks. She can't fight their lead, though. With cartel violence, it is almost never hand-to-hand. There is not often brawling, two people coming to blows. There is the burn of a bullet, the ripping of a body apart, but rarely one on one, with the most physically powerful fighter prevailing.

"Where's my brother?" Lola asks.

"He is safe."

"I need him back."

"Get in the car."

"If I do," Lola says, "will I be taken to him?"

Now Lola sees the smile in the woman's eyes as she tilts her head, studying Lola as if she's smeared her on a slide and shoved her under a microscope.

What do you see? Lola thinks. Then, *What do I see? Are you like me?*

The woman cocks the gun, moves the barrel a millimeter to the right, and shoots Rodrigo in the left knee. The boy's leg goes out from under him, as if there is someone kicking him from behind. The right side of Rodrigo's body follows the left, cartwheeling onto the black pavement. He doesn't scream out in pain, but Lola does.

She doesn't see who shoots next, but when she lands next to Rodrigo on the concrete, she sees Jamie's kicks striding past her. The next bullet rings out close to her head, starting there loud, then getting softer as it whizzes toward the woman in the pink dress.

Jamie keeps shooting, keeps moving forward.

The woman in pink is firing back.

Lola has only her blade.

Rodrigo is struggling to stand. He's got his fingers wrapped around his own gun, but he's bleeding too much to have the strength to get a good grip.

"No," Lola tells him. "Stay the fuck down."

He shakes his head.

"I fucking gave you an order. You need to follow it."

Rodrigo keeps shaking his head. He manages to get onto one knee.

"Stay down or I'll kill your fucking sister."

It is the only way to make him not want to die protecting her. It works.

Jamie and the woman in the pink dress are shooting it out. There are bullets flying everywhere, spinning a web of trajectories across the parking lot. The laundromat's front window advertising fifty-cent soap shatters.

The woman sticking through the roof of the Lexus has her sniper rifle set up. She has yet to take a shot, but Lola knows she's waiting. Lola knows it's her in the woman's crosshairs.

So she runs in zigzags.

They have taught the children this at Blooming Gardens, because there are active-shooter drills now, in this world, even the one west of here where the American Dream is still alive. During the first drill, Lucy had raised her hand and asked to be excused from the exercise.

"Why should I excuse you, Lucy?" her teacher had asked.

"Because I already know," Lucy had answered.

So does Lola, who zigzags across the parking lot now. The sniper can't get a shot. Lola hears the belch of the engine being shoved into gear.

They're going to try to run her over.

They have to. It's their only move.

She is ten feet from the driver's-side door. Five.

She knows the door will be locked. Knows she can't just yank it open and drag out the driver by the long black hair.

So she shatters the window with her elbow.

The glass bites her skin, digging in hard like a dog's teeth, clamping down and not letting go.

She doesn't look at the blood.

The woman is wearing a seat belt. Lola cuts it off her in one swift movement, tossing the driver onto the pavement and taking her seat.

She can see the sniper's ankles from here, sheathed in low-heeled black boots. The woman is ducking back into the vehicle, but Lola slashes her knife across the back of the woman's ankles, severing both her Achilles tendons.

The woman buckles to the backseat in pain, and Lola hates that she's had to take down a car full of female cartel assassins. She wishes she could have failed, if only for the next generation's shot at equality.

The woman has a draw on Jamie. He is too close. Lola taught him better, or at least Jorge or Marcos did. But sometimes men have to walk straight into a fight, because to run in zigzags might be construed as weak, instead of what it really is—smart.

Her pink dress flutters as the wind picks up. She shoots Jamie in the head just as Lola guns the Lexus over her dress, her nothing body, leaving her smashed on the pavement.

When she throws the car back in park, she hears a man's voice, scratchy, over a bad phone connection.

There is a Bluetooth connection in the Lexus. Someone has been listening to the whole encounter.

"Sonya?" the man's voice says. He speaks English with a Southern twang.

"Sonya's dead," Lola says. "The fuck is this?"

There is a pause, then the man says, "You must be Lola."

Lola is silent.

"I have your brother," the man says. "I'd like to get him back to you. But now that you've killed my partner and three of my soldiers, I don't know that we can be friends."

"You want to talk, you need to send better people to pick me up."

"Women," the man says, with a shrug in his voice.

"I didn't order the hit on your partner." Lola feels the lie smooth as lard slide off her tongue, leaving a salty taste behind. "My partner did."

"So you have a partner? That is interesting. I'd like to know who he is."

"I'll bring my partner to you. You bring my brother."

"I'd like that."

Lola gets out of the car and runs to Rodrigo. She gathers the boy in her arms. He weighs almost as much as she does, but she lifts him to his feet and starts to walk him across the lot.

When they get to the corner, Lola begins to yell for anyone who can help.

TEN

AFTERMATH

The sun is high in the sky when Louisa Mae wakes the next day. It must be close to noon. She is in the den, on the sofa, with a blanket over her. There is a soap opera on the television, not loud enough to hear the dialogue, although the actors' facial expressions are clear—yearning, anger, and deceit.

This is her father's room. She and her brother are not allowed in here. She will be in trouble for sleeping here.

Louisa Mae sits up, throwing the blanket off her legs. She is wearing her school clothes from yesterday—blue jeans and a green cotton sweater.

She should be in school.

Then she remembers. It is not the switch flipping from the unconscious to the conscious world, that thin line between dreaming and waking that, when severed, floods the brain with the difference between imagination and reality.

It is the smell. Metallic. Acidic. Blood and guts.

She runs toward the dining room. The house is big enough that she can do that. The smell gets stronger, so strong that when she reaches the kitchen, she doesn't stop to see her dead family framed through the dining-room doorway. She keeps running.

She collides with black fabric, her forehead hitting muscle and bone. She screams into someone's stomach, a man's stomach, she guesses, because there is not the same softness she has found in her mother's flesh when she's buried her head in the same place, seeking comfort from a woman who should have protected her but couldn't.

When her throat is dry from the screams, she bothers to look up, past the black fabric to the face.

The man is Latino. A stranger. He is young, early twenties, Louisa Mae guesses. Is he a detective? But he's not wearing a suit. He's dressed in all black—long-sleeved cotton shirt and cargo pants, lace-up black boots, military-style.

And he is holding a gun. It is not pointed at her, but the way he holds it, casually, makes it seem like an extension of his hand that he can raise and fire at will before she thinks to beg for her life.

He doesn't bother to tell her she will be okay. Yet she knows, in the same way she knows this man has killed before, that he is not going to hurt her.

"Who are you?" she asks.

"I was sent here," he says.

"Who sent you?"

"The people I work for. The same people your father worked for," the young man says.

So it is true. Her father had another business. Something Casey had referred to as "shady," which had sounded more like a word Casey's mother, the town gossip, would use.

"Why are you here?" Louisa Mae asks, because she smells the smell again, the beginnings of rotting flesh. Her flesh. Her baby brother.

"I was sent to kill you all."

She runs now, back to the dining room, its square of flesh-colored carpet framed in a rectangle of hunter green. She falls onto the floor next to her brother and cradles his head in her lap. He is dead, she knows, but she can't let this man get to him.

"It's okay," the man says. He is standing over her, and Louisa Mae doesn't know how much time has passed—seconds, minutes, hours.

She can feel a stiff part of her brother's hair where he hadn't washed out all the shampoo.

"I'm not going to hurt you. I . . . I saw it. What happened."

"You kill children," she says.

"No. I . . . I didn't know."

It sounds false, even to her in her grief.

"I'm sorry. That is a lie."

He speaks with an accent, but his English is clear.

It is only now Louisa Mae thinks to look at her mother. She remembers coming back into the dining room with the gun. She remembers seeing her brother. She remembers seeing her father looking out the front window, hands on his hips, his back to her, the frustration of what his family made him do evident in the way he stood. She remembers her mother in the same position as she'd left her—hands clasped in prayer, head folded.

But that can't be. Because her mother's cheek is on the table, her face turned toward her dead son and her living daughter, her mouth set in a relaxed line, her eyes open and resigned to their fate.

Her mother looks peaceful, the way she imagines someone who has been fired from a job they are not qualified to do might look.

"How did she die?" she asks the man. "My mother?"

"He stabbed her. Steak knife."

Louisa Mae peeks around the cherry-wood table and sees the roughhewn wood of one of the family's steak knives. The set her mother had told Louisa Mae countless times she had picked out for the occasion of her marriage. There had been hope in her mother's voice then, as she went back in time to before, when she didn't know she would end up dead with one of her wedding knives in her side.

"You didn't kill her," Louisa Mae says, not looking up at the man standing over her.

"No." He is telling the truth.

"Would you have killed my brother if he weren't already dead?"

"I don't know."

She sees the man shift his weight from one boot to the other. He doesn't like this line of questioning.

"Please," he says. "You will need to go. They will be looking for you."

"Did you put the blanket over me? In the den?"

"I put you in the den. I turned on the television."

"Why?"

"So you would not wake up in the dark and be scared."

The thought is so ridiculous it makes Louisa Mae bark with laughter. Although maybe, in that moment between sleeping and waking, she would have still been innocent enough to be afraid of the dark.

"You will need to go."

"Go where?"

"To disappear. They will be looking for you."

"I'm not leaving him," Louisa Mae says of her brother. His eyes are closed. She expects him to sigh, indicating a peaceful slumber. At the same time, she knows he is gone.

"You must."

"I won't. Why are you trying to save my life? You're supposed to kill me."

Please, the thought comes, *kill me.*

She thinks of her baby brother, dressed as a plump orange for Halloween, and now the tears come, deep, wracking sobs, and the man in black freezes.

"Please," he says again. "You will need to look like you have been killed too. Or they will send someone else. Someone not me."

"I need to take my brother with me. I need to . . ."

She remembers the conversation that never should have come back into her consciousness, the one she should never have had to give a second thought.

When I die, I don't want to be buried. Her baby brother was claustrophobic. He wouldn't ride elevators or lock bathroom doors. She could not let him be buried. *When I die, I want my ashes scattered on the Pacific.*

Why the Pacific?

Because it is far from here.

Why had they been talking about their deaths? Had she told him her plan, too, or had she tried to stop him from telling her his, as if that would make his death impossible?

"He can't be buried," she says.

The man in black sighs.

"If you will please to help make yourself look dead, I will help you with your brother," he says.

Louisa Mae doesn't need to ask how she can make herself look dead. She just knows. How does she know? Television? Or is this where she belongs, in the darkness, where she knows not to bother looking for the light?

She knows it will be difficult to dislodge the steak knife from her mother's side. What organ has it struck there? A kidney? A lung? She knows next to nothing about human anatomy, she has no map of the organs that have kept her own self breathing and thinking and grieving, yet she knows to plant her feet in the flesh-colored carpet and bend her knees to give herself the leverage she needs to yank the knife from her mother's gut.

Her mother's blood doesn't gush from the open wound because there is no beating heart to push it out.

But when Louisa Mae draws the steak knife's blade across her own arm, the blood comes quickly, bright red, new and young and plentiful.

She lets it fall onto the carpet. She lets enough of her blood out that the police will think she, too, died here.

She looks to the man in black. She has a task—get out of here alive, but make it look like you're dead. Know your enemy.

"What's your name?"

"Juan."

"Who do you work for?"

"A cartel. They are called Rivera."

ELEVEN

BLOOM

She has ensconced Rodrigo in a hospital three neighborhoods away, guarded by Ramon, Lola's oldest soldier. She had called him in the early hours yesterday, and the old man had appeared half an hour later in his short-sleeved shirt and blue work pants. He had brought along a stack of trashy Mexican romance novels, their covers featuring oiled, shirtless men on oiled, bucking stallions. Now, on Monday morning, Lola has tried to stick to the morning routine she and Lucy have shared for the past two years.

Up, pee, wash hands, cook and eat breakfast, pee again, wash hands again, teeth, hair, shower, dress, car. Don't forget lunch.

Jamie is dead. Lola did not tell him to walk into a firefight, but she didn't try to stop him either. Without his cover fire, she would not have made it to the Lexus. She would not have saved Rodrigo's life.

There will be a funeral in two days, thrown like a party by several neighborhood women, because Jamie's family can't afford it.

Lola will have to miss it, because, in forty-eight hours, she will be trading Andrea for her baby brother. She doesn't know yet how she will kidnap her former partner and offer up her white ass to a cartel boss in a city where Lola can't dispute that Andrea holds more power—both in the courts and on the streets.

That is a problem for after the day's normal business is done.

The drive from Huntington Park to Culver City runs the gauntlet of socioeconomic statuses in Los Angeles. Although Huntington

Park is not the poorest of the city's ghetto and ghetto-adjacent sub-urbs, it maintains its share of exhausted, upstanding citizens who struggle with the impossible task of making ends meet after twelve hours pushing a mop across tile or running fabric through a sewing machine. Many of the houses Lola and Lucy pass at the beginning of their morning drive to school have bars on the windows and flashy lowriders in the driveway.

When a red light stops Lola's Honda Civic, Lola tries to distract Lucy. There, across the street from Lola's favorite Mexican restaurant, a place she takes Lucy every Tuesday night, Ricky pedals tight circles on his bike. He intercepts a spindly woman in a knockoff suede suit two decades past fashionable, her paycheck just exchanged for cash. She drops something and keeps walking. He picks it up and keeps pedaling. The woman disappears around the corner, where Lola knows another young man in a hoodie is waiting behind the wheel of a car to pass off a plastic baggie of powder.

She knows because these are her young men, these are her corners, and they are turning her profit.

Even on a day when they are down one soul permanently and one at least temporarily, the deals must go on.

Lola keeps an eye out for black SUVs with tinted windows, and dark men, or women, in bespoke suits or cotton dresses getting out of them. The SUVs might be any federal law-enforcement agency, but the bespoke suits are what separates the criminals from the enforcers.

This rule will apply to Andrea when Lola goes to get her and turn her over to the cartel Andrea is fighting from the shadows.

"Mama!" Lucy cries out from the backseat.

"Get down!" Lola shouts back, a hand reaching into the backseat to shove Lucy's head out of window range. She waits for the shot she knows is coming until Lucy speaks again.

"I just wanted to tell you I saw Isa."

"Oh. I . . . oh." Lola thinks back to Andrea's question—*What would you tell your daughter, about what you do?* Luckily, they live in a shit neighborhood where a possible shot through a car window on a morning commute doesn't linger in Lucy's mind.

Lola spots Lucy's Huntington Park friend Isa walking past Lola's corner boys. Lola is about to jump out of the Civic and tell her boys to step aside, but Ricky screeches to a halt at that exact moment, shooing the boys out of the way so Isa has a clear path. Because of Lola, they know not to approach a child, unless they see one in danger. Then they have Lola's permission to shoot to kill.

"Is she walking to school?"

"She must be," Lola says. Isa's parents don't own a car. Her mother takes a bus to her housekeeping job in Pacific Palisades, and her father hitches a ride with his brother to the Sara Lee factory in Vernon. When Lola allows Lucy to play at Isa's house, she has to mask her horror when Lucy returns, calling Isa "lucky" because she gets free cake for dinner every night. One day, Lola will explain to Lucy that having to eat baked goods as a meal is not a treat, but a prison called poverty.

Even now, to Lola's adult ears, the speech sounds sanctimonious, laced with arrogance . . . and privilege.

But she can help only one little girl, her daughter. There is no room for another.

"Can we give her a ride?" Lucy asks.

"I'm sorry, *mija*. We don't have an extra booster for her," Lola says. Lucy is only in a booster because she is small for her age. Lola is covering another, darker truth she does not want to admit, even to herself. Lola doesn't want Lucy getting used to her friends here. She wants her to make friends at Blooming Gardens, where parents don't have to check their bank balances before they make a purchase because they assume there will always be enough.

"Okay," Lucy says. The little girl waves to her friend, but Isa's head is down, her eyes on the sidewalk, her thumbs hooked under her backpack straps. She has trained herself to be small, not to attract attention, to get through the gauntlet that is the ten blocks between her and school.

"She didn't see me," Lucy says.

She doesn't want to see anything here, Lola thinks.

A few blocks later, they pass the public elementary school, a sprawling beige-and-blue complex. On the playground, harried teachers attempt to wrangle children before the morning bell rings. Young boys hurl themselves from the top of a rust-ridden jungle gym. Little girls move their hips in time to a beat Lola and Lucy can't hear. There are screams from unknown corners—a tunnel, a slide, a filthy sandbox—and Lola hears a snap she hopes isn't a bone breaking.

When Lola looks in the rearview mirror, she sees Lucy looking at the playground, her hands folded on her lap, her legs crossed at the ankles. Is she judging her neighbors or longing to join them?

Lola knows this is a moment when she should attempt to find out what's bothering her child. Lucy is her child, legally, and has been for two years. All Lola had to do to get the little girl's junkie mother's signature on the adoption papers was to hold up a baggie of heroin. A child's value should never be measured in powder, but in that moment, Lola was happy to have the power punch of heroin on her side. They have had many of these rearview mirror conversations, Lucy asking questions about why things are the way they are, Lola trying to find explanations that go beyond "Because they are."

"Why won't anyone stop to pick up that man holding a sign saying he'll work for food?"

"Because he might have a gun."

"Why is that woman yelling at her baby?"

"Because she is tired and frustrated and has no one to help her."

"What about us? Can we help her?"

"We have to get you to school on time."

"Why did that family ask for the receipt when you bought them diapers and baby formula?"

"Because they're going to go back in the store and exchange the things they said were for their baby for cash. Then they're going to buy drugs."

"Oh, right," Lola remembers Lucy saying that day, a troubling response letting Lola know she had uncovered a repressed memory for Lucy. Maybe she was once the baby and Rosie Amaro, her now-dead mother, the woman begging for diapers and formula.

Lola enjoys these rearview conversations more when they aren't directed at society's myriad atrocities, but at Lucy's day. What did she do at school? Did the teacher give her any more challenging books to read? Was Ms. Laura in the classroom when Lucy performed her fourth-grade-level math?

Blooming Gardens, a private elementary school in Culver City, is expanding. With forty students per grade split into two classes, the school needed to add an additional building to its crowded campus of playground, gymnasium, cafeteria, and classrooms. The new building will house a music room, an art studio, and a computer lab to teach students to code—a term with which Lola was not familiar until two years ago, when Lucy came home excited to show her new mother her new skill. Lola can appreciate the nuance required to craft a concise order, even if the soldier in this case is not a human, but a machine. And she likes the idea of Lucy inventing a virtual start-up instead of a bloody drug empire.

Lola was pleased to learn that her sizable donation to help fund the computer lab would secure Lucy a spot in the Blooming Gardens kindergarten class, although that's not how Ms. Laura, the school's director, had put it. Ms. Laura had spoken of an unfortunate illness that took one pupil out of the school at the end of the year. Ms. Laura had mentioned prorated tuition, and Lola had said no, they didn't need charity. Lucy had begun school with the rest of her class that August. Two years later, she is flourishing.

"Charlie!" Lucy cries, opening her door before Lola has a chance to stop the car in the school's circular driveway. Lola slams her sneakered foot on the brake, spitting up a stray rock broken from blacktop.

"Lucy!" Lola yells, and the little girl immediately pulls her door closed again. When she looks in her rearview mirror, Lucy is sitting as still as a portrait, her back straight, her hands and ankles folded. She looks both formal and too frightened to move.

"I'm sorry," Lola says. "I only yelled because I was scared you would hurt yourself."

"No, it was my fault. I should be more careful," Lucy says. The readiness with which the little girl blames herself bothers Lola.

"Go see Charlie," Lola prods.

Lucy says she would like that, but would Lola help her out of the car? Of course, Lola says, having forgotten about the booster seat with its tight straps and pinching buckles. Maria Vasquez never bothered with such a contraption for Lola and Hector, although Lola likes to imagine it was because these $300 Cadillac car seats weren't available when she was Lucy's age.

"Forgot to turn on the child locks again?" The voice that catches Lola bending over Lucy is male, confident, and white.

"My car doesn't have them," Lola says, not bothering to turn around, because she prefers at least two cups of coffee before getting a lecture from that most privileged of species, the white male. Lola overheard a term on the West Side last week, something called "mansplaining," and the term rang so true to her she tried it out on her mother, whose mouth rounded into a circle of confusion even as she changed the subject to herbs that might help Lola sleep. Lola's soldiers had ignored the word when she tried it out in a business meeting later that day, pretending they hadn't heard. From their bent heads and jittery fingers, Lola had known they were embarrassed for her, walking around the ghetto with a white-lady vocabulary.

Lola had realized then she needed more female friends—or even one female friend.

When she turns around, she finds a man, planted like a wise old tree in a young, handsome body. His muscles stretch the fabric of his white cotton T-shirt, and his sandy hair is messy in a way Lola thinks might be achieved only with expensive product. His eyes are blue, his face dotted with sandy stubble that matches his hair. He's wearing board shorts and flip-flops, as if he's just caught a wave, but he smells of the shower instead of the ocean. He wears his smile like a broken-in baseball cap.

"You're Lucy's mom," he says.

"Yeah," Lola says. If this were another mother at Lucy's school, Lola would have said "yes" and smiled and attempted civility. Many of the Blooming Gardens mothers here are former CEOs and department heads, women who worked twelve-hour days and had a dozen or more employees reporting to them, before popping out a baby minus an epidural and updating their Facebook profiles to report they were now CEO of the "X household," answering only to a boss who woke them at all hours and pooped his or her pants. Lola knows she could learn something from these women, who must long for the days of tailored suits and coffee deliveries, even though she herself will never enjoy these perks in her particular line of work.

The men of Blooming Gardens are different. They arrive at drop-off either on their phones or making a big show to their child and all the parents in the schoolyard of switching off their devices to say goodbye to their offspring.

This man, in board shorts and flip-flops, has caught Lola off-guard. Has he taken the day off? But that hair, Lola thinks. It's almost to his shoulders. She doesn't know much about Hollywood, but she has made note of the agents and studio executives at the school. The ones who aren't balding seem to get trims twice a month. Once a year, there is a neat beard grown to raise awareness for prostate cancer, an act Lola can't and doesn't want to understand, but aside from that, a "working father"—another term Lola learned from an eavesdropped white people conversation—keeps his coif neat.

"I'm Charlie's father," the pseudo-surfer says now. "Zach."

"Oh," Lola says, because almost three months into the school year, Lucy is closer to Charlie than to any of her other classmates. Even now, the two of them have begun a game of tag that spans the length of the school. Their laughter is high and sweet and naïve.

Charlie's mother, a thin, quiet woman who Lola imagines was a powerhouse in her former career as an oncologist, was shy about be-friending Lola.

"It looks like they like each other," Charlie's mother had said, scooting closer to Lola at pickup one afternoon, when the two moth-ers were having difficulty wrenching Lucy and Charlie away from each other, promises of ice cream be damned.

"It does," Lola had said, not knowing how to continue the conver-sation. Her prior interactions with the parents at Blooming Gardens had overwhelmed her. Aside from three Asians and a Nigerian family with lilting English accents, they are all white. Still, each mother had descended on Lola at either drop-off or pickup, wanting to shower her, the lone brown lady, with attention. Their bright smiles and trying laughter had only served to make Lola, who didn't laugh for no good reason, feel like more of an outsider.

Charlie's mother didn't laugh without reason either. Lola had guessed years spent telling patients there was nothing else they could do had cured any artifice the woman might have possessed.

"She's a strong girl," Charlie's mother had remarked the day they met, her chin tilting upward to indicate she was referring to Lucy and not her own daughter. Lola hadn't realized until Blooming Gardens that girls could be named Charlie too.

"I think so," Lola had replied. Then, without meaning to disclose anything about Lucy's past, she had blurted, "She had a rough first five years. Her biological mother . . . she was an addict. She made Lucy do some horrible things."

Charlie's mother hadn't given Lola any of the usual platitudes, the "I'm so sorry" or the "How awful" or "Poor sweet girl." Instead, she had taken a few moments to look into Lola's eyes, not unkindly, but examining, as a doctor would a patient, to see if she needed to get more of the story in order to formulate an accurate treatment plan. What she saw there must have been that Lola had told more of the truth than she had meant to. Lola had frozen under the woman's gaze, as if doing so would make her invisible.

"I'm Susan," Charlie's mother had said, offering a calm hand in the face of the shit storm Lola had just thrown at her.

"Lola," Lola had replied, and the woman's handshake, firm and soft at once, had let her know Lucy's secret was safe with her.

Now, confronted with Charlie's father, a fake surfer with a permanent grin, Lola is confused. How had these two humans come together to make Charlie, a bold girl who, at this very moment, is darting from the school door to Lucy and back again, shouting with laughter over nothing?

"Where's Susan?" Lola asks, her tone more challenging than she intended.

"We decided she should go back to work," Charlie's father says. Lola wants to interrupt, to ask why, then remembers that, while this question would be absurd regarding any profession, it is particularly so in the case of a person trained to treat cancer patients. Susan taking several years off to stay home with Charlie must have resulted in some deaths, or, at the very least, a slight shortage of oncologists in the Los Angeles area.

"You work too?" Lola asks.

"I'm a chef," Charlie's father says. "I work nights."

"Where?"

"The restaurant I own," he says. "Mexican food is my specialty."

"Mexican?" Lola repeats. What the fuck is this white-boy man-child doing cooking Mexican food?

Zach has the good sense to blush. "I've spent a lot of time in Mexico. I love the food there more than anyplace on Earth. So I opened a restaurant here."

"Cool," Lola says, but her tone indicates it isn't.

"You and Lucy want to come by for a playdate this week?"

"At your house?" Lola asks.

"Yep," Zach says, rocking onto the toes of his flip-flops and back onto his heels. Lola can't tell if he is nervous at the proposition of the playdate or just can't stand still.

Lola has hesitated to say yes to a playdate with any of Lucy's Blooming Gardens classmates. Lucy has never visited a West Side home. The little girl has never seen a minority bused in to clean another person's shit. Lucy might balk at the lack of bars on windows, and she might think she is doing a friend's family a favor by asking where they keep the guns in their house, so she can make sure she stays away.

"Yes," Lola says now, though she can't say why she's suddenly okay with Lucy visiting Charlie's home. Maybe Charlie's father's casual appearance and extensive research into the country Lola's grandparents came from has lured her into thinking he'd be cool with the gun question, or at least pretend to Lucy that it doesn't faze him.

"Let's say tomorrow, then," Charlie's father says. "It's one of those random teacher in-service days. No school." He doesn't check the calendar on his phone or text his wife to see if tomorrow works for her.

"Will your wife be there?" Lola asks.

Does she detect a wrinkling of Charlie's father's mouth? If she does, does that wrinkling indicate displeasure with her question, or is he stalling for time before he answers?

"Lola." The voice this time is female, but strong and undeniable. It leaves no room for Lola to prod Charlie's father for an answer. Lola couldn't pretend she didn't hear Ms. Laura even if she wanted to.

The school director is tall and broad, her face heart-shaped, her skirts floral and feminine. Two years ago, Ms. Laura had looked the other way when, during Lucy's disastrous and eye-opening school interview, Lola stole a dollhouse—mother, father, and furniture included. Ms. Laura's blind eye won Lola's loyalty, and now the two exist in a world of compliments and kindness, of chaperoning field trips and signed permission slips and nut-free morning snacks.

"Did Lucy tell you?" Ms. Laura asks, her gray eyes somehow brightening blue so Lola knows whatever Lucy didn't tell her is good news.

"Tell me what?"

"The science fair. She won," Ms. Laura says.

Lola looks to Lucy, who has stopped in the middle of a game of tag with Charlie. The little girl, all awkward arms and legs, tags Charlie with a gentle tap, amazed at her luck. Lucy has never been able to catch Charlie, because Charlie has never stood still.

"Right," Lola covers. "Great news." Inside, she is wondering why Lucy kept this accomplishment from her.

"Okay, your turn. Catch me. Catch me, Charlie!" Lucy pleads with Charlie, who has remained still, her eyes on Lola and Ms. Laura, as if the subject they are discussing—Lucy—belongs to her as well. Lola finds the blue eyes of Lucy's pale friend unnerving.

"She can't catch you if you don't run away," Lola calls to Lucy, hoping her words will propel Lucy away from Charlie, even though it is Lola's fault Lucy is here, at Blooming Gardens, instead of in Huntington Park with Isa, her head down, trying to be invisible to the violent world around her.

TWELVE

HIGH LIFE

Half an hour later, Lola pays for parking at an automated machine off Abbott Kinney, blocks from the drop that her baby brother fucked up two years before, setting off a war with Los Liones cartel. Now, Hector is gone, taken by a new cartel.

Goddamn Whac-A-Mole, Andrea had said. Andrea, who'd set Lola up to be the face of whatever war-on-drugs revolution she was staging.

Andrea, her partner, the woman Lola has to kill.

It's too bad, Lola thinks, because she had liked being part of Andrea's world. But was she part of it when the two of them couldn't even sit across from each other at an Italian deli, instead having to sneak a conversation and a cigarette or two out back near the dumpster?

The dispensary is sandwiched between a votive candle boutique and a beach-cruiser rental shop on the Venice boardwalk. A green cross with the name "High Life" in green block letters blinks against a white background.

Lola did not choose the sign or the color of the cross. She hadn't even chosen the name, leaving these details to the people who run the dispensary's day-to-day.

Two white guards lean against the brick wall, one on each side of the double glass doors—bulletproof. Lola had had an opinion about that, and, given the business conducted behind the doors, no one objected.

Even if this were just a legal pot dispensary, the bulletproof glass would not have been out of place. Nor would the armed guards lobbing small talk across the entrance, framed in brick and glass and blue sky.

No one wandering the boardwalk in the middle of the morning will give the dispensary a second glance. To look twice at a place that peddles pot legally in California is to give oneself away as a tourist, a grave sin to any Venice natives—or, at least, those transplants who have chosen Venice as not only their new home, but their way of life.

The guards don't know Lola by name, but they have the good sense to bow to her as she presses the buzzer beside the glass doors and looks the security camera lens in the eye.

"Hi, hi," a familiar woman's voice says, then there is a long buzz and a click that lets Lola know the door is unlocked.

Inside, the woman behind the counter doesn't stop her sales pitch to acknowledge Lola. She is white, with curly chestnut hair and a slight bump in her nose. Her voice tends toward nasal, but still commands attention.

"And honestly, I wouldn't waste time with the brownies. They're too sweet. I've tried telling our bakers to tweak the recipe, but they're still not getting it right. I'm thinking it's partially because they use milk chocolate instead of dark. Of course, at this point, I think I'm just going to have to get in the kitchen and test the recipe myself. So should I put you down for a dozen of the chocolate chip?"

The customer nods. He, too, is white, like the guards, like the female proprietor, like everyone here except Lola, the boss, or one of them. But it is Lola's face people see here. Andrea is a public figure. She can't risk coming here unless it's with a warrant to bust the place.

The man looks like he wants to ask for brownies, but something in the finality with which the woman behind the counter seals his purchase and hands it over the counter with a "Have a nice day" stops him.

No one contradicts Mandy Waterston.

Lola first met Mandy in the midst of a fire that destroyed the heroin supply she and her husband, Eldridge, controlled. As the building burned to black around them, Mandy had whisked Lucy to safety, cartel be damned.

Lola will love her forever for keeping her daughter safe. Andrea was not as forgiving, since she had entrusted Mandy and Eldridge to protect her millions of dollars in white powder.

Now, the husband-and-wife team work the pot dispensary, where they sell grass and edibles up front and keep the white powder safe in the back. It's a perfect setup, with the ability to keep guards out front and bulletproof glass in the windows and doors. Customers must be buzzed in and out. The cameras let Mandy and Eldridge identify any visitors, welcome or not.

Lola wonders what Mandy knows. She had been working for Andrea long before Lola entered the business, although Lola doesn't know how well or for how long. Despite her pride in doing her own research, she had not thought to question a friendship between white women, as if there can't be a threat there.

"How's Lucy?" Mandy asks, restocking the register with cash, some of it clean, some of it dirty and about to be washed by way of fake orders—a dozen brownies here, a bag of grass there. It is not the only way Lola and Andrea launder money, but every little bit helps.

"She won the science fair," Lola says.

"Of course she did," Mandy says, not skipping a beat as she wipes down the counter, realigns the bags of grass under the counter, and calls to the back, "More cookies!"

"Two minutes."

"Remember to let them cool on the racks," Mandy calls back, then, to Lola, "New guy."

"She didn't tell me," Lola says.

"I hired him," Mandy says.

"No, I mean Lucy. She didn't tell me she won the science fair."

Mandy stops dusting the case and looks at Lola. "Huh."

"What huh?" Lola feels her breath coming faster. Surely in the midst of a cartel war and a fractured partnership and her missing brother, Lola shouldn't worry that her daughter is keeping academic success from her.

"That's odd," Mandy says.

"I thought so too," Lola says. She's a beat away from asking Mandy what she should do when she remembers—Mandy and Andrea were friends before Mandy and Lola watched a heroin den burn. She can't be sure how much Mandy knows about the Rivera cartel, about Hector's disappearance, about the hit Andrea had Lola order to ignite a war.

"Have you heard from her?" Mandy asks, and Lola knows she means Andrea. They don't call her by name, even her first, because out of all of them, there is still hope for Andrea to live a legitimate life. Lola protects that hope for her. She is the brown woman drug runner who controls Los Angeles. Andrea is the white woman prosecutor fighting the war on drugs. One can't succeed without the other.

But now, one will have to.

"Yeah," Lola says, trying to keep the scoff out of her voice. She can't assume Mandy is on Andrea's side. She also can't assume she isn't. "We thought it would be a good idea if I checked on the inventory."

"Sure," Mandy says. "Eldridge is back there. He's supposed to be at Starbucks getting me a latte, but he wanted to supervise the new guy."

"I don't know if now's a good time to let anyone we don't know in here."

"Because of the Rivera cartel?" Mandy asks.

"How did you know?"

Mandy lets Lola behind the counter and pulls up the live security feed on a laptop. Four squares showing footage from each of the dispensary's entrances.

"Black SUV, no government plates; tattooed Latino looking at votive candles, another black SUV, no government plates; guy in a tailored suit with enough hair gel to choke one of those stoners trying to do a pull-up at Muscle Beach."

"I wasn't followed."

"I know. They've been here all morning."

"How do you know they're Rivera?"

"Andrea told me to expect them. And to protect you if they came in here."

Lola appreciates the sentiment, but she is the one with the ankle holster and the switchblade in her cargo pants pocket. Mandy is five foot seven and a hundred and twenty pounds, no weapons or defensive driving training to speak of, unless the vehicle in question is her toddler's tricked-out stroller.

Lola also knows the Rivera cartel won't touch her unless she doesn't come through with her part of the bargain—the true boss delivered to them in two days.

"I get it. You can protect yourself."

"Not when the people I work with are busy stabbing me in the back."

"I don't know anything about that," Mandy says.

"I'm going to cut you a break because you saved my daughter's life, but you need to stop lying to me. You know better."

It is the last sentence that gets to Mandy, who doesn't appreciate it when someone speaks to her as if she is a child who has forgotten to cover her mouth when she coughs.

"Are you going to kill her?" Mandy asks.

"What do you think?"

"I think you can do better."

"Fuck does that mean?" In her head, Lola thinks of a phrase she recently heard on television—*white nonsense*. Indeed.

"It means you don't need to kill her. You can destroy her."

The buzzer sounds then, and Mandy's eyes go to the security feeds. There are two white women in workout pants at the door. They're chatting over their reusable Whole Foods bags.

"Did the men watching seem interested in me?" Lola asks.

"Didn't give you a second glance," Mandy says. "But they will if you leave here empty-handed."

Lola doesn't understand. If the Rivera cartel has her brother, they must know she ordered the hit.

Unless Hector hasn't given her up.

She realizes she has been thinking of her brother as the boy he was before he went into prison. Now, he is a man, a soldier.

And Andrea has put him in danger.

THIRTEEN

AUTENTICO

"When I'm back, you'll be in bed," Lola says to Lucy that night. It is past six o'clock, and the November dark has already settled over the neighborhood. Lucy sits in front of a small plate of broccoli, brown rice, chicken, and cheese. Valentine waits at Lucy's feet, head tilted up to beg, the brown fur on her chin starting to show a sad dusting of gray.

"Who will stay with me?"

"Manuel," Lola says. She has fought to keep the handsome ex-cartel hit man out of her bed, but tonight, she'd had to face the challenge of working women across class and race. She'd had to scramble for child care. Lola is fine with her own mother watching Lucy when she is in the same apartment building. She would be able to hear her mother unleashing her television from its wall mount or yanking open and slamming shut drawers to find any old jewelry to pawn. Lola would be able to hear her mother about to relapse, if she were here, on the premises.

But her mother can't fight the Rivera cartel.

Tonight, all Lola's men are here, in the building. They are watching for the black SUVs without government plates. They are watching for the Latinos dressed in suits, shoes polished, hair slicked back, sunglasses at night. They are watching for the men who will be sent to kill Lola and her family.

"Manuel's nice," Lucy says.

"I'm going to tuck you in. He's going to stay in the living room unless you call him. You can lock your door."

Allen, the fat Mexican handed over to Lola's custody at Locust Ridge in lieu of her actual brother, has changed from an orange jumpsuit into a T-shirt too tight for his flabby frame. Her men have kept vigilant watch on Allen until she decides his fate. Tomorrow, she will either hand him over to the warden at Locust Ridge or put a bullet in his brain. She doesn't know enough about him to picture a third alternative, and even then, she isn't sure one exists.

Lola can see Allen from the front window, pacing the courtyard, which Lola has made sure is lit up like a football stadium as soon as the sun goes down. Allen goes from Jorge to Marcos and back again. At first, it looks to Lola like her men are playing the slowest game of keep-away she's ever seen. Then she hears the barks of laughter from her men, the American ones, and realizes Allen needs to use the bathroom.

She pulls and bangs at the window until it opens, an angry mother catching her child bullying, and yells to them, "Get him to a toilet. And don't let me see that shit again."

Jorge and Marcos look up. They didn't know she was watching them, but their surprise lets her know her reaction is extreme.

"Okay, boss," Jorge says.

Lola shuts the window only when she sees Jorge and Marcos marching Allen toward Maria's apartment. Maria will welcome the inmate with open arms and bad-tasting New Age tea. She'll tell him she can soothe his soul, when all he'll really want to do is take a shit.

"What did that man do?" Lucy is there, her hands and mouth wiped clean. Valentine sits beside the little girl, chomping on a lump of grilled chicken she's hoping Lola won't notice.

"Nothing. It's not his fault, what's going on," Lola says, because she doesn't know the specifics of what's going on herself. She knows Allen is most likely a scapegoat, a man the Rivera cartel offered money to be smuggled into prison instead of out, to replace an actual inmate they wanted for themselves. She can't imagine what trouble Allen must be in, to agree to go into a maximum-security prison without knowing she would be coming to get him out. Still, his in-depth questioning will have to be left for later. Right now, she has to go talk to the other head of the snake.

She keeps her smile on as she bathes Lucy, as she brushes her daughter's hair, still stringy, in front of the mirror, and together they count the strokes. She reads to her from *Matilda,* finding comfort in the idea that smart little girls can have shitty parents and still thrive. She wonders if this trait is exclusive to girls, because aren't boys born knowing the world is rigged for them to win?

When Lucy is tucked in and sighing, a certain precursor to sleep, Lola remembers the science fair. She should have asked. Tomorrow her daughter's omission will have lost importance, as most things do when family members reset their minds from yesterday to today, from dark to light.

It is too late.

Lola finds Manuel in her living room. He has the television on low, and he asks her if that's okay.

"Lucy won't mind," Lola says. "She can sleep through a lot."

"And you?"

"And me what?" Her tone makes it sound as if he is the one she is helping, instead of the other way around.

"Do you mind if I watch television?"

"No," Lola says, her tone softer. She finds her hand on his cheek before she can think, then his hand is covering hers, and they are kissing.

He breaks away first, and she asks what's wrong.

"You have work to do."

"I do," Lola says, part of her sad that she wasn't the one to stop things she alone has forbidden here, in her home. But the truth is, she and Manuel don't spend much of their stolen time kissing, and they have never kissed here, in the open, right in the middle of the living room. Their relationship is meant to take place behind closed doors, with sound cranked up to drown them out. Lola wonders now if these rules are less about keeping their relationship a secret from Lucy and the rest of Lola's soldiers, and more about keeping herself untouchable. It is easy for her to see now, in the common area of her living room, that she has designed this relationship with Manuel to keep herself from falling for him.

When she crosses the courtyard to her Civic, unlocked on the street because no one will touch it, she sees Jorge and Marcos returning from Maria's apartment with Allen.

"We got him to the pot," Jorge says. "Sorry about earlier."

Marcos grunts his agreement.

"Don't worry about it. Put him in my car."

"We going on a field trip?"

"Nah. Just him and me," Lola says. She pretends not to see the look her men exchange—she's going by herself in a car with this man almost the size of three of her. They've made sure he's not armed, but even with no weapon, his hands on her throat could squeeze the life from her in the time it would take a traffic light to go from red to green. There would be no caution light.

"Okay" is all Jorge says.

Marcos starts to load Allen into Lola's backseat, as if he is under arrest without the cuffs, but she says, "No. The front."

Marcos obeys.

When Lola has pulled into traffic and left her two soldiers in the rearview, she makes a phone call. Her Civic hums along the ghetto streets, bouncing over a pothole, dodging a plastic grocery sack whose contents are liquid and beige—the color of Latino flesh put through a blender. Lola commands the car with ease as she listens to the ringing of her cell, then the chirpy female voice that answers on the other end.

"Andrea Dennison Whitely's office."

Lola musters a sob as she swerves to miss several children shooting a deflated basketball into a ragged net they've placed in the middle of the street. The children part into two lines, boys and girls playing basketball together, and wave to her. They are neighborhood children. They know her car. They know her name. Lola wonders if the boys have invited the girls to play their game because of her.

"I need . . . Andrea. Where can I find her?"

"—Who is this?"

"Lola Vasquez," she says, stealing a sideways glance at Allen to see if he gives a shit what her name is. He is waving to the children, a fact that irks Lola and makes her take a wide right turn, sending Allen left, away from the window, away from her babies playing in the street.

"Oh, Lola, hi. I'm so sorry. She has a dinner tonight."

"Can you tell me where?"

Lola hears the hesitation in the woman's voice.

"Please," Lola whispers. "He came back."

"She's at El Norte," the assistant says. "But you didn't hear it from me."

The line goes dead, and Lola tosses her phone to Allen. "Google El Norte for me."

She did not call Andrea on one of the burners this time. It was a legit call. As far as Andrea's assistant knows, Lola is a victim of recurring domestic violence. The woman should by no means have given Lola Andrea's location, but Lola can't imagine the DA's Office pays well, and you get what you pay for. If Andrea were to hire a real assistant, to help with both her legal and illegal enterprises, the DA's Office would raise an eyebrow at the exorbitant salary that person would have to command in exchange for their discretion.

To Lola's surprise, Allen has no trouble pulling up an address and phone number for El Norte. It is located on Melrose, in West Hollywood. Unlike in her own neighborhood, parking will be a bitch, and she can't leave her doors unlocked. When you're queen of the ghetto, the nicer parts of the world never feel like a palace.

"What is a restaurant called 'The North' doing in West Hollywood?" Allen asks. He speaks English with no accent. There is an amused undertone to his comment. He finds the situation funny. He must have a shit life.

"You speak English," she says aloud.

"*Sí,*" he responds.

Lola sighs. "And you're a smartass."

"I have my moments." He chuckles.

"Where are you from?"

"San Antonio."

"And the Rivera cartel flew you all the way out here just to put you in prison." She switches to Spanish, surprising him.

"You speak Spanish."

"Yes."

"I try to get my daughters to speak it. They don't want to anymore, now that they're teenagers."

"You have daughters?"

"Three. No sons." He spreads his fingers and smiles, a *What can you do?* gesture that makes Lola like him. For now.

"You're giving me a lot of information. Are you worried for your safety?"

"I am on release from prison to attend my *abuela*'s funeral."

Allen is over fifty. His *abuela* is long gone.

"Have you ever heard of Los Liones cartel?"

"Gone. Dead. Taken down by a woman."

"So you know about the business."

"I was a street-food vendor in San Antonio. I had to pay my share to the powers that be."

"Huh," Lola says. All L.A. street vendors, whether they're peddling meat grilled fresh in open air, fruit sprinkled with chili pepper, or flowers wrapped in cellophane on freeway overpasses, must pay a pittance to the gangs that run them. The pocket change flows upward, eventually fueling the cartel boss. Lola hadn't known San Antonio was the same.

"You're riding in the front seat of my car with no cuffs. How do you think that would look to your bosses if they were following us?"

"Bad. But they're not my bosses. They provided me with an opportunity to earn some money. A lot of money."

"Enough money to potentially stay in prison the rest of your life."

"But you came to get me."

"And I can take you back."

"You can. It will still be worth it."

"Why?"

"Because the Rivera cartel saved my daughter's life."

In the slow crawl of seven-o'clock traffic, Allen tells Lola his story. His daughter Adela had leukemia. Her parents, Allen and his wife of twenty-plus years, couldn't afford her treatment. They sought help from the only source they knew. The Rivera cartel. Much like Lola, the Rivera cartel does favors for its "people." They provide a service in advance, and one day, maybe the following week, maybe the following decade, they "ask" something in return.

Adela is cancer-free and has been for three years. But several days ago, a representative from the Rivera cartel came calling on her father for their favor. Allen would go into Locust Ridge and pretend to be a different inmate serving a life sentence. An inmate the Rivera cartel wanted out. An inmate named Hector Vasquez.

The thought of serving a life sentence did not faze Allen, because, in return, the Rivera cartel had given his daughter a life.

Of course, he can have a life, too, if Lola chooses not to make the three-hour drive back to Locust Ridge tomorrow and turn him over to the sneering prison guard who released him for a long-dead, never-present *abuela*'s funeral.

"Do you know where they were taking him? Hector?" Lola knows the question is pointless. This man isn't even a hired gun—he was a prisoner of the Rivera cartel long before he went into Locust Ridge on their behalf. He was their prisoner as soon as the cancer cells in his daughter's body began to multiply and spread, attacking her life and sending her parents into a desperate downward spiral to save her.

"No," he says. Then, "Right there!"

"What?" Lola slams on the brakes and the Honda squeals with effort. She thinks for a second Allen has seen Hector right here, on this corner of Melrose, where a large sign warns of the consequences of attempting a left turn during rush-hour traffic.

"El Norte."

Lola sees the restaurant's red sign then, penned in a throwback vintage cursive scrawl, punctuated with a prickly green cactus. Jesus

Christ, she thinks, is this where white people go for Mexican food? The location, West Hollywood, is full of bars and clubs and sexual revolutions, all three of which Lola approves of. What she does not approve of is the whitewashing of Mexican cuisine, the smothering of cheese and mole on enchiladas, rendering them impossible to taste. But this is America. More is better.

Still, she does dig the red cursive, scrawled and messy, the restaurant name barely legible.

A valet steps into the street, spotting Lola's signal to pull to the curb before she can look for metered parking. She can't help feeling honored that the valet, a portly Latino not unlike the one riding in her passenger seat, knew she belonged here, in the same place Andrea is dining.

"Good evening, miss," he sings, in a voice both respectful and condescending. In his home country, Lola thinks, he must have meant more than he does here, in matching evergreen valet vest and trousers.

"Yeah, you too," she says, because she is taking in the outside of El Norte, its massive oak doors, the red light and the hip techno pumped out at a perfect volume for conversation. The valet scurries ahead of her and Allen to heave the heavy doors open.

Inside, the light is low, but not dim, like many Mexican restaurants she's been to. This is not a cave but an oasis of warm red light. Lola detects an electronic beat beneath the steady yearning croon of some white lady. The woman's voice over the speakers makes Lola's heart ache, and she thinks of Manuel at home on her sofa, trying to figure out the remote in case he doesn't want to watch Lucy's cartoons. He might like this place. She has never sat across a restaurant table from him.

The same can be said for Andrea.

"Two, please," Lola tells the hostess, who has long blond hair and long legs and a muted smile.

The girl, for she can't be much more than twenty, with spindly legs and heels too tall for a woman who works on her feet, leads them through the spacious scattering of heavy oak tables. Lola recognizes the business diners, the Hollywood agents in pinstripes sealing hand-shake deals as white servers prep tableside guacamole. She spots older men who think they have a chance with the much younger women sitting across from them. She spies a table of actors she recognizes from at least one of the prime-time television shows she keeps on as background noise when she's folding laundry.

What she does not spy is a single Mexican, either serving food or busing tables. Here at El Norte, the most authentic people have been relegated to outside work, parking cars and opening doors for guests.

"You're in luck," the hostess says. "We had a last-minute cancellation."

The hostess shows them a corner table, and Lola wants to ask the girl why she felt the need to point out that this table almost didn't belong to them. Why not just seat them and tell them their server would be right with them? But of course Lola knows—the more desired something seems, the more you want it. That is the flipside of humanity. Most people want to be good, or at least perceived that way, yet they will always grapple for the next rung on the caste ladder, the next thing that will satiate their hunger for more once the initial need is met. Lola knows—she peddles her product to addicts, and maybe she should feel guilty, but the ability to take away their hunger completely, instead of feeding it so it grows too big within them, is something she has forever considered beyond her abilities.

"What's good here?" Allen asks as he sits across from Lola, and she is about to remind him that she has never been here, that this is not the type of Mexican joint she would choose to patronize. Then she realizes the hostess is still tottering above them in her heels, swaying back and forth to the music. Lola wonders if she is nervous speaking in public, even if "public" is just reciting the dinner specials loudly enough that patrons can understand her over the music.

"The sea bass is our special tonight. It's a whole fish, roasted in a salt crust and topped with guava de gallo."

Guava de gallo. What the fuck?

"And of course it wouldn't be a meal at El Norte without our famous tableside guacamole."

"Yeah, we'll take some of that," Lola says, both because she wants this blond girl out of her sight and because she wants to see what ingredients white people think belong in guacamole.

"The hell is this place?" Allen asks when the blond lady disappears.

"I have no idea," Lola says, and for a second, she and Allen are two against the rest, adrift in this upscale restaurant where they should be at home but aren't.

"Don't we get free chips and salsa?" Allen asks.

A short blond server appears, wearing a pasted-on smile and pushing a small cart with a mortar and pestle, a mountain of avocados, and small pewter bowls of red onions, garlic, and lime.

"Good evening. My name is Daniel, and I'll be preparing our signature guacamole right here at the table for you."

"Leave that shit here. We'll make it," Lola tells him.

"I'm sorry, ma'am, I can't leave the guacamole ingredients tableside."

Lola pulls two hundred-dollar bills from her cargo pants pocket. She doesn't showcase the switchblade she keeps there, but she doesn't hide it either. "And bring us some chips and salsa, okay?"

Daniel dashes from Lola's table to the hostess stand. She knows they're on borrowed time. Allen seems to know it too. He has already knifed open three avocados from the pile, smashing the meat into the bowl and squeezing lime juice on top of it.

"Lots of salt," Lola says, standing.

"Where are you going?"

"Bathroom," she lies. She is not scared to leave Allen alone. He has fulfilled his obligation to the Rivera cartel. His daughter's cancer is in remission. Lola has gotten him out of prison and planted him at an upscale Mexican restaurant. He has time to kick back and enjoy some tableside guacamole.

Lola weaves through the tables of patrons. Daniel is already at another table, this one populated by four women pushing sixty, with pulled faces and bellies constricted under flowing silk tops. He sees Lola and stumbles over his speech about the salt-crusted sea bass. She feels a sense of triumph, but only for a second, because one table over, in a darkened corner, Andrea is throwing her dark hair back, laughing.

Lola has never seen Andrea laugh before. She is a nervous woman, buzzing from one meeting, one thought, one victim, one killer to the next. She takes both her careers, as a prosecutor and as a drug lord, seriously. She moves with the raised shoulders and bent head of someone who knows she is pretty but can't accept that people will look at her. The few times Lola has seen her confident—striding down a Venice street to meet one of her former front men, Eldridge Waterston—she has been alone and out of context. In the courtroom, Andrea speaks of violated little girls in her own little-girl voice. Lola has wondered if this is a trick—speaking in a small voice to force people to sit up and strain to hear what she has to say. Lola has never had to speak in public. She is a voice society wants quiet, the angry third-generation immigrant who commits heinous acts like trafficking narcotics and lifting her community out of poverty. No, Lola's story is too dark even to be trotted out for purposes of giving hope to the next generation.

Andrea sees Lola in that instant. She doesn't stop laughing, a fact that pisses Lola off. Andrea knows Lola has a blade in her pocket. She knows this restaurant is full of corners better for shivving than a prison shower, because no one here knows to keep looking over their shoulder.

She knows Lola has come here to decide whether she should live or die.

"Would you excuse me a second?" Andrea puts a hand on the tall, dark-haired man Lola recognizes as her husband, Jack, a psychiatrist who specializes in the treatment of addicts, from narcotics to opiates to sex. When Andrea touches him, it is both to show her affection and to help herself out of her own chair. She is wedged in the corner, her three companions' heads turned away from Lola. But they all watch Andrea leave, and when they do, Lola spies a silver-haired man in a three-piece suit, and his wife, a woman with high cheekbones and pumped-full lips, dressed in tailored royal blue. Even sitting down, Lola can tell the woman, who is pushing sixty, has wide hips, probably from children. First wife, she thinks, approving of the silver-haired man's marriage. Before she met Andrea, who dangled a sliver of her West Side world in front of her, Lola would never have known the difference between a first and second wife. This, she thinks, is upward mobility.

Lola follows Andrea, who parts the crowds with a bowed, meek head and ducks left past the bar, toward a little Zen garden nook outside the bathroom. From here, Lola can see inside the restaurant's kitchen, and now she spies all the Mexicans, deep-frying tortillas and breaking them into bits, salting the hot fried pieces and squeezing lime juice over the top, like Allen just did back at their table but faster, not letting any seeds escape.

"You know this place has a Michelin star?" Andrea says to Lola, in a trilling tone that lets Lola know Andrea thinks someone might be listening.

"The fuck is that?"

"It's a big deal for a restaurant."

"You know what I think's a big deal? That no Mexican restaurant I go to has a Michelin star. And this one's got all the Mexicans in the back, with the white people on display."

"A valid point," Andrea says with a sigh, turning around so she and Lola are standing side by side, both their backs against the cool concrete of the Zen wall. Lola can hear the little waterfall below them, somewhere under the wistful techno beat.

It takes Lola three of the techno bass beats to get her back off the wall and her hands around Andrea's throat. The flesh is even, a slick coat of moisturizer making the skin smooth, not oily, under Lola's rough fingers. Maria puts lotion on her neck now, telling her daughter most women forget to moisturize their necks because they're too busy worrying about the crow's feet at the edges of their eyes and the smile lines at the corners of their mouths. Maria's own face is stretched taut and sad from years of drug use and skipping food in lieu of heroin. Her neck is the only part of her that looks like it hasn't been sick her whole life.

Lola feels the viscera beneath the thin skin of Andrea's throat. Esophagus. Vocal cords. Her voice.

Lola has her former partner down close to the fountain now, and Andrea is looking up at her, her own fingers clasping Lola's hands. She doesn't claw, and Lola finds Andrea's lack of desperation for her own life annoying.

She squeezes harder. She wants to feel Andrea's blood vessels bursting. She wants her eye to be drawn not to the huge diamond sparkling too bright on Andrea's ring finger, but instead to Andrea's own eyes, the clear green of them, beginning to disappear into the back of her head.

Still, Andrea does not fight back.

Lola relents, telling herself it is because she must keep Andrea alive in order to hand her over to the Rivera cartel. The nagging voice inside that must be her conscience tells her no, she has released Andrea because Andrea did not beg her to do it. She has released Andrea because Andrea has made what should have been a fight to the death into a battle of wills.

Andrea must know not to fight a battle she can't win.

"Why?" Lola manages. Is the music too loud for her to bother trying to say more? Or is it her emotion—emotions, rather, anger and worry and fear, for her brother, for the fact that she couldn't strangle Andrea with her bare hands, and it wasn't because Andrea's death would be bad for business.

Andrea drags herself onto the fountain's concrete edge. Her fingers dip into the water, and she lifts her dark-brown hair and splashes the back of her neck with the cool, clean liquid.

It does not escape Lola's notice that Andrea avoids splashing her face. Even with Lola's hands just off her throat, Andrea does not want to risk messing up her makeup.

"I had you start a war with the Rivera cartel because you're the only one who can win it." Andrea's voice, scratchy from strangulation, is still a song, soothing and seductive, and Lola wonders if she is any match for this particular white woman, whom she once saw as a mere equal.

She also wants to believe her former partner. She wants to think this is the whole reason Andrea had her start a war, but Lola knows that can't be.

Lola feels Andrea's hand on hers. She glances down at the glinting diamonds, the red nail polish.

"Someone's coming."

They stand again with their backs to the wall. Andrea holds Lola's hand behind her back, as if she is a dog on a long leash being allowed the illusion of freedom.

Seconds later, the silver-haired man from Andrea's table appears around the corner.

"Andrea. Jonathan's trying to talk us into dessert. What do you think?"

"The churros here are to die for," Andrea says. "Lola, meet my boss. Raymond Ewing."

Lola recognizes the name, not from a movie screen, but from the local news, and now she places the silver-haired man, whose baritone has watched over her from press-conference podiums as she folds sheets and shorts. He is the district attorney of Los Angeles.

"I'm helping her through her . . . domestic situation," Andrea says, because Raymond sees Andrea's hand touching Lola's, and the older man is curious. The touch would make sense if what Andrea's saying were true, but Lola is not a victim of domestic violence. She is a drug trafficker on Andrea's payroll. So why is Andrea holding her hand? To convince her she is loved? To convince her she can win a war against a beast of a cartel? She, a lone woman with five men she trusts completely, one, her brother, already captured and likely smuggled south of the border to Tijuana or beyond, a recovering addict mother, and an abused, adopted eight-year-old daughter?

"She's a very special woman," Andrea says to Raymond, and Lola knows the purr in her voice is meant for her, not Raymond.

"An honor to meet you, Lola," the DA says, and here, in the restaurant's cool, dark hallway, Raymond Ewing shakes Lola's hand.

Andrea leans in for a cheek kiss, Lola's first not from an older

Latina who first would pinch her, then exclaim how big she was getting. Andrea's lips brush her skin, so Lola can't tell if this is, in fact, a cheek kiss, or something she has never experienced—the air kiss.

"Meet me out back in half an hour."

Andrea lets go of Lola's hand, using it to steer Raymond back to their table. Lola doesn't realize that she's taken a churro from a basket in the window between restaurant and kitchen.

When she bites into the fried dough, she tastes sweet and salt, coupled with the slight spice of cinnamon. Her eyes widen with pleasure, and when she comes back up for air, Zach, Charlie's father, is staring at her.

As he wipes his hand on a white towel and steps out of the kitchen, Lola realizes she must have known all along—Michelin stars, district attorneys, Hollywood agents in pinstripes. Only a white chef could command this caliber of crowd in a Mexican restaurant.

"Hey," Zach says, his arms open, his smile genuine, as if he expected her to show up at his workplace.

"Those were for your friend's table," he says, nodding to the churro still in Lola's hand.

"I'll pay you." She had planned a snappier response, something about how Andrea would get over it, but instead she takes a decisive bite of churro, content in her choice to keep quiet.

"Tell me," Zach says.

"What?" Lola says, mouth full of buttery sweet dough. Zach can't know the storm she just resolved in her own mind.

"How's the churro?"

"Beautiful," Lola says, and a sigh accompanies the word, spoken unexpectedly in earnest, so that Lola has to wonder if there is a different Lola learning to operate on the white side of Los Angeles, and, if there are two Lolas, which one is real?

FOURTEEN

HORIZONS

Lola has never ridden in Andrea's apple-red Audi. This is a different car from the one Andrea parked outside the apartment of Lucy's biological mother the day Rosie Amaro drew a shard of glass across each arm, sealing Lola's fate with Andrea's. It is a different car, but it was the same color and model as the one that sat outside the apartment that August day.

It was the day they realized inside each of them lived both a hero and a villain, or, at least, it was the day Lola realized it.

She does not know how many characters coexist in her former partner, who, sometime between tucking away her half-eaten order of churros and her zipping up to the back of the restaurant in this very car to tell Lola to get in, has changed clothes.

Now, as they do a steady sixty up the Pacific Coast Highway, the ocean to their left, mountains and houses on stilts to their right, Andrea is in dark jeans and a dark hoodie. She has scraped her hair back into a ponytail. She drives with her left hand, the hand with the diamond, and to her left, the sand of Will Rogers State Beach glitters white in the black night. Beyond the sand, the ocean is a black hole, so that any stranger to a beach would think it is the sand that is the star.

All that changes, Lola knows, with the light. The ocean glows blue and white, reaching for the sand, pulling back. The sand is littered with sticks and algae and glass and trash.

The light switches the stars.

Lola knows where they are going even before Andrea slows somewhere past the Malibu KFC Lola has seen only once before, two years prior, when she came up this way for the first time. She had wanted to stop and take a picture, to memorialize the fast-food chain common to both the crumbling houses of Huntington Park and the glass mansions that line America's West Coast.

Andrea signals as soon as she brakes, letting the cars behind them know she will be making a left turn. The move will bring them as close to the ocean as they can go without plowing the Audi into the water, chasing the waves and sinking at the impossible task.

The guard at the gate knows Andrea and waves her through. She waves back. He does not ask what she is doing here close to midnight. He nods to Lola, too, and she, too, waves, as if she knows the answer to the question she wishes he would have asked.

The parking lot is close to empty, but Andrea takes one of the spaces farthest from the entrance. Lola wonders if she is concerned about getting a scratch on her car, something Lola does not have to worry about with her Civic. She expects scratches and dings, side mirrors crumpled into doors. These wounds are so common, not only in Huntington Park, but in all of Los Angeles, that it has never crossed her mind to retaliate, to track down the citizen who thought better of leaving a note with name, number, and insurance policy information.

Maybe Andrea has parked far away because she wants to leave the closer spaces for those who need them, not the physically handicapped, but the loved ones dropping heroin addicts at the doors, this place a Hail Mary, the end of a long road Andrea does not wish to make longer by taking up a close space.

New Horizons Rehabilitation Center is quiet this time of night. Lights-out, Andrea tells Lola on the walk up to the double front doors, is nine p.m., sharp.

Patients are expected to sleep, even with the weight of what they've done under the influence of the white powder Lola and Andrea peddle on their minds.

How do they sleep? Lola wants to ask Andrea. *Isn't that asking a lot of them? How does my mother sleep?*

The man at the front desk gives Andrea another wave. He is fat, with a mustache and a receding hairline. Lola knows the addicts themselves work the front desk. The only other time she has been here, it was a tall bleach blonde with a Southern accent and zero tolerance for the bullshit perpetrated by her own kind. Lola can't picture this man snorting coke or shooting up heroin. She can't imagine him doing anything but sitting behind a desk, watching the television too low to follow the story.

"He might be asleep," the man says.

"That's okay," Andrea says. She signs the visitor's log with a name Lola doesn't recognize.

"What's with the name?" Lola asks as they walk a long hallway. She has wondered if this place uses fluorescents at night. During the day, the sunshine floods in through floor-to-ceiling glass. Now, at night, the light is soft and blue.

"You'll see," Andrea says.

"How did your husband beat us here?"

This is, after all, the rehab facility her husband, Jack, owns. Lola can't imagine he drove all the way from West Hollywood to Malibu to maybe sleep, as the guard had warned.

Lola doesn't understand why Andrea signed the visitor's log at all, given that her husband isn't a patient but the doctor in charge.

"Jack's at home," Andrea says. "I didn't tell him I was coming here."

"Where did you tell him you were going?"

"To deal with work."

"And he believed you?"

"He wanted to," Andrea says.

There is something in her comment that Lola wants to file away for later, in case she ever marries. The lies we believe to preserve what we have. The lies we tell our loved ones to preserve their sense of safety. The lies we tell them so they keep loving us.

Andrea stops in front of the closed buttery wood door of Room 432. She plucks a clipboard from a bin attached to the wall and reads the paperwork there. Lola knows Andrea is not a doctor, but she must know enough about the physical devastation of addiction from her legitimate career as a prosecutor to be able to read a patient's chart.

Andrea nods agreement with whatever treatment plan she is absorbing, then deposits the chart back in the bin, which matches the buttery wood of the door.

When Andrea opens the door, she does not let Lola see what's inside.

"Wait here," Andrea says.

Lola doesn't have time to agree or protest before Andrea disappears inside, shutting the door behind her.

The fat man from the front desk appears and calls, too loud for this quiet place, "Would you like a glass of water?"

Lola holds up a hand to let him know it's okay, she doesn't want one, because she doesn't want to disturb the silence here. When the man's footsteps retreat, it is so quiet she can hear the ocean just beyond the glass windows, the waves crashing and retreating, the ebb and flow of white noise.

So that is how the recovering addicts can sleep.

So how does my mother? Lola wonders again.

"You can come in," Andrea says through a cracked door.

Lola has to step so close to the wood she can smell the newness of the timber. It is only then that Andrea opens it all the way, and even then, she stands between Lola and the patient.

Lola recognizes him immediately, even though he is turned on his side away from her, so that she sees only the bare skin stretched over his spine. She is close enough to count the vertebrae before it occurs to her that she has covered the eight steps from door to bed with Andrea still standing between her and the boy on the bed.

Because he is still a boy, even though Lola puts his age at close to fifteen. He is still a boy because he is white, with a smattering of golden strawberry hair that doesn't match Andrea's. He is still a boy because he did not grow up in Huntington Park, but in a neighborhood where it is normal for testosterone-fueled teenagers to cruise around in brand-new Range Rovers not borrowed from their parents, but given to them on the occasion of sixteenth birthdays.

This boy was not driving the Range Rover that landed on the corner across from Avila's El Ranchito.

This boy was in the backseat, the lowest on the totem pole of teenagers.

This is the boy who picked up the baggie of heroin dropped under the front tire and escaped with the white powder because Lola came running from the shadows to distract the police with a tale of an abusive boyfriend and a stab wound.

"This is my son," Andrea says. "Christopher."

Oh, shit, Lola thinks. Then: *Thank God.*

Because now she understands why Andrea started a war with her name on it. Now she understands what she had considered before to be her partner's betrayal, but now realizes is retaliation.

Christopher turns to her, and Lola recognizes the clear green eyes of his mother. Even in a haze, they see her.

"You," he says.

Me, she wants to say, but can't. Her voice is gone. Andrea may as well have choked it from her with her bare hands, as Lola attempted to do to her an hour ago but couldn't.

"It was the first time he tried heroin. He ODed," Andrea says, to fill the silence, because Lola does not need her to tell her this part.

This part is from any after-school special. This part is memorized, seared in the brain, textbook.

This part is her fault.

FIFTEEN

IRRECONCILABLE

When Lola arrives home from New Horizons, it is just past dawn. Andrea had driven her back to El Norte, where Lola hadn't thought to worry about Allen and how he would get back to the neighborhood that wasn't his. He was gone, as of course he had to be, because the restaurant was closed, but her car was still there, abandoned by the valets who must have left hours ago.

She hopes Allen is on a train or bus back to San Antonio. She was never going to take him back to prison, she realized, even if it meant cops knocking at her door. Now she can plead ignorance. Now she doesn't have to lie.

"I have a spare key," Lola had assured Andrea, even though her partner hadn't shown any concern for how Lola would get home. She is not a child. She is a drug lord who almost killed her partner's child.

Then, as Lola had started to exit the passenger's seat of the apple-red Audi, she had turned to ask Andrea, "What can I do?"

How can I make this right? How can you forgive me?

Andrea shrugs one shoulder. She was different on the drive back, her silence fraught with the sight of her son, of his skin stretched over his spine. Lola had watched after the immediate shock of recognition as Andrea attempted to cover Christopher with blanket after blanket, to warm up a chemical chill in his bones that would not seem to go away.

Lola remembers trying the same thing as a girl the first few times her mother attempted to get clean.

The chill doesn't go away, Lola had wanted to tell Andrea, but of course Andrea must have known and not cared. Not cared because this was her child.

Lola had found Manuel on her couch, sitting up, the remote in his hand, but his chin tucked to his chest in sleep. She had sat next to him in silence. The television was playing an infomercial, some sort of kitchen contraption that sliced fruits and vegetables one second faster than the kitchen product advertised a half hour prior. After this infomercial, there is one for a cream that claims to rid its users of turkey neck.

Lola doesn't know how long she's been sitting here, her thigh touching Manuel's, when Lucy appears, dressed in a cotton play dress peppered with pineapples, a print unfit for late fall in most parts of the country, but perfect for Los Angeles, where the temperature holds fast at seventy-five past December. Lucy's arms are exposed, and Lola notices the little girl's biceps for the first time, rounded lumps of muscle under skin plump with youth. Lola feels a pang of sadness for the five-year-old Lucy she adopted two years ago, the girl whose arms were skinny, formless strings, who was so clearly a child.

"Mama, we have to go," Lucy says.

The curtains are closed, but Lola knows from the infomercials that it can't even be seven a.m.

"Where?"

"Charlie's."

Lola gives Lucy a blank look, and the little girl sighs with a disappointment as deep as her seven years can imply.

"The playdate."

The playdate. Lola had forgotten, of course she had forgotten, trying to save her brother's life and starting an unwitting war with an entity that, a week ago, she hadn't known existed. Zach hadn't mentioned it last night, or had he, in between her perfect bites of churro that came after her inability to throttle Andrea and her field trip to discover the havoc she had wreaked on another woman's child.

But now she remembers. Lola had caught Lucy pawing through her closet yesterday, plucking out dresses and skirts, never pants, then tossing them aside with small puffs of what Lola realizes only now must have been disgust. Once, Lola had caught Lucy standing in front of her mirror in the very dress she is wearing now, hands clasped in shyness behind her back, hips swaying back and forth, back and forth, saying, "No thank you. I'm not hungry."

Lola had seen it, but she hadn't seen it. The preparation for the playdate with Charlie. Her daughter wanting it to go just right.

A blurry several hours later, Lola stands at the door of Zach and Susan's Venice home, Lucy at her side, her small hand slipped into Lola's until they hear footsteps. Lucy's hand disappears, and Lola watches her little girl stand on her own, wanting to be separate from her.

Lola consoles herself thinking that Zach and Susan, a restaurateur and an oncologist, live in a smaller house than she would have imagined, a bungalow, really, steps from the beach and squeezed between other identical bungalows. Cars squeeze through pedestrians to reach tiny garages where they fit, fender touching wall, bumper touching door. Walking shirtless surfers bark laughter, carrying boards as easily as a single bag of groceries . . . or the smallest pistol, not sparing a second glance for Lola and Lucy. They have eyes only for the ocean.

The door opens, and Zach appears, pulling on a T-shirt over muscles Lola tries to pretend she doesn't see, but when Zach's head reappears, his sandy hair tousled, his smile isn't one telling Lola he caught her staring. It is a grin free of guile, of genuine happiness to see them.

"Hey," he says. "Come in. Charlie's in the playroom."

Lucy disappears into the house at jet speed, pineapple skirt flying behind her, and Lola thinks again of her daughter's refusal to consider pants. It strikes her for the first time now that she should worry— where is her daughter getting the idea that she's a girl, so she must wear skirts? Lola glances down at her own cargo pants, olive green, with a reddish stain Lola hopes is watercolor paint from Lucy's hobby and not work-related. She should be more careful with her own clothes, she thinks. Then, immediately—she should resolve the drug war she's entered as an accidental general. It is the least she can do to make up for what she did to Andrea's son. It is the least she can do to save her own brother's life.

But now she can't turn Andrea over to the Rivera cartel. Now she has no leverage.

Now she must focus on the playdate in front of her.

Lola finds herself standing on a square of white linoleum tinged brown with dirt and sand. The house smells of salted ocean and sea breeze, with a hint of fish and Febreze. The carpet just beyond the linoleum is brown, a color that might hide stains, but also mutes the natural light from the windows beyond that open onto the Pacific.

"I don't spend much time inside," Zach says. "I prefer the deck."

Lola follows him without a word. They pass the playroom, which is also the bungalow's main living room. Lola clocks vaulted ceilings and dark carpet, spill-resistant in color if not quality, and a flat-screen playing *Doc McStuffins* at a volume she considers too loud. She feels a crunch underfoot and lifts her Puma to find a pulverized cheese curl. This is not the kind of house Lola expected Susan to keep, but is this judgment unfair? Susan is a doctor who cures people of cancer, who calls to tell them she has good news and bad, whose voice must remain calm, even when she is giving a patient an approximation of his or her time of death. Is it a shock to Lola that this woman doesn't have the time to vacuum the carpet? Or to hire someone from Lola's own neighborhood to do it? Lola looks at Zach—what's he doing all day, and why doesn't she blame him for the state of the bungalow?

Charlie greets Lucy with an aggressive hug, putting her to work at a dollhouse with instructions to "make the boy and girl doll fall in love." To Lola's surprise, Lucy sinks to her knees with a doll in each hand, her eyes intent with purpose. She is going to obey Charlie's order. Lola fights the urge to grab her daughter by the hand and pull her away from this dirty house and back to the car, parked three blocks away for the bargain deal of ten bucks cash. But they are little girls, playing, and a little bossiness is better than everything else Lucy has endured.

Zach has one hand on the smeared glass door when he looks back to make sure Lola is still following him. "Coming?"

"You got any food?" she asks instead. She knows nothing about West Side playdates, but she knows when the children of her neighborhood come to visit Lucy or just show up at her doorstep with no explanation save for a hanging head and a belly bulging with hunger, Lola puts out a spread: guacamole, pico de gallo, chips fried fresh from lard-speckled tortillas, white-meat chicken pressed and fried into whole-wheat floured dough. She serves filtered water in colorful glasses. She allows a single piece of dark chocolate for dessert.

Would any of her male soldiers do the same?

But Zach responds with a grin. "Thought you'd never ask."

They step into the kitchen together, and Lola feels her stomach flip-flop with the pleasure of expectation. Zach is a chef. Zach will deliver where most men could not.

"I bought this place for the kitchen," he says, his hand already lifting a cast-iron skillet from a childproofed cabinet.

The countertop is granite, the double range a stainless-steel brand called Viking. Lola has heard of it before—overheard, actually, in the school pickup line as two white mothers discussed a kitchen remodel that was almost ending one of their marriages. When she had arrived home that day, Lola had Googled the brand. The most reasonable range she could find started at $6,000.

The windows in Zach's kitchen are long and wide, the floor a soft hardwood that makes Lola wonder if she should have offered to remove her shoes. She steals a glance at Zach's own bare feet, then finds herself staring at his calves, plump muscle under tanned skin, his leg hair such a soft blond she can make it out only when the sunlight hits him just so. She finds herself slipping her right foot into the heel of her left Puma, hoping Zach doesn't hear it clunk to the floor. She hurries to remove the other shoe, looking at her bare toes, painted dark purple by her own hand. She is not so good at coloring inside the lines, but from a distance, no one can tell.

Zach moves a thick serrated blade through fresh jalapeños so fast she can't tell where one slice ends and the next begins. She sees only the whole motion, a blur of beauty that, reduced to single parts, would be rough and violent. When the pepper is diced into equal-sized squares, Zach smacks his knife into the center of an avocado and twists, revealing the light-green flesh, squeezing it from the rough peel with gentle hands.

Lola thinks of Hector, her baby brother, bound and gagged, wrung out from hours of interrogation and torture.

She thinks of Andrea, standing over her son's bed because a mother watching her child suffer can't be bothered to rest.

What is she doing here, Lola thinks, on the West Side, with her daughter, when there are so many problems to be fixed? Is this what it's like for all working mothers, torn between the small moments with their children and the life-and-death stakes of the outside world?

Now Zach has corn tortillas frying in cast iron, a smattering of solid fat coating them. He smashes a black-bean mixture over the tortillas, squeezes lime juice over the top, then sprinkles on Cotija cheese.

It is a meal Lola could make at home, she thinks, except it would take her three times as long.

Then Zach serves her a black-bean-and-cheese quesadilla with guacamole and jalapeños on the side, a sprig of cilantro as decoration, and when she takes the concoction in her hands and lifts it to her mouth, she knows before she even takes the first bite that she could not have created this.

"How is it?" Zach asks, his grin so wide Lola knows he already knows the answer.

Lola wants to tell him to take her to bed right now, forgetting the two seven-year-olds playing dolls in the next room, with its dirty carpet and loud cartoons. Her whole body tingles with the flavor of Zach's creation.

He can see it, and he moves closer to her, so close that if she stood, they would be standing chest to chest.

He leans in to kiss her, and Lola thinks of Zach's wife, Charlie's mother, and somewhere in her chest her moral center pounds to make itself heard. Maybe if Susan were a neighborhood chica who split her days between the local nail and hair salons, her nights downing just enough tequila to ensnare a one-night stand, she would have felt differently. But Susan fixes people. Susan saves lives.

Lola takes them.

"No. Susan," she murmurs into Zach's ear, catching a sharp waft of cheap shaving cream that somehow doesn't detract from the quesadilla she is still chewing, even in the midst of beginning an affair.

"We're separated," he breathes back, and she smells the bubblegum scent of children's training toothpaste on his breath, the kind Lucy used when she first came to live with Lola because the other stuff was too harsh on her tummy.

Now the children's toothpaste, the crushed cheese curl, the shitty carpet, and the too-loud television all make sense. A man lives here. A man who doesn't clean or shop for cosmetics, a man who bought this bungalow for the kitchen and abandons the rest of the place like it's an unwanted child.

"Why?"

"Work," Zach replies, and Lola wants to ask whose work—his Mexican cooking or his wife's cancer-curing, but she doesn't get the chance, because there is the pitter-patter of little-girl footsteps Lola recognizes even on carpet as her own daughter's.

She knows before she looks up that Lucy will be standing in the doorway, her cheek and one side of her body hugging the wood, her hands behind her back. A warning bell sounds in the back of Lola's brain—she should have said something to Lucy earlier, about not having to obey Charlie.

"Mama, I need you," Lucy says, and the words, a toddler's, not her seven-year-old's, add a pitter-patter to her own heart—my little girl needs me—before Lola recognizes the pitter-patter turning to a thump, from love to fear. Why does my little girl need me?

Zach clears his throat and steps back, unsure if he should be listening or talking. Instead, he wipes the cast-iron skillet with a dish towel and returns it to the cabinet, seasoned and unwashed, used and loved.

"What's the matter, *mija*?" Lola asks, kneeling to Lucy's eye level, but the little girl won't look at her. She is staring at Zach, his back to her as he moves from sink to countertop, swiping random pieces of granite with his towel, slinging the towel over his shoulder, unable to leave the two to their private conversation because they are blocking his doorway.

"We should get home," Lucy says, in a voice so different from her toddler's plea that Lola wonders if she saw something that upset her. Did she see Zach moving in toward Lola? Did she think Charlie's father was trying to hurt her mother? To Lucy, anything sexual equals hurt. It was a long time before adult Lola unlearned the arithmetic she'd been forced to pick up in childhood. Even now, Lola can let Manuel climb atop her in the dark, but she can't look at his body, naked, vulnerable, in the sharp light of morning that cuts through her apartment's cheap blinds.

"Okay," Lola says.

"Charlie!" Zach calls. "Let's say goodbye to Lucy."

Zach does meet her gaze, and she can see, despite his inability to clean any room but the kitchen, that he knows something has soured between their girls. She sees the question there, directed toward her— *What do you think happened?* Lola responds to his unasked question with a shrug, trying to pretend she isn't both salivating at the prospect of learning the truth while also fearing the darkness she knows can pass, not just between an adult and a child, but two children left to their own devices to explore what makes them happy, what makes them cry, and what hurts.

"Goodbye, then," Zach says at the front door. Charlie is nowhere to be found as he nods an awkward goodbye to Lola, and she to him.

The walk to the car is silent, but Lucy slips her little hand into Lola's. In the Civic, Lucy allows Lola to concentrate on finding her way out of Venice, a cesspool of one-way streets, the only section of Los Angeles Lola has found not to be situated on a grid, its twists and turns and lack of logic enough to dizzy anyone who is not a native.

Finally, on the freeway, Lola asks, "What happened? Did you . . . see something?"

Lola is thinking of herself, of Zach, of them discussing his separation and the reason, of the kiss.

Instead, Lucy blurts, "It was Charlie's idea."

The words send a ripple of fear through Lola's soldier-sinewy body. On the steering wheel, her trigger finger, the one she has used to seal the fate of many an enemy, begins to tap the leather, ridding itself of nervous energy that has built up in her fingertip, wanting to get out.

"What was Charlie's idea?" Lola asks, fighting to keep her voice even.

"Calling Mary. Inviting her for a playdate."

Mary is another girl in Lucy's class, a shy, bespectacled smart girl with few friends other than books.

"What playdate?"

"One that wasn't true."

Lola feels her cheeks burn hot. She wants to turn the car around, to spin the wheel back toward Zach's bungalow and shake Charlie until she feels something akin to empathy, but she would settle for pain.

"It was a prank, Mama, and I wanted to tell you, but I couldn't. I didn't do the right thing."

Lucy's little-girl tears spill forth in heaving cries. Snot bubbles from her nose, and Lola can see in the rearview mirror that her daughter is lapping up her own snot with her tongue, trying so hard to keep the pain inside.

"Oh, *mija*," Lola says. "Yes, you did."

"But it's too late. Mary must have gone to Devon's, and Devon's mama isn't going to know what's going on, and they're going to turn her away."

"You told me. That's what matters." Lola looks at Lucy, making sure the little girl sees her as she says, "I'll fix this."

At home, while Lucy falls into a deep sleep fueled by the exhaustion that comes with carrying guilt, Lola scans the Blooming Gardens address book for Mary's name. Under "Parents," Mary, like Lucy, has only a mother listed. Lola dials the number, and the woman who picks up screams into the receiver, "Haven't you tormented my daughter enough?"

Lola hears a little girl's crying in the background, and all Lola can say at first is "I'm sorry. I'm Lola Vasquez, Lucy's mother, and Lucy feels horrible about what happened."

The woman must not have expected an apology, because she is silent. Her silence silences the crying child behind her.

"Ms. Vasquez—"

"Lola."

"Lola, it doesn't sound to me like your child is the problem."

"No," Lola says, "but she let it happen. And she will make it up to your daughter."

"We don't need pity."

"That's not what you'll be getting," Lola says, and when she hangs up and puts her head in her hands, she wonders if she will get through this week without hurting anyone else.

The answer comes at her, sharp, like a tack hidden in carpet: *Not unless I let someone else hurt me.*

SIXTEEN

BLOOD-RED TAPE

The parking lot behind the Coroner's Office is empty because the government has cut its funding. It is closed on some weekdays now because it can't afford to stay open. Louisa Mae herself has not kept track of what day it is, but this is what Juan has told her.

What day was it her family died? She can't remember. Halloween? She sees her brother as an orange. Herself as an apple.

She sees her brother's still head in her lap.

When did it rain? Louisa Mae sees drops clinging to the parked car's windshield. When did it stop? How long has she been sitting here?

Juan said it would be easier if he went in alone. It hasn't occurred to her until now that because the Coroner's Office is closed, there should not be anyone inside to even let him in, so how is it Juan will escape with her baby brother's ashes?

"Don't worry," he had told her. "I will bring him to you."

It was a stupid request, because her family is dead. There is nothing she needs to worry about ever again, because everyone she could ever worry about is gone.

She is twelve years old, and her life is over. Isn't it?

She shuts the question deep in her brain. She opens the passenger's-side door. Juan drives a nice car, something foreign, maybe a BMW. She knew her mother's car was a Mercedes only because her father made such a show of announcing what Louisa Mae would have called a brand instead of a make or model.

There is a shudder from the nearby dumpster—a man in a uniform with a name tag stitched over the left breast pocket is disposing of a bulky black trash bag.

"No," Louisa Mae says, because she feels certain it is her brother's body in that bag, suffocating, scared and unable to get out.

She runs for the man, squeaks out another "No."

But he doesn't see her or hear her. He turns his back and walks back into the building.

She has to catapult into the dumpster off the hood of the lone shitty pickup truck in the parking lot, three spaces over from Juan's might-be BMW.

This is the dumpster of a Coroner's Office. It hits Louisa Mae as she lands. There aren't eggshells and old lo mein noodles.

It stinks of rotting human in here, even if there are no actual bodies. Everything in here has been body-adjacent. Everything in here is complicit.

"Complicit" is a new word from school. She stumbled across it in a book. She did what she had always done with a word she hadn't recognized. She had looked it up in the dictionary. According to *Merriam-Webster,* the word meant "to do wrong in some way."

In what way? To shoot your father for killing your brother? To shoot your father while his back was turned? Was that self-defense?

She finds the black bag closest to the top. It is hefty. She tears at it with fingers slippery from sweat.

Inside, she finds paper. So much paper. Case files. Murders. Lives ended. Lives destroyed. There are photographs, too—wives and daughters, fathers and brothers.

Where is her brother? Is he in here?

Why doesn't she want to bring her mother too?

Because my mother didn't do the only thing a mother must. My mother didn't protect me.

She wants a mother who isn't silent. She wants a mother who will take charge.

Does such a woman exist? If so, she has yet to meet her.

"Louisa?" Juan's voice lobs over the top of the dumpster and lands on her like the ping of the first raindrop—startling and, therefore, annoying.

I'm here, she thinks but can't say. Is this where she wants to stay, among the Coroner's Office detritus?

There is Chinese food, she sees, a paper sack with a fortune cookie and carton spilling out. Someone must have gotten delivery.

She hears Juan's boots walking away, most likely back toward the car. He must have checked there first, because he told her to stay there, not to worry, that he would bring her baby brother back.

She doesn't know if she will be able to climb up and over the dumpster. She doesn't know if she wants to. Her baby brother isn't here. She had hoped to find him in the black bag. Then she could run into the building and find the man with the name tag sewn onto his work shirt, and she could punish him for throwing her baby brother out like trash.

But she has already killed the man responsible for her brother's death. She has killed her own father.

She has found it is not enough.

How will she get out of this? Who is there alive to make her better? Who is there alive to fix her?

The braided rope sails over the dumpster and almost thunks Louisa Mae in the head.

"You must come out now," Juan says on the other side of the black metal.

"I can't," Louisa Mae whispers.

"You must. He is waiting for you."

"No," she cries out.

"Keep your voice down."

"He doesn't want to be buried. He can't be waiting for me. His body—"

She is up and over the black metal side of the dumpster without the help of Juan's lifeline.

She crosses the parking lot at a sprint. The double doors are still unlocked, she's guessing because whoever's inside is waiting for Juan to come back in.

She recognizes the smell of formaldehyde because they've been dissecting frogs in biology class. She was surprised when, after the first cut spilled the frog's guts, she had been okay eating pickles with her hamburger at lunch.

She had a strong stomach, she remembers thinking.

Now she stops in the white tiled hallway to vomit into a large black rolling trash can. When she looks up from heaving, Juan is there. He holds out a blue-and-white checked handkerchief for her to wipe her mouth.

"He is not going to be buried," Juan says.

"Then why did you say he was waiting for me?"

"Because you will want to say goodbye. Before his body is burned."

"Where is everyone?" Louisa Mae asks, almost before Juan has finished explaining, because her brother is dead, and hadn't she already seen him dead, his head in her lap? Doesn't she already believe he is gone for good?

"I have paid an assistant coroner to cut his fishing trip short. He is going to perform the cremation upon his return, then we will take your brother."

Juan starts to roll the black trash can toward the double doors.

"Where are you going?"

"I must get rid of any evidence of you and your life."

It is a sweeping statement, Juan letting her know he is ridding the world of any sign she is still here.

He is erasing me, she thinks, and it is the first time she stops to wonder why he, a cartel hit man, is helping her escape with her life by faking her death.

It is only a fleeting thought, though, because she has turned away from Juan, away from the double doors leading out, and toward the double doors leading in.

She sees her brother's head on the autopsy table. She sees his blue lips. She sees he is not himself, even from here.

It is so cold in the autopsy room. There are other bodies, too, one a naked older man who is too fat to be her father. Her mother must be here, too, but, as in life, she remains an invisible background presence easy to ignore.

"Hello," Louisa Mae says to her brother. She swears she sees his mouth twitch into a quick smile, like he used to when he was a little baby and heard her voice in his sleep.

But that can't be. He is dead. She is alive. Her job now is to give him the goodbye, even at age eight, he knew he would want.

Juan was wrong—she does not want to say goodbye. This is not goodbye. Goodbye will be at the place her brother wanted his ashes scattered. She can delay goodbye.

"See you in the car," she says instead.

SEVENTEEN

SYNDICATE

"I know it hurts," Lola says, pulling a brush through the thin, knotted strings of Lucy's hair. It is coal black. Even when Lola has washed, conditioned, and dried it, it doesn't shine. Lola makes sure Lucy gets plenty of fruits, vegetables, and vitamins. Her daughter is finally closing in on a normal weight. She has grown an inch or two. Still, Lola can't raise the little girl's hair from limp to vibrant. She knows it shouldn't bother her. Lucy is healthy, the trauma of her childhood reduced to repressed memories. Lola doesn't want to be sexist, but she can't help thinking a lovely, full head of hair would make the little girl happier, if not now, then at some point later in her life.

"Good enough" is all Lola says now.

"Can I rinse?" Lucy asks.

Lola nods. "Go ahead" and Lucy sinks into the bathwater with a relaxed sigh, reminding Lola of Andrea and the concrete wall and the Michelin-starred Mexican restaurant. One night later, she still remembers the strong, tender feeling of Andrea holding her hand, of that same hand stealing a churro from a basket, of Zach catching her. And of earlier today, of the moment in his kitchen when their daughters were too quiet to be up to good, when he had almost kissed her.

As Lucy flips and flops, turning from belly to back in the soapy water, Lola wonders how she will keep the promise she made to the Rivera cartel boss she didn't kill: to bring him her own partner, Andrea, in exchange for her brother's return.

She has only tonight to figure out a plan.

"I'm done," Lucy announces, standing up tall and naked and slippery in the tub. Every night, Lola holds her breath as she lifts the little girl from the tub and wraps her in a towel to keep Lucy from shivering. Lola doesn't know enough about being a mother to know when she should stop supervising baths—when does she not have to worry about Lucy drowning or falling and hitting her head? Ever? She does know the moment when she's lifting Lucy's wriggling body from tub to towel makes her more nervous than contemplating her next move in a cartel war. That is business. Lucy is personal. And Lola finds that, because she had her brother sent to prison for a murder she committed, she now feels confident in Hector's ability to keep himself alive under pain of torture, a confidence that wasn't there before Locust Ridge morphed him from boy to man.

Lola can't take time away from Lucy, from her operations here, to fight a war for Andrea in Mexico. Still, if she doesn't turn Andrea over tomorrow, this war will continue, and Hector will wind up still captured, still tortured, and finally dead, unless Lola finds him of her own volition. Her guess is, the sole surviving leader of the Rivera cartel, the man she spoke to over the Lexus's Bluetooth, might be holding her baby brother hostage just across the border, maybe in Tijuana. She's not going to go hunting Hector down on a hunch. She's not a cop. She wants proof before she acts. And she wants a plan.

Lola reads two more chapters of *Matilda* to Lucy, kisses her on the forehead, and smooths her hair. She hands Lucy a stuffed Donald Duck, bought legit from the Disney Store for fifty drug dollars. The little girl hugs the asshole duck closer and flips onto her side, her toes kneading into the mattress like a kitten trying to get comfortable.

Lucy asks Lola if she can ask for forgiveness for what she and Charlie did today.

"No," Lola says. "Only for what you did."

Lucy absorbs this information, then nods her understanding to Lola. But instead of asking her mother for absolution, Lucy turns to her bed and falls to her knees, her hands clasped. It takes a good twenty seconds for Lola to realize Lucy is praying.

Religion is not something Lola has taught her. Faith is something

Lucy has for no good reason. Maybe they are intersecting now that Lucy is older and can grasp just how wrong her early childhood was.

You would need faith to get beyond that evil, Lola thinks. Does she have it?

She pulls on a charcoal hoodie that smells strongly of Tide. As she descends the concrete stairs outside her apartment, Lola thinks of CNN and the news that detergent causes cancer, that anything that will get your clothes or your house clean will kill you. She inhales the scent in the quiet night air. She can hear boys' voices two blocks away, shouts and barks of laughter that, to her, equal peace, because raised voices are not the ring of bullets.

She wonders when Rodrigo will be able to rejoin the ranks of boyhood. She sent him fried fish and tortillas, his favorite meal, via Ramon, today. He will need physical therapy. She will pay. His parents won't even know where the money is coming from.

Maria's place is dark. Lola's mother goes to bed before nine and rises at five. Lola wonders if sleeping through the dark hours, when drug dealers prowl the streets freely, helps keep addiction at bay. She is not a night person, either, but she is also the boss, not a Crenshaw Six corner boy.

Lola finds Manuel asleep on one side of Maria's overstuffed, L-shaped sofa. A telenovela turned down plays on the television. He is staying close now that there's a war on. All Lola's men are.

When Lola gets closer, she sees Manuel's eyes are closed. But a second later, his eyelashes, long and lovely, flutter, and his eyes widen as if he's woken from a nightmare.

He sees her standing in front of him, her hoodie pulled close, her hands jammed in its pockets. She is not one to seduce with lingerie and heels, with a come-hither glance that would be wasted in the left-over light of an onscreen telenovela. She prefers her shell of a hoodie, with its soft scent of carcinogenic laundry detergent and ability to swallow the shape of her stomach and breasts, so that she is a lump it would be tempting to toss aside.

"Sorry," Manuel says. "I drifted off."

If Manuel were Garcia, her ex, he would ask her if she wanted him to come upstairs. But Manuel does not ask her. He stands up and reaches his own hand, big, with black hairy knuckles that cancel out the femininity of his eyelashes, and she takes his big hand in her small one. His hand rests atop hers, but he does not let her lead the way up the stairs. Instead, he walks beside her, allowing her to be not the boss but his lover, if only for the next twenty-seven minutes.

When it's finished, he rises from sweaty sheets, pulls his jeans back on, and leaves her alone in the shadows of her bedroom. He goes back to being her soldier, walking the perimeter of the apartment complex to keep an eye out for danger, and she goes back to being the boss, with the problems of her people on her shoulders alone.

Hours later, the rising sun hits her face, causing a flush in her already hot cheeks. Wednesday. Fuck this day.

"Coffee?"

Shit. Manuel. Here beside her in bed. Lucy will be up any minute.

"You have to go," she says now.

"Okay," he says, with not even a shrug of exasperation at the command.

"No, I . . . What do you want to do? Do you want to stay?" Even today, a shit day, Lola loves the feel of Spanish rolling from her lips, every word a small burst of tongue and teeth.

"I can go."

"I know you can, but I'm asking—"

"How do you take your coffee?"

"Cream, no sugar."

As Manuel disappears into her kitchen, Lola thinks of Garcia, of the way he could never separate Lola the girlfriend from Lola the boss, and how Manuel just accomplished with a simple question what Garcia never could. Shit. Manuel is here. Manuel is making her coffee. He has stepped over a threshold. He is her people, her soldier. He speaks her language, the one she never used growing up but every time she speaks it she feels the scents and sights and sounds of a country she has never seen.

Lola pulls on her standard uniform of cargo pants and wife-beater. She will throw on a cotton sweater for school drop-off. She will see

Zach there. The thought makes her freeze, her left foot halfway in its Puma. Is he the one she imagined crossing the threshold? Or would she be embarrassed to have him here, with the dirt-bare courtyard and the mushrooms growing under the stairs and the beige carpet that absorbs all the nastiness of life and hides it?

Zach can never see this place, she thinks, which is good, because she's fucking someone else.

Lola pads into the living room and sinks into the sofa, which smells faintly of salt and sweat and Lucy's shampoo, baby shampoo, because Lola doesn't want to risk hurting Lucy's eyes when she's rinsing the suds from her strings of wet hair at night.

A knock at the door brings her to her feet, and she notices a shooting pain in her right foot as she pads across the wood floor to answer. She recalls the night she killed the head of Los Liones cartel, prying the green glass shard from her foot and bringing it up to slit the man's throat. She has felt no residual pain from that injury, until now. Maybe it is a warning—*Don't see who's there*.

She opens the door to no one. A quick scan of the courtyard shows only a black cat skittering across the lone picnic table. Lola is about to take this as a bad sign, but Valentine is behind her, her bark deep and repeated and dangerous.

"Inside," Lola says in an even voice, pointing to the living room. Valentine shuts her mouth and retreats, her tail between her legs.

There is an envelope on the mat. Lola has become accustomed to this version of communication in her line of work. In fact, she is relieved, because she knows the note inside will enlighten her as to Hector's well-being. She rips it open and removes a single sheet of copy paper. She reads the expected note written in standard font, single-spaced, not taking up even a third of the page: *"Let's make a trade. Your partner for your brother. Forty-eight hours are up."* The note goes on to give a time and place.

Lola shows the note to Manuel. She translates it aloud in Spanish as his eyes scan the English words, of which he might know every other one.

"It is a trap," he says.

"I know," Lola says. Garcia would have waited to hear her own analysis of the situation before agreeing with her.

"I will go," Manuel says.

"You're not the boss."

The word sends a tingle of pleasure up Lola's spine. Then she remembers Andrea, the woman whose identity Lola is supposed to give today, because Lola is no longer the shadow leader. That honor belongs to Andrea.

EIGHTEEN

IN THE BLACK

"Place puts dill in their bacon," Garcia says, as if he has been to this place before, as if Lola is not the one who suggested it.

Grub is tucked between nondescript two-story Hollywood post-production houses where a lot of Blooming Gardens dads are either editing or yelling at editors about the films and television shows they've directed. There is ivy growing on the outside walls of the restaurant, which looks more like a house. There is no street parking unless you're lucky enough to get here when another patron is leaving.

Lola has parked her Civic several post houses down, in an empty lot with an open gate and a sign threatening to tow. No one is working now, though, even in the late morning hours of a Wednesday. Editing, she has learned from the angry men on cell phones giving notes at drop-off, is a dark art. Men slouch on couches, feet up, dinner ordered so late indigestion is inevitable. The story is told frame by frame, revised, picture by picture, to say something different no one knew was there until just now, with this perfect arrangement of shots and sound.

"The edit is the final rewrite of the script," one dad had explained to her, as if Lola had asked what it was like to be an editor. She hadn't. It sounded very much to her like being in control, pulling strings, or, at least, pulling them at the behest of the director, the real person in charge.

"Food's good," Lola says, and it is, but she doesn't have much of an appetite. Her eggs and bacon have grown cold on her plate.

Garcia hasn't thought to ask why she wanted to meet here, in Hollywood, for brunch. He has not brought up their falling-out, the one that involved her pulling a knife on him and chasing him out of her strip-mall parking lot.

Garcia must have considered her actions that night a compliment, the hysteria of a woman in anguished lust with him.

"More coffee, please," she says to the waitress with a sigh.

The woman, white, in a plaid shirt and clean, dark jeans, replies, "Sure, sweetheart." There is a hint of complicity in the waitress's voice, a wink, as if she understands the situation—Lola on a brunch date she wants to end.

No shit.

Most of the people here look like they've come straight from hiking, and Lola guesses they have. If you look up Seward toward the Hills, you can almost see the Hollywood sign. It's a popular trail for locals and tourists alike, or for the locals who want to show their tourist friends a good time. Lola has had this hike recommended to her several times by Blooming Gardens mothers, who must do weekday morning hikes while their editor husbands sleep off their puppet nights.

Los Angeles is odd like that. No one works when they're supposed to.

"But the thing is, I do still have feelings for you," Garcia is saying.

"Huh?"

"I fucking love you," Garcia says.

Lola does not want to hear these words, not ever, but not now in particular, when she catches the white man's glimpse across the room. The same waitress who called her sweetheart goes to refill his coffee cup, but he shakes his head no and puts a protective hand over the top.

He says something to her that makes her scurry away, but Lola can't imagine this man—white, in pressed pants and a button-down shirt—would bother to exert his power over a waitress. Not here, not in Hollywood, not at brunch, where his whiteness and his ironed clothes and his crossed legs and carb-free plate keep his cover intact. He is not *not* a threat, because a white man with flecks of purpose-

ful gray sitting alone at brunch reading a novel by someone named
Vladimir Nabokov automatically exudes power over the sweaty hik-
ers, younger, more female than male, in the place. It's just that he
doesn't need to make threats to be seen as the most powerful man in
the room.

Because that's what he is.

"I don't know," she says and sighs again.

This is not like her, and Garcia should know it. She used to think
he never spoke out against her, never put his weight behind one decision over another, because he did not want to blur the lines between
boyfriend and soldier. Now Lola wonders if Garcia never bothered to
read her signals at all.

"I'm fucking tired," she says.

Her language draws the eyes of the table next to them—four
women, all white, all in yoga pants, although one wears a hideous
yellow sweatshirt Lola can tell one of the other women is biting her
tongue to keep from mentioning. These bitches have been saying fuck
this and fuck that all brunch, but that is okay, because this is their
place. Put a Latina in here using foul language and someone's bound
to call the cops.

Today, let them.

Today, she feels sort of shitty for what she has made up her mind
to do. She knows Andrea lives five minutes from here, even in the
late-morning tourist traffic. She could run up the hill and grab her
from her house, the house she's never seen except on Google Maps but
whose number and street she knows by heart.

Then she remembers Andrea's son, Christopher, shivering in his
hospital bed way out on the edge of America.

Lola's heroin put him there.

Lola deserves this war Andrea placed on her shoulders.

"I have to pee," she says. She gets up and heads for one of the two
gender-neutral bathrooms. Both are locked. She lingers next to the
white man's table.

"That him?" the white man asks without looking at her.

"That's him."

"Your partner."

"My partner. Where's my brother?"

"So that's it. No breakfast. No nothing."

"I had breakfast."

"You barely ate."

Thanks, Dad, Lola wants to say, but it feels wrong, not only because she has never had a father, much less one who worries if she doesn't eat, but also because this man is the voice on the other end of the Lexus Bluetooth, the other leader of the Rivera cartel.

The one she didn't kill. Yet.

"There's a Dodge Charger outside."

"How far away?"

"Right outside."

But how did you find parking? Lola wants to ask. That part will have to remain a mystery, though, because she is going to get her brother back. She is going to fuck Garcia, not in the way he wanted, and have Hector back and buy herself time to re-up—arms, soldiers, money, drugs—for all-out war.

Garcia is too busy scrolling through his phone to notice when she slips out. She has memorized the cartel boss's face. She has not paid the check.

The keys are in the Charger. There is a banging coming from the trunk.

Can it be?

She pops the trunk. She holds her breath.

Hector jumps out, hopping on the concrete like it's hot and he's not wearing shoes, because even though it's not hot, he is barefoot, and his feet are bloody.

"Lola," he says when he sees her.

"Hector," she says back. "I'm here to take you home."

NINETEEN

YET

Hector spends his first night home on Lola's living-room sofa. He asks her if it's okay to turn on the television, because he is used to all the noise in prison.

"Okay," Lola says, and she finds a cooking show where four people pretend to be friends and share tips on different themes. This week, they are discussing how to give a low-key dinner party.

"You don't want to spend your entire party at the stove. So make sure you do all your prep work in advance. When your first guest walks in the door, you should be ready to greet them."

No shit, Lola thinks.

"The hell is this?" Hector asks.

Lola shrugs, thinking again of the phrase *white nonsense.* But how can it be white nonsense if she has found herself watching it, folding a load of her daughter's clothes in the middle of the day, the same time a stay-at-home mom would be around watching television? She is on call twenty-four hours a day, seven days a week, she can't take a sick day—as a popular cold-medicine commercial explains the plight of a stay-at-home dad. Lola had felt her heart leap when she saw the man speaking to his "boss"—a toddler staring up at him from a crib.

Is the world changing? Or does television first have to reflect the world people should want in order to make it true?

"You get enough dinner?"

Maria's friend Veronica had descended on the apartment with freshly fried flautas, still sizzling, the filling too hot to touch tongues.

She had ordered Lola's men to unload the rest of her car—enough enchiladas, rice and beans, flan to stock a funeral of someone very important.

"From the neighborhood," Veronica had explained.

"For what?"

"No reason," Veronica had said, because of course no one can know Hector is home, yet everyone does know.

Lola knows he can't stay with her permanently. It's been twenty-four hours since she was due to return "Hector Vasquez," real or stand-in, to Locust Ridge. At some point, the cops will show up asking questions. They haven't bothered with the at-least-triple homicide in the strip-mall parking lot. Brown people killing brown people. But they'll get to it—maybe some earnest white detective who wants to make a difference will insist he investigate the case of the missing inmate.

Lola can appreciate such a fictional character, though she prefers when the winds of racism blow in her favor.

"How are your feet?"

"Fine."

"You have to stay off them."

"How? I can't stay on your sofa."

"You can tonight."

"How did you get them to give me to you?"

"I gave them Garcia."

"The hell they want with him?"

"Nothing. But they don't know that." Yet.

"So they don't know about the white lady?"

Hector does not know Andrea's name. None of Lola's soldiers do. This is by design, both for their own protection and for Lola's. If they don't know information, they can't give it under duress.

The next morning, Lucy knocks on Lola's bedroom door.

"There's a man on the sofa."

Lucy must have seen Hector at some point before he went in, but Lola can't remember a specific time.

"That's my brother."

"So he's my uncle?"

Lola doesn't say anything, doing the math that shouldn't take so long in her head.

"Yes. He is."

"Is he going to stay here?"

Lola hears the rising panic in her daughter's voice, and she wants to take back the word "uncle," because maybe, to Lucy, it does not have a positive connotation.

"Where did he come from?"

"Three hours away," Lola tells Lucy, because she does not want to get into the whys and hows of prison, not during the morning rush of getting both herself and Lucy out the door and to school before the last bell rings. She also doesn't want to lie to her daughter.

Manuel is coming through the front door when Lola makes her way through the living room. He stomps his boots as if he's shaking off sand or snow, hot or cold, some natural wonder turned nuisance.

"*Hola,*" Hector says.

"Hi," Manuel says, wary because this man is using his language, when he's so used to Jorge and Marcos refusing.

"I'm Hector. Lola's brother."

The two men shake hands on Lola's threshold, because of course Hector must have let Manuel in. He does not have a key.

Manuel watches Hector hobble back to the sofa.

"Your feet," Manuel says, as if Hector isn't aware, but Lola guesses it is just because he does not know how to express the weight of his concern in English.

"Yeah. Sucks. Went through some shit."

"I know," Manuel says.

"Lola tell you?"

"No."

Manuel is excited now, sitting on the sofa next to Hector, who looks to Lola—this okay? Lola is too surprised to see Manuel removing his boots, then his socks, as if he is about to stretch out for a nap, unaware of the fact that the people who live here have just begun their day.

"See," Manuel points, a smile on his face. Yet his feet . . . they are scarred red, slish-slashed skin on his soles like several tic-tac-toe boards.

How is it Lola has never seen these marks?

Who did this to you? Lola wants to ask, although of course she knows.

"Cartel," Manuel says.

Hector doesn't look to Lola for permission now. He lifts his bandaged feet onto the sofa so Manuel can see the combat medicine Lola put in action last night, wrapping them as he sucked in air to relieve the pain.

"Cartel," Hector says.

There is a moment of connection between two men in Lola's life. War wounds.

She almost lets them have their connection, and she would, if Lucy weren't one room over, putting shoes and socks over her own soles.

"Put your fucking feet away," Lola hisses to both men, and they do, but there is a shared smile between them: *Silly Lola.*

Lola thinks of the green glass shard, the one she pulled from her foot, gushing blood, as she slashed the head of Los Liones cartel.

I understand, Lola thinks. Manuel should know—he was there.

Lola doesn't have to tell Hector to start folding the sheets and blankets she pulled over the sofa last night. He has folded them neatly, as he must have had to do in prison.

"What next?" he asks her.

The question lets Lola know he, too, knows. All she has done by turning Garcia over to the Rivera cartel is buy them some time.

"You taking me back?"

"You're not safe in Locust Ridge. Not until this war is over."

"And then?"

Lola doesn't know.

"Keep him safe. And hidden," Lola says to Manuel, who nods.

Lola drops Lucy at school. Then she's walking to her car like it's any other day, but she's going to drive east instead of west, having made an educated guess as to where in the city her next target might have landed. She isn't even to her car when her iPhone rings.

Lola's iPhone, the one phone she owns that's not a disposable burner, is the one where she saves photos of Lucy and Valentine, with Maria sometimes caught in the background. Her mother doesn't know how to photo-bomb, but she does have a knack for walking into the room right as Lola is trying to capture family photos that, she hopes, will let Lucy know her family is, if not normal, loving.

The background photo on Lola's screen is a selfie. Both Lucy and Valentine have crowded onto Lola's lap. Lola and Lucy are laughing because there isn't room on Lola's sad excuse for thighs for both Lucy and Valentine, yet there they are, perched and supported. In one corner of the frame, Lola sees a pocket of triceps that belongs to her own lean arm. In the other corner, Maria has walked into the room, mouth open, black-gray hair escaping from a hurried ponytail. Lola can tell from the photo—which she has examined in detail many times—that Maria is about to apologize for ruining the picture, instead of jumping out of the way.

Lola uses this phone to accept calls from school when Lucy is sick, or for other parents to call Lola and extend invitations to join the committee for the Blooming Gardens annual fund-raiser. This last call has yet to happen. Still, this is the phone Lola answers when she's playing Mom, because when you have kids, needing to drop your phone into the river so it can't be traced back to a drug drop is no excuse for not being there when they need you.

Lola doesn't recognize the number that comes up on her screen now, as she turns, catching one last glance of her daughter disappearing to the double doors of Blooming Gardens. Her little girl doesn't spare a backward glance for her—her eyes are peeled, Lola guesses for Charlie. Even though Lucy cried herself to sleep after their last playdate, Lola knows it will take more than one prank to let Lucy know Charlie is bad fucking news. Lola declines the call and wonders if she should make a scene, separate Lucy and Charlie, tell her daughter some girls are assholes. If she does that, Lucy will turn on her. If she doesn't, maybe one day Lucy won't think it's so bad to call the least popular girl in school and make a fake playdate.

"You declined me." The voice behind her is white, male, with an undertone of laughter that could be either confidence or nerves. Is that undertone the reason she knows this man is white? Is the mixture of confidence and nerves a recipe for entitlement? "Hey, Zach. Didn't recognize the number."

"Oh, right." He laughs. His laugh is easy, as if he isn't afraid to let his guard down and use it. "I got a new phone."

The phone Zach holds up is an older model, something Lola thinks is called a Droid. The last time she saw him, didn't he have an iPhone too? If his ex-wife took his phone, Zach's divorce must be getting nasty.

"I was wondering—"

Lola knows what's coming. She has never dated a white man before. She went from Carlos to Garcia to Manuel, if she can count Manuel. She shared her life with Carlos before she shot him between the eyes for either becoming someone she didn't know or being a person she couldn't see all along. She and Garcia foraged for furniture and door-mats and had dinner and talked about their days until her growing power overpowered him. Now he's in the hands of a white cartel boss because he wouldn't stop asking her to take him back. Manuel has stayed the night only once, by accident. Even in her small apartment, she has compartmentalized her life to protect what really matters— Lucy. She does not want to be the kind of mother who brings home different men for her child to meet. Even if some of them are decent, there is too much darkness to risk.

"Would you have dinner with me?"

Lola has never heard these words, spoken in this order. She has heard versions, yes, but she and Carlos got together over high school lockers. She and Garcia got together over Carlos's dead body. Dinner was something prepared on your own stovetop, served in the kitchen, and eaten to survive.

"Okay," Lola says.

"Tonight?"

The rules of dating have not etched themselves into Lola's brain. She can recall with frightening quickness the street value of a kilo of heroin or a gallon of milk at the local bodega. It has not occurred to her until now that Zach has waited the requisite forty-eight hours from the time Lucy and Charlie had their playdate to approach her. She does not know until it's too late that saying yes is giving in too easily.

"Okay," she says, wanting the words back as soon as she says them. She is tired. Her brother is in danger. She is in danger. Lucy is in danger. She will have to change her sweatpants to jeans. She can't wear cargo pants and a ribbed tank on a date. Likewise, she can't dress like the women in her neighborhood, with cleavage boosted out of their belly shirts and hoop earrings the size of Ferris wheels. All Lola can think when she sees these hoops is how easy and painful it would be to rip the metal rings through cartilage, to tear apart the ear.

"Great. I'll pick you up."

She has the good sense to say no to this. Like Zach, she has a 323 area code, but her world is several away from his.

"I'll meet you."

"Great." He gives her an address and tells her the reservation is under his name. He'll see her tonight. He is halfway to his car, his keys out, the fob chirping the driver's-side door of his used Acura open, when he turns.

"Did something happen the other day? With the girls?"

Yes, Lola thinks. *I think your daughter's an asshole.*

"What'd Charlie tell you?"

"That there's this unpopular girl," Zach says, then looks around to make sure he's not hurting any child's feelings. The gesture causes Lola's breath to catch in her chest. It is the first thing Zach has done in this conversation that doesn't reek of privilege. "And they called her. And Lucy played a prank."

All Lola's goodwill sinks from her heart to her toes, leaking onto the manicured Blooming Gardens grass. She hears a mother polite-shouting after her child to come back for his lunch bag. Behind her, a father screeches into his cell phone that he told his assistant he would be late this morning, and she needs to be proactive, goddammit.

"Is that not what you heard?" Zach asks.

"No," Lola says. She shakes her head, her black hair whipping fast over the white of her T-shirt. She is not having dinner with the asshole daughter's asshole father who just called her own daughter a liar.

Lola can't help herself. She gets in Zach's face, the Spanish flying from her lips fast and hard. "Listen, motherfucker, you got a lot of fucking nerve calling my daughter out like that. Maybe you want to pick on someone your own size."

Parents have stopped to stare. The three lone children left in the yard abandon the jump rope they were sharing and scurry inside the school. Zach holds up his hands in surrender as Lola's own fingers close around the blade in her pocket.

"Look, I'm not calling your daughter a liar."

"You speak Spanish?"

"I do. But I also got the intent. I know Lucy's telling the truth."

"How would you know that? You've met her, what, once?"

"I know because my daughter's the liar."

Lola backs up two steps, then forgets if she meant to charge to her car or just stand down.

"Charlie's having trouble . . . with the divorce. I'm trying to cut her some slack, as long as what she does isn't hurting other people."

Lola thinks of Lucy, crying in the backseat of the Civic as they traveled the vast distance from Venice to Huntington Park in a lane of sluggish traffic, west to east.

"You need to punish her for this shit," Lola says.

"And now I know that."

Lola realizes she and Zach have been speaking Spanish this whole time, that the parents stopped in the yard have stopped to stare not because they know Lola was about to pull a knife, but because the language the white man is speaking to the brown woman is not necessary outside of eavesdropping on a housekeeper's conversation or asking where the bathroom is at a five-star Mexican resort where the entire staff speaks English.

"I'm sorry," Lola says.

"It's nothing," Zach says.

Still, he has seen her Huntington Park side. He knows there is something deeper there, something animalistic. Zach knows that she was about to pull a weapon, and that she would not have been afraid to use it. What she can't tell is if he minds seeing a glimpse of her true self.

"So . . . dinner?" he says.

Who the fuck is she kidding? She can't inflict her world on him.

"Not tonight," she says.

She gets in her car and pulls out of her parking space too fast. She dials Andrea's office number. The assistant who picks up is male this time, with a booming, caffeinated voice.

"Andrea Dennison Whiteley's office," the assistant says.

Lola was going to play the cool, calm CI. She'd already played the frantic-female, damsel-in-distress card when she had called the office for the location of Andrea's dinner Monday night. It does not escape her attention now, Thursday of the same week, that Andrea has a different assistant. Lola wonders if her trickery is the cause.

"Fucking help me!" Lola screams into the phone, although she didn't plan it. As the cautious minivan in front of her refuses to make a left turn on yellow, Lola finds small satisfaction in deafening Andrea's new male assistant.

"I'm sorry . . . ma'am . . . are you still there? Could you tell me the nature of your emergency?"

Who is this guy, a fucking 911 operator?

"He fucking beat the shit out of me," Lola continues in Spanish, because she's betting this dude doesn't speak it, and that somewhere deep, dark in the recesses of his open, slightly racist mind, he might see her native tongue as a threat.

To her surprise, the male assistant rattles off a response in Spanish. There's a slight accent, as if he didn't start learning the language till he hit high school, but Lola stands corrected.

What is it with white male Spanish speakers today?

"Can you get someplace safe?" he asks.

"I think so," Lola says.

"Where?"

"Grand Central Market. Twenty minutes."

"How will she recognize you?"

"I'll recognize her," Lola says, and hangs up.

She has to stop this war.

Downtown, Lola finds parking a block away and pays fifteen bucks cash for the privilege. She could have parked farther and spent less, but fifteen bucks isn't so much, and getting a chance to pay in cash, to pass a dirty ten for clean, is a welcome opportunity in Lola's life.

She thinks of providing for Lucy in case something happens to her. She bets Andrea has a life-insurance policy, something that will provide for her husband—if he even needs it, running his five-star rehab facility in Malibu with both his wealthy clientele's money and the trafficking profits Andrea cleans there.

She wonders if Andrea knows that a life-insurance policy will do her addict son no favors.

Grand Central Market is not busy at this time of morning. It is pushing ten, a time when many downtown workers have just arrived in the office and can't yet justify a coffee break. Lola hasn't been here since Maria brought her and Hector as children to ride Angels Flight, the tram across the street that chugs uphill to give patrons breathtaking views of the city. Maria had bought both children fruit with chili powder from a street vendor below, and Lola had been too nervous before the tram ride to eat it. When they were back on safe ground at the bottom, Maria had yanked the uneaten fruit from Lola's hand and tossed it into the trash, calling her daughter wasteful. She had sent Lola to bed that night without dinner. It was a rare glimpse of what life with a sober Maria would have been like.

Angels Flight is closed now, maybe for repair, maybe permanently, and Grand Central Market, which Lola remembers as an open-air haven for cheap produce and spices, is now a high-ceilinged, white-painted showcase for restaurants.

Lola sees Andrea before Andrea sees her. She is seated alone at a small, white table for two. There is a bagel and lox in front of her, a coffee in her hand. Her hair falls in loose brown rings around her face, sharpening her already sharp chin and jawline. She flips through note cards—a speech?—and Lola sees her mouth move, her finger poised to punctuate whatever words she has just mouthed. Definitely a speech. A server from the deli refills her coffee without her having to ask, then retreats to the corner, where he and another server watch their only customer. From here, they could be her henchmen, having cleared a space for her in a very public arena. When they spot Lola, their eyes narrow, as if they don't trust her, despite the fact that they are both brown, and so is she. Still, Lola knows what they are thinking when they see her: What does she want with lox and capers and red onion?

True, she doesn't much care for smoked salmon, and she wonders if it's only because she grew up Mexican American and not Jewish that she prefers ceviche. Fuck those two waiters for assuming, though.

"Hey," she calls out in Spanish. "Get me what she's having, please."

The server who refilled Andrea's coffee nods, as if she's speaking English and he knows the language only well enough to understand but not respond. What an asshole.

Andrea doesn't look up from her speech. Lola catches a glimpse of key words written in Sharpie on the pale-blue cards—"honored," "fight for you," "love this city."

"What's the speech for?" Lola asks, then regrets the question, because it's stupid. Andrea is a prosecutor. She makes speeches to give victims closure and justice. She makes speeches to put pieces of shit behind bars.

She makes speeches to sum up a world of problems that should be too big to put into words.

"It's nothing," Andrea says, thwacking the note cards into sharp order on the table before she twists a rubber band around them and tucks them into her handbag.

The server appears. "What can I get for you, miss? We have many fine pastries—"

"I already told you, I'll have that," Lola says, her hands crossed over her stomach, her ankles stretched out and crossed on the floor. She is taking ownership of this deli, and she might not know the name of what Andrea's eating—is it lox or salmon? She doesn't know the difference, but she knows she can damn well eat it too.

The server spends a long time writing on his pad. Andrea looks at Lola. Lola is wondering if Andrea has the power to tell this guy to scram.

"He your spy?" Lola asks when he disappears.

"He's overzealous because he's meant for more. In his country—"

"Yeah, I'm sure he's a fucking doctor. We all are."

Andrea settles in her own chair, and Lola sees she has made her partner smile.

"Most girls from Texas eat this stuff?" Lola gestures to the bagel, the cream cheese, the capers.

"Austin's pretty progressive. If you call Jewish delis progressive."

"I don't. Not like there's a bunch in my neighborhood," Lola says, but the fact that Andrea didn't flinch when she mentioned her birthplace has not escaped Lola's notice. Andrea does not like to talk about her childhood in the Lone Star State. Lola knows where Andrea lived during law school, but she doesn't know the name of the Texas town where she was born. She assumes Andrea had a mother and father, but Andrea only mentions her husband when Lola brings up family. There is a dog, too—an Australian shepherd named Vanilla, a cream-colored monster with fluffy salon hair. Andrea has a photo of him on her desk. It is the only personal photo in her office Lola has seen.

The one time Andrea caught her staring at the photo of Vanilla the dog, Andrea said, "We run four miles a day, Vanilla and I." Lola knew what Andrea was really saying—*I'm watching you watch me. I'm watching you try to read me. I see you.*

The night Andrea took Lola to see her son in rehab is the only time Andrea has let Lola gape into a very personal window of her life. Until that night, Lola had not known Andrea, too, was a mother. In their line of work, Lola doesn't blame Andrea for not keeping pictures of her kids where anyone can see what they look like.

Try as she might, Lola has never seen Andrea. That was a mistake, one she intends to right. They are sitting across from each other in a stalemate, but a stalemate can't last.

They sit in silence, the crowd at the market starting to pick up. A woman in her fifties wanders in, asking for a platter of smoked salmon for a party she's giving tonight. She needs to feed thirty people, although she doesn't know how she's going to squeeze them all into her loft. Lola has heard the term "gentrification"—the taking of a poor person's neighborhood and selling it to the wealthy—but she has never seen the term personified as she does now. The woman in front of her wears khaki Capri pants, a jewel-toned top, and a man's cotton collared shirt that swallows the rest of it whole. There are streaks of paint on the shirt, as if she's been using it as a smock, and a clot of electric-blue paint clumps a section of her ash-blond hair into a tiny tumor above her left ear.

"I'm fighting your war," Lola says.

"You're perfectly capable."

"And you're soft on drugs."

Andrea sits up a little straighter. "Have you been reading the Internet?" she asks, her sharp chin resting in her hands, a little girl putting on a show of apathy. But Lola knows, just from the fact that she sat up, that she's gotten Andrea's attention.

"Something like that," Lola says. "Soft on drugs, hard on pedophiles and domestic offenders."

Andrea's neck lolls back, her hair spilling over the back of the chair, her spine going slack so Lola thinks she might slide off the chair, slippery as a cracked egg sliding from shell to skillet.

"I believe there's a saying for that," Andrea says. "Pot. Kettle. Black."

Lola has heard this saying before, although it wasn't featured in her house growing up. She has long ago filed it somewhere in her brain under the category of "white-people phrases," along with things like "Bob's your uncle," a phrase that makes sense only if you're likely to have relatives named Bob.

"Understand this: My brother is home. That's the only reason I'm not slashing your fucking throat right now."

"That's fair."

"What I don't understand is why there's no record of Andrea Dennison Whitely before 2006. According to the Internet, you've only existed for the past ten years."

Lola doesn't get to clock Andrea's reaction, because here's the server, carrying three separate plates for the bagel, the cream cheese, the fixings—capers, red onion, slice of tomato. It takes him a full thirty seconds to arrange the three plates in front of Lola, and she fights the urge to leap from the table and rip open his throat as he places her cloth napkin on her lap. Is that something servers do? Or is it one of a million ways men are allowed to touch a woman's body without her permission?

"Would you like to know what it is?" Andrea asks. "My name from before?"

"I'll figure it out," Lola says. She spreads cream cheese on half of her bagel, tempted to squish everything into a single sandwich, but she sees Andrea has used each half as a separate whole.

"I'm sure you will. But I can speed up the process."

"I'm not in a hurry. I'll destroy you when I feel like it."

Andrea nods, tapping her fingernails on the white table. They are painted dark purple. Lola can't make out a single chip in the polish.

"You. Not the Rivera cartel," Andrea says.

"They want you," Lola tells Andrea. "They know I have a partner. Even if they don't know it's you."

"You're their match. Not me," Andrea says. Her fingers, long and slender, continue to tap the tabletop, then fish the note cards from her handbag.

"Tell me why you started this war."

"Because you sold heroin to my son, and he overdosed."

"The real reason."

"Or?"

"I take you down."

"You'll need to know where I came from if you want power over me."

"I didn't say I wanted power."

"You destroy me, you'll have more."

"Answer my question."

"I started this war because Los Angeles needs a new front woman."

"What for?"

"Would you like to see?"

Lola would.

TWENTY

PRESS

Lola stands on the steps of the Los Angeles Hall of Justice, facing large black boxes of cameras shouldered by men in cargo shorts. She watches the reporters—eager blond women with arched, frozen brows leaning so far toward the camera it looks like they are straining for a kiss. The male reporters are more relaxed, their arms crossed over their chests, as if they've seen this kind of press conference countless times. Lola sees hints of orange makeup on the men's bronzed cheeks, but she also sees the wrinkles the male reporters don't feel the need to cover. She looks from women to men—eager, relaxed, prepared, whimsical.

The sun hovering over the downtown skyline is the color of fire.

When Andrea moves to the podium, Lola has to squint to see her, even though she can't be more than ten feet in front of her.

Lola stands behind the podium with a group of victims Andrea has helped—battered women and abused children. Lola doesn't know where she fits among them, although her cover, or, more to the point, her excuse for being in her wealthy white-lady partner's life, has always been that she is an abused woman. Andrea first noticed Lola when she was taking a kick to the stomach from Hector. Then Andrea mistook Lola for a true victim, and Lola mistook Andrea for a true prosecutor. To be fair, both women are both of these labels, but the lines of their categories smudge until Lola is the one doling out justice and Andrea is running from a past Lola is now determined to find.

"Good morning," Andrea says.

Lola spots Raymond, the silver-haired man from El Norte, standing to Andrea's left. To her right, Lola recognizes Jack Whitely, Andrea's husband. He's traded his white doctor's coat for a tailored suit and tie. Lola wonders why Andrea spent the morning at Grand Central Market with her, Lola, instead of with her husband, who has appeared only when the cameras do, careful to stand the requisite two steps behind her for the news conference.

Are they fighting because their son is stuck in a hospital bed on the edge of the Pacific? It would not look good for a doctor who claims to specialize in helping addicts recover if his own son were revealed to be one of his patients. It would not look good for a prosecutor either.

"I want to thank you all for coming. I'm here today because I want to express my gratitude for the man who started my career, who has taught me everything I know. The man who showed me how to dedicate my work—and my life—to the idea that there should not be different justice for different people, that the scales should be balanced and fair, regardless of race, religion, or income. Raymond Ewing has not only helped me, he has made it possible to help everyone here."

Andrea makes a sweeping gesture that lumps Lola in with the other victims, who, Lola's realizing now, are a pleasant, nonthreatening blend of white, black, and Latino. One Asian woman stands on the fringes, and Lola can't tell if it's because she feels isolated, or if she doesn't want to rub shoulders with the black woman she's keeping at a distance of at least two feet.

"So it's only fitting that I celebrate Raymond as I announce my own candidacy to become your next Los Angeles district attorney."

Lola notices the crowd beyond the reporters for the first time as a whoop erupts. The reporters turn, their mics and cameras stuck out in the air like so many butterfly nets, hoping to capture anything that will sound sharp in five seconds or less. Unfortunately, the crowd is hell-bent on claps and whoops, and as the reporters turn back to Andrea, they find a demure girl, her head bent, a small laugh at her lips.

Andrea's tendency to use her feminine wiles has not escaped Lola.

She thinks of Andrea taking her hand at El Norte. She thinks of Andrea's lashes fluttering over the white chipped coffee mug a mere twenty minutes ago. She thinks of how Andrea is the reason the Rivera cartel abducted Hector, and how she, Lola, has yet to destroy Andrea.

Lola looks at Andrea's soft curls, at the glint of long, milky flesh beneath. She pictures blood freed from a vein, staining the milky pale, and she pictures herself standing over Andrea as the woman crumples to the concrete steps beneath her feet.

Then Lola feels the beginnings of tears at the edges of her eyes. Is she turning soft? Is she hesitant to kill Andrea because this woman is her key to the legit world? Does she want to become Andrea, because being Lola is no longer enough? Has she realized there is only so far she can go in her own neighborhood, her own class, her own race, only so far she can run from her own shitty past?

"Together, we have no limits," Andrea says as soon as there is a large enough gap in the applause for her words to be heard.

And heard they are. The crowd roars. The victims, some of whom Lola is sure don't speak English and were told there would be free food if they showed up, look to one another, unsure what to do.

Lola shows them. She raises her hands in a polite clap. She does not whoop—a whoop from a minority female victim would come off too aggressive, and Andrea needs her victims to appear victimized.

Lola hears the crack first and, although she knows it's impossible, thinks she sees the pointed metal of a bullet as it parts the air above the crowd. Not one of the reporters thinks to duck. Even though they are often on the scene in the immediate aftermath of violence—a drive-by, a hit-and-run, brains and blood and metal mingled on asphalt—in their worlds, a crack like this, under the din of celebratory applause, might signify something as innocent as fireworks. It doesn't matter, though, because Lola knows the bullet is above them, aimed at the stairs, at the podium, at the milk-pale skin that covers Andrea's skull.

Lola lunges forward, her arms spread, and tackles Andrea. She smells the deep sweet of her perfume, feels the light coat of slick sweat mixed with it, a glaze atop Andrea's unblemished face. Lola takes her to the concrete with her, smashing Andrea's cheek to the hard, sunlit and sizzling stairs.

"Get down!" Lola yells, once in English, then again in Spanish, but the victims behind her already know to drop, squatting, to their knees and cover their heads with their hands. The reporters and Andrea's supporters are slower, looking around first, their eyes wide with something like disbelief that this could be happening to them. But they are in downtown L.A., on the steps of the Hall of Justice, watching a powerful woman announce that she plans to seek more power, and, of course, Lola thinks, there is a man behind a rifle somewhere above them who can't stomach this. What she doesn't know is if this man is your run-of-the-mill defendant released from prison and bent on revenge against the prosecutor who put him there or if he is a member of the Rivera cartel, the organization Lola thought had mistaken her for the gatekeeper of drug trafficking for the whole of Los Angeles.

"What the fuck?" Andrea says, her breath coming in one short heave before she corrects it and begins to inhale and exhale at normal intervals. This is a trick Andrea must have learned in her past life, the one that began in Texas, the one she erased.

"Someone shot at you," Lola says. She is inhaling and exhaling herself, normal, nothing to see here, because, while a sniper attempting to pick off a powerful white woman is new to her, the bullet spinning and cracking through city air, aimed to spatter skull and brains to pieces of gray and white, isn't.

Andrea moves to stand, but Lola pulls her back down. Her cheek is scratched red from the uneven pavement, from Lola holding her face to the concrete, and the five neat red lines on her milk-white cheek are so symmetrical they could be from an enthusiastic cat scratch.

"Stay down," Lola says. "He could still be out there."

"Where?"

"I don't know. Above us."

Lola peers around the wooden podium to the parking garage across the street. It is four levels, full of cars in all variations of make and model—Bentleys to Nissans to an ancient Volkswagen van—

because this is downtown Los Angeles, and everyone, regardless of class or income, needs a dose of the Hall of Justice from time to time.

"I don't see anyone," Lola says, but she is sure the shot came from one of the top levels. If she makes a break for it now, she might be able to catch the shooter. She is not armed, not with a gun, at least, but she is good with her blade, and there is enough rust on its tip to make anyone about to be stabbed with it wary of tetanus as well as a knife wound. "I need to get closer."

"No!" Andrea says, her turn to pull Lola back to the ground with her. "Stay with me." Lola wants to ask Andrea why her, and shouldn't her husband be the one scurrying over to shield her body with his? When Lola looks up, she sees Jack watching the brown woman covering his wife's body with her own. His head is tilted, curious, and he is standing, while everyone else on the stage is still crouching low.

Already uniformed cops are swarming the scene. Of course they must have been nearby, directing traffic around the Hall of Justice, where news vans were parked, blocking the steps.

"Ma'am, are you okay?" The cop who approaches them can't be more than twenty-two, fresh-faced, blond stubble buzzed into a crew cut atop his head. His blue eyes pierce Lola's, because his question is not directed at Andrea. It is directed at her.

"I'm fine," Lola says, ignoring his hand, although she wants to take it, to let this cop know she is happy he is here, that he picked the brown woman over the white one to care for first.

Andrea is already standing, pushing away a blanket that another uniformed officer, older, stockier, is holding out to her. Why a blanket? Lola can't imagine the LAPD trains its officers to treat cold as the priority problem after someone takes a shot at you, although she saw it happen one night in Venice over two years ago. She just wasn't paying attention because Hector had just cost her four million large in cash and product, fucking up a drop to help the white pixie tweaker the cops couldn't wait to keep warm.

"I'm fine. I'm fine. I don't need that blanket," Andrea says, but then Lola sees the slight quivering of her shoulders, the clicking clatter of her teeth as she talks. Shock. Lola is certain from the breathing technique she watched Andrea execute earlier that she has survived a shooting before this one. The theory surprises Lola, coming to her fully formed—Andrea has walked through trauma. But Andrea can't accept the blanket—there are cameras here. She has just announced her run for district attorney. She can't give anyone the impression of womanly weakness.

Lola scoots out from behind the podium as Raymond Ewing makes his way to Andrea. Lola gives the current DA credit for not putting an arm around her, and instead, the two, boss and protégée, stand facing the parking garage.

"The shot must have come from there." Andrea points, and, once again, the cameras are raised, capturing Andrea's eyes, the resolve there as she faces the place where a sniper just took a shot at her.

Lola slips past the other victims, most still kneeling with their hands atop their heads, looking like they're surrendering to the police, staying down until told to rise.

Lola doesn't wait for permission. She's going to find the shooter before the police have a chance. Because if anyone is going to kill Andrea, it will be her.

TWENTY-ONE

ROCK PAPER

Lola crosses Temple at a walk-sprint, not because she is injured, but because she has to dodge the cars taking the downtown street too fast. Drivers lay on their horns, brakes squeal, and one man plows past her, revving his truck's engine and catching her eye as his tires just miss the tips of her toes. She knows the white man was putting her, the brown girl, on notice—*This is my country. I can run over you if I want.*

But he hadn't. Lola could take this as progress in America's race relations. Instead, she figures it has more to do with the white man's cowardice, his inability in the eleventh hour to make the kill.

She does not have that cowardice. When she finds the man who would have killed Andrea, she will kill him.

A man and a woman, both white, dressed in courtroom professional attire, exit the parking garage as Lola enters. She knows they must be headed to court, having shelled out the requisite twenty-five bucks it costs to park this close to the place that doles out justice. She wonders if they are plaintiffs, defendants, or attorneys. But the woman looks up, and Lola notices her puffy eyes, swollen as bread dough, her pupils tiny brown dots lost in the rest of her face. Both the man and the woman are wearing black, Lola sees now. Mourning. The man has a steadying hand on the woman's back.

Have you lost a child? The words are a second from escaping Lola's lips. It is her own worst fear, losing Lucy, and potentially the only fear that would cause her face to swell with bloated grief. She can't imagine having the ability to pull on a black suit, to take a parking ticket at the entrance to this garage, and to wait for the green light to cross Temple and hope for justice for her child.

Then she thinks of Hector, of school mornings when Maria hadn't given them dinner, of him devouring the cereal Lola poured with the hunger of an animal. She thinks of how he ate so fast he spilled milk, wasting what little food she was able to scrounge for them. She thinks of Hector peering up at her, waiting for her to yell, and she remembers telling him it was okay, everybody spills.

Now her brother is home, but she let him languish too long at the hands of the Rivera cartel while she has played West Side white lady, dropping Lucy off, picking her up, eating things like bagels and lox with the woman running for district attorney.

"Shit," she says, loud enough so the grieving couple hears her. "Sorry."

The man and woman look at each other, surprised this woman has apologized to them for her language. Lola sees the sad half smile they give each other.

"It's okay," the woman says. "This place—" Her gesture encompasses the overpriced parking lot, the busy street beyond, and the Hall of Justice, stacked tall and square like a wedding cake.

"I hope things go your way in there," Lola says, her nod encompassing all the same places.

"Did they go yours?" the woman asks, stepping toward Lola, the dots of her eyes searching Lola's face for an answer Lola doesn't know.

I make my own justice, Lola thinks, but she can't say that aloud, because who would, and also because this woman is not looking for the truth. If she's lost a child to murder or drugs or even negligence, the truth is too bleak and too much.

"Yes," Lola says, and the woman finds enough comfort in Lola's answer to turn and walk back to her husband.

Lola bursts into the stairwell knowing she's lost precious time, knowing if the police are looking for her later today, they will know she came over here to confront the would-be assassin. They will track down the couple, and the two grieving parents will be able to place her at what is about to become a murder scene.

It will be only a matter of time before they knock at her door to ask about the shit that went down in her strip-mall parking lot the other night. But this takes precedence, because this shooter tried to gun down a prosecutor.

The assailant could have run out a back entrance. But how would he walk down the street with a sniper rifle? He would have to pack up first. He would have to have a bag whose contents he could hide. Lola doesn't know much about sniper rifles. She deals in semiautomatics, weapons that give a burst of quantity shots over quality. But this is the second time she's encountered one this week, so she's going to have to learn.

She heads to the roof, figuring she'll start there. The police will be here as soon as they've secured the scene across the street. Shit, Lola thinks this time, the couple will be walking into the aftermath of a crime scene. Lola wonders if the post-trauma will upset them, with their puffy eyes and their numb walk up the stairs. Will it force them out of their grief-stricken fugue state, or will it stir hope somewhere inside them to see other people going through some violent shit?

By the time Lola gets to the roof, five floors up, she is out of breath. She does not work out. She is skinny with tight, light muscles. She can't breathe, but she does have her blade, a small, prodding hunk of metal that jabs her just enough when she sits to remind her of its presence.

The air up here is crisp and fresh, with a tiny tinge of brisk that signals fall in Los Angeles. Unlike the lower levels, packed full with neat rows of cars and SUVs squeezed into compact spaces, there are only a few cars whose owners bothered to make the trek up all five ramps. She imagines the car on the first floor, its turn signal blinking, waiting a full five minutes for another car to back out, the driver telling himself he was saving time, while the car behind him sped past him and up to the roof, no waiting, always moving. Lola is more like the latter imaginary driver. She doesn't like to stand still. Now she counts twelve cars in all. She walks the gamut of Bentleys, Benzes, Hondas, and Acuras, her fingers playing with the handle of the blade in her pocket.

Andrea's would-be assassin is here somewhere. Lola's heart speeds up, and when she licks her lips, she tastes blood, salty and metallic. She must have bitten her lip in her hunger for the kill.

When she sees him, he has his back to her. Not smart, she thinks. Not like a professional assassin. The rifle he used to take the shot is still aimed at the Hall of Justice. It's resting on its stand, the scope still in place. Is he planning to take another shot?

When he turns around, Lola knows he was expecting her.

"Look, lady, my boss told me to do you a favor. Take out the white lady," he says.

"Fuck you," Lola says. The curse lights a fire in her, and with a flick of her wrist, her blade is out, and she is striding toward the sniper rifle. It is a weapon that requires precision and patience. Its handler's most important skill is the patience to wait for the perfect shot.

The assassin, a wiry Mexican with a black mustache who must be sweating underneath all the black, is the first to run. Even with the rifle, which he doesn't pack, he is faster than Lola.

The stairwell stinks of mildew and cleaning supplies. Lola's Pumas clang on the metal, so loud she can't hear the assassin's footsteps in front of her. By the time she gets to the first floor, her eyes are burning so hard with fury that she can't remember if there was a single bystander in the stairwell.

When she gets to the bottom, even before she opens the door onto the street, she knows the man is already gone.

"Shit," Lola heaves as she bursts through the ground-level door. The L.A. sunshine smothers her face, and her eyeballs hurt so much from the bright that she has to bend over, her hands on her knees, to keep from falling to the pavement.

The arms that encircle her are a man's, but the way they touch her is not the way one of her soldiers would touch her. They move around her waist, landing on her tummy with a tenderness that could turn to animal in a split second.

"Manuel," she says.

"Yes," he replies.

"We have to get out," she says, and she isn't sure what she means. Out of Huntington Park? She has never lived outside the city's boundaries. She has bought her milk at the same bodega. Get out of Los Angeles? And go where?

"Where is your car?" she asks Manuel.

"At the market," he replies.

Because you followed me there, Lola thinks. *Because you wanted to make sure I was okay.*

"I didn't ask you to do that," Lola says.

"Still, I am here," Manuel replies. He doesn't shrug off the fact that he has followed his boss without permission. He looks her in the eye, his shoulders squared.

Across the street, Lola sees a black SUV with tinted windows waiting at the red light. Even though they are not in a war zone, but a city where even a cartel SUV might bother to obey traffic laws, there will be shots if they stay here. Still, she can memorize the plate number. She is good at remembering . . . and good at holding grudges.

"Let's go," Lola says, giving a quick jerk of her chin in the direction of the market, even though she knows Manuel knows the way.

He matches her, stride for stride, and having him beside her as her Pumas pound pavement, left, right, left, right, the strike of her foot rolling from heel to toe, heel to toe, she begins to relax into the pace that, for her, is a sprint, but for him an unknown exertion. When she risks her own precious energy to give Manuel a sideways glance, she sees his mouth open, but his face isn't red, and his breath is even.

Why should she care if he is only making her think her pace is challenging for him? Is it because in running, this most basic of human instincts, women can never be equal?

As they turn the corner into the market, the aroma of spices hits Lola hard as she swallows air, trying to catch her breath. Cumin, chili, turmeric, all invade her sinuses, and, while she relishes them in her food, she does not want to breathe them. She fights the urge to lean over a trash can and vomit.

"Stay here," Manuel says. "I'll bring your car around. I won't be more than a minute."

He takes off, moving at the same relaxed sprint he did with Lola, the difference being she could no longer match his pace now that she has stopped once.

TWENTY-TWO

LOCK

Late that afternoon, after Lola has picked Lucy up from Blooming Gardens, Manuel calls the other soldiers and asks them to please come over. There's been an emergency. Lola listens to his tone as he passes on her order, which, in his mouth, comes out as a request. His English is choppy, lilting, soft. She doesn't know how her original soldiers—Jorge and Marcos—will take Manuel's order, which they must know is coming from her. She is unsure if the divide between the American and Mexican factions of her operation is growing or collapsing. Ramon, the older Mexican, doesn't count. He is old. He couldn't give two shits about the battles of youth—money, sex, power. He wants to do a good job, whether it's cleaning a floor or cleaning up a body. Manuel is different. He doesn't speak Jorge and Marcos's first language, and, whether or not Lola's two original soldiers know it in their conscious minds, there must be some tell that he is fucking the boss.

Lola doesn't hear the end of Manuel's conversation, though, because she finds Lucy on the living-room floor with Isa, the neighborhood girl with long, shiny black hair who lives a handful of blocks away in a first-floor apartment with bars on the windows.

"No," Lucy says, "put your doll there. They should hug."

The two girls are sitting in front of the dollhouse Lola took away from her first visit with Ms. Laura, the Blooming Gardens director. Lola doesn't like to say "stole," because Ms. Laura never named it, and Lola does not consider herself a thief.

"Oh" is all Isa says in response. Then the little girl does as Lucy has commanded, jamming her male doll up against Lucy's blond, blue-eyed fake sexy Barbie. It does not escape Lola's notice that, in this scenario, Lucy has chosen the white, weird-as-fuck-proportioned female doll for herself. The heroine. Isa is relegated to the blockhead man, jamming himself up against the lovely lady in vain.

Lola feels her stomach drop. It is the first time Lucy has shown signs of becoming like Charlie. Lola has never noticed this trait at Blooming Gardens, where Lucy and Charlie run off their excess energy in the schoolyard before being called into class. But Huntington Park is not Blooming Gardens. In Huntington Park, Lola is in charge. On the West Side, Lola is visible only as the "other," a quiet, brown woman who most other Blooming Gardens parents must assume is only able to bring her daughter to their school because of a diversity quota and financial aid. These assumptions are wrong on both counts, but Lola has never corrected them, because she can't correct what the white Blooming Gardens parents have never had the balls to voice. It is frustrating, not being able to slap them down.

"Now, kiss," Lucy commands, and again Isa obeys.

Then Isa looks to Lucy, waiting for the next order.

"Isa," Lola says, "what do you want the dolls to do?"

Lucy looks up, caught, not because Lola's tone is angry—it is even. If you speak softly and evenly enough, Lola has found, people will lean forward not only to hear you but to see if they can detect danger in your voice.

"I don't know," Isa says.

Lola sits on the sofa, and Lucy wriggles up next to her.

"See, Mama?" Lucy says. "She doesn't know."

Lucy lays her head on Lola's shoulder, and Lola wonders if she is being played. Is her little girl frightened Lola will punish her for forcing Charlie's make-believe alpha-female bullshit on Isa, the ghetto girl who can't afford Lucy's posh private school? Or does Lucy not see how what she is doing, while innocent in the scheme of beatings and drugs and molestation that made up her childhood before Lola took over, is at the edge of wrong?

"Give her your doll," Lola says.

"What?" Lucy looks up at her mother, her eyes wide in the way of children who believe they are being wronged.

"She can be the heroine for a little. Let her have a turn."

"No," Lucy says, pulling White Privilege Barbie to her chest.

"Lucy." Lola's voice takes on a mother's warning tone, one she didn't know she had, because she has never thought Lucy would have to be scolded about the need to share a Barbie doll.

"I don't want to," Lucy screams, and before Lola can stop her, the little girl has wriggled out from under her mother's arm and disappeared into her bedroom.

Lola's hand goes to her mouth. She is a typical woman in shock, until she realizes Isa is watching her. When Isa notices Lola is looking back at her, she looks away, flinching, as if Lola might raise a hand to her.

"Isa," Lola says, "it's okay."

But Lola doesn't know if it is. Manuel enters, methodically checking all the locks on the windows and doors, and Lola remembers then that she needs to get her daughter and her baby brother to safety. Now that the Rivera cartel knows to go after Andrea, Lola has no more leverage, at least not until she knows who Andrea really is.

Lola knows how to protect Lucy's life. She does not know what to say to Lucy to make her understand that what she's done to Isa, while not criminal, is still wrong. And it's okay to be wrong, to fuck up, to make mistakes, and to ask forgiveness. *But,* Lucy might point out, *it wasn't okay for my real mom. The one you coerced into slitting her wrists. You didn't forgive her. Wasn't that wrong, too, Mama?*

No, Lola thinks, *because junkies never think far enough beyond the fix to remember they need to ask forgiveness.*

Lola leaves Isa in the living room with all the dolls. The door to Lucy's bedroom is locked. It is an agreement Lola and Lucy have—at almost eight years old, Lucy is allowed to lock her door. Lucy is allowed privacy whenever she wants it. Even here, out of her dead junkie mother's house, a locked door is the only way Lucy can sleep at night.

"Lucy," Lola says. She hopes her voice is gentle but firm.

"Go away," Lucy says.

"Okay," Lola says.

"No!" Lucy speaks in a scream now, and Lola knows the scream comes not from anger, but fear.

"Then let me in," Lola responds.

Lola hears the stomp of stubborn little-girl feet on cheap carpet—Lucy jumping off her bed and padding the five steps to the door. One day, Lola will ask Maria if her seven-year-old self ever thought throwing a tantrum was an option. If it was, Maria probably doesn't remember.

A second later, the lock clicks, and Lucy opens her bedroom door. It can't have been more than a minute since she was in the living room with Isa, smashing blond Barbie against boring Ken. Yet the child's eyes glisten, red and watery as a bloody stream.

"Oh, Lucy," Lola says, and Lucy pours into her mother's arms and tries to cling to Lola's skin with all she's got—arms, nails, feet—until she is standing entwined with Lola.

"Do you love her more?" Lucy says, and Lola can tell from the little girl's heavy breathing that Lola's body is crushing her. She tries to move back, to give Lucy space, but Lucy steps forward.

"Who?"

"Isa," Lucy says in a whisper.

"What?"

"You gave her my doll."

"I don't love anyone more than I love you."

Lola feels Lucy's body relax, and her breath begins to come in even counts.

"Why would you think that?" Lola tries, holding her own breath at a question she never would have thought life-or-death.

"Because you took her side. You asked her what she wanted to do."

Lola must choose her next words with care.

"Isa doesn't have some of the . . . advantages you do."

"What's an advantage?"

"Your school, for one. It's a really good school."

"Isa goes to school. She doesn't have to drive far to get there."

"She doesn't drive at all. She walks. Because her parents are working too hard to drive her."

Lola can't see Lucy's face to tell if any of what she's saying makes sense or matters, because Lucy is pressed against her tummy, trying to burrow there.

"Isa doesn't have money," Lucy says, Lola's flesh muffling her little-girl voice. "But we do."

"We do."

"Money is good," Lucy says.

Lola wants to say something about how that's wrong, sort of, that money is good, but it's not everything. Even money won't cure some things, like a mother who lets boyfriends molest her child. But she can't tell Lucy that her own mother would have still fucked her up, rich or poor. Junkies always find a way to fuck up and fuck over the people they should love the most.

On cue, Maria Vasquez sails in, carrying a basket of baked goods through a front door Manuel must have locked. For a second, it is magic, Maria appearing on Lola's threshold in tight jeans and a flowing floral top. She's had a pedicure, and her toes are a light, bright pink that would be more suitable for summer.

Isa, who Lola had forgotten was in the living room, hops to her feet with a yelp, like a kicked puppy, and Lola thinks, *You've got the right idea, kid. Fucking run.* But once on her feet, Isa freezes.

Lola says only, "Where did you get that basket?"

"It was on your doorstep. So I brought it in."

Manuel appears from the kitchen, and Lola looks to him, because she's got Lucy on her skin and can't move the ten steps from the little girl's bedroom to the front door without pushing Lucy to the floor and scaring the shit out of both children present.

"Mom," Lola says, her tone too cheerful to be addressing her mother. Lucy looks up at Lola, knowing something's off, and Maria's face is screwed up in confusion. "Turn around. Put the basket back outside. And come right back in."

"No," Manuel says. "I'll take it."

Lola is glad for the interception, even if he is disobeying a direct order.

"Girls," Lola says. "Stay here."

Lola manages to step out of Lucy's arms. It is a full-body experience, extricating herself from the child's iron grip of claws and long limbs and thick skull.

"Stay inside with them," Lola says, low, to Maria, who nods.

"Maybe they'd like a muffin." Maria gestures to the basket.

"Mom." A warning this time, and, to Lola's surprise, Maria understands.

"I'll get them a snack from the kitchen."

"Wait," Manuel says when Lola gets to the door. He steps outside first, gives three hand signals, then nods to her. "Okay."

Lola steps from dark apartment to sunlight so bright she has to let her eyes adjust. She looks to the roofs of the two longer sides of the U that make up her court. Somewhere up there, even though she can't see them, she knows Jorge and Marcos are armed and waiting to take a shot at any stranger who approaches the building.

With Manuel beside her, Lola bends down to pluck a small rectangle of card taped to the basket's cellophane wrapping. The cellophane squicks and squeaks at Lola's touch, and she jumps back with the card in her trembling fingers.

She opens the white envelope and reads, "Thank you for your business. Best, High Life Dispensary."

Lola doesn't know if the dispensary where Eldridge and Mandy Waterston sell edibles and guard her supply makes a regular practice of sending gift baskets. She can't remember if she's ever received a package on her doorstep that isn't a threat, a deadline, a dictation of terms for an exchange of life for money. But there is no threat here that she can see. Just an address in Texas. Maple Lane in some shit town Lola has never heard of.

It was Mandy Waterston who told Lola not to kill Andrea, but to destroy her instead.

It is Mandy Waterston who is giving her Andrea's beginnings.

TWENTY-THREE

FIRSTS

Lola is two blocks from Eldridge and Mandy Waterston's house when she starts to feel heat coming over her in waves, ebbing and flowing. If she watches closely, she thinks she will be able to see the sweat spring from her pores, but she can't focus. She has to open the window and stick her head out, taking in the salty air that whips past her as the Uber driver speeds south on Venice streets.

He is taking Lola to LAX, where she will board her first flight. It is Friday morning, and she has just left Lucy at the Waterston household, having called her daughter in sick to Blooming Gardens. Mandy had laminated a schedule for Lucy's time at their home—wake, breakfast, dress, free play, park, lunch, rest, art, chores, dinner, bath, bed. Lola had approved the schedule, but asked that, if Mandy were taking Lucy outside the house, that she let Sergeant Bubba, Andrea's LAPD insider, know, so that he could send a black-and-white around to keep an eye out for any Rivera cartel soldiers.

"I'll guard her with my life," Mandy had said, her arms crossed over Lucy's chest, the little girl pulled into her body as if she belonged there.

Of course Lucy must remember that Mandy shielded her the night Los Liones cartel almost murdered all of them.

Mandy will guard Lucy with her life; Lola just doesn't know if Mandy's life will be enough.

She can't focus now, her eyes not landing on a café here, a spiritual bookstore there, another goddamn candle store, Italian food, a bungalow, a glass mansion, Whole Foods.

Lola could not allow Hector to stay at her place, yet she couldn't place the burden of housing a convicted murderer on Eldridge and Mandy. Instead, she had dialed Sergeant Bubba herself and requested that he put Hector to work at his house, a two-bedroom would-be teardown in El Segundo he spends all his spare time renovating. Lola had warned the sergeant that officials from Locust Ridge would be launching a manhunt any day for their escaped inmate, but Bubba had laughed and told Lola not to worry—he'd heard some riots broke out there earlier this week because some cartel leader got shivved.

"Power vacuums," Bubba had explained, "are a bitch."

There is no Mrs. Bubba Lola knows of, and if there ever were, she's guessing the woman fled when her husband turned addict narc, one of the countless souls willing to abandon everyone behind for a little white powder. Then a little more. And a little more.

She ducks back into the Uber, a Prius. The Middle Eastern driver is cranking rap, old-school hardcore stuff, with lots of talk of fucking and sucking. It is not the lyrics but the beat that bothers her, causing the space behind her eyeballs to ache. She catches a glimpse of herself in the rearview. She's as pale as a brown woman can be. Why is her forehead sweating? She is cold. Is this a fever?

It could be, except for her heart. It is speeding up, keeping time with the breaks of sweat, the ebb and flow of something like fear.

This is panic.

The flight. The leaving. The war. The crowds.

Lola goes the wrong way at the curb, and by the time she finds the correct escalator for her gate, she is afraid she'll miss her flight. She has arrived two hours early, but she imagines that is not enough time, that someone like her, a banger, will be selected for "random" extra screening.

The TSA agent, a hefty black woman who's shooting the shit with another hefty black woman, stops her conversation to bark at Lola that she needs to have her ID and boarding pass out. There is a problem with her carry-on too. She did not know to remove liquids. Her toothpaste is taken, as is her soap, because she has not stayed in enough hotels to know if shampoo and other toiletries come standard.

She knew enough to check the bag with the knife.

She is barked at again by a gate agent, this one male, too skinny, with a reindeer tie even though it is way too early in the holiday season for that shit. She tries to picture Manuel wearing a tie like it.

She realizes she has never seen any of her soldiers in a tie.

"Miss, you'll need to board with your group."

But, Lola thinks, *I was here first.*

And she had been. Two hours early to the gate. There had been enough time to purchase food and eat it, even at the sit-down restaurant in the terminal, something called Lemonade, with a clear glass case showcasing colorful salads and sandwiches.

Lola had remained in her seat at the gate, afraid of missing an important announcement.

She is seated in the last row of the plane, near the bathrooms, and the older woman next to her is reading a paperback western with cowboys on the cover. Lola writes her off as a Texas racist. She pulls her seat belt so tight it presses into her stomach.

The older woman asks, "Are you all right, dear?"

Lola feels for a second that she is not, that she's about to burst into tears, but this is not something she does.

"I'm all right, thank you," Lola mumbles, and the old woman goes back to her book.

Takeoff is difficult. Lola doesn't know how it works. She grips the armrests, and the old lady next to her puts down her book to look out the window. Does that mean something? Why would she put her book down unless she needed to focus her entire attention on surviving takeoff?

Something in the cabin beeps three times, and then the male flight attendant's voice booms over the intercom. "Ladies and gentlemen."

There is a long pause. No one seems concerned, though. The man across from Lola powers up his laptop and starts to work on a quarterly sales report. She wants to tell him to put that fucking thing away, that no one has said it is okay to turn on electronic devices.

"It is now okay to turn on your electronic devices."

Lola releases her breath in a sharp exhale. She feels a tap on her shoulder. It is the older woman, her seatmate, holding out another book to her, this one with a cowboy and a Native American.

"Would you like something to read?"

Lola stares at the cover and doesn't know if she should be offended. Cowboys. Indians.

Distraction.

Lola starts to read. By the time the plane lands, she is on page 138, and the cowboy, a loner whose wife was kidnapped by the Native American's tribe, has just snuck into the village to rescue her. The only problem is she's fallen in love with the chief, the Native American on the cover.

Lola is shaking her head in disapproval as the plane's wheels touch the ground. There is a whooshing of air, and Lola thinks this is it, this plane can't stop. There's a hiccup, as if the pilot is pulling back on a horse's bridle, and then the plane goes from out of to under control in a recognizable instant.

Everyone switches on their cell phones, but nobody removes their seat belts until the plane halts at the gate. There's a ding, the seat-belt light goes off, and then it's a mad dash to stand, grab bags without banging fellow passengers over the head, and . . . wait.

By the time Lola gets behind the wheel of her rental car, a sea-blue Toyota Corolla, she has waited two hours: in the restroom line, at baggage claim, in the rental-car line.

She is driving away from the airport when she wonders if Andrea has ever flown out of it, and, if so, under what name.

She drives for hours, always with one eye on the rearview to see if she's being followed. The roads get smaller, going from eight lanes to four, down to two.

As the sun sinks in the sky, she is the only car on a two-lane highway leading into a town called Jasper. She pulls onto Jasper's Main

Street at six p.m., when many of the businesses downtown are turning their signs from Open to Closed.

Lola parks her car and steps out. There is a café called Marshall's.
Lola can smell the fry grease from here. There is a bookstore, a law
practice, an accountant, a shoe repair, a consignment shop, all lined
up and uniform, with what she assumes are apartments above them.

She finds the lone hotel next to a pizza place. A woman shuffles to
the front, and Lola sees the same goddamn cowboy novel she couldn't
put down on the woman's table. A television blares the six o'clock
news. It smells of cooking meat.

"Hi, there," the woman says. She doesn't ask Lola how her day is
going. She doesn't ask what brings her to town. She keeps her head
down, takes Lola's credit card, and only asks how long Lola plans to
stay.

"Just tonight," Lola says.

The woman tells her there's free breakfast tomorrow, in case she
wants to fuel up before she goes back south.

"Back south?"

"Yes," the woman says, puzzled at Lola's surprise.

But of course Lola knows from her research that the US–Mexico
border is only fifteen miles from here.

*Isn't that where you're going? Back south? To Mexico? Where you came
from. The place that must be your home.*

No. I'm going to 1451 Maple Lane, Jasper, Texas.

*Oh. It's just . . . we get so many . . . though not usually in this hotel.
This establishment has the finest free breakfast in Jasper.*

But Lola says nothing, and the woman can't defend her racist assumption unless Lola calls her out first. Instead, Lola takes the key the
woman gives her and finds her room on the second floor, up a staircase
and hallway carpeted in gray-blue. The whole place is quiet, and Lola
would whisper if there were anyone to talk to.

At the end of the hallway, two white men in jeans and sport coats
speak in low voices. They stop talking when they see Lola.

They tip their hats to her—cowboy hats. Lola thinks again of the
older woman on the plane reading the cowboy novel, and the racist

woman at the desk reading another cowboy novel. She hasn't read enough yet to know if it's the cowboy's or the Indian's novel, but she can venture a guess. Still, she is relieved it is a series. She would like to keep reading.

She finds her room is cozy and clean, with the same blue-gray carpet from the hallway. There is a television with all the channels Lola could want and won't need. There's a Bible in the dresser drawer, and a floral-patterned armchair and ottoman with a blue blanket thrown over the back. Over it, there's a reading lamp with powerful light. The overhead light is soft, nonthreatening.

Lola splashes her face with water in the bathroom. She changes into khaki pants and a floral cardigan. She places the red ballet flats she wore the first time she visited New Horizons Rehabilitation Facility, undercover as the sister of one of the white meth-head princesses housed overlooking the Pacific. This is the outfit she wears when she needs to fit in with "normal" society. It is the outfit she wears when she wants people to buy that she might be one of them. It is the outfit she wears that makes middle-class white people afraid to question her belonging.

Rich white people aren't fooled, and rich people don't care if they insult her. Middle-class people are too close to both gaining and losing on life's seesaw. They've gotten comfortable, and they don't ever want to go back to being uncomfortable.

Lola is rich. Her earnings place her in the country's top 1 percent, but she is not middle class. She is outside of class. Her place is without a place. Her place is also Los Angeles, the city that keeps her secrets.

Her place is not Jasper, Texas.

She navigates the rental car to Maple Lane. It isn't far, less than ten minutes from the boutique hotel, but the driveway is one of ten other driveways on either side of the road that lead back under trees, their respective houses blocked from view. It is full dark now, and Lola thinks of parking her car on the street and walking up to the house, because the car isn't nice enough to fit with her disguise. Still, it is a rental, and she can say the car company ran out of Range Rovers.

She takes her bag, vintage Vuitton, purchased with clean cash as opposed to snatched from the back of a truck. This bag she keeps sealed and tucked away at the top of her closet, because she never carries a bag. If she's out with her soldiers, they carry her wallet. She's like the queen of England that way, she figures.

She had thought about waiting until morning to come here, to see Andrea's beginnings, but she has figured, if the people inside are Andrea's parents, that this is the time they are most likely to be home—night, washing up after an early dinner.

When the house emerges from the dark under the trees, Lola is not disappointed. It is large brick, two stories, and it would go for several million dollars on the West Side of L.A., not that there would be a lot wide enough to hold it. L.A. houses sprawl back, Texas houses sprawl out.

The dining room at 1451 Maple Lane is lit up from inside, and a white man in his sixties carries a single plate from the table into another room at the back of the house, presumably the kitchen. A few seconds later, a tall, older woman appears, gathering the rest of the dishes into her thin arms, and disappears through the same doorway.

They are an older couple who has just finished dinner. So far, Lola is right about her presumptions.

She clears her throat before she rings the bell, preparing her most educated voice, the one she uses in parent-teacher conferences at Blooming Gardens, the one she uses to say that her career is going so well, but she fears Lucy is suffering because of it. No one in these conferences asks about Lola's career, what it is she does, they just absolve her of her guilt. Easy to do, if you don't know the extent of the sin.

The house smells like pine needles and slow-cooked pork. The man opens the door, and at the same time, a motion detector light pops on, showing him Lola, but he squints, his vision blurred by the sudden light.

"Hello," he says, but it comes out a question.

"Hi. I'm so sorry to disturb you. I think I'm . . . Mr. Atherton?"

"Yes? I'm Mr. Atherton."

Lola has practiced this part, of course, and she knows the couple who lives here is called Atherton. If she had looked further, she would have been able to determine their income, their former life's work, but she likes to be surprised. Right now, she knows they are James and Judy Atherton, and they have two children—a daughter named Anne Catherine, and a son named Christian.

Anne Catherine is in her late thirties.

"I'm Teresa Condell," Lola says. "I went to school with Anne Catherine."

"Oh, oh, yes, of course," James Atherton says, then, in the vein of every television sitcom dad Lola has ever seen who has no fucking clue what's going on, James turns and calls for his wife. "Judy! Woman here to see us, by name of Teresa . . . what was it?"

"Condell." A white name. Let them think she married into the race.

"Teresa Condell?" Judy Atherton comes into the front hallway wiping her hands on a dish towel peppered with sunflowers. "I'm sorry, dear, my memory must be slipping—"

"College. Sorry. College friend. UCLA."

"Oh," Judy says.

"I had to come here for work. I'm an attorney."

"Immigration?" James is interested again.

"Yes." No.

"Come in, dear. I was just about to serve the cobbler. You do like cobbler, right?"

Lola has never eaten cobbler, but she knows from cooking shows that it is fruit with butter, sugar and flour crumbled on top. There are worse ways to spend a night when you're at war with a cartel.

"Love it. But do you happen to have any ice cream?" Two years ago, Lola would never have asked, but if she's going to have cobbler for the first time, she wants to do it right.

Two minutes later, Lola is seated at the dining-room table with James and Judy. The first bite of cobbler stings, like her first bite of sushi, in a way that makes her eyes roll back.

Judy is thrilled, so much so that she tells Lola she'll be right back. There's something Lola should see. Her departure leaves Lola alone with James, who is thin but doesn't stop eating to make small talk.

He finishes his cobbler in four neat bites, all with equal parts cobbler and vanilla ice cream. Then he turns his attention to his black coffee, and to Lola.

"Anne Catherine's doing really well now, you know."

"I'm so glad to hear it. She's always been such a loyal friend." *Fuck you, Andrea.*

"She's got two children, older boy, younger girl." *Get well, Christopher. And why didn't you tell me you had a daughter, Andrea?*

"And wouldn't it be nice if we could all marry a doctor?" Lola laughs, her proven assumptions making her bold. This is it. She is speaking to her partner's father. She just ate cobbler Andrea's mother baked.

What made Andrea run from these people? Why did she have to hide under a different name in a different city?

"It'd be nice for you ladies, that's for sure. My Judy, she's one of the lucky ones."

"Oh, I forgot, Anne Catherine said her own father was a doctor."

"Gastroenterologist. Forty years next May."

"Fascinating."

Judy returns holding a shiny photo collage wreathed in red and green. It reads "Merry Christmas from the Flynns."

"That's Anne Catherine now. With her husband and their two little ones . . . well, not so little anymore."

Judy places the photo card in front of Lola, who gets her first glance of Anne Catherine.

The woman is blond. She is short. She has gained weight, presumably from two pregnancies and the stress of being a doctor's wife, because after growing up here, in a brick mansion, it must seem like stress to be a doctor's wife.

Anne Catherine is not Andrea. So what the fuck is Lola doing here?

She checks her cell phone and makes her apologies. "I'm so sorry . . . work. May I?"

Judy and James gesture toward the kitchen, and she starts through the doorframe. There is no one on the phone. She wants access to more of the house. She needs to turn it upside down to get the key. Why did Mandy send her here? What is she doing halfway across the nation when her daughter is back in L.A., her brother hiding out in an LAPD officer's home while the Rivera cartel looks for their lost hostage?

She sees the pencil marks on the doorframe before she reads the two names, girl above boy. A growth chart, used by families Lola has seen on television to mark the passage of time.

The names there are not those of James and Judy's children.

TWENTY-FOUR

THE EDGE OF AMERICA

Louisa Mae does not like the way the sand that borders the Pacific feels on her toes. It is midmorning, and even though the wind whipping around her is cold, the sand feels like it shouldn't be so hot.

Juan is at the snack shack, a distant speck from here, where she stands, alone. He told her he was hungry, that a burger and fries sounded good, but she has been traveling with him for three days now, and he doesn't eat the kind of food she presumes they serve at the snack shack.

Her clothes aren't right for the beach. She is in jeans and a sweater. She has had to take off her socks and sneakers to dip her feet in the water. She is the only person on the beach now, in the middle of a weekday morning in November.

She knows Juan wanted to give her privacy. She has tried to figure out why he saved her when the Rivera cartel, her late father's employer, paid him to kill her and her entire family.

"Did you have a daughter?" Louisa Mae had ventured over egg whites, fruit, and toast at a roadside diner in what she thinks was New Mexico, but might have been Arizona. The diners blur, as do the mile markers that clicked off, counting Louisa Mae's journey west, to the edge of America.

"I don't have any children."

"But you have killed them?"

He had not answered the question, but he hadn't looked away either.

"Why didn't you kill me, if I didn't remind you of your daughter or your sister or some other girl you knew?"

"Because I saw myself."

Juan had signaled the waitress for the check, and Louisa Mae had wondered what he meant. She is a twelve-year-old girl. He is a twentysomething cartel hit man. He has not tried anything with her. He has made sure they have separate rooms in the roadside motels where he pays cash. It was only in New Mexico it had even occurred to Louisa Mae that his taking advantage of her was a possibility.

Still, he had kept his hands off her, and now she looks back to the beach café where she sees him sitting at a concrete table under a closed umbrella. He has his hands and ankles crossed. He is looking everywhere but at her, standing at the place where the water meets the land, holding her brother's ashes in a vase with no lid. She has held him on her lap the whole way to California, and she has kept one hand on the vase, the other over its open top. She has told Juan to slow down when she felt the ride get too bumpy, and he obliged.

Now, she is here, and it is time to say goodbye to him.

There is an emptiness here, at the edge of America, the sense of shock she felt at the death of her family, at her killing of her own father, that aches more in the sunshine. Here, there is nothing and everything.

She does not want to be alone, but she knows, as soon as her brother's ashes are scattered, that is her fate for the near future. She will not go into the system. Juan has gotten her new identification, a new passport and birth certificate, and he has put a month's rent and a security deposit, in cash, down on an apartment in an area of the San Fernando Valley that has a good school district.

"Why?" she had asked him.

"Because you are like I used to be. At a time when I could have gone either way."

"You mean not joined the cartel?"

Again, just as she was getting somewhere, he had not answered.

She has been beside him this whole journey, and on some level, she knows he is not the cartel hit man with a heart of gold, like Gary

Oldman in *The Professional*. He came to her house earlier this week because he intended to put a bullet through her head and her baby brother's.

Now, at the edge of the earth, one foot on land, one in the water, she realizes Juan is the closest thing she has to family.

"Hey!" she calls, raising one arm to wave him over. He doesn't hear her at first, and then, he is slow to rise to his feet. He has a manila envelope tucked under his arm, and Louisa Mae knows that inside is her new life.

"You should do this alone," he says.

"How do you know? Have you scattered a loved one's ashes?"

"I didn't love my family."

"I loved my brother."

"What was his name?"

"You must know it. We were all on your hit list."

"I know it. But you will need to say it, to say goodbye." Juan says this as if it is something he doesn't know from firsthand experience, only through stories or rituals passed down through other people's loving families.

"Who will be left?" she asks.

"No one."

Juan has made it clear that the Rivera cartel will be on his trail, that he can't stay with her because to do so, after he has risked everything to save her, will once again jeopardize her life.

"Your father stole their money. They will punish him, even in death. They will take your life," Juan had told her at another diner, over chef's salads that were more iceberg lettuce than anything else.

"They think I'm dead."

"But they know I am alive. And that I did not come back from killing you."

Now they stand with the vase at the ocean.

"Tell him goodbye," Juan says.

"Goodbye," she echoes.

"His name."

It is the name that catches in her throat, that makes her insides ache. She failed him. She is the reason he is dead, because she couldn't protect him.

She deserves to be here, alone. There is no one who can save her now.

"Why didn't you kill me?" She tries again.

"Because I saw myself in you," he says again, but this time, he continues, "I saw you kill another person, shoot him in the back, when he couldn't defend himself."

"Something you would do?"

"Something I have done. But it doesn't make me special."

"What does?"

"The same thing I recognized in you. Not that you are capable of killing. But that you enjoy it."

Louisa Mae doesn't feel anything at this statement. She doesn't know how she felt when she pulled the trigger and dropped her father. She knows only that the act didn't make her sad. Maybe growing from child to adult will complicate these feelings, but for now, she is numb.

"You will be okay," Juan says. "When I leave."

"I want the new me," she says. It sounds grown-up, self-aware, as if she's read a book on motivation or seen a charismatic speaker.

"You will have her. As soon as you say your brother's name."

"Goodbye, Christopher," she whispers. She heaves the vase as far out into the water as she can without letting go, wondering why she doesn't want to risk breaking it now, when the ashes that used to be her baby brother are scattering across saltwater.

She turns to Juan.

"Who am I now?"

He hands her the envelope, and she opens it. She reads the birth certificate.

"Andrea," she says.

TWENTY-FIVE

BLUR

Back at the hotel, Lola locks the door and sits on the still-made bed. There is a rectangular silver tray with two chocolates and an orange. A folded card reads "Welcome, Ms. Vasquez."

The names notched in the Athertons' doorframe were Christopher and Louisa Mae.

"A shame, what happened to those children," Judy Atherton had said.

James had snorted, and Judy had shot him a dirty look that let her husband know she would talk about them if she damn well pleased.

"Those children . . . it was their father who was the monster, laundering money for the cartel."

"The cartel?" Lola had widened Teresa's eyes.

"The one that operates around these parts," James had said, waving off Lola's rival as if they didn't matter, because he is white and a doctor and doesn't have to worry about doing shitty things to protect his family.

"Rivera," Judy Atherton had said. "Anyway, the father, he started stealing from them, and they retaliated. Killed the whole family. The boy was beaten to death, the mother stabbed with a steak knife, the girl . . . they never found her body."

I did, Lola had thought.

"Just so much of her blood. Here, in this room."

"Got to pay cash for the house because of it," James had said, approval of his own actions apparent in his voice.

Alone in the hotel now, Lola needs noise. She turns on the television and cranks up the volume on a game show. She should leave, she knows that, because this is Rivera cartel country, but there are no flights out until morning. She could start driving, but that would take days, so she stays here, sitting up straight, the ceiling fan cutting a swath through the air. The edge of her red ballet flat is too close to the chocolate and the orange. It bothers her. She knows the soles of her shoes must be dirty, and yet she can't seem to will herself to move even the few inches it would take to kick her shoes onto the floor.

She should eat. She knows that, too, but the distance from her body to the telephone is too great.

She is tired.

She wakes later, though she's not sure how much later, to a different game show, and someone banging on her door.

One ballet flat has fallen to the floor. It is still dark outside.

She slips on the other shoe and runs for the bathroom. She locks the door behind her.

There is a window in here, right over the nice washstand with clean blue towels, folded into neat rectangles. It smells of cinnamon and lavender, two scents that Lola doesn't think go together.

She tries to unlock the window, but the latch doesn't give.

Whoever was at her hotel room door has stopped knocking. There is silence, and Lola thinks maybe she can go back out to the bedroom, pack her few things, and get the hell out of here. She'll leave the chocolate.

Then she hears a closer knock, this one on the bathroom door.

"What do you want?" she says to the door. She has locked it, though she knows that doesn't matter—it is a flimsy door even she could kick in.

"You," the male voice on the other side says.

It is one word, and Lola can't tell for sure if she knows the man doing the talking. Is there an accent? Is English his native language? With one word, one small piece of evidence, is it possible to tell?

"I don't have any money," Lola says.

"I'm not here for money . . . Lola," the man says, and Lola wonders at the pause between the statement and her name. Was he debating whether or not to use it, as if this is a hostage negotiation?

There is a glass vase full of sunflowers next to the towels on the washstand. Lola pulls out the flowers, shaking water onto the floor, and grabs the vase.

The man on the other side warns her that if she doesn't open the door, he will kick it in. She believes him, and, five seconds later, he keeps his promise.

She is ready with the vase—broken glass has brought her luck in the past, but this man is on her too fast for her to see his face.

"I didn't come here to hurt you," he says.

His firm hands toss Lola onto the unmade queen bed. The same hands wait for Lola to settle, to stop kicking—a damsel in distress tactic she knows is a waste of energy. For a second, she doesn't see the male shape beyond her. Instead, she clocks the whirring blades of the ceiling fan, the blare of the television—louder now that the flimsy door to the bathroom is open—and the quilt, rumpled from holding her resting body.

When she does take him in, she sees a white man in his early forties who looks ten years older. She sees a leather jacket and distressed denim. She sees his hands in his pockets, because he has no need to train a weapon on her. She sees a shrug in his look, an apology for tracking her down here, maybe, but she can't know for sure until she asks.

"Sergeant Bubba," Lola says to one of LAPD's finest.

A former narcotics officer, Sgt. Bubba McMillan went too deep undercover and got addicted to coke. After several stints in rehab, the LAPD has stashed him in Vice, where he rescues drug-addled hookers and throws them in Andrea's husband's fancy Malibu clinic to detox. He steals drugs from evidence rooms, too, big stashes that never seem to make it into the logs, but he doesn't snort or smoke or inject the various powders . . . anymore. Instead, he turns them over to Andrea, who keeps them far away from her husband's rehab facilities and the addicts within. Andrea traffics to the lost causes, the ones who will never kick the habit, and while Lola's partner might not think of herself as a Good Samaritan, Lola knows for fucking sure Bubba thinks he's doing good, giving back to the community and helping addicts— hot, white female addicts mainly, as far as Lola can tell—kick their habits, stop using, stop turning tricks, stop fucking up.

"Hey," Bubba says, and this time his shoulders shrug with his face. He keeps his hands in his pockets. "We should talk."

"What? Why?" She thinks of Hector, staying with Bubba.

"You're needed back in L.A."

"Is it my brother?"

"It's Andrea. She's disappeared."

"Disappeared?" The word sends a tingling chill shivering from Lola's tailbone to her brain, the cells there freezing like she's just bitten into a hardened chunk of ice cream with both her front teeth.

"Do you know who took her?" Lola asks.

"I didn't say she was taken. I said she disappeared."

Lola swings her legs from the foot of the bed to the side to face Bubba, her right arm level with her right shoulder as she holds the blade she managed to dig out of the nightstand toward his face. When Bubba gulps, she knows he knows she wouldn't mind scarring his face to remind him who's in charge. It wouldn't serve her cause—Bubba hasn't fucked her over, yet, and he might know something about where Andrea's gone or been taken.

"Don't get fucking smart with me," Lola says, not recognizing her own voice, which sounds sure, privileged, a voice that expects Bubba to listen to her. Is this privilege a result of holding the blade, or is it two years of Blooming Gardens and Culver City and watching white people in their element?

"Sorry," Bubba says, and Lola feels a leap of excitement ripple through her as Bubba, the cop, raises his hands in surrender to her. "I'm worried about her. I don't know if someone took her. I don't know if she skipped town."

"Have you talked to her husband?"

Bubba nods.

"What did he say?"

"That she would never willingly leave their kids."

The words are a hammer to Lola's chest, cleaving it open, spilling her guts onto the comforter's medicinal pink flowers.

"She . . . has more than one?"

Bubba's hands lower, and Lola can tell he is surprised at her own surprise.

"You didn't know?"

Lola shakes her head, even though she knows she doesn't need to. Bubba is a cop, trained to read people, and right now, she's a goddamn open book.

"How old?" Lola asks. Before she met Christopher, she had thought of Andrea as a career woman, someone who would have kids later in life, maybe with the help of science and test tubes and enough money to make a life happen.

"Twelve and fifteen," Bubba says. "Girl and a boy. Boy's not doing too well."

Lola knows.

She does the math and comes up with a number—twenty-two. Andrea was twenty-two when she gave birth to Christopher, the son she named after her dead brother.

"Christopher and Rayna," Bubba gets in as Lola is opening her mouth to tell him she doesn't need to know their names, because she already knows she will do whatever she needs to do to get their mother back.

Lola thinks back to her own experience as a fifteen-year-old, un-able to discuss, over giggles and twirls of hair at school lockers, the possibility of losing her virginity, of letting a boy touch her here or there, when she had already been touched and prodded all over, not for money, but for her mother's fix. Instead, fifteen-year-old Lola wished every morning that her mother would disappear on a heroin binge, giving Lola and Hector a few days or months of peace. Even though she had never experienced any other existence, she knew in her bones it was wrong to wake up wishing your mother dead—not that she was wrong to wish Maria dead, but that her mother should behave in a way that made her daughter want her to be alive.

Lola is willing to bet Andrea's kids do not want their mother dead, at least not in the way Lola had—salivating with pleasure at the thought of Maria, completely still, skin turning from brown to white, lying in an alley with a needle in her arm. Equally satisfying was the thought of police not being able to identify their junkie mother or find Lola and Hector to share the news, giving them a time of peace before foster care. But Maria's death, somehow a given as her addiction lingered, as countless innocent and guilty lives have come and gone, has never come to pass.

"I'll fucking deal with it," Lola says.

Bubba doesn't say anything. Maybe he wants to be the hero here, the person who discovers Andrea, bound and gagged and powerless.

"Who else knows?" Lola asks.

"No one yet. Jack can hold off the press, he thinks, tell them she's laying low after the assassination attempt, but that'll only last a day or so."

Twenty-four hours. Another fucking deadline. Lola has to get her boss back, give Andrea's children their mother, and stop the fucking war Andrea started.

TWENTY-SIX

MOTHER

The house on Bronson Canyon stands two stories tall. Gray stone peeks out from under the ground-to-roof ivy, and the roof is black-shingled with a pitched arch. The grass is green, of course, and trimmed, with a light spattering of rust-colored leaves on top that could have been allowed to stay purely to give the indication to passersby that this house knows it is fall. In the driveway, Lola sees Andrea's candy-apple red Audi sedan parked next to a black Mercedes SUV.

Jack must drive the family car, Lola thinks, toting kids from home to school to practice.

She stays in her own red car—which would appear dull next to Andrea's—for another minute, telling herself it is to scope out the neighborhood, although she's got her men here to do that too. Jorge, Hector, Marcos, and Manuel are parked in two separate cars, borrowed from Jorge's uncle's chop shop, on two separate ends of the street. They will spot any cartel SUVs or warm bodies, but so will every other wealthy white person on this quiet block that's just starting to wind up into the mountains under the Hollywood sign. And even if they didn't, Lola has kept watch on the block long enough to notice the LAPD black-and-white making a pass every ten minutes. She's guessing Andrea refused a full-on security detail, but the LAPD is determined to protect their potential future DA regardless.

It takes Jack Whitely a minute to open the door, and when he does,

Lola smells something baking—an apple pie, maybe, although she doesn't use her own oven enough to know for sure.

"Hello," Jack says. His tone is friendly, if not upbeat. He is a tall man in his late thirties, with piercing blue eyes and a kind smile. He is handsome, without a doubt, and, while Andrea is a good match for him physically, Lola wonders if Jack has ever fucked around on her. She has found it is often not enough for men to be equal physically to their partners—they are trained early on to believe they deserve more.

"Hi," Lola says. "Can I come in?"

"Oh, yes, of course. I'm sorry," Jack stands aside, and a big furry sheepdog crashes into Lola, its tongue lapping at her calf, bare below her three-quarter-length cargo pants.

"It's not a big deal," Lola says. She takes a moment to pet the dog, stealing glances around Andrea's front hall. There is a portrait of a younger Andrea, her nose wrinkled in laughter, holding a baby on her lap, a girl toddler glued to her mother with eyes and limbs.

"Are your children home?" Lola asks Jack.

"Rayna's upstairs. Christopher is . . . away."

Lola does not mention she knows that part, because part of her was hoping she didn't, that he would tell her Andrea had lied about that, too, that the boy she saw in that hospital bed wasn't really her flesh and blood.

"Can I get you something to drink? We have coffee . . . regular or decaf . . . some tea . . ."

"I'll have water," Lola says, and Jack nods, turning toward the back of the house and what Lola thinks must be the kitchen.

When he realizes he has forgotten to invite her back, he stops. "I'm sorry. Please, come with me."

Lola has never met a doctor socially, if this occasion can be deemed a social one. Doctor visits were not a regular part of her own childhood growing up. Her mother sent her to a free clinic when she turned thirteen. Maria had instructed her daughter to tell them she had started to bleed—she hadn't—and that there was a new boy in her life. The new boy was a man, and for once in her life, Maria was planning for her daughter's future, to that time several months ahead when Lola's body would prove itself capable of carrying another life. The doctor at the clinic, a Latina with a bob haircut and a short, stumpy frame, had asked Lola the bare minimum of questions—height, weight, date of last menstrual period, had she ever been pregnant—before performing a quick pelvic exam and scratching out a prescription which she handed to Lola before she shook her hand. The whole thing had taken three and a half minutes. Lola had wanted to ask the doctor, a brown woman, a single question—How did you get here? To her, college, medical school, the scratching of a pen across a prescription pad, seemed leaps above her world, where she considered any day she got three meals in her brother's stomach a victory.

Now she considers the fact that she can pay for Lucy's medical and dental visits with cash, out of pocket, a victory.

Andrea's kitchen is all granite countertops and new tile—a modern gray that calls to Lola's mind the saying "clean slate." The appliances are all steel and shiny. Lola sees her own face in the refrigerator door's reflection—it is a sharp, brown heart, framed by charcoal sticks of hair. Her boundaries are blurry here—a house where she doesn't belong but has been welcomed anyway.

Jack was expecting her. Sergeant Bubba had told Andrea's husband the limits of what he, a vice cop, could do, especially given the theory that Andrea's disappearance was not voluntary. Lola doesn't know how much Jack knows about his wife's illegal activity, but she's figuring, given Andrea's tendency to launder money through Jack's rehab clinic, that he must know at the very least that he needs to turn a blind eye to the things he shouldn't know.

Now, Jack gestures to one of the black, half-egg-shaped barstools at the edge of the counter. Lola imagines Christopher picking at breakfast here, complaining that he's not hungry as eggs grow cold and bacon fat congeals. Lola stares at Andrea's cabinets, painted black, wondering what kind of plates are inside. She is sure Andrea's dishes match, but she finds herself hoping for at least one missing or broken piece, something no one but Andrea would notice but would ruin the whole set for her regardless. Lola thinks of her own dishes—a mismatched hodgepodge of sunflowers and blue Chinese teapots and large polka dots, all of them chipped and washed, rinsed, and reused.

"When did you last see your wife?" Lola asks after Jack has placed a mug of coffee in front of her. He has forgotten she asked for water, but Lola doesn't feel right correcting him, not here, on his turf, with his brow furrowed with worry for his wife.

"Yesterday," Jack says, but he's looking beyond Lola, and when she turns, she sees him looking at a portrait centered behind her on the wall.

The girl in it is Andrea, Lola is sure of it, without ever seeing what Andrea looked like as a child. Lola recognizes the pert nose, the pale skin, the soft brown hair falling in curls around a sweet smile. The boy beside her shares many of the same physical qualities, including the smile, which seems to light her pale features from inside. Andrea's arms are wrapped around the boy, whose face is flushed with pink, maybe embarrassed at his sister's love for him, or at least embarrassed that the photographer can see it so plainly, even through the filter of a lens.

"Is that Andrea's brother?" Lola asks, but only because Jack has caught her staring. She already knows the answer to the question.

"Yes," Jack says.

"Does he live around here?" Lola asks, then feels her heart start to thump faster in her chest, because again she knows the answer.

"He's dead," Jack says. "Passed away," he corrects himself, as if Lola needs the censorship. She does appreciate that he considers her worthy of the whitewashing. "A car accident."

"When?"

"Not long after that picture was taken. I never met him."

Lola hears a twang of regret as Jack's voice cracks, a boy's uncertainty betraying his man's body.

"They lived in Texas," Lola states.

"Yes."

"And her father?"

"I don't know . . . she wouldn't talk about him."

There, Lola thinks, there is the answer to Andrea, to her need to prosecute perpetrators of domestic violence, to be on top of everyone—men and women, to protect children from violent fathers, to not give a shit about a black man caught with a dime bag of weed. Andrea must have spent every moment since attempting to erase the male power and dominance she didn't want anywhere near her DNA.

"When did you see her?"

"Yesterday," Jack repeats, and it's the first flash of stress she's seen from him. Why are you making me repeat myself, he must be thinking. "The day after the press conference . . . where I saw you. You were there."

Lola feels Jack's blue eyes on her, maybe seeing her for the first time—slight, no more than ninety-eight pounds, thighs even a man his size could snap like brittle twigs, hair long, black, hanging to her waist, and tiny muscles stretched under the skin of her upper arms. Here, in Andrea's house, Lola is unarmed. She does not have her blade, but that didn't stop her from doing a quick sweep of Andrea's kitchen, finding the knife block on the countertop, although she doesn't think a knife will do the job when it comes to getting Andrea's doctor husband to trust her.

"Who are you? Security? A private investigator?" Jack asks.

"Is that what Sergeant McMillan told you?"

"He just said you would help me find her."

"I will."

"He told me your name. Lola." Jack waits, and Lola knows he expects her to offer her last name, maybe an address, or at least the name of her neighborhood. Instead, she stands, still and silent. "It just seems, if we're going to be honest, I should at least know your last name."

"It's better if you don't," Lola says.

"I'm a doctor. I can say you're a patient, if anyone asks."

"The people who'll come asking for me don't give a shit about that doctor/patient privilege stuff."

Jack takes this in, his handsome brow knitting and un-knitting over his blue eyes, and Lola realizes how clueless this man must be, whether by choice or not, to his wife's business endeavors.

"What does your wife do for a living?" Lola asks. Her voice sounds foreign, even though she's speaking the same language as this doctor, unaccented English.

"She's a prosecutor. For the District Attorney's Office." Another pause. "Do you want to write this down?"

"No," Lola says. "What else?"

"What else what?"

"What other businesses does she have?"

"No other businesses."

Lola takes a long sip of coffee. It's delicious, still warm and dark. She pictures the black liquid rushing through her veins, setting her blood tingling. When she looks back at Jack, he is looking at her, questions he doesn't want to ask poised on his tongue.

"Are you saying she was into something else? Something that could have gotten her hurt?"

Lola has a choice. She can come clean to Andrea's husband, tell him she and his wife run the city's largest drug-trafficking empire, peddling powder to upper, lower, and the disappearing middle class. She can tell him about the Rivera cartel, about the remaining founding father whose partner Andrea ordered shivved in a maximum-security prison. She can tell him Andrea is her partner, and that even though Lola is the one who sold his son his first heroin, Lola's still the best bet he's got for tracking Andrea down before these cartel dickheads tear the mother of his children limb from limb and crumple her into a barrel of lye so he will never be able to identify her and her children will never know if their mother is dead or alive.

"That's what I'm asking you," Lola says instead.

"No," Jack says, shaking his head so vehemently Lola knows this man must have chosen not to know the bad things about his wife. She wonders if Andrea broached the subject, even came clean, and Jack looked at her with his angel-blue eyes and told her she was being too hard on herself and working too much.

It is strange, what we choose not to know about the people we love. Lola's mind recalls Lucy, dictating to Isa, the poor ghetto girl, how she learned to play at her West Side white friend's house, and how quick the transition from victim to would-be bully was for her. Lola wonders what else Lucy is doing to the poor girl when Lola doesn't see, or chooses not to.

"Dad!" The voice from upstairs is female, half yell, half whine, in the tone of white teenagers Lola has seen on television. She herself never mastered the art of whining—she had no one to listen, and if you have no one to listen, whining loses its appeal.

"Yes, Rayna?"

"Who's down there with you?"

Jack looks again to Lola, who shrugs and takes another sip of coffee. She doesn't know what to call herself, in relation to Andrea. They have never discussed titles or made their working relationship official. Still, Lola knows she will not sleep until she finds Andrea and returns her to her family.

"A friend of your mother's," Jack says, shooting a questioning glance to Lola—*Is that okay?* Lola nods in response to the question Jack didn't ask out loud.

Two seconds later, Lola hears socked feet thumping on the hardwood of the stairs, and Rayna appears. She is tall, with long, skinny limbs she hasn't learned to control. One day, Lola sees, Rayna will have her mother's grace, the ability to produce beauty by reaching for the coffee creamer and the security of speaking in soft tones because you know you deserve everyone's undivided attention. Rayna has brown hair tinted with auburn, the same pert nose turned up at the tip. It is a physical trait Lola knows Andrea must fight—a literal turned-up nose—when she's speaking to victims.

"Hey," Rayna says, a white-socked foot kicking out in front of her as she walks toward Lola. Andrea's daughter tosses her brown hair over her shoulder and heads to a frosted glass door, framed in white. The pantry. When she opens it, Lola sees labeled tins of coffee, flour, and sugar. There's a row of cereals, some sugary, some claiming "whole-grain goodness." There is a shelf of canned beans and tomatoes, a large sack of brown rice, and a clear glass jar of corkscrew pasta, tinted brown to indicate wholesomeness. Rayna's eyes scan the items before landing on a snack pack of Frito's, which she digs out, rips open, and begins to crunch.

Lola shoots a look to Jack, who understands her unspoken question—*Does Rayna know her mother is missing?* Jack shakes his head, and Lola nods approval. It is best to shield children from darkness.

"Have you heard from your mother?" Jack asks, casual. "I need to ask her what she wants to do for dinner."

"I'm not her keeper."

Fucking teenagers, Lola thinks. She can't remember if she was ever a bratty shit to her own mother, because if you're a bratty shit to a junkie who can't process that you're trying for attention, were you ever a bratty shit?

"I know you're not," Jack tries, in an even tone Lola knows he must use on his addict patients, people who can barely tolerate being soothed, whether they're high or low or sweating and writhing through detox. A soothing voice is not what calms a junkie, and it is not effective on a teenage girl either. "But I need to talk to her. Did she call you? A text, maybe?"

"Yeah," Rayna says, digging a smart phone from the back pocket of her slim fit denim. "This morning."

"What time?" Lola speaks to Andrea's daughter for the first time, and Rayna's eyes lift from her phone screen to meet this strange brown woman's. Lola sees a challenge there—*Why do you care?*

"Rayna," Jack says, a warning tone creeping into his doctor voice, making it what she imagines is a father's.

"Ten thirty-eight," Rayna says.

"What did she say?" Jack again.

"That she was going to be busy at work for the next few days, but that she was thinking about me and wanted to send me lots of love," Rayna paraphrases with a roll of her eyes in her voice, and Lola wants to tell this teenage girl not to take her mother's love for granted. She pictures cartel henchmen standing over Andrea, each taking a limb, each pulling her apart. Lola wants to paint this picture for Rayna, to see if she can make Andrea's daughter leak tears for her mother, but then she stops herself—if the Rivera cartel found Andrea, took her, tortured her, killed her, Rayna will have plenty of time for an attitude adjustment.

"I'm guessing she'll show her face here again in a few days," Rayna says.

"Why's that?" Lola asks.

Rayna looks to Jack, who nods to his daughter. "Because it's what she always does before a trial."

"Which trial?" Lola asks. She feels certain there is no trial, but she wants to know how much Rayna has heard about the assassination attempt against her mother. She understands Andrea's determination to keep the police away from her home, her haven, her clueless, eye-rolling teenage daughter.

"I don't know. Probably some wife beater turned killer." Rayna delivers this line with a pointed look at Lola. The girl wants to see if she can shock her. *Good fucking luck,* Lola thinks.

"She took clothes for about a week," Rayna continues.

"What clothes?" Jack says, and Lola hears in his question the hope he's been able to hold back until now. Her own heart leaps in her chest—Can it be true and not just foolish optimism that Andrea has skipped town of her own accord?

"Casual stuff, mainly," Rayna says. "Which I guess is weird, if it's the trial thing. And she left her running shoes in her closet. Which would also be weird, because she always runs before court to clear her head."

"That's something," Jack says. "All right . . . all right."

Of course, Lola knows that, right now, nothing is all right. Rayna seems to sense it, too, shifting her weight from one long, thin limb to the other, setting aside her half-eaten bag of Frito's. When the girl looks up, she has the good sense to have tears in her eyes.

"Is Mom okay?" Rayna asks.

Lola assumes Jack hasn't told Rayna about the assassination attempt on her mother, but even if he hasn't, the girl has a smartphone.

Even though it's Saturday, Lola assumes Rayna has friends from school who must have provided the headlines Jack might be trying to keep from her. Then again, Rayna and her friends are most likely upper-class white teenage girls, and Lola doesn't imagine they give much thought to the news. Still, Rayna knew enough to realize that her own theory about Andrea disappearing for a trial didn't add up, and she cared enough about her mother's disappearance to check her closet for missing clothes. Someone needs to give this girl some credit.

"Someone took a shot at your mother," Lola says. "Because of her . . . high-profile position. And now she's done the smart thing. She's left town."

"Hey," Jack protests.

"Dad, don't," Rayna interrupts. "I know . . . about the shot."

"Who told you?" Jack demands, raising his voice for the first time. Lola recognizes the impotence there, the inability to yell at his wife or his child, transferring to the determination to go after whoever told Rayna the truth.

"It's not important," Lola says, because Rayna looks frightened, not because she thinks her father might hit her, but because she doesn't recognize this version of him.

"Should we tell him? Christopher?" Rayna asks. The addict son, abandoned in his father's rehab clinic, suffering unspeakable horrors, as all addicts must if they want to leave their demons behind.

"Yes," Lola says.

"No," Jack says, shooting Lola a seething look. His fists are clenched. His eyes red-rimmed. He would hit her if his daughter weren't here, Lola thinks, but that can't be. Andrea wouldn't tolerate that shit.

"If you don't, you risk him hearing it from someone else. He's in recovery. He's not dead," Lola says. She thinks of all the times Maria was in recovery and Lola had thought she and Hector would be better off if their mother were dead, if all hope of a recovered mother were lost, so they could move forward.

Lola knows she is right about Christopher, though. And just when

Jack is nodding agreement with her, they hear a series of shattering explosions from the front room, a room where Lola was not invited but now is running toward as she yells for Jack and Rayna to get down and stay in the kitchen.

When she gets to the living room, an untouched wonder of white furniture and teak wood, she finds the bay window glass shattered into a million little pieces on a rug even she knows must have cost thousands of dollars.

TWENTY-SEVEN

FLIGHT

The street outside Andrea's house is so quiet, Lola can hear a bird chirp. The wind lifts a tree branch above her head, and when she hears a twig snap, she reaches for the blade that's not in the pocket of her cargo pants. Jack appears behind her, and the sight of this white-collar white man outside the bullet-shattered glass of his bay window doesn't fit.

"Get inside," Lola shouts, when she knows her voice should be calm. "To the bathroom. Take your daughter, lock the door, and get in the tub. Then call the cops."

Lola hears shouting from down the street, and when she follows the source of the noise, she finds a woman stopped in the middle of Bronson Canyon, pointing after someone or something that has already disappeared. A large white poodle, taller than Lucy, dotted with fluffy white curls, stands beside the woman, its leash dropped on concrete.

"That way!" the woman screams when she sees Lola. She is older, maybe sixty, with silver-white blond hair stretched into a ponytail, and Lola guesses from her clean cream skin that she's had more than a few Botox treatments.

"What's that way?"

"The shooters!" the woman cries.

A car turns onto Bronson from Franklin. The driver of the black Volvo tricked out with rims and tinted windows accelerates, and Lola pushes the woman out of the road. She grabs the poodle's leash and runs for the sidewalk, diving atop the white woman, covering her body with her own. The woman smells of lemon and sugar.

"Are they going to kill us?" the woman asks.

"Not you," Lola says, and she realizes she should climb off this woman, leave her alone with her poodle and her plastic surgery so she can live. The Rivera cartel wants Lola's head, and they won't mind taking an innocent one to make sure Lola dies.

"Hey!" It's a man's voice she hears as she stands, half-turned toward the street, knowing her back shouldn't be to that car. But when she looks up, it's Manuel, Jorge, and Marcos, all together. Jorge and Marcos have stuck Manuel in the backseat, but they have included him.

"Let's get you out of here, boss," Jorge says.

The white woman raises her head from clipped grass and screams at the sight of three brown men in a tricked-out, tinted Volvo.

"It's them," she tells Lola, as if Lola isn't brown, too, and about to get in the car.

"What?"

"The shooters," the woman says.

"The fuck's she talking about?" Jorge again.

Manuel tries in English. "Lola, we have just arrived to get you."

"What he said," Marcos says, jutting a thumb toward the backseat.

Lola looks to the woman, who's not too scared now to be standing, wiping the grass stains from her white cropped pants, and moving toward the car.

"Isn't it you?" the woman asks, squinting her eyes, which are blue, like Jack's, like every person in this white-people neighborhood.

"Think you're confused," Lola says.

The woman shakes her head. "No. I'm not like that."

"Sure you're not," Lola says. "Get the fuck on home."

The woman's shoulders straighten, and she looks Lola in the eye. "Thank you. For getting me and Donald out of the way."

A white woman with a poodle named Donald. Fucking world, Lola thinks.

"What car were they driving? The men you saw?"

"It was a black SUV. Very clean. And the driver tossed his ciga-rette into the street. I saw his sleeve. He was wearing a suit."

It's good intel, and Lola should let the woman go back to her multimillion-dollar house and her dinner prep and her dog walking, but the words hang in the air before she realizes she's spat them there.

"Any of these motherfuckers wearing a suit?" Under normal cir-cumstances, she would not refer to her men as "motherfuckers," but when she sneaks a glance at them, even Marcos is grinning.

"No," the woman says. Then, "I was wrong. I'm sorry."

"It's cool," Jorge calls from the car. "Boss . . ."

We've got to go, Lola knows Jorge wants to say but won't.

"We go now, Lola." Manuel says what Jorge couldn't. Both Jorge and Marcos turn to look at him, the handsome Mexican cartel defector.

"Shit, you're gonna get it now," Jorge says, and Marcos's laugh is deep and guttural. The white woman has had the good sense to take off at power-walk pace. Lola hopes the woman will bar her door and phone the police, in case Jack proves incapable of following directions.

Lola is hesitating because there is another car, one with Hector, her baby brother, behind the wheel, at the other end of the street. But when she peers up the hill toward the Hollywood sign, she doesn't see the Nissan Altima.

"Where's my brother?" she asks.

The three men look to each other, confused.

"Up the hill."

"Don't see him."

They follow Lola's gaze, and Lola watches it register on all their faces—Hector's car is not there.

The first bullet grazes her ear, coming from nowhere, and Lola thinks of the twig snapping, no more than ninety seconds ago. The sound conjured visions of a man's boot crunching a tiny slice of wood on grass. She had looked around, she had looked down, but she had not looked above her, to the giant oak tree that towers over the street outside Andrea's house.

Manuel is out of the car, dragging her back even though she's al-ready running toward Andrea's house.

"The tree," she says in English, then again in Spanish.

Manuel pulls his weapon, tossing Lola into the car like she's a half-full duffel bag, but Lola claws at the tan cloth of the interior, screaming no, not to shoot, not yet.

She scrambles back out of the car, her Pumas kicking at Manuel as if he's coming for her and not the shooter who just tried to explode her head.

"Stop! I said stop!" Lola never screams her orders. This is not how to lead. But her brain stem takes over, her nails clawing at Manuel's face as he tries to aim. He is so surprised he all but drops the gun into her hands. He is surprised again when she raises it back, pointing it square in his face, between his lovely eyes, the rugged, ruddy skin drawn into a pinch there.

"Lola, it is okay," Manuel says. He raises his hands in surrender, and Lola sees the tension go from his shoulders, the adrenaline drain from his body, a body she knows well despite her best efforts not to. She knows the identical red welts on his lower back, symmetrical as if planned by a ruler and a doctor's Sharpie for surgery, but instead from his father's belt. She knows the gash puffed over with pink-and-white tissue on his forearm from the knife his father used to come after him the night Manuel finally retaliated. She knows his wrists are red from handcuffs, not from the Mexican police, but from his kidnapping by a band of guerrilla civilians trying to fight Los Liones cartel. They had caught him, and they hadn't known what to do with him, so they handcuffed him in the middle of their town and watched him. Manuel had told her, as she pretended not to listen, of the women and children and their mouths, some gaping, some—those who had lost loved ones to the violent Los Liones—set in a firm line.

"I never killed a child," Manuel had told Lola.

"Get in the car," Lola says to him now, and Manuel does, ducking down low to fit into the Volvo's backseat. Lola can see the muscles bristle across his back, under his white T-shirt, and she catches a whiff of clean, deadly bleach as he passes beneath her.

The second shot zings past Lola's head and hits a tree behind her, burning through the thick trunk of the bark and sizzling, just for a second, before sticking there. If she were police, she would want that bullet collected, bagged, and logged, to prove the identity of the person shooting at her now, to put them behind bars. If she were police, she would have to worry about chain of custody and technicalities and unpredictable juries. But she is not police. She is Lola.

She crosses the street at a walk. She hears sirens now, coming from a faraway place that Lola imagines is safe. But for her, Bronson Canyon has become a war zone. She makes it to the base of Andrea's oak tree before the next shot sings into the street behind her, sinking into the asphalt with a dull thunk.

Where is Hector?

She looks up, through leaves the season has turned red and gold and brown, and sees the barrel of a gun instead of her would-be assassin's face. It is not a sniper rifle, maybe because the shooter knew he wouldn't need one to pick her off, walking out of Andrea's house, crossing the white woman's cut grass sprinkled with just the right amount of fall foliage. This scene in Andrea's yard, with Lola staring up the oak tree and the shooter staring down the barrel of his weapon, will not be an assassination, executed from afar. This will be a murder.

In an instant, he is on her. She doesn't see him, just boots rushing down the tree toward her face, wanting to stomp her. Then he is on top of her. The first blow lands on her right cheek. The world goes liquid, the tree above her swirling into a fall tornado, the sky above darkening. The second blow lands on the left side of her skull, rattling bones and brain and teeth. Something inside her chips, and she pictures a piece of gray matter falling away into her bloodstream, like a tree branch swallowed and dissolved into rapids.

Then she sees the gun, dropped on the ground so that her attacker can use his fists. He is a blur of brown skin and black hair above her. Blood runs into her eyes, and pain blurs all her other senses. Still, her fingers reach for his gun, and she feels warm metal on her skin like a gentle kiss, dissolving the tension, soothing the pain.

It takes less than a second to raise the gun and pull the trigger. When she does, she sees red spewing from her attacker's brown skin. She sees the blur above her fall off the side of her body.

She claws at her eyes, trying to wipe the blood from them, but only succeeding in smearing the red liquid and further blocking her vision.

The wail of sirens swallows her now. The cops are close. She thinks of her men, three brown bangers parked in a tricked-out Volvo across the street. She hopes they left her here and got themselves to safety. She hopes Manuel will remember to make Lucy eat her broccoli before she polishes off her mac and cheese. Then she remembers she pulled a gun on Manuel, pointed it between his eyes, and she wonders if he will forgive her.

Where is Hector?

Now, much closer than the voice, she hears footsteps crunching leaves, unafraid to warn her of their approach.

She feels a man's hands pulling her warm body to standing. "The cops."

"We can make it." It is Manuel, speaking in Spanish, even though Lola hears the muffled voices of Jorge and Marcos next to them, dealing with the brown man she shot.

She sees him still on the ground. He is the man who tried to assassinate Andrea on the steps of the Hall of Justice.

"You take his feet. I'll grab his arms. Hurry."

The words run together in a single stream, and Lola feels she is underwater, weightless, as Manuel starts to lead her to the Volvo.

He has to let go of her to wrangle the assassin's body into the back of the car.

It is then the Altima reappears, from somewhere, and Hector is at her side.

"Where did you go?"

"I was there," he says.

The three men have gotten the assassin's body into the Volvo's backseat. There is no room for Lola.

Still, Manuel says, "Get in."

"We need to keep her separate from the body," Hector says, and the three men agree.

She is in the passenger's seat of the Altima within five seconds.

Then, Hector is driving up into the Hills, away from the man she killed, away from the cops who are turning onto Bronson, the red bubbles spinning atop the black-and-whites.

"This is the first time," Hector says, a minute later, as they wind up the narrow road, the big trees bending to touch over them.

"Huh?"

"The first time we've been alone since you got me back," Hector says, and Lola realizes he is right. As a leader, she feels alone almost all the time, yet never is.

When Hector kills the engine, they are parked at the foot of a hiking trail. He has the windows rolled down, and Lola can hear the babbling of a brook somewhere nearby.

"The fuck is this place?" Lola asks.

"A hiking trail. I found it."

"When?"

"Just now," Hector says.

He gets out and opens her door for her.

"We should clean your wounds."

He is right. The Rivera cartel shooter got her good. She feels the salt metal of blood coming from her lip. When she tries to swipe it with her tongue, she feels more drying beneath her nose.

Have I ever been allowed to go to a hospital?

As a little girl, Lola had to stay away from emergency rooms because her mother feared Child Protective Services. Now, as a drug trafficker, she has to stay away because she fears the cops identifying her as a person of interest in a shooting.

Will I be the kind of person who isn't scared to go to an ER if I move us to the West Side?

Hector washes her face himself. He uses water from the brook, which is closer than Lola would have thought. Hector's hands are larger than she remembers, but maybe that's because she hasn't paid attention to the size of his hands since he was a boy.

"I'm glad you're back," Lola says.

"Back from where? Prison? Or Mexico?"

So the Rivera cartel did take him to Mexico.

"What did they do to you?" She doesn't want to know but has to ask. His hand is on the back of her neck, steadying her as he cleans a vicious gash above her left eye.

Hector gives a bark of laughter at the question. It startles her, and he doesn't apologize.

"The fuck you think they did?"

"I'm so sorry." Lola's head hangs without Hector's hand to support her, and then her brother's arms are around her, pulling her close. He smells of sick and sweat, as if he hasn't showered in days, but that can't be.

"When you were a little boy, and you were scared," Lola says, "you used to sweat. Like you're doing now."

"Tell me more."

"You were scared of umbrellas. So much so when you were a toddler I'd just put one across a doorway if I wanted you to not go in a room."

"Never rains here."

"No," Lola says. "It doesn't." *But still, we had an umbrella. Why? When Maria was out scoring heroin and selling all our other shit, why did we always have an umbrella?*

Hector's hug gets tighter. Then he is pushing her down. She knows it will be cold even before he puts her head under the water.

"Why?" she manages, but of course she knows. She cut off his trigger finger. She made sure he did time for a murder she committed. She ordered him to carry out a hit that got him whisked to Mexico for torture by a rival cartel.

She has grown him from boy to man, and now that man has come for her.

She thinks of fighting him, she thinks of Lucy, and she tries. She forces her feet to kick, but she is so tiny under him, and she can't breathe. The water is so cold. His hands are on her neck, holding her down, and she tries to use her own hands to paw at him, but she is so slow.

The last thing she hears before she surrenders is another man, shouting in what she thinks is Spanish. The sound lulls her to sleep.

TWENTY-EIGHT

MOURN

Lola wakes to whispers and the tin tang smell of canned vegetables simmering on a cheap stove. She hears a mix of male and female voices—*How long . . . what happened . . . who was there . . . what man . . . a man in a tree. . . . What's a grown-ass man doing in a tree?*

Veronica, her mother's longtime best friend, appears above her, the older woman's narrow face looming large, her brown eyes as wide as moons. Lola feels the unexpected urge to wrap her arms around the woman, who was the only adult to rock her to sleep in childhood, to teach her to brush her teeth up and down instead of side to side, and to show her how to fill her plate with half vegetables, one-quarter meat, and one-quarter starch. It was Veronica who instructed Lola in the fine art of French braiding her own hair, pulling each strand so tight Lola would yelp, and Veronica would apologize, following up with, "You have to suffer to be beautiful."

A second later, Maria appears beside Veronica, and Lola sees how similar the two look—wholesome neighborhood gossip and sad-ass recovering junkie—now that age has started to steamroll any gains or losses life experience might have provided one or the other.

"Is she okay?" It is Maria.

"Yes, yes," Veronica says, and it comes out a tsk. "Your daughter is strong. You give her some credit. Go check the soup."

Maria nods and wanders away. Veronica lays a cold hand on Lola's cheek, bending down to kiss her.

"Don't you make me a liar," Veronica whispers in Lola's ear, so close Lola can see the dry cracks in her red lipstick. Her mother's friend hasn't thought to touch up her makeup, a strange occurrence. Now Lola realizes Veronica must be worried about her, words of wisdom to Maria be damned.

"What . . . happened?" Lola asks. She tries to scoot over so Veronica can sit next to her on the brown cushion she only now recognizes as belonging to her own couch.

"Some crazy banger took a shot at you," Veronica says. "I've told you time and again, only bad things happen outside this neighborhood."

Lola's mind tries to recover all the memories of bad happening in this neighborhood—children shot, children hungry, young Lola afraid to fall asleep in her own bed—but they flood her brain to bursting, and all she can say is "I need water."

"Yes, yes," Veronica says, another tsk, a toss of her hand, but she doesn't move to get it. A second later, a man's hand appears in the narrow frame of Lola's vision, handing Veronica a soap-spotted glass Lola also recognizes as part of her own mismatched set.

"What else does she need?" It is Manuel. Lola would know his hand, specked with sun spots and a thick patch of black hair, even if it weren't for the rolling lilt of Spanish bass that makes up his voice.

"Nothing, nothing," Veronica says, giving another toss of her hand, and Lola feels her heart drop when Manuel's hand disappears. He is gone.

Come back, Lola thinks. *Come back.*

"*Mija,*" Veronica says. "I know. About your brother."

Lola sits up too fast, and Veronica holds back the water glass to keep Lola's jerky movement from spilling it. Her eyes throb, and she can't feel her head. Her living room goes wavy around her, until all she can see is bodies—male and female, some in dresses, others in jeans—standing a safe distance from the couch where Lola has been resting. Is it the same day that her baby brother tried to drown her in a peaceful brook way up in the Hollywood Hills?

"What?" Lola asks. "Where is Lucy?" Lola has not seen the girl since she picked her up at Mandy Waterston's on the way home from LAX and dropped her off here.

"The girls are at Isa's. Her mother is there with them. Now, tell me what happened."

"What happened with who?"

"Hector. I know you got him out of prison to attend your *abuelita*'s funeral. May she rest," Veronica murmurs and crosses herself. "It is sacrilege, *mija,* what you have done."

Lola tries to stand, but her knees give out and she falls back onto the sofa, which smells like dog. Valentine must need a bath. Usually, Lola bathes the pit every Sunday night after Lucy goes to bed. Valentine stands tall and quiet in the tub, waiting as Lola dips a plastic cup into the warm water and pours it over her chocolate-brown back. When Lola has soaped the dog up and rinsed her clean, Valentine waits for permission to step from tub to towel, then continues to stand still as Lola wipes each paw dry.

This cartel war is affecting her dog's cleanliness. It is destroying her family's traditions and rituals. It has stolen her brother. It is time to end it.

Maria reappears with a too-full bowl of steaming-hot soup. "Here. I cooked for you," Maria says, in the voice of a woman expecting to be thanked for what a mother should do with no thought of expecting kind words in return.

"Is it Campbell's?" Lola asks, finding her voice louder and more certain than before.

"Yes," Maria says.

"I don't want it," Lola says. "Don't keep that canned shit in my house."

For once, Veronica does not jump to her junkie mother friend's defense, instead staying beside Lola, who tries to stand again. With Veronica's help, Lola is able to leave the couch, and the people in the room begin to come into focus—Jorge, Marcos, Manuel, Ramon, Señora Ocampo from downstairs. They all sit on folding chairs that have been set up at the other end of the room, as if they are attending Lola's wake. But there is no food.

"There's no food," Lola says.

"They're worried about you. They're not hungry," Veronica says.

"We need food."

"I will get it," Manuel says.

No, Lola thinks. *You are a guest. You don't get to do my grocery shopping.* But once again, her voice is gone. All she can do is plod toward the kitchen, feeling Veronica's thin hand on her elbow, somehow holding her up.

Lola searches cabinets and finds crackers and tortilla chips. There is fruit in the refrigerator—strawberries and blueberries—and cheese that doesn't come in individually wrapped rectangles of plastic.

"Lola, honey." It is Veronica again. Lola has placed all the ingredients on a platter, somehow assembling an acceptable cheese plate, but the soup . . . she can smell the soup, its processed sodium scent permeating the carpet and cushions, stinking of bad childhood dinners thrown together without a parent, of too-hard homework pondered over a card table that served as a kitchen table until Maria pawned that too.

Lola heaves the hot pot over to the sink and watches the red liquid fill the sink, weak as watered-down blood. She flips on the garbage disposal and lets it grind the fake vegetables to a pulp she can't see.

Now she can walk without Veronica.

"Where are you going?"

"I have to serve them something."

"Mija." Veronica's hand is back at Lola's elbow, this time to stop her. "You should know. The police are here."

"What? Where?"

"They're waiting out front."

"Why didn't they come in?"

"They don't have a warrant."

"How long have they been out there?"

"Half an hour. Maybe more."

Lola takes the cheese plate with her as she goes.

"Let me come with you," Veronica says.

"There's more cheese and fruit in the refrigerator. Take care of everyone in here."

Veronica nods, knowing enough to know she doesn't know how the fuck to talk to cops in a way that will help her drug-trafficking surrogate daughter.

Outside, the sky is gray, the wind lifting the palm leaves in the trees that line the street beyond Lola's courtyard. One cop has his back to her, but the tan trench coat gives his status as detective. The other cop wears a gray trench coat and holds a cup of Starbucks coffee with a smiley face Sharpied next to his name—Kyle.

"Hi," Lola says, peeking around the screen door in the tentative way they should expect from a Latina with no criminal record. "I have food?" It comes out as a question because she will ask them permission for everything. It is the only way she will make it through this conversation without cuffs.

"Are you Lola Vasquez?"

"I am. I . . ." Lola trails off.

"Yes?"

"I'm sorry, I know you ask the questions, but I just . . . is something wrong? My aunt is very worried."

"Your aunt?"

"Veronica. The woman who asked you to wait out here. I'm not feeling . . . well."

Shit. She has forgotten to check a mirror. For all she knows, her eyes are bloodshot, her face bruised. What does a person who was almost drowned look like?

And why is she still alive?

She has to check to make sure she is wearing pants, and she sees someone has changed her from the cargo pants she wore to Andrea's and into a pair of black yoga pants she didn't know she owned.

"Do you know the current whereabouts of your brother, Hector Vasquez?"

"I don't . . . is he missing?" Lola tries, but she can tell even through her bloody eyes and swimming head that the detectives don't believe her. They exchange grim glances right in front of her, as if she is not smart enough to make it worth their while to hide their strategy.

The detective in the tan trench coat sighs. He is tall and thin, with a chestnut mustache that curls up at the sides. Lola wants to offer him a pair of scissors, just to snip off the ends. She should write a letter to the LAPD, petitioning them to forbid facial hair in any form.

"You signed him out of prison for your grandmother's funeral last week. He was never returned."

I was supposed to return him Tuesday. It's Saturday. If you wanted him that bad, you should have asked for him sooner, Lola thinks. Then she remembers Sgt. Bubba's intel—that there had been riots at Locust Ridge, the result of a power vacuum. One she, Lola, had not meant to cause. She knows too much, so she does what she has to—she pleads ignorance.

"He . . . but I thought . . ." Lola can't see her way ahead in the fog of her brain. She should have seen these two detectives and their predictable line of questioning coming. It is not their fault—it is their job to follow up when a convicted murderer goes missing from a short prison sabbatical. Lola feels the confession on her lips, that they don't need to worry, because, until she gave him the order to take out the founding father of the Rivera cartel, her baby brother had never killed another person. That was her—she killed Darrel King, saving Hector's life, yes, but he is not the killer the law says he is.

Until he tried to drown you, the voice in Lola's head that isn't her but is says.

The anger snaps her neck and spine straight.

"You see my eyes?" She points, stepping closer to the detectives. The one with the smiley-face coffee cup steps back, then realizes it shows weakness and steps back up. The tall, mustached detective doesn't move. He looks tired, Lola sees now, with black circles under his eyes and lips downturned because it must be too much work to even lift them into a straight line. He wears a wedding ring. Maybe he has a new baby at home.

"You see my face?" Lola continues.

The detectives exchange glances, confused this time, as they both start to realize they might have underestimated her. It is a look Lola has seen countless times on countless faces—male, female, black, brown, white. Regardless of race or gender, the look is the same—raised eyebrow, one downturned corner of the mouth, maybe even a sucking-in of the cheeks meant to express outrage at having been fooled.

"We do," the gray overcoat says.

"Yes," the tan overcoat says, just to say something.

"Who do you think did this to me? You think I beat my own self up?"

"No," Gray Overcoat replies.

"I don't . . . . did you?" The tan overcoat must be really tired.

"You got a kid at home?" Lola shoots at him.

"Six weeks."

"Yeah. I can tell."

The tan overcoat shifts his weight from one scuff-loafered foot to the other, embarrassed to be called out by this battered Latina holding a lame cheese platter.

"How bad is my face?" Lola asks them.

The gray overcoat peers closer. "Yikes," he says.

"Yeah. It's bad." The tan overcoat sighs again.

"My brother's a shithead. Turned on me. Tried to drown me. Then ran. I did him a big favor, pulling all those strings to get him out. I thought he was a good person. I thought he loved me. Loved us." Lola bows her head, but she can't cry over Hector yet. She's not sure if it's because she still feels she can salvage their relationship, or if she's just too angry to make room for any other emotion.

"Oh shit," the gray overcoat says. Lola thinks, with his job in law enforcement, that he's seen worse shit than a beat-up woman lamenting the criminal brother she never thought could be a criminal.

"When's the last time you saw him?"

"Today. When he drove me up into the Hollywood Hills and tried to drown me."

"Why would he do that?"

"I tried to get him to go back to Locust Ridge. But he wouldn't get in the car. He got so angry with me. And then . . ." Lola trails off because she wants them to fill in the rest of her story with their own imaginations. Lola does not like to lie to cops.

"Are you going to find him?" Lola looks up, widening her eyes to make up for the lack of tears.

"We'll try," the tan overcoat says with yet another sigh.

"Here's my card. Call us if he contacts you."

"Yeah, for sure," Lola says and waves them away, pretending to stare at the card, which gives the gray overcoat's full name: Kyle Esterman. Lola is surprised Starbucks got it right. To them, she is Love or Lala or LA. She doesn't mind the last one.

"One more thing," Kyle Esterman says. She should have expected this, a cop trying to catch her off guard.

"Yes?"

"There was a pretty bad altercation in a strip-mall parking lot around here during the time your brother was out. Do you think—"

"Yes," Lola says. "I think he's capable of anything."

This part is true.

"Lola?" The man's voice she hears now doesn't belong to either detective. Lola recognizes it, even in the haze she's feeling again now that she is off her tiny stage.

A second later, she sees full-body Zach turning the corner of the stairs, taking in her body, her bloodied face, the cheese getting too warm to be eaten.

"Are you okay?"

"Yeah, sure," Lola says. She wants to ask him what he's doing here, on her turf. She doesn't remember giving him her address. Then she sees the cops are between her and Zach, on their way out.

"These men bothering you?" Zach asks, and Lola recognizes a hint of white alpha male in his tone, a beast waiting to be unleashed.

The tan overcoat sighs, pulling his badge. "LAPD, sir. Please let us pass."

"I'll let you pass when you tell me what you're doing bothering her."

"You two married?" Kyle Esterman asks. "'Cause honestly, we don't owe you an explanation."

Lola finds it difficult to understand why she is rooting for the cops in this situation.

"It's fine," she says, loud enough for Zach to hear, but it doesn't seem to make a difference, because the white, laid-back chef charges the cops, about to plow into the gray overcoat in a way that lets Lola know he's done this before.

It takes Lola darting between them, absorbing the blow, to keep Zach from assaulting an officer of the law.

A second later, she is on her feet, brushing tiny concrete remnants from her yoga pants and apologizing. "Please. I'm so sorry."

Zach sits on the pavement, head down, and now he is apologizing too. "I'm sorry. I'm going through a divorce. I shouldn't have . . . that was wrong."

The two detectives exchange another glance. Lola can tell from the sun it is late in the day, that if they decide to arrest Zach, they will not make it home to their respective dinner tables, to wives or girlfriends or bawling newborns.

"Daddy?" It is Charlie, eyes widened and dry like Lola's a few minutes before, who breaks the tie. Lucy trails behind her, mouth shut tight, hands clasped in front of her. "What's wrong?"

Zach looks from the ground to the two detectives. "Daddy made a mistake."

"What kind of mistake?"

"Nothing," the gray overcoat says. "Nothing. You folks stay safe."

Then they are gone, and Lola turns to Lucy.

"You were at Isa's. What's Charlie doing here?"

"Abuela said she could come over."

Fucking Maria.

"And I just came to pick her up . . ." Zach tries, hands on hips, breath coming in slight hefts. He is shaken up.

"I'm sorry, Mama," Lucy whispers, and now Lola understands something else has happened between the two girls. Lucy will tell her when Charlie is gone. Lola needs to get Charlie to go away.

"Boss." It's Jorge, on the stoop, and he comes to Lola to whisper the rest once he sees the white stranger and his white kid. "You need to stay inside. He's still out there. He knows where you live."

Hector. Her brother. The man who can take away the most important person in Lola's world.

"Mama," Lucy says. "Can't you stay?"

Lola sees the glance Charlie tries to shoot Lucy's way. *Lucy wants her gone. Get her out of here,* the voice again.

"Zach, there's been an emergency. I have to go," Lola says. "It's best if you leave."

Zach nods, "Thanks for letting Charlie come over."

Lola nods acknowledgment, although she had no say in the matter.

"Mama, stay," Lucy says when they are gone.

"I'm sorry, I can't. But I'll be back," Lola says, bending down to speak to Lucy, and when the little girl nods, Lola is more nervous about what awaits her at home than she is about what she has to do now.

It is Manuel who walks her to her car, the two of them not speaking or touching, but still connected. When he opens the driver's-side door for her, she looks at him.

"It was you. You saved me from my brother."

Manuel does not confirm or deny. He bows his head.

The fact that the man she's fucking had to save her from her own baby brother, the villain she didn't see coming, does not make her angry this time, the way she was angry when Manuel was trying to stuff her into the Volvo and get her out of Andrea's neighborhood.

It makes her sad, because Manuel has solidified his status as her soldier, and he has let her brother get away. Lola notices the knife wound at his throat, a flesh wound, but one that must have allowed Hector time to run.

Now, her baby brother is hunting her in Huntington Park, she has a cartel to defeat, and the only woman who can help her do it is missing.

She kisses Manuel out in the open because they both know it will be the last. It is time for a fresh start.

TWENTY-NINE

HOME

Light rain beats the puddle-shaped concrete slabs that lead Lola from car to front door. The house, two stories, modern, is floor-to-ceiling windows, raindrops slipping down them in slow suicides, plopping in fat ovals on the ground.

Lola left her umbrella in the car, because she can't use it without thinking of Hector.

Mandy Waterston stands on the covered porch, a coat not meant to withstand water pulled over her shoulders, her curly hair limp. When she sees Lola, Mandy straightens and shakes the water from her hair, as if someone else's eyes on her make her go from falling-apart to fine.

"Were you waiting long?" Lola asks. She has pulled a belted coat over her own ribbed tank, something snagged at a thrift store in Huntington Park years ago. The coat's threads have started to unravel, the buttons hanging and able to be removed with the swift poke of a finger. Lola needs new clothes.

She needs a house. She can buy this one, if she likes. She has the cash. She has Mandy. She can get Lucy out of Huntington Park, maybe not away from Charlie. She has yet to speak to Lucy about what happened. Lola knows shit went down, but she doesn't know how shitty or who got shit on in Charlie's sociopathic little-girl game.

"Don't worry. Rain. Traffic was horrible. I haven't been here long at all," Mandy says. Then, as Lola nears the door, "What's with the blood?"

"Sorry. Long story. Should be all bandaged up."

Mandy knows better than to ask any more questions. "Would you like to take off your shoes?"

Lola understands Mandy is not asking, so she bends down, unties her Pumas, and leaves them on the scratchy welcome mat next to Mandy's flats, pale-blue numbers with a logo stuck to the tops. Mandy's shoes are bigger than Lola's.

It is Sunday, Open House day in Los Angeles, but this is the kind of house you see by appointment only. Inside, the house is light despite the gray sky above and around its walls of windows.

"The glass is bulletproof," Mandy says, not bothering to point out the Viking range, the vaulted ceilings, the walking distance to the mega–Whole Foods that Lola read about in the house's online description.

Lola cocks an eyebrow.

"Owner is a very successful film producer who may or may not be an arms dealer for the Israelis."

"Shit," Lola says.

"He wanted something larger for his guests."

"Where does he live?"

"No clue," Mandy says, pretending to admire the fireplace, set in stone, burning a gas log brighter than anything Lola has seen in nature. Mandy is lying—she probably has that fucking arms dealer on speed dial—but it doesn't bother Lola, because she has asked a question to which she has no business knowing the answer.

Does she have business here, in Venice, the place where she first made her name by fucking up a drop and losing $2 million in cash and $2 million more in heroin that neither Los Liones cartel nor Mandy's husband, Eldridge—or Andrea, as Lola learned—were willing to concede? Los Liones insisted they were owed $4 million. Eldridge—Andrea's front man at the time—insisted on $4 million. The only thing the two parties had agreed on was that someone had to pay, and for a few weeks, Lola thought that someone would be her.

Hector, she thinks now. She didn't fuck up that drop. Hector did.

"Come over here," Mandy says.

Lola does, Mandy drawing her under her arm, pointing through the fog of cold L.A. rain. Lola sees a brick wall a block away, a three-way intersection she doesn't recognize in the daylight . . . at first.

"That's where it happened, isn't it? The drop?" Mandy asks, like she needs Lola to tell her the answer.

"Yeah," Lola says. "Wonder if that fucking dog still lives there."

"He wouldn't shut up, would he?"

That night, Eldridge had tossed a pockmarked blond meth head from his car to the middle of the street and fled the scene. No one else had been in the car, unless Lola had missed Mandy.

"You were there?"

"I like to see what the men do all day." Mandy winks at Lola, and Lola knows she'll never know if Mandy was there, hiding in the backseat of the Chrysler, or if maybe later, getting ready for bed, Eldridge had mentioned the dog, a huge German shepherd whose owners should have listened when he kept barking, trying to warn them bad shit was going down.

The move to Venice will not be an easy one for Lola. She can pay cash, so she doesn't fear the escrow process or even the money laundering. The physical move will be simple. Lola and Lucy don't have much furniture worth carting from Huntington Park to the West Side. Jorge can find a truck to borrow for the day.

The other part of it, the part Lola can't define, causes a tightening in her stomach, her guts flopping like empanadas in slick, hot grease. Lucy already goes to school with West Side kids like Charlie, but will the Charlies of the world ever accept her? Is Lola giving Lucy more or less of a future, moving her from Huntington Park to Venice? And is she betraying her people, selling out for a Viking range, a backyard where Valentine can sunbathe as her chestnut beard goes gray, a neighborhood where her child doesn't have to fear a drive-by?

"I know you don't give a shit about the school district, because Lucy will be doing private, but it's great," Mandy says.

Lola feels the kitchen tile on her bare feet, cold and calming and grounding. The house smells like no one has lived here, really lived, cooked and fucked and fought.

Mandy sniffs the air like she can hear Lola's thoughts.

"Too new," Mandy shakes her head. She brings her hand to her mouth like she expected a cigarette there, and Lola thinks of Andrea, of the cigarette she snuck behind Bay Cities only a week ago. "You'll get past it. You just have to cook—something with lots of garlic or tomato. Maybe fry some meat." Mandy's nose turns up in a way that again reminds Lola of Andrea, who's missing, and Lola wants her partner here, her backstabbing bitch of a partner, to tell her it's okay to spend this much money, that she's worked hard for it, that she deserves it. That no one's ever going to take it away.

But these would be false promises. And Andrea always tells the truth, when prompted. She copped to setting Lola up to start a cartel war as soon as Lola confronted her. Lola has to give Andrea credit for that. Maybe absence does make the fucking heart grow fucking fonder.

"Have you talked to her?" Lola asks. She has not mentioned the small town in Texas, or the discovery of Andrea's past that Mandy helped her uncover. To do so here, in broad daylight, seems like too much. This house is not hers, not yet, and she is not ready to reveal her secrets, or Andrea's, here.

"No," Mandy says. "I don't know that she can make calls. I don't know if it's safe."

"Do you think the Rivera cartel took her?"

Mandy laughs, a deep, guttural release of tension, as if what Lola has posited is not only ridiculous, but impossible.

"She would never let that happen."

Mandy's words make Lola think of God, or whatever supreme being or combination of energy watches over everything and nothing, doling out vengeful, incorrect justice, pain, and love. If she were as bad at her job as God is, she'd be dethroned and pulled limb from limb, dissolved, and scrubbed from history. To Mandy, though, maybe Andrea can do no wrong. It is not the Rivera cartel that is in control, but Andrea. Lola thinks again of Garcia, of how he never questioned her leadership, and how it almost destroyed the empire she hadn't yet built.

Then she thinks of Zach, and realizes that, even though he is the professional chef, she would not be ashamed to cook him dinner in this kitchen.

"Has Andrea disappeared before?"

"She's got kids," Mandy says, as if that answers the question.

"I met the girl at her house."

"Right. That one," Mandy says, encompassing all of Andrea's daughter's bad attitude and unknowing privilege in three words.

"And I met her son."

Mandy sucks in the air around her as if this is news, and maybe it is. Then Lola sees the sadness on Mandy's face, appearing there before she can cover it up.

"Are you friends? With Andrea?" Lola has never thought to ask. To her, Andrea operates independent of feelings. Yet she remembers Andrea taking her hand in the back hallway of El Norte. Was it just to make Lola feel special?

"We've known each other a long time," Mandy says, but only after a silence lasting more than five seconds, less than ten.

"And you know her past?"

Mandy gives the slightest nod.

"How do you know her past?"

"Well, we're close to the same age, aren't we?" Mandy says.

"So she came out here from Texas, after . . . when the Rivera cartel thought she was dead. Were you in school together?"

"We were," Mandy says. Then, as if this house has heard too much from its non-owners, "Would you like to see upstairs? It has a killer master suite. Vaulted ceilings, all windows."

"So people can watch me sleep?"

"So you can watch over the world," Mandy says, in a tone that lets Lola know she's not joking. "This is not a house meant for curtains."

Try venetian blinds, Lola thinks. Then, *But this—the West Side—is not your world.* Lola finds herself putting one foot in front of the other. The stairs are carpeted in black and brown.

"Lucy would have a hard time falling down these. Good traction," Mandy says. "And of course, if you have more—"

Mandy doesn't finish the sentence because she wants to hear Lola's thoughts on a second child.

"I'm young," Lola says.

"Right."

"Are you having more?"

"I'm not so young."

"But you have money."

"Yes. We'll probably have another," Mandy says, and knocks wood. "Maybe twins. Get it out of the way."

What is "it"? Lola wants to ask. *Late-night feedings? Liquid poop streaked on every diaper? Sleepless nights?* Lola has never given birth, never waddled the halls of her dingy apartment after pushing a baby out of herself, unable to think straight because she hasn't slept or eaten. She has never been sucked dry by a helpless, wailing being totally dependent on her. She wonders how it feels to be spent physically, yet filled to the brim with love and angst, resentment and sadness for all the things from which she will never be able to protect her children.

She wonders if she will ever have the courage to pass on her genes and pray to nothing for the best biology can offer to a fucked-up ghetto girl like her. For now, there is the pill she swallows every night, protecting her from looking into her biological child's eyes and wondering how she fucked them up before they were even born.

"Twins. Sounds like a lot of work," is what she says aloud.

"There's always help."

For women like Mandy, there always is.

Eldridge's wife steps aside so Lola can enter the master bedroom first. It is big and full of light. The walls that aren't windows are painted stark white, a color Lola imagines belongs in a mental institution, the kind where patients go to escape their own thoughts of devastation, destruction, and disease.

"It's beautiful," she says, and she can feel Mandy nodding, even though Lola has her back to her.

Lola looks out the back window. For the first time, she notices the wooden swing set. There are two swings, red and green, set on yellow ropes. The grass is too green, and Lola can see that each blade is the exact same length.

"The lawn is turf," Mandy says, and Lola isn't sure how this woman can read her thoughts.

"Does that mean fake?"

"It does."

"How much?" Lola says.

"For a fake lawn? A pretty penny, but remember, it's a one-time investment."

"For the whole house."

"Same answer."

"Can I afford it?"

"With cushion to spare."

"I'll take it," Lola says.

The walk downstairs is silent. Lola doesn't know if there are papers to sign or hands to shake. Will Mandy call someone now, maybe the current owner, to share the good news?

"This is a wise investment," Mandy says when they're both standing at the threshold. Lola realizes Mandy is showing her out, which feels strange, because isn't this her house now?

Of course, Lola knows it isn't. She has never purchased a home, but she has heard the term "escrow" thrown around like a beach ball tossed just above a short soul's head. She knows it means a kind of purgatory that lasts at least a month, and of course there is the inspection to make sure the pipes won't burst or the foundation isn't cracked.

"Don't worry," Mandy says. "It's a lot easier when you're paying cash."

Lola feels she should ask how it will work. How are Mandy and Eldridge going to clean her cash? Bit by bit, to make her eligible to purchase a wealthy white person's home on the West Side? Or is it already done, through the pot dispensary and the strip mall, the day-to-day of Lola's operations she's had to cede now that she's too busy?

When they are downstairs, on the threshold between staying and going, Lola asks the question she has wanted to this whole time. "You never wanted me to destroy her, did you?"

Mandy smiles. "I wanted you to understand her."

"Is that why you sent me to Texas?"

"Yes."

Lola had expected an argument from Mandy, but the clarity of her answers leaves Lola speechless. But there is one more question she needs to ask. "Where is she?"

Mandy goes to the granite countertop of the kitchen and scratches out an address on the back of a receipt she digs from her handbag.

"She'll be glad to see you."

THIRTY

MEAN GIRL

The call comes shortly after Lola has navigated her Civic over the speed bumps of West Side streets. The last thing she remembers thinking before her cell phone rings is that, in Huntington Park, cars and trucks, from roller-skate- to industrial-size, plow down neighborhood streets where children play, where lives are conducted on two-way asphalt—jump rope, drug deals, conversations between people who share too little space. In her soon-to-be-former neighborhood, there is little regard for the brown lives seeking respite from whatever happens to them behind the closed doors of cramped homes. When there is too little space, a life spills into the street.

On the West Side, there are speed bumps to control the power of passing cars. In Huntington Park, there is nothing but straight, smooth asphalt, meant to burn rubber and excess aggressive energy. White energy, from outsiders passing through. The very last thing she remembers thinking is that she is happy Lucy won't have to worry as much about the speed of passing cars.

Then, the phone. Her ring tone now is Flakiss, whose songs never apologize for the fact that their rapper is a woman. Lola finds her music both relaxing and empowering. This ring tone belongs to her personal cell, not the burner she keeps beside it in her bag. Ramon, the old cartel cleaner with a knack for technology and forgery, recently helped install her email. Now she can see messages from Blooming Gardens, most of them warning of childhood diseases like pink eye and the norovirus, some asking for money, others subtle warnings of what will happen if a parent chooses not to sign up for a fund-raising committee.

Lola does not recognize the number on the caller ID, although the area code—323—belongs to Huntington Park . . . and a hundred other enclaves of Los Angeles, from Hancock Park, with its old-money mansions shielded by ten-foot shrubbery and wrought-iron gates topped with polished black points sharp as fireplace pokers, to West Hollywood, home of Los Angeles's largest gay population and a surge of high-end restaurants and boutiques, Zach's among them.

One day, Lola thinks, she will meander Melrose and hem and haw over a single top that costs $300, one she won't have to pay for in cash because the money stacked high in her bank account will be clean.

To do that, she has to find Andrea, and she has to end this war. Whether or not her brother kills her first is the variable.

"Hello?" Lola says into her phone.

"Ms. . . . Lola?"

"Yes . . ." It is a guarded, drawn-out yes, as if she is waiting for the caller to challenge her so she can deny ever affirming her identity.

"This is Carmen Zapata. I am Isa's mother."

Lola knows who Carmen Zapata is. She has spoken to her many times, over wilting produce at the neighborhood bodega, or in passing on the street when Lola is out walking Valentine and Carmen is headed to or from the bus stop, with its dusty glass encasement for waiting patrons, in order to commute to one of her two or three jobs.

"Yes, Carmen," Lola says. She can feel the other woman's fear rippling through the phone. There is something Carmen Zapata does not want to tell Lola. Lucy, Lola thinks. Her heart heads north of her chest, trying to cram itself into her esophagus. "Is it Lucy?"

"Yes."

Fuck. Lola does not pull over, as she knows she should. Instead, she feels her foot, her big toe clawing at the edge of her Pumas, pressing on the gas. The Civic belches over a speed bump, almost zooming over a black cat that darts into the street at the last minute. Lola swerves to miss it and almost sideswipes a shiny electric-blue Tesla. She hadn't known they made them in that color, she remembers thinking, then wondering how she can think about that when Carmen Zapata has just told her there is something wrong with Lucy.

"What is it?" she asks, pulling over and blocking the driveway to a two-story Spanish-style monstrosity, built to the edge of the lot so the dogs Lola can hear barking inside have no place to run around.

"She is fine. Physically," Carmen says, and Lola feels like a balloon pierced and popped, deflating and sinking to the floor in scraps of useless rubber.

"But?"

"My daughter is not."

Isa.

"What's happened to her?"

"We're at the hospital. Lucy is here too. You should come."

Carmen gives Lola the address, although she is too familiar with the local hospital in Huntington Park. It takes her twenty more minutes to get to the one-story brick mess. To Lola, it has always looked like someone repurposed a strip mall, and maybe that is what happened. She parks and moves from the Civic to the front door at a flat-out sprint, a pace she recognizes in several other fellow patrons peppered across the sidewalk. A man pushes a wheezing old woman in a wheelchair at breakneck speed. A high school boy, propped up by two friends, hops along with a stab wound in his thigh. Lola beats them all to the entrance, because she is the one in good health, the one least in need of the medical care behind the double doors, streaked with debris from ghetto air and bodily fluids from suffering patients.

The lobby is low and squat, lit dimly, with a wall clock that ticks like a bomb over the nurses' station. The ring of the phone is constant, and somewhere in a back office Lola can hear a copier churning out paperwork, the lifeblood of any life-saving organization.

No one at the front listens to her when she says she's here to see Isa Zapata. As soon as an older Latina nurse with an eyebrow permanently raised in the name of skepticism discerns Lola is not family, she points her toward a row of cheap plastic chairs—bright orange, for God's sake, as if someone melted down prison jumpsuits and re-formed them into hospital waiting room chairs.

I should buy them new chairs, Lola thinks, although surely the chairs can't be what you notice when you are wounded or waiting to hear the fate of a loved one who is.

Lola ignores the chairs, because now the high school boy with the stab wound is being lowered into a wheelchair he claims, with all the bravado one can muster when bleeding out, he doesn't need. There is a commotion as he rails at his friends, at the nurses trying to wrangle him, and the blood pours from his gaping wound.

"Sit the fuck down." Lola's voice is low and firm. It calms the bra-vado, the rage, the frantic pace of this place where ghetto warriors come to die.

The high school boy tilts his head, as if he's getting his first look at an exotic creature in its natural habitat.

"You . . ." he says. "You're . . ."

"I'm Lola," she says, and this time nobody stops her as she rounds a corner, peeking in doors and behind curtains, trying to find Lucy or Isa or Carmen. Some of the suffering faces she sees are familiar—they are her neighbors, after all. Some think she has come to pray with them, or to change the conditions in this long, low place with two postage-stamp windows per fifty patients. She will have to beg the forgiveness of her people, though. Today, she's here on her own personal emergency.

Isa is behind a curtain, not stashed out of the way to suffer in pri-vate. Single rooms are more expensive, and Lola is certain Isa's parents don't have health insurance, that they are lucky to eke the cash they do out of their employers, because health insurance for employees would mean less money the employers would forget they have for themselves.

The little girl is conscious, her breathing labored, and her parents stand over her with their hands crossed in front of them. At first, Lola thinks Carmen and her husband Emilio are praying. Then she realizes they are afraid to touch their daughter, because this is the closest they have come to losing her.

It is such a sad scene that Lola does not want to disturb it. Surely it does not belong to her. Then she sees Lucy in the far corner of the curtained square, sitting in another one of those goddamn orange chairs, her head bowed, her face streaked red with the stains of old tears.

This scene does not belong to her, but that little girl in the corner does.

Lola feels a tug to go to Lucy, as strong as a rope pulled tight between them, feels the wind knocked out of her belly in a whoosh despite the fact that no one has laid a hand on her. Something has shifted, gone from innocent to adult, and Lola hasn't felt the floor giving out like this in her entire life, from nights spent cowering in her childhood bed, to feeling her brother pushing her head into a cold, clean babbling brook.

"Lola . . . Ms. Vasquez." Carmen Zapata leaves her own labored-breathing daughter to stand beside Lola.

"Call me Lola," Lola says. She can't remember now if Carmen has used her first name or not in the past. The formality doesn't fit here, in this cramped, curtained square of shitty hospital. Here, they are all in the trenches of war—against violence and death, against infection and poor hygiene and a population unable to scrounge up enough money to earn their loved ones' lives.

"What's going on?" Lola asks, trying to keep her voice even, but it pitches up, like a hysterical mother's would, if said mother were white, wealthy, and unaccustomed to losing the lives of those around her.

"She . . . my daughter—"

"Isa," Lola says.

"Sí, Isa, yes," Carmen continues, shifting her weight from left foot to right, her husband standing silent over Isa, who's trying to rest under the dingy sheets of her shitty hospital bed. "They were playing, Isa and Lucy. Lucy and Isa," Carmen corrects, putting Lola's daughter's name first in a way that makes Lola sink even further. Why would a mother do that, put another woman's child first?

"Yes," Lola says, solemn, as if she's answering a question on cross-examination. One-word answers. Yes or no. Tell the truth, but tell as little of it as possible, and whatever you do, make it make sense. She pictures Andrea walking the courtroom floor in front of her, dressed in a tailored suit, her confidence both permeating the room and invisible. Visible confidence in a woman is often construed as aggression or arrogance. Lola can't remember if Andrea taught her that, or if she's known it from birth.

"Isa got on the roof of our apartment building. It is not tall—only two stories. And she jumped."

"She jumped?"

"Yes."

Lola now recognizes the churning in her stomach. It is the knowledge that this is not the full story, and there is something in Carmen Zapata that won't let her tell Lola what really happened. First there was the "Ms. Vasquez," then the putting of Lucy's name before her own daughter's.

Here, inside these four walls of sickness and death and poverty, and maybe because she's just paid what will soon be cash for a $2 million house on the West Side, she has forgotten her original title. Huntington Park is her domain. Its citizens come to her when they need help, and they steer clear of her when doing anything, legal or illegal, that could put them on her bad side.

"Mrs. Zapata," Lola says. "I can tell you're holding something back."

Carmen looks to Lucy, who looks away.

"What did Lucy do?"

Carmen herself can't meet Lola's eye as she whispers, her head turned away from both her daughter and Lucy, as if she doesn't want Isa having to rehash the memory.

"We're late on our rent. Very late. We will be evicted by the end of the week if we can't pay."

"I'll pay it. How much do you need?" Lola doesn't stop to consider the nerve of Carmen Zapata, demanding that Lola pay her for the truth.

"No," Carmen says. "What I'm telling you . . . I'm not asking for a favor. It is part of the story."

Rent money. Eviction. Helping the helpless, just a few letters off from hurting the helpless.

"Okay," Lola says.

"Lucy told Isa if she jumped off the roof, Lucy would get us, her parents, the money to pay the rent."

There it is. The drop. Lola's stomach wads itself into a knot. She feels the rope that ties her to Lucy stretch tighter, no longer a connection, but a noose.

Lucy's head snaps up as if there is something pulling her from behind, someone forcing her to look at Lola, her mother, who didn't grow her or carry her in her stomach, but who has forged the connection between them that won't sever, despite the fact that Lola feels the bile in her stomach turn to rage, her safety zone. For the first time, Lola wants to march across the room and slap her daughter, to make her feel the pain she has caused her friend and her family. A thought flashes across Lola's mind, of her jumping on Lucy and clawing at her face until she begs for Lola's mercy.

The thought stops her breathing. She knows it is wrong. She hopes it is just a thought. She is thankful, however, that there are other people in this room right now, a necessary buffer to keep her from saying or doing something she will regret. She is not a bad mother, she thinks, even if she is thinking like one. She is not Maria. Then again, Maria was never one to lay a hand on her children.

"Oh shit," Lola says softly, having to look out to the hallway, unable to face the truth of the evil inflicted on a poor girl by her own wealthy daughter.

"I know." It is Carmen Zapata who speaks, and Lola feels the woman's hand on her arm, and Lola lets Carmen lead her from the curtained room to the hallway, where Lola sees a supply closet like a beacon. She tears open the door, and Carmen is right behind her, catching her while she shuts the closet behind them with a free hand.

Carmen can't be older than her, Lola thinks, looking up at the woman through tears, her head resting on Carmen's shoulder. There are lines around her eyes and mouth, a few stray gray hairs salting the black. But right now, to Lola, Carmen is the one with the power to forgive.

"I'm so sorry," Lola manages between wracking sobs.

"She is your daughter," Carmen says. "She is not you."

"My mother . . . she was bad," is all Lola can manage.

"She is your mother. She is not you."

Lola hugs tight to Carmen. Her hair smells of grease and salt, as if she's been working with food, or maybe just cooking for her family, but underneath there is a hint of something calming—lavender, maybe, like the hotel in Jasper? Lola has never been good at identifying smells associated with positive things. She knows blood, with its tang of iron, and she knows shit and piss and smog. The only nice smells she can think of are meant to mask underlying rot, but the rot is always still there.

"What can I do?" Lola asks.

"It is not for me to say," Carmen says.

"Please."

"You might think of punishing her," Carmen says. "To keep her from doing this kind of thing again."

"And if she doesn't stop? If she is a monster?" Lola can't believe she has come to this conclusion about Lucy, about her own daughter. Since she's said it aloud, is it a foregone conclusion?

"You will love her still. You are her mother," Carmen says.

"Have you ever felt this way? About Isa?"

Carmen considers the question, then shakes her head. "Not Isa."

Lola feels the knot in her stomach tightening.

"But my son. He is trouble. He will go after the girls. I must watch him every minute, and I know one day he will break our hearts."

"Have you ever thought of harming him?"

Carmen pauses again, not afraid to speak, but trying to remember. "Yes. I have."

"But you haven't hurt him?"

"I will think to, but I won't. That is the difference between a good mother and a bad."

Lola feels the tension drain. She has to hold on to Carmen to keep from puddling on the floor, and once the feeling of despair has passed, she has the good sense to feel ashamed of herself for seeking comfort from the mother of the girl Lucy harmed.

"Are you ready to talk to your daughter?"

"Yes," Lola says, and when Carmen opens the door of the supply closet, the light of the hospital is much brighter.

THIRTY-ONE

PUNISHMENT

The drive from the hospital to Lola's courtyard apartment takes less than ten minutes. Lucy sits in the backseat, as she always does, looking at the black night sky and the stucco houses with their barred windows. Lola looks from the street to her white knuckles, gripping the steering wheel instead of her daughter's throat. For the first time, she is afraid to be alone with Lucy. She is afraid her work life will bleed over into her personal life.

Twice, Lola looks in the rearview, about to ask her daughter why, or to tell her this isn't the Lucy she knows. But that's the tricky thing about trauma. It could be years before it manifests. Lola's had custody of Lucy for two years, enough time for the abuses her biological mother, Rosie, wove into the fabric of her dear daughter's being—tiny strands, thin as thread, but strong enough to hold together her brain, her heart, and every other organ that makes Lucy Lucy—to begin to show themselves as whole cloth.

So Lola stays silent, because she is not ready for whatever answer Lucy might give. Back at the hospital, once Lola stepped out of the supply closet, she had called Mandy Waterston on a burner phone and asked that $9,500 be transferred to the Zapatas' lone bank account—checking, no savings—by end of day. Another $3,000 would be wired directly into the hospital's accounts payable to settle Isa's medical bill. Carmen and her silent husband had refused to accept Lola's money, but when Carmen snuck out to pee, and her husband had gone for coffee bloated with grounds, Lola had reached into Carmen's purse and photographed a check from the cheap blue plastic book. She had read the account and routing numbers off to Mandy, not knowing the difference, but Lola's ignorance hadn't seemed to bother Eldridge's wife.

The whole time, Lucy had stayed quiet in the corner, her head tucked into her chest, her knees pulled up so that her sneakered feet rested on the orange seat.

"Don't put your feet up on that chair," Lola had said. "They're dirty."

She did not yet know of a punishment fit for Lucy's crime, and now, driving home, she has yet to say anything else to her daughter beyond accusing her of having dirty shoes. And isn't that the mother's fault, not the child's?

In the apartment, Maria has dinner ready—jarred spaghetti sauce and multigrain pasta, the only kind Lola keeps in the house, because, given a choice, Maria will pick processed white over wholesome grain every time. Maria's unquenched longing for crap food—slices of sick orange cheese between pieces of shiny plastic, cheese puffs, balls of chemicals deep fried and rolled in more pulverized chemicals, packaged sugary snacks whose cakey insides stick to human gums long after they've been consumed—is one of the most consistent characteristics of Lola's mother.

"Who wants Parmesan?" Maria shakes the green can with the gaping holes in the top. Lola has asked Maria to use the fresh Parmesan in the cheese drawer, but she is willing to make this concession because she would rather Maria find comfort in this green can than at the wrong end of a needle.

"Lucy, are you hungry?" Lola asks. She expects to see the little girl's cheeks burning with shame. She expects Lucy to want to escape to her bedroom, but, of course, when you've had the childhood both Lucy and Lola have, a bedroom does not mean solace.

Safety in numbers, Lola thinks.

"I'm really hungry," Lucy says. It's the first time she's spoken since Lola entered Isa's hospital room and saw the sweet, sweating girl fighting pain to stay awake. Lola had made sure the hospital knew to give Isa pain medication, as much as the law allowed, and to charge it to her. Whether true or not, Lola imagined the hospital might be skimping on care where they could on Isa's case, because they knew her parents couldn't pay.

"Good," Maria says.

When they are all three seated at the table, Valentine sitting beside Lucy, who barely has Maria beat at being the most likely to drop food, Maria asks the question she was never sober enough to ask her own children.

"How was school?"

Both Lola and Lucy roll their eyes. It is a question that transcends age, race, even violence, in its stupidity.

"It's Sunday," Lola answers for Lucy. Even if Maria had her days right, she couldn't listen to her daughter go on about lunchtime or recess or any of the should-be innocent pieces that make up a second-grader's day.

"Oh," Maria says, dumping more canned Parmesan on her pasta. Lola realizes she has just caught her mother stress eating. There must be palpable, sticky thick tension in the room if even Maria can pick up on it.

"I hurt someone," Lucy says.

Maria nods, sucking more pasta into her mouth, showing herself open and receptive to any horror Lucy might reveal.

Fucking NA, Lola thinks. She knows her mother goes to meetings, that organizing doughnut and coffee preparation is central to Maria's sobriety. She is glad, of course, that Maria has structure to fill her days where heroin once did. Lola does not care for the acceptance of any and all wrongs, no matter the scale. If you've done fucked-up things, should you really be forgiven, or should you be made to live in shame so you don't repeat your mistakes?

"You can tell me," Maria says now.

"Tell her," Lola says, conscious she and her mother have just said the same thing, Maria an open and willing receptor, Lola wanting Lucy to say out loud what she did to Isa to shame her.

"I hurt Isa. She's my friend. I dared her to jump off the roof of her parents' apartment building."

Maria's face doesn't change. Lola thinks of her own reaction to this news. She remembers running to the supply closet. She remembers clinging to Carmen Zapata, then, moments later, thumbing through the woman's checkbook and snapping a photo of the account numbers, all, she told herself, in the name of good. Now, sitting over jarred spaghetti sauce and canned cheese, Lola knows all she did was force this family to accept what they might think of as charity, but which Lola knew to call penance.

"Okay," Maria says, her voice low and even, a soothing balm that settles over the sizzling air of the kitchen with its dingy linoleum and old electric stove, where the cooking time for each of the four burners varies widely. Lola thinks of the Venice house she has bought, of the Viking range and the hardwood floors, of the floor-to-ceiling windows crying the first rain of the season.

"Have you ever done something like that, Abuela?" Lucy asks.

Abuela? Where the fuck had Lucy gotten that term? It is the second time in as many days she has heard Lucy refer to Maria this way. Granted, it is a language-lesson Spanish term, like "dress" or "water" or "toilet," the necessities for navigating the shopping and eating and shitting of a new country.

"Not like that, no," Maria shakes her head.

"But . . . other things?"

Lola is amazed at the audacity of her daughter, shining an innocent light on the woman she's now calling her grandmother.

Yes, Lola thinks, *lots of other things.*

"Of course," Maria says. "We are all human."

Lola rolls her eyes again, like she's a teenager whose mother did things worthy of eye rolls—not letting her go to a party with no parental supervision, insisting she finish her homework before she could watch television. The things her mother did were not eye-roll material. They were material for trauma and addiction and the constant second-guessing of herself, asking every day if, in her life as both a drug trafficker and a mother, she would turn into an irredeemable fuck-up. *No,* Lola realizes now. *Not if. When.*

Still, Lola can't dispute the fact that Lola now sits across from her fuck-up mother at her kitchen table, eating a meal Maria, who she'd thought could never be redeemed, has prepared.

"Would you like more cheese?" Maria asks Lucy, and Lucy nods.

Lola watches the white powdered clumps fall from can to sauce, watches Lucy mix them in so they'll melt. She watches her daughter, able to eat after what she did to Isa, and she knows that, if she punishes Lucy now, she will regret whatever she does tonight in the morning.

Lola stands and scrapes her plate into the trash, eliciting a whimper from Valentine. On a normal night in this kitchen, Lola would explain to Valentine that tomatoes are acidic, not good for her belly, that they will keep her up all night. She would try to make Valentine understand she was doing something that hurt her right now in order to avoid a greater hurt later.

Valentine does not see it that way. She never does. In that way, tonight feels like any other night, instead of the night that could turn Lola into a bad mother.

"I'm going out," Lola says.

"But you just got here."

Lola had never imagined, when her mother got sober, that she would turn into every person's mother, tossing passive-aggressive comments into the ether to see which ones stuck.

"Work emergency," Lola says. Maria knows what Lola does for a living and chooses to ignore it. For Maria Vasquez, the denial of her daughter's profession is a must, not because the way Lola earns her living shames her, but because the product her daughter peddles will kill her . . . if she ever asks enough questions to figure out where Lola keeps it.

"You should wear your coat," Maria calls as Lola starts out, a reminder Lola needed and never got as a child, but not now, when she has just turned twenty-eight.

"I will," Lola says. When she leaves, Maria has her teacup halfway to her mouth, the story of Lucy daring Isa to jump off a roof written off to that vast abyss of shit in Maria's brain that she must file under "humanity" before forgiving and forgetting. Lucy is looking at Lola, her eyes wide, the daring she displayed at dinner, peppering Maria with questions and confessions, gone. She wants Lola to tell her she still loves her.

Lola does. And she will. But not tonight.

But when she reaches the front door, Lucy is already there. Lola sees the little girl's eyes, big with tears.

"Will I ever be better?" Lucy asks.

"You are," Lola says.

Lola opens her arms and bends down to envelop her daughter. She feels the sting of Lucy's tears on her bare shoulder, and she realizes she has ignored her mother's warning about a coat. A second later, she feels the pinch of tears fighting to stay in her own eyes, but it doesn't work.

"I'm sorry," Lucy says. "I don't know why I did it. What's wrong with me?"

"There's nothing wrong with you," Lola says. "Did someone give you the idea? To do that to Isa?"

"Charlie," Lucy says. "She said if I didn't, she'd call the police and they'd send me back to Mexico."

Lola's face flushes red with rage. She buries her cheek in the black straw of Lucy's hair, air catching somewhere in her lungs so it hurts to breathe.

"I love you," Lola says, finally, the trapped words escaping her in a desperate rush. "And you are not going anywhere. This is your home, just as much as it is Charlie's."

"She said I wouldn't have a mother in Mexico."

"I don't want you to worry about this anymore. It's not going to happen. I am your mother. We live here."

"Huntington Park?"

Lola thinks of the Venice house, of infiltrating the world of Charlies and their second glances at brown skin, followed by pasted-on smiles and pretend friendliness.

"Not just Huntington Park. Los Angeles. It belongs to all of us. It will keep us safe."

Lola doesn't know what brings her to say that last bit, except that in that moment, she feels every square of this city—race and class and money and shit and art all strung together across hundreds of miles of freeway, suspended in air thick with car exhaust—fighting to care for each and every one of the people who calls it home.

THIRTY-TWO

FUCK

L ater that night, Lola sets out to find Andrea at the address Mandy Waterston had given her, but after her conversation with Lucy, she makes a stop in Venice to fuck Zach first. Her visit takes him by surprise, but not so much that he doesn't follow her lead to his second-floor bedroom and onto the bed with a wooden frame too plain not to be expensive. The sheets are dark red, a perfect color to match bodily fluids, and although by now Lola can tell when sheets have a high thread count, this cotton scratches her skin enough to know that Zach's sheets are new, washed maybe once. She straddles him on his dark-red sheets, and he is shirtless beneath her, his muscles rippling under tan skin in a way she wishes she could enjoy. She lets his thumbs hook into her hip bones as she rides him. She tries leaning down close to him to let him take control, but he pushes her back up.

"I want to see you," he says.

You fucking will, Lola thinks, and then she is moving again, in slow circles around his big dick—because of course he has a big dick, and he is moaning beneath her, surrendering, before she speeds up again. Zach goes still before he starts screaming, and Lola wonders if he would sound the same were his screams to stem from pain instead of pleasure.

"That was . . ." But he trails off. Like every man Lola has ever fucked, he can't talk afterward.

Lola could but doesn't want to. She's got shit to do. She pees and checks her face—still bruised from her altercations with the Rivera cartel assassin and the man she used to call her baby brother. Zach didn't ask because she was there to fuck, and they'd done so in the dark. She doesn't get dressed again before she flips on the lights and pushes back Zach's blackout curtains to reveal the same floor-to-ceiling windows she will have in her Venice house.

"Might want to keep those closed. I've got nosy neighbors."

"Is that what you have?" Lola asks, her head tilted. She is standing naked, ass to window, tits to Zach, but the fucking she just gave him has drained his ambition.

"Huh?" Zach asks, turning full surfer bro post-coital.

"Where's your daughter?" Lola can't bring herself to say that bitch's name. She gets back on the bed. Zach presses himself against her.

"At a friend's."

"What, so she can terrorize more than one girl?"

"Huh?"

It is difficult, this part—telling him in a single breath what Charlie said to Lucy, and what Lucy did to Isa in order to keep Charlie from having her deported.

"Your daughter needs to take responsibility for what she's done," Lola says.

Zach sits up, the sheet covering his balls. "She made a joke."

"That's not a fucking joke," Lola says, and she resists the urge to add *where I'm from,* because whether you grew up in Bel-Air or Boyle Heights, deportation should not be a fucking joke.

"You're right," Zach says, but he can't resist a grin.

"I am," Lola says, and she's going to teach him that she is, because this night, fucking him into honesty, has taught her he won't be able to learn on his own.

It is late, past midnight, when she leaves Zach snoring, and, according to a quick text from Maria, "Lucy sleeping . . . zzzzzz lol." She makes three quick turns in Venice to make sure she's not being followed, then exits the only part of L.A. she can't seem to navigate without GPS, because it's the only part not built on a grid of rectangular blocks, each one a straight line that hits another straight line until Lola's city streets are nothing more than a mass collection of tic-tac-toe boards.

Lola doesn't recognize the address Mandy Waterston gave for Andrea's location. It is a house in South Central proper, not South Central adjacent, like Lola's Huntington Park neighborhood.

Lola's Civic moves through Compton, which has turned from a no-go zone to a haven for Starbucks and Foot Lockers housed in fresh stucco strip malls. If Lola didn't know better, she would place the intersection where she's stopped now, with its uniform Spanish-tile roofs and cream-colored adobe walls, as somewhere smack in the middle of suburban Simi Valley. It is only when she pulls off the main thoroughfares that she begins to spot the telltale signs of the ghetto—lowriders up on bricks, young men with dark skin gathered on a corner, not doing anything threatening, but letting any visitors know they're watching. There are bars on the windows, and Lola imagines that, during the day, old women in housedresses, slippers, and curlers ease down the street, their weight shifted to walkers draped with grocery bags—milk, flour, eggs, more plastic curlers.

The address Mandy gave belongs to a pale peach house. Like every other house on the block, there are bars on the windows. The lawn has long since grown into wild weeds that part in all directions. Somewhere in the back, a dog gives a warning bark. Lola doesn't have to see the dog to know it's fucking huge. There is no doorbell, so Lola knocks on the flimsy front door. Her knock comes out small, hollow, so she knows the door is no more than plywood.

The man who answers is brown, like Lola, with a single gold tooth top front. His other teeth are real but yellow. Lola knows because he smiles when he sees her, as if he were expecting her but wasn't sure when she would show.

"*Hola*," the gold-toothed man says, and for a second, Lola thinks he is going to open his arms wide to hug her. Whatever he sees in her face causes him to step back instead, and Lola doesn't wait for an invitation to cross the threshold.

"Is Andrea here?"

Lola looks around the place—dark wood floors, shabby floral-print couch, linen curtains stained black with dust and dirt. The room is dark except for a sliver of moonlight that illuminates a big-screen television hung above a fireplace Lola assumes does not work. The television is off, but she can still see the pixels on the screen, burning out as slowly as a candle snuffed. This man was watching it before she showed up.

"She is," the man replies.

Lola moves toward the kitchen, and he doesn't stop her. The linoleum floor is stained brown from what Lola hopes is just coffee and grease. The appliances are old, a fact Lola would be able to tell from the refrigerator's rattling hum even if her eyes were squeezed shut.

But her eyes are open, which is how she sees the heroin on the kitchen table. Three men sit amongst a pile of powder, pocket knives, and cellophane. When they catch Lola looking, they nod. Or are their heads bowing to her? Either way, they recognize her as a friend.

"This way." The man with the gold tooth beckons for Lola to follow him.

The hall is dark, with gilt-edged portraits of the Virgin Mary and the baby Jesus lining both sides. At the back, under a mirror that shows Lola only her top half, stands a shelf of lit prayer candles, blinking and blazing, not giving enough light for Lola to see her feet as she passes what she guesses are bedrooms but can't say for sure, because their doors are closed.

The man opens the door at the very back of the hallway, leading Lola into a bedroom—a small square that's probably larger than the other small squares Lola passed to get here. The walls are white. Like Lola's current bedroom, the closet doors are double sliding mirrors that show her her own image even when she doesn't want it captured, like a surveillance camera whose footage has gone from grainy to good.

Andrea sits on the made bed. Her shoulders are hunched, her knees pulled up to her chest. Lola can't tell in the light borrowed from the hallway's prayer candles, but she thinks Andrea might be rocking back and forth, back and forth.

Lola goes to Andrea and sits beside her, trying to pry a hand from her knee to hold in her own, but Andrea gives a violent shake of her head. To hug Andrea now would be like hugging a loaded gun with a faulty trigger, so Lola eases off.

Lola had thought her partner was safe. Maybe Mandy thought she was. Maybe the house was. Maybe the men outside aren't their employees, but their captors.

"What did they do to you?"

Andrea laughs, throwing her head back in an easy way that used to scream power and confidence, but now seems sad and hopeless.

"You came," is all Andrea says.

"Of course I did."

"Even though Hector caught up to you."

Lola will ask Andrea later how she knows about Hector. There could be a simple explanation—maybe she's still speaking to Jack, her husband, or maybe Andrea has people watching her house and reporting back here, to whatever this place is. Lola doesn't believe Andrea would seek refuge in a heroin den. Even though Lola doesn't know much about politics, she can't imagine Andrea allowing herself to potentially be caught here, with several hundred grand worth of heroin instead of dinner on the kitchen table, unless major shit has hit the proverbial fan.

"Yeah. Wish I could say I took care of it," Lola says. "But he got away."

"I'm sorry you had to go there," Andrea says, her voice cracking so she has to shift it to a whisper. "To my house. That I put you at risk. With the Rivera cartel . . . and with your brother—"

"It's nothing," Lola says. She wonders what would make Andrea risk her political career and her family's safety, not to mention exchanging her $2 million Bronson Canyon home for a South Central heroin den.

"Why are you here?" Lola asks.

Andrea doesn't answer.

"I know," Lola says. "About your family. That the Rivera cartel killed your parents, your brother. That your father owed them money."

"No." Andrea shakes her head.

"You don't need to lie to me. We're in this war together."

"Then you need to know the truth."

"What is the truth?"

"That I don't know what to do. I mean, I know what to do," Andrea continues at a whisper, speaking so low Lola has to lean closer to hear her. She is not hearing Andrea. She is hearing a little girl. "He found me."

"Who?"

"I'll show you. I think I can do that." Andrea rises on wobbly long legs, as if someone has fastened her with stilts and demanded she run before she walks.

"Careful," Lola says, catching the sharp edge of Andrea's elbow in her palm. Lola feels the pale skin there—it's drier than she would have thought, as if Andrea hasn't been taking care of herself.

Facing each other now, Lola gets her first glance at Andrea's face. She sees the crow's feet etched deep into the grooves of each eye socket. Her green eyes are too wide, as if she's trying to tell Lola they are both in grave danger. Her lips are dry and cracked. Now that Andrea is standing, Lola can see she is wearing sweatpants—not the black, stretchy yoga pants that go for sixty bucks a pop at specialty women's athletic stores, but the gray cotton polyester blends found in a three-pack at any Walmart. Her T-shirt is gray, too, and Lola can make out a faint stain on the pocket just above Andrea's small left breast. Ketchup? Lola doesn't let herself believe it could be blood. Andrea doesn't get her hands dirty. That is Lola's job.

Andrea leans on Lola, a slight limp in her step that Lola hopes comes from simply sitting too long. How long has she been sitting on that bed? Was she suspended there, like canned fruit in a Jell-O salad, until Lola arrived and broke the mold?

"This way," Andrea says, not gesturing one way or the other, and unable to move forward without Lola's help.

"Which way?"

"Left."

Lola heads for the closed door one bedroom over from the one where the gold-toothed man helped her find Andrea.

"Would you like me to open it?"

Andrea takes a long breath, her head going to Lola's shoulder before Lola knows it's happening.

"I don't know," she says. "I can't do it."

"What's in there?" Lola asks, unsure about wanting the answer.

Andrea laughs again, head thrown back, cracked giggles escaping her throat.

"Open the door," Andrea says, her voice still no more than a whisper. For a second, Lola doesn't know if Andrea actually said the words, or if Lola's own curiosity made her imagine them.

She turns the fake gaudy gold knob and finds the door giving. She can hear Andrea sucking in her breath next to her.

The man on the bed is the same man Lola saw at Grub. The man who took Garcia. The man who gave her her baby brother back. Except now, this man, the remaining head of the Rivera cartel, isn't wearing a shirt, his pale skin sagging over muscles that have long since gone limp.

Lola thinks she sees bruising that could be bed sores on half the older man's back. She has seen bed sores before, not because she has cared for the elderly, but because Maria once checked herself into rehab at a teenage Lola's insistence and refused to move from one side of her heroin-riddled body to the other, creating a line of wounds she would finally roll over to point out to Lola every time her daughter came to visit.

Now, in this dim square of bedroom, Andrea's breath speeding up next to her, Lola exhales.

"It's him," Lola says, relieved, because here is the reason they are at war, this man who presumably had Andrea's family killed, the man who took her brother hostage, the man who needs to die to end this war.

"He's the reason I had to disappear," Andrea says.

"What's his name?"

"Wayne."

"Where did you find him?"

"He found me."

For a second, Lola thinks she's got it all wrong, that Andrea, in her sweatpants and crow's feet, is the captive here. Yet she seems able to move freely about the house, to get up off her own bed and make her way over to this one, to have a guest the men packing heroin will greet with polite nods.

"Where is he from?"

Lola is expecting to hear that the man is from Mexico. She is trying to get Andrea to parse out the information, because sometimes a story of trauma is easier to tell that way. Yes-or-no questions. Concrete answers. What time. Where. What day. What were you wearing.

Instead, Andrea says, "Jasper. My town."

The old man looks up, as if he's realized the two women are discussing him, and the smile he gives Andrea contains no warmth and no mirth. It is cold and cruel, bloody lips curling around snarling teeth.

"Did you know him? Before he found you?" Lola takes a step closer, as if this man is a lion behind the bars of a zoo cage and she's a tentative child. In truth, she wants to see his face closer in the candlelight. When she sees what she thought she might—the pert, upturned nose—she knows his identity before Andrea says it.

"He's my father."

THIRTY-THREE

PAST LIFE

Lola sits with Andrea at the kitchen table in the South Central heroin den. When they appeared in the kitchen doorway, which should have been too narrow for them both to stand side by side but wasn't, the wood seeming to bend to accommodate both their bodies, the three men at the table made quick work of cleaning up their product. In seconds, expert fingers removed every speck of powder from the table's hard surface, and the men disappeared into another corner of the house, one Lola hasn't seen that's set off the kitchen's other doorway, a narrow space between the electric stove with a broken burner and a microwave on a wobbling plastic cart.

Lola had smelled the tang of vinegar and the char of burning, letting her know the men might have been testing the product for purity. Now, several minutes later, the kitchen smells like nothing but stale air and old cooking. Andrea had tried to push open the window over the sink, which looks right onto a concrete wall. Her arms gave out, though, and instead, she crumpled into a kitchen chair.

"Sorry," she said to Lola. Had she been apologizing for her inability to open the window, for the residual scent of the substance that is both responsible for Lola's childhood trauma and the source of her power present-day, or for the fact that she's holding her father hostage one room over?

Lola had held up a hand to indicate that whatever it was for, the apology wasn't necessary.

Now, Lola is ready to hear Andrea's story.

"Did you know your father was alive?" Lola begins. She thinks of the only trial she's ever seen Andrea prosecute, of the domestic violence victim who told her tale of trauma in yeses and nos, in clauses instead of full sentences, never giving more information than Andrea had asked. Andrea must have told the victim how to speak in a court of law. She must have given that woman a voice. It is Lola's job to do the same for Andrea now, in this dim kitchen where enough heroin has passed in the past hour to get them all thrown in prison for a good twenty years, if someone chose to prosecute.

"No."

"When did you realize he wasn't murdered along with the rest of your family?"

"Right before my son . . . before he overdosed."

On my heroin, Lola thinks, but that's wrong. They are partners. The sin belongs to both of them, but Andrea is the boy's mother. She can't shoulder this particular burden, and Lola won't let her.

"He found me. I didn't see him, but he made contact."

"Why didn't the cartel have him killed?"

"Because he started making them money again. Then he worked his way up. It's been so long . . . turns out everyone loves a comeback. Not just Hollywood."

"And you had no idea?"

"I had no idea until he showed up looking for a turf war. With me. His daughter."

"Wasn't he happy you were alive?"

"No."

"Why not?"

"Because the cartel didn't shoot him that night. I did."

Lola sits back and lets this information sink in. Andrea shot her own father. She shouldn't make assumptions. She should ask why, but she thinks of Andrea's pet projects—domestic violence, child abuse, lost children, prey.

"He was violent, and you killed him."

"I tried to."

"Self-defense."

"I shot him in the back," Andrea says, and she meets Lola's eye, a witness reading the jury.

"Good," Lola says.

"Not good enough. He must have walked away . . . I don't know how . . . I thought I saw his body. I thought he was dead. But I was . . . I was in shock."

"You came to Los Angeles?" Lola asks.

"I did."

"And lived on your own?"

"Yes."

How?

"Where was your mother? Didn't she protect you?" As if mothers always protect their children. It's a shift in the line of questioning, one more suitable to the hostile nature of a cross-examination, but sometimes, it's better to startle the truth from someone, the way she sometimes startles Lucy to get rid of the little girl's hiccups.

"He killed her," Andrea says. Her eyes are on her hands, her right hand fiddling with the wedding ring on her left. She has not taken it off for this trip to her past life. In many cases, the past tries to tear us from the present, but if you can find an anchor—a ring—Lola thinks, maybe you can remember who you are in the life you like best. "And then?"

"I killed him. Or I thought I did."

Now Andrea looks at Lola, one side of her mouth turned up, her breath whooshing from her in relief, and Andrea doesn't have to tell Lola that she is the first person to hear this story.

"And your brother?"

Andrea doesn't answer. She fiddles with the ring, spinning it on her finger, which is too slim to hold it.

"What happened to Christopher?" Lola asks.

"My father beat him to death." Andrea speaks this sentence in a rush, and Lola realizes she is the first to hear this woman talk about her brother. Andrea's mouth is wide, her breath coming in gasps, and Lola takes her partner's hand in her own.

"Then you came here."

"I came here."

Los Angeles.

"There was a man in Texas, the man sent to kill us. He told me his name was Juan. He saw the whole thing. I think he was in his twenties. Although I can't say for sure. I was twelve. He had thick hair, dark brown. He was good with documents. I don't mean fake IDs so you could go to a bar a few years early. I mean changing whole lives. Helping people disappear."

"Like you."

"Like me."

"How did you pay him?"

There is a flash of anger in Andrea's eyes. Lola didn't need to ask the question—it isn't her business.

"Not like that. Not the way you're thinking."

Lola hates that Andrea could read her thoughts, but she isn't surprised. Both of them work thigh-high in shit on both sides of the law. Of course Lola's mind, and Andrea's too, must jump to the dark before considering other possible options.

"He saved my life for free." Andrea looks at Lola. "And I haven't seen him since."

Lola wants to ask how a twelve-year-old girl made the trek to Los Angeles with fake identification, found housing, pursued an education that went through law school, then settled down with a psychiatrist husband to raise their two children in the hills below the Hollywood sign.

"The Carpenter District," Andrea says.

"What?"

"You're wondering how I did it. The Carpenter District is an L.A. Unified School District in the Valley. Public school as good as any private one. I went there. Met good friends."

"Like Mandy."

"Like Mandy. Got accepted to Harvard Westlake on scholarship for high school, then UCLA for undergrad and law school."

"But you must have needed someone to sign all those forms. How did you pay for housing?"

"I had a one-bedroom in Studio City. Clipped coupons. It was a game. It was fun."

"But you must have had some way to get money."

"I took all my father's papers with me when I left. I found a lot of questionable practices in his corporation's books. So I blackmailed his business partner, because I thought he was still running the business. My father let me think that."

"Until now."

"Until now."

Andrea smiles at Lola, something akin to her old smile, the one that radiated confidence and implied she knew something Lola didn't.

"Would you like a drink?"

Andrea doesn't wait for Lola's answer. Instead, she pulls two juice glasses, spotted white not with heroin, but with the spilled powder of a dishwasher capsule. She pours tequila to the brim of each glass and brings it to the table.

"I don't know why they drink the cheap shit here. They make enough money to afford better."

"Because you never know when the money's going to stop."

"That's easy," Andrea says. "Never."

They clink glasses. Andrea drinks deeply, not flinching as Lola watches the burning liquid travel from her mouth down her throat, water over a rocky stream. Lola takes a sip of her own tequila and does flinch, because it is truly shitty. She bets this one swallow will leave her with a headache tomorrow.

"Here's to ending this war," Andrea says.

Lola feels the tequila churning in her stomach, like a violent family member arriving at a holiday table already drunk and brandishing a gun. She recognizes pieces of Andrea's past catching up to her, Lola's, present.

"How do we do that?" Lola asks, though she already knows. *Never ask a question in court if you don't already know the answer.*

"We have to kill my father," Andrea says.

THIRTY-FOUR

GLASS HOUSES

The beach is dark black, the only light coming from the grains of sand beneath Lola's bare feet. In Malibu, this far north of the Santa Monica Pier and the littering tourists that swarm it, the sand is as clean and white as the caps that top the waves crashing and pulling back, crashing and pulling back. Lola wants to get her feet wet, but she knows the water will be too cold.

Behind her, Andrea and Jack's glass beach house is lit from top to bottom in glowing, warm yellows. Jack isn't there. It is only Andrea and her father inside, with Lola's men—Jorge, Marcos, Manuel, and Ramon—keeping watch on the Pacific Coast Highway that borders the house's front side. Lola can hear the cars rushing the four-lane road, rich people headed from beach house to civilization and back, many of them tipsy at this hour of the night, when anyone not doing something illegal should be tucked safely in bed.

Andrea had reached her Rivera cartel contact, a man with a filtered voice who called himself El Médico. Lola hasn't heard the man's voice, but she's certain he's not a real doctor in anything but violence and destruction and maybe peddling white powder at market price or above. Andrea had arranged an exchange—the Rivera cartel's leader for an end to this war.

Lola is the one who asked that they be near the water, but it is only now, facing the cobalt ocean with its whitecaps, which she'd hoped would be angrier tonight but instead are light and sloshing, that she feels the rush of adrenaline she can't deny she craves, despite being a mother and the top of a trafficking pyramid. She could choose not to get her hands dirty, as she knows Andrea has done, pacing in the house behind her, afraid to pull the trigger on her own father. Yet she is out here, in the dark, with the ocean, Mother Nature's most dangerous weapon, at her feet.

"Lola," she hears his voice before she sees him.

"Did you have to be told where I was to find me?" Lola asks. She has had a hard time with the fact that Hector had not found her before this. He has never lived in or near her courtyard apartment, but she would have been easy enough to track down, to shoot between the eyes if he'd really wanted to.

"I've been keeping an eye on you," Hector says.

When Lola turns to face him, he is not close enough for her to see the smile she knows is on his face.

"Would've thought you'd find me too," Hector says. "After what I did." And it's true. Lola could have devoted her many resources to finding her baby brother and making him pay for trying to drown her, but she hadn't. Was she biding her time, or was she afraid of what she knew she must do to him if and when she found him?

"Why?" Lola asks. *Never ask a question if you don't already know the answer.*

"You set me up," Hector says. "You knew what would happen to me if I killed that man in Locust Ridge. And you gave the order anyway."

The answer is what Lola expected, but she has succeeded in her true aim. Hector has stepped toward her, his chest puffed, his voice taking on a tinge of anger. He is much taller than Lola, has been since he was eleven, but she is not scared. She doesn't even bother to step to him, to puff up her chest. Instead, she crosses her arms.

"It's cold out here," she says.

The comment about the weather angers him more.

"You need to take responsibility for what you've done."

Lola smiles at him, a kind smile, full of pity, but part of her is sad that he is taking the bait just as she predicted.

"Would you like to try to kill me again, Hector?" she asks.

"I could."

"Sure."

Her lack of confidence in him angers him even further. He steps so close she can smell the residual ice-cold freshness of mint on his breath, as if this is a date and he's wanted to make sure he's prepared for an innocent kiss. In an instant, his hands are around her neck, and he is choking her.

Lola feels her mouth open, feels herself gasping for air. She is losing oxygen, but still she looks Hector in the eye just so he can see that, even as he chokes the life from her, she is not scared of him.

The first shot seems to come an eternity later, when Lola is thinking her face must be red, when her brain is begging her for air. She is losing her ability to process, but she can tell the shot came from somewhere behind Hector, and that it is not aimed at her.

She has anticipated a gun battle, but it is still difficult not to jump up immediately when Hector's hands release her and she falls to the ground. She wants to see if her baby brother has been shot, and, if so, if it's a flesh or fatal wound. Instead, she finds her knees wobbling under her, her head spinning in a space that's as dark as the space around her. She sees Hector facedown on the sand, but for a second she can't place him in her life. She needs air to do that. Who is this man and why does she care?

A few more breaths and it hits her—he is her brother. And she was wrong—he has never become a man. He is still a little boy, and she is supposed to protect him.

"Hector," she cries out before she dives on top of him. There are more bullets now, coming from her side and from his, a war raging above the two siblings who have taken refuge in the sand.

Lola smells salt and seaweed here, and even though she and Hector are not underwater, it seems like they are. The noise above them, of bullets ringing out into nighttime ocean air, sounds faraway. The noise that Lola hears at a deafening decibel is not the shootout above her, but her baby brother's sobs, loud and wracking as the deadly water behind them, coming on strong, then pulling back.

"Hector," Lola says. "Shhh . . . don't let them hear."

They are back to their shitty childhood apartment, to the living-room closet that smelled of canned soup and clothes slicked with their mother's junkie pre-fix sweat. They are hiding so Maria won't find them, and Hector is crying, not because he fears being pimped out, but because he doesn't want the bad men to come after his sister.

What has happened to us? Lola wants to ask him, but he is her sobbing baby brother, and it is his job to ask the questions and her job to answer them.

"I'm sorry, Lola," Hector says. "They're coming for me."

"Who's coming for you?"

"The Rivera cartel. It's not personal . . . it's just . . . I didn't follow orders."

It takes Lola a second to understand what Hector is saying. He has not come after her of his own volition. He has pushed her head underwater and circled her throat with his hands at the behest of someone else. Someone who is not her.

"They gave you back so you could get close to me."

"So I could kill you. And I . . . I failed."

There is another shot, this one closer, and Lola presses her baby brother into the sand, sheltering his body with her own.

"Why?" Hector asks in a gasp between tears.

"I don't know," Lola says, because she doesn't know how they ended up here, on two separate sides of a cartel war, clinging to each other.

"Can I come back?" Hector asks.

"Hector. Keep quiet," Lola says. "They can't hear you cry."

Hector swallows a sob.

Then, Lola says, "We have to stand up."

She doesn't know if this is the best option, but it seems like the only way to get the shooting to stop is to enter the line of fire. It was the same when they were children, hiding in a closet. Stomachs would start to growl, Hector would have to pee but refuse to go in his pants, and Lola had known that, whatever was behind the door waiting for them, they would have to look it in the eye.

"I can't."

"I'll help you."

"You can't do that in front of them."

"Don't worry about it."

Lola shoulders her baby brother, propping his arm not over her shoulder but onto her waist, making it look like he is the one holding her, and not the other way around.

She looks from one side to the other. Behind her, her men stand with weapons trained, and though she can't be certain from this far away, it looks like the Rivera cartel is a bunch of fucking gringos. The shooting has stopped. They have stood up in the middle of a standoff.

Then someone in the dark pushes him to the center. Andrea's father. Showered and clothed in white linen.

Lola spits at the sand, a petulant move, but she is not feeling grown-up tonight.

Marcos and Manuel lead Andrea's father to the middle ground. No one from either side takes a shot, because the white man is the asset. Lola wonders if this man has told the rest of his organization that the opponent they're facing is not the brown woman spitting on the sand tonight, but his own daughter. Andrea used her to start a cartel war all because she wanted to punish her father. Lola wonders what lengths she would go to to find her own father, to get his attention, to ensure that he couldn't turn away from her ever again.

But now Andrea's father knows who his daughter has become, and there's nothing to stop him from sharing that information with the rest of the world if he leaves tonight alive.

He has to die, and Andrea won't be able to kill him.

"Everyone put their guns down," the white man orders, his voice even and calm, yet loud enough to be heard over the crashing ocean waves.

The white men on the other side start to obey their leader, and Lola sees her own men looking to her to see if they should also comply.

"Fuck no," Lola says, because there can be no standoff with no weapons.

"I want a peaceful resolution," Andrea's father says, with the expectation that his wants come first.

"First you promise to leave Los Angeles," Lola says. "Get off our turf." "Turf" seems like the wrong word to encompass a city spanning so many miles that even flying over its square blocks and Spanish tile roofs takes forever.

"We will," Andrea's father says. Lola doesn't have to wait long for the condition. "But we'll take him with us."

He means Hector. Next to her, Lola's lovable fuck-up brother stiffens, and Lola thinks Andrea's father can't know about what just happened in the sand. He can't know Hector begged Lola to take him back, that he became a traitor to the Rivera cartel as soon as he said those words. He can't know, but he seems to, and it is only now Lola realizes she is gripping her brother's hand, that they are standing in accidental solidarity against the white and brown soldiers surrounding them.

"No," Lola says, because it's too late. She can't give Hector back. They will torture him and kill him and toss him in the ocean or in a vat of lye, never to be mourned.

She has to keep him safe, at least until their mutual external enemy is extinguished.

"It's only fair," Andrea's father says. "You didn't give me the real boss when I gave you your brother."

"Huh?" Then Lola remembers Garcia. She doesn't have to look to know for sure that the white soldiers on the other side of her have raised their weapons again.

"Now I have to take one of yours. Unless you don't want me to take your brother. I'll settle for one of them too," Andrea's father says, nodding first to Marcos, then to Manuel. But Marcos and Manuel have not fucked up. It is Hector who endangered the whole crew at their very first drop for Los Liones cartel. It is Hector who forced Lola to take Darrel King's life. It is Hector who turned traitor with the first promise of women and wealth she is sure Andrea's father has made him, then turned back as soon as he and his sister dropped to the sand to avoid the gunfire above them.

Then Lola sees her, standing at the edge of the white foam waves lapping at the sand, ready to take her. Lucy stands in a sea of white foam and white men. To their credit, the men lower their weapons as the girl comes forward.

Lola does not have to think before she says, "Take him." It is her hand that pushes her own brother forward, toward torture and pain.

Hector shakes his head, "Lola. Don't do this."

"Go," Lola says.

"I can't."

"You can take care of yourself. She can't. Look at her."

Hector does. He bows his head, shamed, and starts walking.

"Lola." It is Manuel, soft, compliant, and Lola knows what he is asking. *What should we do with this white man?*

"Let him go," Lola says.

Marcos and Manuel release Andrea's father. This was not part of the plan, but neither was Lucy, and neither was Hector coming back to her side. But Lola has not been able to see until tonight that Hector's loyalties still flip and flop, a fish on dry land dancing for whoever will give it water first.

Lucy is walking the sand, too, putting one foot in front of the other as if she is on a tightrope and not miles of California coast.

"Look at me," Lola says.

Lucy is close now, maybe twenty feet, and Lola fights the urge to run to her. If she does, she will be in the middle of her men and those of the Rivera cartel. She will expose herself to a head shot. She will do what feels good now but will sacrifice any future of motherhood she might have.

She has to trust that Lucy can do this. She can walk to Lola.

But now Lola sees the headlights come on, the four vehicles' headlights on the white man's side. She doesn't know how they got here, but each vehicle is at one quarter of a rectangular square of beach. Lola knows before she sees the rope what they are going to do.

"No!" Lola screams, and she is running, her feet digging into the sand, her arms trying to help her take off. Her ankles are sinking when the shot rings out, the men of the Rivera cartel trying to keep her from her little girl, who stops walking when she hears the shot, who doesn't know to hit the ground.

"Get down!" Lola says, but maybe getting shot won't be worse than the fate Andrea's father wants for her little girl.

She sees the four ropes crossed in the middle at the same time Lucy does, each one extending to a separate vehicle.

"Stop," Andrea's father says to Lola.

Lola doesn't.

The next shot stings her shoulder, skimming some flesh off the bone. She is bleeding.

"Stop, or we tie her up," Andrea's father says.

Lola stops.

Lucy looks to her mother.

"Come here," Lola says.

"They'll shoot me," Lucy says.

"No," Lola says. "They won't."

"It's strange," Andrea's father says. "When your own child won't obey you. My little girl shot me in the back. How do you explain to her that what you're doing, you do for her own protection?"

"Lucy," Lola says. "Come here."

"Will you keep me safe?" Lucy asks.

"Yes."

"Can you?" Lucy says, a follow-up.

"Yes," Lola lies, because if Lucy believes it, that will make it true.

The little girl takes her first step forward. Lola is conscious of the waves crashing on sand, louder now, and a ringing behind them. Is it a trick her ears are playing on her, or is there really an alarm?

Another step. Another. One foot in front of the other until Lucy reaches Lola, who gathers her daughter in her arms and runs back to her men.

"Take her inside," Lola says after she gives Lucy a cursory look for scrapes and bruises—nothing. The white men have treated her fairly, she thinks. "Are you okay?"

Lucy nods. "They gave me ice cream with sprinkles."

"Okay. Good. Marcos and Manuel will take you inside."

"Someone should stay with you," Manuel says.

"No. I have to do this alone."

"I will leave you my gun," Manuel says.

When Lola doesn't take it, Manuel lays his weapon on the sand at her feet.

Then they are gone, and it is just Lola, watching the pre-show carnage. Ropes, rectangles, and Hector, who is only a light brown speck in the dark now, but who must know what's coming, because he screams her name, "Lola!"

She starts toward him as the white men bind his wrists and ankles, each rope attached to one of the four vehicles. They are going to pull him apart, limb from limb, and they are going to make it take all night.

The closest beach house besides Andrea's is a good hundred feet away. Maybe someone will hear, but maybe the glass on that house, like Andrea's, is soundproof, because rich people move to the ocean only to shut it out.

They have Hector tied quickly, and Lola, fifteen feet away now, sees the white man nod. It is beginning. The vehicles rev their engines, and with the first press of foot to gas, Hector screams, his joints popping and cracking, Lola imagines, even though she can't hear over his yowls of pain.

"Lola!" Hector cries again. Or is she only imagining he is calling her name?

The next time the vehicles inch forward, Hector's screams are inhuman, loud and twisted and guttural, and Andrea's father catches her eye. He smiles at her, and his smile is not unkind.

"Are you planning to shoot me?" he asks. It is only now Lola realizes she must have picked up Manuel's weapon, because she is holding it at her side.

Another scream from Hector, and Lola is close enough now to see the twisted limbs, the beginnings of broken bone, the sweat popped on his brow, as if they are not only pulling him apart but roasting him.

The pain is too much. This is too much.

"I asked you a question," the white man repeats. "Are you going to shoot me? Because even if you do, they aren't going to stop."

"I know," Lola says. She raises the weapon. The white man doesn't break a sweat.

Then, she swings the gun to the right. She is a good shot. She aims for the point between her baby brother's eyes and squeezes the trigger.

A second later, his screams stop. The vehicles' engines are killed. So is her baby brother.

Andrea's father did not expect this. She swings her gun back at him.

"Untie him. Leave him on the sand. And get the fuck out of my city," Lola says.

It is only when she is walking away from her brother's dead body that she notices the sirens—how long have they been blaring?—and sees the storm of uniforms coming at the Rivera cartel's white entourage with weapons drawn. Andrea is rushing from her house, doing a good impression of a damsel in distress because her goddamn father is not supposed to be alive, and Hector is not supposed to be dead. Gray Overcoat and Tan Overcoat rush toward both women. Andrea catches Lola first, but Gray and Tan aren't far behind.

"Are you okay?" Tan overcoat.

But Gray overcoat doesn't wait for an answer, and now that he's close, Lola sees he is holding out a blanket. She steps aside to let him drape it over the future district attorney, but Gray Overcoat turns and wraps Lola in the blanket's warmth, and nothing has ever felt so good.

THIRTY-FIVE

HOMECOMING

Lola sits across from Andrea at Bay Cities, but unlike every other time they've ever met, they are not in the back alley. Today, they are sitting across from each other at a table facing Lincoln. Today, Lola is trying something new—maple turkey with Havarti and hot peppers on an Italian roll—because at last she knows what Andrea orders, and she wants to try it too.

"Add salt and pepper," Andrea had said. "It makes all the difference."

Today, Lola's partner eats with gusto, letting mustard spill from her own sandwich. Andrea has a pile of thin napkins next to her, and she grabs three from the stack to wipe her mouth. All she manages to do is spread the mustard to the corner of her cheek.

"Let me," Lola says, upending her bottled water and dabbing at Andrea's mouth as if she's a child with no patience and no impulse control. Lola has learned about things like impulse control since sending Lucy to Blooming Gardens, the school that just expelled Zach's daughter, Charlie, when Ms. Laura received an anonymous recording in the mail. On it, Charlie's voice could be heard threatening Lucy Vasquez, another student and classmate, with deportation. When Lola had outfitted an unknowing Lucy with a tiny wire, she had counted on Charlie being a repeat offender, someone so privileged she wouldn't get up off her lazy second-grade ass and think of another threat to get Lucy to do her bidding.

The expulsion of Charlie caused Susan to seek full custody of her daughter, and when someone leaked the tape to the *Los Angeles Times,* the bleeding-heart liberals who frequented a white chef's restaurant for authentic Mexican food stopped coming. Now he is labeled a racist and a fraud. Lola could have killed him, but, by exercising some impulse control, she came up with a much better punishment.

She and Andrea have purchased his restaurant out from under him.

Andrea pours some salt-and-vinegar chips onto the plastic wrap Lola has spread under her sandwich.

"I can't eat all these," Andrea says.

Lola licks the salt and vinegar from the chip, letting the flavor sting her tongue and shock her taste buds to life. She has never tasted anything so delicious.

It is a Saturday afternoon in December, almost a month after Lola killed Hector and left Andrea's father alive.

At the funeral, Lola got to see her mother's grief, crying over Hector's coffin in a Huntington Park funeral home that still used Styrofoam cups and powdered creamer. Lola could have afforded something here, in Santa Monica, where the cream would be fresh, organic, and enhanced with DHA, but she had known Hector would have wanted to be buried at home, in Huntington Park, a place denied him so long, what with prison and his turning traitor.

"I'm so sorry," Lola had heard her mother whisper-cry over Hector's peaceful body. "The things I did to her . . . that I made you witness . . ."

Maria hadn't said more, because the tears had overtaken the words Lola was longing to hear. She had fought the impulse to stride to her mother, to shake her shoulders and demand she finish her thought. But it wasn't meant to be, because Lucy had tugged at Lola's sleeve and apologized for asking, but could Lola tell her where the food was, because Isa was here, and Lucy wanted to welcome her friend with some cake.

A young woman approaches Andrea, who's not in her trademark tailored suit, but dark jeans and a deep-purple cardigan.

"Excuse me, Ms. Whitely? I'm a first year at UCLA Law, and I know you went there, and I just wanted to wish you luck in the election and let you know I'm in awe of you and everything you've done."

It is a speech straight off a teleprompter, Lola thinks, except this girl, fresh-faced, jeans and a T-shirt, struggling to stand up straight with a book bag pulled tight over both shoulders, speaks it all in one breath.

Andrea reaches across the table to shake her hand, and the girl turns red. "It's an honor to meet you—"

"Candace."

"Candace." Andrea squeezes the girl's hand, and Candace lights up like a goddamn Christmas tree.

Forty-eight hours after his arrest, Andrea's father hanged himself in his cell at the Twin Towers. He had no visitors that day except the prosecutor responsible for his case—Andrea Dennison Whitely.

"And this is my associate, Lola Vasquez," Andrea says to Candace. The white girl shifts her focus to Lola. Again, the younger woman waits for Lola, the elder, to extend her hand, which she does.

"Nice to meet you," Lola says.

"What do you do for Ms. Whitely?" Candace asks, a decent question which Lola doesn't bother to consider disrespectful, because Andrea is running for district attorney, a position without a partner.

"A little bit of everything," Lola says.

"Nothing," Andrea says. "Lola doesn't work for me, Candace. She works with me."

"Oh, okay. Sorry," Candace says, in a tone so accepting that Lola sees this world, the West Side white world, open up in front of her like the ocean on an L.A. winter day like today, seventy-five and sunny, blue sky dotted with puffy white-gray clouds.

"Is this a working lunch?" Candace asks, then instantly finds her hand at her mouth, like she's gone too far.

"No," Andrea says. "I'm helping her move."

"Wow. You must be a good friend, Ms. Whitely," Candace says.

"I can be." Andrea laughs, but Lola knows she is not joking.

Andrea leaked the story about Zach's racist daughter to the *Times*. Andrea would not let Lola do the dirty work of killing her father.

Andrea made sure one of the Rivera cartel henchmen took the fall for Hector's death so Maria would not have a sin that could be considered higher than her own to hold over her daughter's head. Lola could have blamed Andrea for the events leading up to Hector's death, but, in truth, Andrea exposed Lola to the truth about her brother—he was a traitor, he was weak, he wanted Lola dead.

Then, Andrea introduced her family to Lola's over dinner at her Bronson Canyon home. Jack poured Lola one of his signature Manhattans, which Manuel refused because he was driving that night. Rayna fawned over Lucy, shifting from bratty teen to role model with an ease Lola found both frightening and normal for a girl Rayna's age.

And Christopher, home from New Horizons, had emerged from his room to sit at the table with the woman his mother said it was important he meet. He hadn't remembered Lola from that night, because now her arm is healed, and she wasn't screaming, so Lola had extended her hand and said, "It's nice to finally meet you, Christopher. I've heard so many wonderful things about you."

And Andrea's son had said, "Likewise."

Now, Rayna emerges from Bay Cities, and she is saying, "You have to hold my hand, Lucy. There's too much traffic on Lincoln."

Lucy obeys, even going so far as to look both ways, as if the Bay Cities patio that overlooks the four-lane Lincoln Boulevard is the road itself.

"We got strawberry oat bars," Christopher announces as he helps Lucy onto the concrete bench.

"One for each of us," Lucy says.

"One for each of us." Rayna smiles.

"You have to finish your sandwich first," Andrea tells her daughter, and Rayna flashes back to bratty teen with a roll of her eyes, one Lucy catches, and Rayna sees, because Andrea's daughter switches back immediately.

"Lucy, do you think we can finish our sandwiches?" Christopher asks.

Lucy nods as if she's been given a grave task. Lola watches her daughter bite into white bread and chew, and she feels nauseous, yes, at having transplanted Lucy to the West Side, but Hector is gone. Hector was Huntington Park—hiding in the closet to keep away from Maria, poring over math worksheets at a splintered kitchen table, scrounging for breakfast to keep their bellies from rumbling.

Lola is sick of feeling guilty for her good fortune and for the death of her brother. She can no longer stomach the well-wishes of her Huntington Park neighbors, people like her mother's best friend Veronica, who brings casseroles with too much cheese and grease for dinner every night, because she knows Lola must be too upset to cook. She is tired of apologizing for having money and a work ethic and for becoming more than she was ever meant to be.

It is a new day. It is, in fact, moving day.

"And of course you'll need a decorator," Andrea says, then with her voice lowered, "I have someone, but he's an addict and might relapse. Is that okay?"

"I'm not picky," Lola says, and she finds her hand on Lucy's head, stroking her daughter's black silk hair. Lucy takes another bite of her sandwich, and another, filling up her belly so one day she will be more than Lola.

In the end, that is all that matters.

Still, the privilege snaps at her heart, and she says to Lucy, "Why don't we invite Isa for dinner tonight?"

"Okay!" Lucy says, excited to see her friend, her real friend, the one who has known her the longest.

Lola does not have any friends from childhood, a traumatic, isolating time. So she looks across the table at Andrea, with her pert nose, supervising her teenage daughter's vegetable intake, smiling small as she watches her son wolf down a strawberry oat bar instead of white powder. Then, she gives Lola one more piece of advice: "And of course you'll need a security system."

"Is she running for office too?" Rayna asks in earnest.

"Maybe one day," Andrea says, in a tone that lets Lola know her friend believes it.

ACKNOWLEDGMENTS

This book would not exist without the people who create the space for me to write. Thank you to Veronica Gomez, Lucy Valdizon, and Lillian Lopez. The work you do is invaluable.

I want to thank my editor, Nathan Roberson, for his thoughtful critique and for making sure this book is everything I intended. I also want to thank Eve Attermann, my agent and champion, for making all this come true.

More thanks to Blake Fronstin, Oly Obst, and Devon Bratton. And, of course, to Amanda Segel and Denise Thé—your friendship, talent, and guidance continue to mean the world.

Thank you to my parents for never blinking when I said I wanted to be a writer. Thank you also to my mother and mother-in-law for reading this book chapter by chapter and asking for more.

Thank you to David for navigating the world when it is too much for me, and for loving me even when I am too much.

Thank you to Leah and Caleb for all the love, challenges, and joy you've given us.

ABOUT THE AUTHOR

Melissa Scrivner Love is the author of *Lola*, winner of the John Creasey New Blood Dagger. She was born to a police officer father and a court stenographer mother. After earning a master's in English literature from NYU, Melissa wrote for several television shows, including *Life*, *CSI: Miami*, *Person of Interest*, and *Fear the Walking Dead*. She and her husband live in L.A. with their children.